Murder on Everest

Books by Charles G. Irion and Ronald J. Watkins
The Summit Murder Mystery Series
Murder on Everest
Abandoned on Everest (a prequel to Murder on Everest)
Murder on Elbrus (Summer 2010)
Murder on Mt. McKinley (Winter 2011)
Murder on Puncak Jaya (Summer 2011)
Murder on Aconcagua (Winter 2012)
Murder on Vinson Massif (Summer 2012)
Murder on Kilimanjaro (Winter 2013)

Books by Charles G. Irion
Remodeling Hell
Autograph Hell
Car Dealer Hell
Divorce Hell
Roadkill Cooking for Campers (Wild Game Cookbook)

Books by Ronald J. Watkins
Unknown Seas
Birthright
Cimmerian
Evil Intentions
Against Her Will
A Suspicion of Guilt
A Deadly Glitter
Alter Ego
Shadows and Lies
High Crimes and Misdemeanors

Murder on Everest

A Summit Murder Mystery

Charles G. Irion
and
Ronald J. Watkins

www.SummitMurders.com
www.IrionBooks.com

IRION BOOKS

Copyright © 2010 by Charles G. Irion trustee C.I. Trust, Summit Murders LLC

First Edition 2010

10 9 8 7 6 5 4 3 2 1

Library of Congress Catalog Card Number: 2009938527

ISBN: 9780984161805   Trade Paperback

Cover Design by Johnny Miguel, www.johnnymiguel.com
Book Design by The Printed Page, www.theprintedpage.com

Irion Books
480-699-0068
4462 E. Horseshoe Rd.
Phoenix, Arizona 85028
email: charles@charlesirion.com
www.IrionBooks.com

Printed in the United States of America

Dedication

To Tenzing Norgay and Sir Edmund Percival Hillary, the first

PROLOGUE

The wind whipped my face. I wiped my goggles with my gloves and stared directly into the blizzard, searching for shadows or any sign of life.

We'd left Camp Five at midnight—more than seventeen hours earlier—and I was beyond exhaustion. My lungs were raw. Every breath I drew burned like cold fire. I fought a nagging cough that threatened to consume me. For two hours, I'd not climbed and my body temperature had fallen precipitously. Little feeling remained in my feet and hands and I was in danger of frostbite. I could sense my internal organs starting to shut down and a deadly lethargy engulfed me. I didn't have long.

The snow was so thick that I could scarcely see more than two feet before me. The wind howled with a ferocity I'd never experienced. To stand erect, I had to lean into the gale. If the wind suddenly stopped, I'd have toppled over.

I reached across my right shoulder and turned the knob of my oxygen bottle. At 28,700 feet, I was breathing air with one-third the oxygen of sea level. The richer mix poured into my mask as I inhaled for a long minute, feeling better, stronger.

After a luxurious few seconds, I forced myself to turn the flow off and pulled the mask aside since it seemed to suffocate me without the oxygen. I doubted that I had enough left to reach Camp Five, where the Sherpas had stored vital spare tanks. But if I had any chance of escaping the Death Zone, I had to preserve all of the oxygen that remained.

I glanced ahead, but could see nothing except the blinding white of the storm against the darkening backdrop of the dying day. I couldn't be certain any of the climbers and Sherpas between here and the Summit had heard the distress call. My own radio was dead.

No one was coming, I told myself. And if somehow they did, no one would see Derek and me there against the outcrop, some distance from the main route to the Hillary Step. I turned my back to the wind and trudged to the wall of stone and the forlorn figure lying there.

I knelt, leaned forward, and shouted into Derek's ear. "I can't see anyone!" I gasped, sucked three breaths of air, and shouted again. "Can you stand up?"

Derek Sodoc had sat down against the rock four hours earlier. His right hand and forearm were extended awkwardly to the side, frozen solid since he'd lost his glove even before I stumbled upon him. He hadn't uttered a word in half an hour, but earlier had reported that he could neither feel nor move his legs.

I took the thin air into my lungs and coughed violently, my sides hurting so badly that I thought I'd broken a rib before regaining control. I shouted again. "Can you stand up? I can't lift you!"

Derek said nothing. He sat, partially lying against the outcrop, as unmoving as the Sphinx. I gripped his jacket awkwardly with my gloved hands and tugged, but I was so weak myself—so near death—I had no chance of raising the man to his feet. I paused to breathe, drawing the thin air across my burning throat, feeling again as if I was suffocating. I leaned down and placed my face almost against Derek's ear. "You must help me! No one is coming! There's no time left. Stand up!"

The effort nearly did me in. Losing my balance, I tumbled to the snow and ice, the wind howling to a crescendo. I lay there drawing unsatisfying gulps of air. I closed my eyes. It felt good resting here. Just a few minutes. I began to drift.

But part of me knew better. This was one of the ways that you died on Everest. If you lay down in the Death Zone and stayed down, life drained from you until you ceased to exist.

With every reserve of willpower and strength, I forced myself to my feet. I looked at my watch, turning it toward the fading light: 5:32. It would be dark in less than half an hour.

I faced the storm again and struggled across twenty feet. Again I stared into the blizzard, but could see nothing, just a furious white, and could hear nothing but the roaring wind. I knew that if I walked much farther, I'd go straight over a precipice or into a crevasse. More than one climber—brain depleted of oxygen, functioning with the intellectual capacity of a five-year-old child, exhausted, and numb—had simply walked over a cliff to their death.

I saw nothing. No shapes. No climbers. No one to help.

In the growing twilight, I was now seeing phantasms, dark dancing shapes in the blizzard. At first, I'd thought they were figures coming toward me out of the storm, but soon recognized them for what they were. I'd heard of the phenomenon, but had never previously experienced it. It was unsettling and just one more sign of how close I was to death.

I turned my back to the storm and slowly made my way to Derek. Bracing with my right hand on the rock, I leaned down, drawing five or six gasping breaths as I did. "I have to leave, Derek. I have to leave you."

I could just barely make out my friend's eyes through the ice that had formed like a death mask on his cheeks and eyelids. There was no movement. They were black, deep as a still well. I wondered if he was dead already.

I drew three more gasping breaths, leaned nearly against Derek's ear, and shouted, "If you cannot stand, I have to leave you! Stand up, Derek! Stand up!" Again, I pulled at his jacket. Again there was no reply, no offer of help, nothing.

I slowly straightened. I looked at my watch. 5:41. If I didn't leave now, I faced executing the Hillary Step back to Camp Five in the dark—and climbers attempting it alone, at night, died. That was where Bruce Herrod had been found in 1997, dangling from a rope after he'd attempted the descent in the dark.

I looked back at Derek, who was almost certainly dead. I leaned down, drew several burning breaths, hacked violently, and shouted over the howling wind. "I'm going! I'm sorry. I'm so sorry."

As I began to straighten, something caught my forearm. I looked down. Derek had grabbed me, placing a hand across the top of my arm. His eyelids fluttered and his frozen lips moved. His eyes were bottomless, black as coal. I leaned down and pressed my ear to Derek's mouth. I could barely make out the words.

"Don't … leave … me."

ONE

There is an air of excitement as you prepare to enter the great unknown, to lay your life on the line, for no other reason than you want to.
—Quentin Stern, www.AbandonedonEverest.com

"Do you think it will fly?" Tom Bauman said, eyeing the aging helicopter.

I examined the enormous ramshackle Russian Mi-17 helicopter more closely. "I suppose." Big as a school bus, it had clearly seen better times. Beneath the many dents and scratches, traces of the original camouflage paint showed through.

"We're nearly a mile up here," Tom said as he reexamined the craft. "The higher we go, the thinner the air. The thinner the air, the less the lift." He sounded skeptical. Handsome, thirty-six years of age, of average height with a solid, fit frame, his hair was prematurely graying. We had only met the previous night in the hotel bar, but had formed an instant liking for one another.

Two short men in stained coveralls appeared from within the helicopter, removed a panel from its side, and peered at the innards of the helicopter.

"I suppose if they'll fly it, we're safe enough," Tom added.

I laughed. "They're Nepalese, and trust karma."

I sniffed the air, taking in the mélange of aviation fuel, urban pollution, and crop smoke commingled with the intermittent cool mountain breeze. *Only here,* I thought, *only this place smells like this.* I wondered once again why I'd returned.

Kathmandu International Airport is the end of the line for most travelers. Certainly it was for me. It offers no international transfers, so this place was a point of egress or ingress. Despite its name, it was little more than a single long runway, not much larger than a county airport in the United States.

Nepal was the poorest nation in a region of poor countries. The facilities certainly made the point. The most conspicuous presence was two very large hangars reserved for the Nepalese military, its planes, and helicopters. Little of the equipment that required electricity actually worked. Anything that could be done by physical labor was. Toward the terminal, Nepalese workers, small and swarthy, swarmed over the small mountain of baggage.

An attractive couple emerged from the building wearing brightly colored parkas, each carrying a light bag. They might have been models for an outdoor magazine. The tall, very fit blond haired man was Peer Borgen. His only slightly shorter companion was Tarja Sodoc. They were laughing.

"Have you met Peer?" I asked.

Tom shook his head. "I know Tarja, of course."

The woman smiled broadly as she and Peer reached the helicopter. "Hello, Scott and Tom. Good to see you both again." She extended her hand, European style.

Hers was a face that had graced a thousand tabloid pages. Her smile was warm and seemingly genuine, her white teeth as perfect as God or a skilled orthodontist could create, her skin finely textured with just a touch of red on the high cheeks, her long blond hair like silk thread. She was the goddess of many men's dreams. If she had a flaw, it was her pale blue eyes, which never varied in their calculation.

We shook her gloved hand. "You know Peer, of course," Tarja said to me, "but I don't believe you two have met." She introduced Tom.

The noted Alpine climber and renowned mountaineer grinned like a child. He had a broad Scandinavian face, dark grey eyes set wide apart, fleshy lips prone to a smile, and sunglasses balanced atop his blond hair. He was instantly likeable. "Good to meet you, Tom—and to see you again, Scott." He spoke English with only the slightest of accents. He glanced up toward the azure canopy overhead, tossing a shock of long blond hair back from his brow. "Who would have thought we'd be back so soon, eh, Scott?"

He grinned as he turned his attention to the helicopter. The two men had closed the panel, but were arguing as they walked off. "Do you think that thing will get off the ground?" Peer said.

"We'll soon see." The speaker was Calvin Seavers, the expedition's physician. He'd just walked from around the other side of the helicopter. "Did you know one of its tires is nearly flat?"

"I'm sure they'll fix it," Tom said.

Calvin glanced at a nearby ground crew. "You have more confidence than I do." Just under six feet tall with a robust physique, his hair was thinning. He wore wire-framed glasses and spoke with the cadence and mannerisms of a man with New England roots.

"Have you all read the book?" Peer asked like a naughty child.

Two months earlier, a book entitled *Abandoned on Everest* had been released, giving a highly sensational account of the previous year's tragedy. Many on the expedition had not fared well in the telling.

No one answered at first.

"You didn't talk to that weasel Stern, did you?" Tarja said to me. Calvin had been her husband's good friend, while Tom had not been there.

"No," I answered.

Tarja eyed me. "Well, someone did. I intend to find out just who."

Peer grinned. "What do you care? I thought you liked press?"

Tarja glared at him. "Not when they tell lies that make me look bad, I don't."

"Well, I read the thing on the way over," Peer said lightly. "A worthless piece of fiction. The author is clearly not a climber."

Tarja glared at him as she said, "You can afford to be magnanimous. He never said you had herpes."

A stiff wind from the mountains gusted and I turned to catch it with my back. It was early in the season and winter was in an erratic and slow retreat.

Calvin glanced about as he zipped his parka. "Has anyone else noticed that it's an armed camp?" he said, gesturing toward the nervous guards near the terminal.

"The military controls the airport now," I said. "There's a line of infantry on the other side of the field; each soldier is holding an AK-47 at port arms."

Kathmandu, Nepal's capital, was a city of 700,000, a significant number of whom lived in abject poverty. In the span of two decades, it had grown from an exotic city firmly rooted in the medieval ages to the most modern in Nepal—and little pleasant remained about the place. Sitting within a high mountain valley, smoldering cremation pyre platforms along the Bagmati River cast a perpetual pall of smoke mixed with dust across the city. From the distance, it resembled nothing so much as a brownish dome. The mingled smells were sweet and sharp, acrid and distasteful: cooking oil, dung, human excrement and urine, kerosene and diesel fuel.

The city itself existed in a form of controlled chaos. Driving rules meant little. Sacred cows wandered freely, adding to the disorder. I had noted a cattle grid across the entrance ramp to keep them off the runway, so we at least had that going for us. The intersections were choked with cars, two-cycle rickshaws, and motorbikes. Just beyond the city limits, fields were burned between crops, adding still more smoke to the mix. The high, dry air also meant routine bush fires. Lung problems had become a serious issue with the local population and no climber wished to expose himself—or herself—to a single day here more than was essential. Breathing on Everest was enough of a chore without the crap from Kathmandu in your lungs.

"Do you think there's any truth to the rumor about an imminent Maoist offensive?" Tarja asked.

"Who can say?" Tom answered. "Some guy at the bar last night told me they erupt without warning."

"I thought the Maoists were the largest party and part of the government now?" Peer said.

"Not all of them came down from the mountains," I answered.

"The sooner we are out of this place, the better," Peer said, slipping dark glasses across his eyes. "All these guns make me uneasy. Only that makes this tolerable."

"That" was the distant Himalayan mountain range. Glorious against the clear sky, its magnitude was diminished only by its distance from us. But Everest, the reason we had come, was lost over the horizon.

"Look down, it is dirt and filth," Peer said. "Look up, and it is divine."

"Why Peer, you're a romantic," Tarja said without a smile.

He glanced at her. "I climb mountains. Of course I'm a romantic. Let's get this over with. The worst risk any of us will face these next weeks is riding in that thing," he said, gesturing toward the helicopter. He reached down, picked up his bag, and strode toward the open door. Tarja followed.

Once the couple was beyond hearing range Tom said, "Was it true?"

We knew what he meant.

"What do you think?" Calvin said.

Tom pursed his lips. "She doesn't seem the grieving widow to me, I have to admit."

I watched the couple climb athletically into the helicopter.

The year before, I'd been part of the much-publicized Sodoc Foundation Everest expedition that had ended so tragically. Derek was dead, his frozen body up on the shelf above the Hillary Step, along with that of the expedition leader, Reggie Maul, and three Sherpa guides. Just over a dozen other climbers from various expeditions had perished on or near the summit that season, making it the deadliest since the deaths of George Mallory and Sandy Irvine in 1924.

I glanced at Calvin, who'd been there with me, then at Tom, who had not, and wondered if any of us would join the count this year. I'd certainly never expected to be back.

"Were they up to something?" Tom asked.

Calvin ignored him. I shrugged.

"And Peer was on top when Derek died, isn't that true?" Tom said.

Calvin looked at me when he answered. "I was at Camp Four. I don't know where he was for a fact."

"Yes," I said. "Peer was returning from the summit when the call for help went out. But the storm had hit by then and I never saw him. My radio went down, as did they all. We were blind and deaf up there."

"What happened?" Tom said to me. "The story in that book can't be true."

"I've never read it. As for what happened, God knows. I certainly don't. Just my little piece of it and even it's a haze."

A ruckus near the terminal drew our attention. Emerging with a train of baggage handlers were Crystal Hernandez and Rusty Landon.

"Careful," Calvin said. "The media has arrived."

"Seriously," Tom said, turning back to me. "I'd really like to know what took place. There have been so many different stories that I'd welcome talking to someone who knows."

"Perhaps later." I turned to the approaching newcomers. "Hello, Crissie, Rusty."

Crystal was thirty-five years old with pleasant if earnest features. She had about her the cynical, clutching air of most reporters I'd known, suspecting everything, constantly looking for the angle. Her companion was the cameraman, Rusty. Tall, with a shock of bright red hair and freckles, he was all angles. I had known them both the previous year and thought I'd never see either of them again.

"Scott," Crystal said. "Doc, good to see you. What brings you two on this quest?"

"I can't speak for Scott," Calvin said, "but I'm here to pay homage to Derek, to see that his body is recovered and that he gets a proper burial."

Rusty set his camera bag down and snorted. "Even in death, the rich get it better."

"What's that supposed to mean?" Calvin said.

"There are more than two hundred bodies up there. Climbers stay where they fall. There's a reason for that—and you know it. Why are you here, Scott?" Rusty asked. "I seem to recall you vowing you'd never set foot on that mountain again."

"I'd say 'vow' is a pretty strong word—but yes, I never intended to return."

"He should be here," Calvin said defensively. "He and Derek were friends."

"So was I, Doc, so was I," Crystal said softly.

"Let me ask you a question, Calvin," Rusty said. "How many people are going to die finding Derek's body and getting it down to Base Camp? Two, three, half a dozen?"

"Perhaps none."

Rusty snorted. "Right! All those dead climbers are still up there because you *can't* bring them down. They've either fallen into a crevasse or they fell off a ridge, and you can't get at them, or they just lay down and froze to death and are stuck in a block of ice. Those you can find. Hell, you can't miss them. You can practically walk to the summit on bodies. Nobody has the energy in the Death Zone to haul anyone down. And what's the point? Dead is dead."

"Rusty, enough," Crystal said.

"I mean it," he continued. "Old man Sodoc's got all the money in the world. He thinks he can buy his son's body off that mountain. Hell, he's the reason Derek's dead to begin with! What does he care who else dies?"

"That's enough," Crystal said. "Load your gear."

Rusty gave her a look and moved back to the porters, carrying most of their gear, shouting and waving his arms. I couldn't hear the words, not that it mattered. The helicopter's engine began the familiar whine of start up.

"So why are you going?" Calvin asked, all but shouting to be heard.

Crystal eyed him. "It's my job. We're recording this expedition."

"You're kidding."

"Not at all. SNS is going to air this as a four-part series next fall. If it's good enough, it will run during sweeps week."

"I think I'm going to throw up," Calvin said.

"That's why the company sent us," Crystal said with a softer voice. "But I'm here for Derek." With that, she shouldered her bag and stepped off toward the door of the helicopter.

"Is this true?" Calvin asked.

I shrugged. "It's the first I've heard of it, but it sounds about right." Motion caught my eye. "What's that over there?"

Beside the tarmac, a holy man in orange robes, assisted by at least five others, was officiating over a bleating goat.

"I heard they're slaughtering a goat to get this thing in the air." Calvin laughed as if he'd seen everything and walked to the waiting helicopter. I glanced toward the goat and spotted a knife glinting in the sun. I turned my attention back to the tarmac. Approaching was a Sherpa, wearing a broad grin. We embraced.

"How are you, my friend?" Dawa asked. He was dressed in traditional Sherpa attire: a long inner shirt over a pant-like woolen garment, both of which were covered by a heavy, coarse, wraparound robe reaching just below his knees and fastened at the side. He wore a sash and high boots of wool with leather soles. From Base Camp on, he would be dressed as a Western climber.

"Good. And you and your family?"

"All well. I had not expected to see you so soon."

"Things change."

Dawa's smile vanished. "You should not have come. No good can come from this."

"Maybe we'll have better luck than last year."

The man shook his head. "Not luck. The holy men say it is a bad time for Sagarmatha. Many Sherpas don't want to go. The gods oppose the climb, just like last year. We should not do this. We should pray instead and ask for forgiveness for our sins. Christians do that, don't they, Scott?"

I thought a moment. "Yes, but not often enough."

❧❧❧

The Sodoc Foundation Everest expedition the previous year had been the most publicized climbing event in history. Every resource of the senior Sodoc's worldwide media conglomerate had been employed to cover it and no expense had been spared. Crystal and Rusty were two of the company's most experienced crew—and avid amateur climbers themselves. With the latest in digital electronics, live reports were possible from elevations not previously known. The expedition had been as much a media event as a legitimate effort to summit Everest.

For more than a decade, Sodoc News System—or SNS—had recorded the exploits of its founder's son, Derek. Handsome, affable, and fortunate, he'd had every benefit in life. But rather than follow in the extraordinarily successful steps of his father, Michael, the young Derek had chosen the life of an adventurer, where his father's wealth and the fame of his name could not buy success.

When it was clear to his father that no amount of persuasion could convince his son to join the family corporate empire, Sodoc had elected to make his son a celebrity and capitalize on his fame. Every one of his climbs had been lavishly covered and became a television special, dating back more than five years. He appeared regularly on cable television, hosting his own show, *High Adventure!*

Last year's expedition was to have been the culmination of Derek's climbing career. Having summited each of the highest peaks on the six other continents, Everest was meant to be his crowning glory. SNS announced its intention to turn the climb into a major documentary. Instead, the climb and expedition had ended in disaster. Rather than glory, Derek had found his grave not far from the top of the world.

Now the same team was here to recover his body.

I didn't like it. Rusty had a point. Why Derek and not others? Hell, fabled George Mallory was still up there. No one had seriously argued he be brought down once his body was located. If Everest was good enough for Mallory, why not for Derek Sodoc?

And Rusty was right about something else. It was dangerous in the Death Zone. People died routinely from slips, malfunctions, the altitude, unexpected weather, bad judgment, or bad luck. Especially bad luck. It was difficult enough asking climbers and Sherpas to attempt the rescue of the living stranded in a storm—rescue efforts that often resulted in their own deaths—but to risk lives because a rich man wanted to bury his son?

No, Dawa was right. This was bad. Everest was sufficiently dangerous without adding media to it. You could try to do whatever you liked on the mountain. You could set out to make a movie or just climb the thing. You could collect a skilled team to get your son back if you had a mind to and the money. But mixing missions was a very bad idea.

I could see no good coming from this.

A Nepalese in an orange jumpsuit standing beside the helicopter door caught my attention and gestured for me to climb aboard. I shouldered my bag and turned toward the helicopter just as I spotted a car stopping beside the tarmac. Whoever was in it had managed to evade the mob at the terminal entrance. Expecting an army general, I was stunned instead to see Diana Maurasi emerging from the rear door.

Spotting me, she grinned as she walked briskly over and gave me an embrace and a kiss. "Hi, stranger. Surprised?"

"Surprised" was putting it lightly. The last time I'd seen Diana had been on television at my home. Until recently, she'd been the anchor for the SNS Evening News, a spot she'd held for two years of modest ratings. She'd been elevated to the position with much fanfare, but the previous month had stepped down with the announcement that she'd soon be hosting her own morning show. Her stint as evening anchor might have been a failure, but it had done nothing to diminish her celebrity, a status I had as much to do with as any other event or individual.

"What are you doing here?" I asked. Dawa retreated from us and climbed into the helicopter.

"Covering the expedition. Let's get on board before some reporter spots me. My presence is supposed to be a secret." She tugged at my arm and we climbed into the loaded helicopter, an attendant slamming the door behind us.

Peer looked up from his seat beside Tarja, registered surprise, and then approval. No question, Diana was one attractive woman. She took a seat toward the rear and gestured for me to sit beside her. We buckled up as the engines roared.

The heavy machine seemed glued to the ground at first, then slowly we were rising and moving forward at the same time. The lumbering craft gathered speed as it crossed the runway, gaining altitude as it raced away from Kathmandu, and civilization, toward the distant Himalayan Range—and Everest.

Two

On the far horizon, the mountain range stands,
remote and obscure. Only as you approach it do you
realize its enormity. It makes any normal person seem
puny, as nothing. It is with great excitement you
confront your destiny and begin the high adventure!
—Quentin Stern, www.AbandonedonEverest.com

In the fall of 2001, I was a first lieutenant in the U. S. Army. A few days after the attack on September 11, my unit had been transported from the United States to a former Soviet air force base in southern Uzbekistan. There we'd stayed briefly in the dilapidated barracks as manpower and equipment were flown in.

A British and American air campaign against the Taliban began on October 7. Twelve days later, as part of Task Force Dagger, my four-man Ranger team was inserted by helicopter into the Panjshir Valley on the Shomali Plain—some fifty miles north of Kabul, the capital of Afghanistan, home to Osama bin Laden and al Qaeda.

Fluent in Dari, the most widely spoken of the Afghan languages, I contacted General Fahim Khan, one of the leaders of the Northern Alliance which controlled not quite one-third of Afghanistan and had been at war for some time with the Islamic fundamentalist Taliban controlling the rest of the nation. A Taliban suicide bomber had murdered the revered leader of the Alliance, Ahmed Shah Masood, on September 9 and the anti-Taliban forces were in disarray. Part of my assignment was to assure Khan of the American commitment to help them in defeating the Taliban.

The ongoing air campaign told the Northern Alliance leaders that an offensive might succeed, so General Khan agreed to engage the Taliban. My team mounted horses and swaddled ourselves in native garb, much as Lawrence of Arabia had during the First World War. Accompanied by Northern Alliance forces, we scouted the Taliban defenses, and I began calling in air strikes. The initial Alliance attack had quickly broken through the lines. Within days, Khan's forces were at the gates of Mazari Sharif, a key provincial capital. It fell after a bloody four-hour battle.

Khan turned south, advancing rapidly against light resistance toward Kabul, with me and my team leading the way. Each time the advancing forces met with significant resistance, I called in air strikes, after which the offensive continued. General Khan and his men were delighted, dancing in ecstasy whenever distant airplanes dropped 500-pound bombs on the defensive positions. Mine wasn't a job I could do from safety and, as often as not, I was forced to expose myself to enemy fire. Every time I did, the Afghans greeted me with wide grins.

On November 10, the Northern Alliance forces were within striking distance of Kabul, with just a single defensive line between them and the Taliban. That afternoon, five riders approached from the northeast. Stepping down from her horse was Diana Maurasi, Middle East correspondent for SNS.

Just twenty-four, she was known more for her looks than her talent. I'd seen her on television once or twice, enough to recognize her. She'd been stationed in Jerusalem when war broke out and I never learned how she managed to get to the rear of the Northern Alliance advance. I suspected that she'd flown to Pakistan and worked her way north and west from there. It had been both daring and stupid. This was no place for a Western civilian—especially a woman.

"How you doing, soldier," she said as she approached.

I'd been speaking with Khan. "What are you doing here?" I demanded.

Diana was wearing traditional male Afghan dress and had ridden with her face covered, much as I did when on horseback. "Reporting the war. And it's been hell getting here before you guys won it. What's the hurry?"

"You've no business being here. This is no place for a woman."

"You sound like my dad, only he's not as good looking."

General Khan approached. "You're the reporter from SNS I've heard about?"

"That's right. You must be the man in charge." She extended her hand. "Let me clean up and get the camera set then we'll do that interview. I've got uplink capacity, so if we time it right, we can go live." She gave me her winning smile. "See you later, soldier."

That night, Diana Maurasi was the sensation of the desert camp. The Northern Alliance forces fought without women and were impressed with this Western woman who'd found a way to them across hostile country. Walking about the camp, she clearly enjoyed the attention.

Before turning in, I'd taken her aside. "Do you have any idea the danger you are in?"

"No more than you, I would think."

"This is my profession. I'm supposed to be in harm's way. It's what I've trained to do."

"You think I'm any different? The war is here. I'm not going to sit in an office and let the others do the work. General Khan knew I was coming. He needs the publicity and so does this war. It's the twenty-first century, soldier. Time to get with it."

Three minutes of her interview with Khan that first night had gone live. The intrepid SNS reporter—perky, pretty, and tenacious—became an overnight sensation. I reported her presence to my superiors and received orders not to offend the lady.

The next day, my team and I rode out on reconnaissance and spread out across the waiting line of advance. Diana arrived behind me without warning.

"I can't let you go with me," I told her. "Get back to camp. There's going to be fighting today."

"You aren't giving me permission. General Khan did. As for fighting, that's what I'm here to cover." She steadied her horse, then said,

"So where do you think the Taliban forces are dug in? Across that ridge up there?"

That was exactly where they were. I had just called in the air strike against them. "What the hell. Get your cameraman ready. That entire ridge is about to go up."

I stayed aboard my horse as Diana and her cameraman prepared for the shot. The forces with us were talking excitedly among themselves. They were always happy when the enemy died at long range.

High above, I spotted the contrails of the B-52s. We didn't see the bombs falling, but suddenly the ridge came alive as bomb after bomb exploded.

"Hey, soldier," Diana shouted, and I turned my head. She snapped a picture. "Thanks," she said with a wide grin.

Diana then stood in front of the motion camera, holding her microphone as the bombs pounded the ground behind her. I learned later that SNS had cut into normal programming to air her report. "The last stronghold of Taliban forces is being destroyed this very moment behind me," she said in that cadence unique to news reporters. "American-led Northern Alliance tribesmen are marshaled for the final assault on Kabul." I drifted away from the camera.

We entered the capital the next day.

One week later I was stunned to see my photograph on the cover of *Time* magazine. Fortunately, my face was covered and I was not identified except as an American officer with an advance team of Rangers who'd led the offensive and called in air strikes. Those up the chain of command knew it was me, but since I was never publicly identified, said nothing.

After the occupation, I stayed in Kabul as the Northern Alliance and some 10,000 Marines who'd arrived prepared for their offensive against the last Taliban redoubt in Tora Bora, near the Pakistan border. My team and I were housed at the Mustafa Hotel in downtown Kabul. A U.S. Army-supplied generator supplied the hotel with four hours of electricity a day, providing the hotel luxury available nowhere else in Kabul.

A few days after the *Time* cover came out, Diana approached me in the bar.

"Mind if I join you?"

"You will whether I want you to or not."

She grinned. "I see you're getting to know me. So what's your name? I can't keep calling you 'soldier,' and your men call you 'lieutenant.' You must have a name."

"Only if you don't use it."

"What's the matter? Don't like a little fame?"

"No, I don't. And who gave you permission to use my picture?"

"I didn't need it. You're safe with me. What do I call you?"

"Scott will do."

"Okay, Scott. Buy a lady a drink?"

What followed was a torrid affair fed by the uncertainties of war. Overnight Diana had become a celebrity. The network had ordered her to file from Kabul, as they didn't want to risk her near the fighting. Each day, she'd cover another aspect of the city—the refugees, the former tyranny of the Taliban, the rebuilding of the city. I worked from SOF command just outside the city, but found most of my nights free.

By late December, Diana was flown back to the States for a new assignment as White House correspondent. I stayed in Afghanistan during Operation Enduring Freedom. I was promoted to captain and discharged in early 2003.

We had bad luck after that. I finished my Ph.D. at Columbia in New York City while Diana was assigned to Washington. We continued to see each other, though less frequently. By the time she'd been made anchor and transferred to Manhattan, I'd completed my studies and was working for the Center for Middle Asian Studies in western Massachusetts. We'd not seen each other in more than two years.

I glanced at my fellow travelers seated along the walls of the helicopter—two groups facing each other—and sized them up. Since SNS had decided to cover this as a news story, it was clear enough why Diana was on board. Someone had decided her career needed a boost—though how that would come from an expedition sent to recover the dead son of a man with more money than Croesus and the practical power of a potentate—was beyond me.

SNS also explained why Crystal and Rusty were here. They already knew the terrain and had demonstrated their climbing skills. They'd covered Derek virtually every moment of that ill-fated climb. I expected Diana was about to get the same treatment.

But what was Calvin Seavers doing here? The man had taken valuable time away from his practice for last year's expedition, when he'd also served as team doctor. He and Derek had been very close and he'd taken Derek's death hard. Would he really have come so far, at such expense, merely to recover his body? That didn't seem reasonable. And if memory served correctly, the good doctor had suffered a bit of frostbite last year.

As for Tarja, who was now smoking a cigarette, her being here made no sense at all—even less than did Peer's presence. The Norwegian was presumably going to attempt another summit, but that hadn't been how he'd talked when we'd left the mountain.

Then there was Tom Bauman. All I knew about the man was that he'd been involved in business ventures with Sodoc. I couldn't imagine what connection existed between that and this expedition. Though the man appeared fit enough, he'd mentioned no climbing experience of any kind.

This brought my thoughts to the father, Michael Sodoc. Just three weeks before, the chairman of the Center for Middle Asian Studies had asked me to go to New York City and meet with the senior Mr. Sodoc. "He's making a substantial contribution to the center, but asked to meet with you first," he'd said.

"Why?"

"I have no idea. But he spoke with me personally, not through a representative, and he's not a man to whom you say no."

The next day, I was at the Global News building in Lower Manhattan, international headquarters for SNS, which formed a portion of the Global News empire. The CEO's office occupied a spacious corner on the floor just below the penthouse, where I understood the man lived in a form of Eastern opulence.

Michael Sodoc, the Americanized version of his Central European name, was an internationally known figure, though his history was enigmatic. A senior American government official, irritated that Sodoc was not giving money to his political party, once publicly suggested the vast fortune came from drug money. He'd been forced to retract the statement and quietly resigned a few months later.

But the origins of the Sodoc wealth were only understood in the broadest of terms, while even less was known about the early life of the man himself. Presumably about seventy years old, Michael Sodoc was reportedly born in a village in Carpathian Ruthenia around the time of the Second World War. Having been divided and handed over to various conquerors through the centuries, most of the region was then part of Czechoslovakia.

One rumor said that Sodoc was Jewish, another that he was Armenian, still others that he was Ukrainian, or Romanian, a Turk or a Gypsy. The list, and speculation, was endless. He never said. What little was known was that he was an early orphan. He'd drifted and ended up in Budapest, where he'd been active in the Hungarian uprising of 1956—as either a young man or a child, depending on what age you gave him. He'd fled the country when the Russian tanks rolled on the city and had been granted asylum in the United States, where he briefly attended college, dropped out to go into business, and was later granted citizenship.

While still in his twenties, he'd acquired control of a small, rural weekly newspaper. Over the next decade, he turned it into an influential—and highly profitable——suburban chain. He'd invested heavily, and successfully, in real estate as well, and in 1977 bought a local television station. In 1981, one year after CNN began, he launched his own cable news network, the Sodoc News Service. With deregulation, Sodoc acquired the nearly bankrupt *New York Examiner*, quickly turning it into a profitable tabloid, the first of several.

But his empire had scarcely begun. The holding company was named Global News and it expanded ravenously throughout the world, being the first to move aggressively onto the Internet. Though rich by any standard, Sodoc become enormously wealthy when he followed George Soros' lead in 1992 and joined in selling the British pound short. His fortune was now estimated in excess of $10 billion.

Sodoc's personal life had been less illustrious. His first wife, married while he was beginning, had produced just a single child, the son, Derek. She'd committed suicide the following year, under circumstances never satisfactorily explained. His second wife was an Italian baroness. Theirs had been a volatile relationship that produced no children. The divorce had been so unpleasant that for a time Sodoc lost publishing and broadcast rights in Italy. His current wife was a former Russian beauty with rumored ties to the Russian mob. Since their marriage, Global News had become the dominant news provider in the former Eastern Bloc. She was reportedly pregnant.

❦❦❦

After a short wait, I was ushered into the presence of the great man. I'd scanned Sodoc's history in Wikipedia the previous day, but was not prepared for his enormous size. At six feet, four inches, he weighed just under three hundred pounds, but did not seem fat in the least. Bald, with dark glittering eyes, he appeared decades younger than his purported age.

"We'll have coffee here," Sodoc said by way of introduction, gesturing toward a corner table with a commanding view of uptown. His grip was firm, the smile fleeting, before we sat. It was just the two of us in the spacious, richly appointed office.

"I have little time for small talk, Mr. Devlon," Sodoc said. "I'm sure you understand. I take it you were a friend of my son's."

"Yes, I would say that. We met just over two years ago on a climb in South America. I ran into him later in Australia. When Reginald Maul contacted me about joining last year's expedition, he mentioned that Derek would be on it. I was uncertain about going. A few weeks later, Derek called to persuade me."

"Why uncertain?"

"I'd never climbed above 23,000 feet, and I've never been an avid mountaineer. I'm more a rock climber. You don't tackle Everest unless you are ready for it."

"And Derek was?"

"Oh, yes. If any climber in the world was prepared for Everest, it was Derek."

Sodoc savored that thought a moment before speaking. "But you went, despite your reservations?"

"I wouldn't call them 'reservations.' It was more a certain hesitation about whether I was up to it, but Derek wasn't one to take no for an answer. I'm sure you know that. Plus, I liked Reggie and he had an open slot. I agreed to portage equipment just so it was clear I wouldn't necessarily attempt a summit."

"Yet you did."

I reached for my coffee cup. "Yes, in the end I went for it."

"So tell me what happened. I've read that book. It struck me as irresponsible. You didn't talk to the author, did you?"

"No. I've not discussed the climb with anyone."

Sodoc watched me. "Still, the book makes a number of claims. It says my son could have been saved."

"As I said, I've not read it."

"Could he have been saved?"

I paused before answering. "That's a difficult question to give a single answer to. The fact is that he wasn't saved despite the best efforts of any number of climbers, three of whom died in the attempt, while another lost his feet. Could he have been saved? Yes, if things had gone differently. But the point is that they *didn't* go differently. They happened as they did and in the end, he died up there. I don't say that to be cruel. It's just the way it was."

It seemed to me as if some of the energy had gone from the man. When he spoke, it was in a much softer voice, almost a whisper. "Tell me about it."

I played with my coffee to stall for time. At last I said, "I don't know how to tell it. Really."

"Try. He was my only child."

I didn't know if the man was accustomed to pleading. I doubted it. But there it was. "I can only relate my personal experience. In those conditions, with diminished oxygen, gale force winds, forty degrees below zero, all but blinded, unable to hear anything but the storm,

nothing seems quite real. Looking back on it, it's difficult to recon-
struct events in any way that makes sense. But I'll try."

For the next several minutes, I told Sodoc of the expedition, fast-
forwarding to the final, tragic day when our party had attempted to
summit.

It had begun at midnight on a bright, clear, moonless night; the
path clearly marked and roped in the snow. We'd made good initial
progress to the South Summit not long after daybreak. By then, the
party was strung out, as often happened on summit attempts.

Shortly after noon, a storm struck with little warning, creating
blizzard conditions. We had become separated in the limited visibility and fierce wind. Derek consumed all his oxygen and lacked the
strength to go on or even to make it down Hillary Step—the single
technical obstacle between him and the relative safety of Camp Five.
I had found him, summoned help before the radio failed, and then
waited in vain.

The story I told was a close approximation of the truth.

Sodoc said nothing, taking it in with fierce concentration. When
I stopped, my mouth dry, a slight tremor in my hands, the man said,
"Why didn't you carry him down yourself when it was clear no one
was coming?"

"It was never clear no one was coming. At any moment, help might
have stepped out of the storm. With the radios out, I had no way of
knowing. And I couldn't carry him by myself."

"Why not? You look strong enough."

"As I said, it's difficult to convey what it's like up there. You barely
have the strength to stay on your feet. The rule is if a climber can't
walk, he can't be saved. And Derek couldn't walk."

Sodoc pulled himself more erect and spoke with vigor. "Others
have been saved in similar conditions."

"That's true to a point, but none in the condition he was in or
from where he was. Each situation is unique. All I can tell you is that
I hadn't the ability to lift him up and get him to, then down, the Step
alone. Two of us might have managed, but I doubt it even then. In
similar situations, even in ideal weather, it can take ten climbers to
manhandle someone in his condition."

"Why didn't you go for help? That seems obvious enough."

"Today, sitting here, sipping coffee, it does seem obvious. All I can say is that I was near the limit of my own strength. With the storm, I couldn't see beyond the tips of my gloves at arm's length. If I'd strayed too far, I wasn't certain I could find him again. And Derek begged me not to leave him. In his shape, no one wants to be alone. What I did was remain with him, then every few minutes I'd move to the route the climbers would take of they'd heard my call for help and responded, hoping to intercept someone. That seemed to me the only way to save him. It just didn't happen."

A veil crossed Sodoc's eyes. "I don't find your answers satisfactory. You're still with us, I see, with all your fingers and toes."

"True enough. But more than seventeen climbers died that day on or near the summit. Derek was just one. Our expedition lost five of them. Only seven climbers in all got off that mountain alive. One of them no longer has his feet. To my knowledge, not a single climber in trouble in that storm made it back down. That's the truth of it."

Sodoc gave me a long, steady stare before saying, "I have just one last question for you. My son was already dead when you left him?"

Without hesitating, I said, "Yes, he was."

The meeting didn't last long after that. Sodoc got to business, clearly the place where he was most comfortable. An expedition was returning to Everest. I was to go along and help. If I refused, he would make no grant to the center. The implication was that the man would also make it his life's mission to destroy the center and my career.

"What am I returning for?" I asked, confused at the speed with which events were moving. An expedition took up to three years to plan, not a few weeks.

"It's for my son. For his memory and because I cannot bear to think of his body lying out there for all to see, exposed to the elements. I've seen the pictures of Mallory, his body looking like marble against the rock, his face frozen into the mountain. I'll not have that. You and the others are going back to do what you should have done in the first place. You're going to bring my son down from there. You're going to give him a proper service. You're going to show him the respect he's due."

The mound of gear was stacked mostly to the rear of the roaring helicopter and the Sherpas had clustered there, hunkered down and quiet, as was their way. The racket made reasonable conversation impossible.

Through my window, I saw the countryside racing away beneath us. We'd left the city almost at once. Below were cultivated fields in asymmetric patterns.

I turned to Diana and leaned over to speak. In her bright red coat, her face was small and her complexion pale from too much time indoors. I pressed my lips nearly to her ear and said, "I can't believe you're doing this."

She turned toward me. "The anchor thing didn't work out, as the whole world knows. They're giving me a new show. It's a good deal, very lucrative for the network. This is meant to remind the viewer that I'm the daredevil type, just like the old days." She grinned.

"It's dangerous, anywhere from Base Camp on up. People die from heart attacks or edema every season. Even Base Camp is no cakewalk, at 18,000 feet. There's no way to know in advance if you're vulnerable."

She patted my arm. "Once the body's back at Base Camp, I'll cover the memorial service, focusing on interviews with the great climber's friends—and an abundance of shots of the grieving widow. It should be very touching."

I looked toward Tarja, who was laughing and leaning over to kiss Peer. "That will be something."

Diana grinned. "Won't it, though? Interest is running high since the book came out. People want to know the true story of how Derek died. There's talk of a movie. We'll work segments in over a few days about that, and then cover the service live from the top of the world. It will make great theater. Anyway, you're here, soldier."

"The center was pressured."

She laughed. "You're telling me you're going up Mt. Everest to save your job? That doesn't sound like the man I met in Afghanistan."

"There was a hint about destroying my life as well, not that I took it seriously." The helicopter banked sharply and, out the dirty window, I spotted the landing zone. "Just tell me you're not going to summit."

She grinned again. "Of course not. How stupid do I look? Anyway, the network's not about to risk my fair body. They've got too much invested in me." Then she met my eyes. "With you here, nothing's going to happen to me."

⌐⌐⌐

I closed my eyes and leaned back in the seat. The helicopter lurched and turned sharply to the right, a sickening sensation.

Fun loving, amusing, and occasionally thoughtless, Derek Sodoc had approached the conquest of Everest with the same single-mindedness he'd taken to each of his summit attempts. From all appearances, he relished the role in which he'd been cast by life. But the previous year, it had become apparent to me that the younger Sodoc was driven by demons and that, for all Derek's protestations to the contrary, his father exerted a relentless influence on him. I'd heard Calvin arguing before the summit attempt that Derek was in no condition for it, that he needed to return to Base Camp and its relatively richer air to recuperate for a few days before revisiting his decision to make the effort. But it was nearing the end of that narrow window Everest usually grants each spring and, if he'd done as Calvin wanted, Derek might miss the opportunity.

"Dad wouldn't like that," was all I heard.

Such foolish motivations had influenced the entire expedition. Add cameras, satellite phones, laptops, and reporters to such an enterprise, and priorities became twisted.

Of one thing I was certain. Sodoc had overshadowed Derek all his life and I had not the slightest doubt that the old man had pushed his only son to his death. And that, I decided, was the real reason we were here—to assuage a father's guilt.

And perhaps also to find someone the man could blame—other than himself.

⌐⌐⌐

I had flown home from the meeting with Sodoc feeling angry and manipulated, as well as more than a little guilty. I'd never expected to meet the man. I knew that no version of the story about his son's death would have been satisfactory. I'd certainly thought hard to come up with one that might be.

Back home, resigned to the inevitable, I climbed into the attic where I'd placed my gear from the previous year and carefully laid it all out. As I did, the smell of Nepal brought a rush of memories—a few good, but most of them unpleasant.

I examined each item critically. Some would still do, having been properly broken in. Others were worn and shabby. Still others had to be discarded. I made a list of what I'd need to buy before leaving. That included an ice ax, I reminded myself.

Returning from Everest, exhausted, emotionally spent, and guilt ridden, I'd vowed never to return. I'd meant it. Standing in my living room as I packed my gear, I wondered why I hadn't thrown this all away. If I really hadn't intended to return, why keep it?

In the helicopter, I looked at the woman sitting beside me. Diana wanted to know why I was really on this expedition. So did I.

⌁⌁⌁

The aging helicopter shook violently and then dipped unpleasantly. I glanced along the walls where the Sherpas and Western climbers sat. The Sherpas seemed to be taking this much as a child might a roller coaster ride, while several of the climbers looked ill. Dawa caught my eye and gave that shy smile so common to the mountain people.

Beside Peer, Tarja sat, seemingly unconcerned about the unsettling ride. Her behavior the previous year had only served to reinforce the prejudice I'd formed against her from scanning grocery store tabloids while standing in line.

She was model-tall, but with the hard body of a career athlete. She'd been on the U. S. Winter Olympics team at one time, but had never competed. For two or three years, she'd been the "other woman" in a New York society love triangle. It had ended badly for her and I'd next read her name when her marriage to Derek Sodoc became public. The first time I'd ever seen the woman in person was on the approach trek to Everest the previous year.

Friendly enough, she was always in search of the camera. That struck me as a peculiar way to spend your life. She'd traded on her celebrity status these last years and I'd taken her appearance on the Everest expedition with her new adventurer husband as just one more step in a lifetime of fame for doing what was essentially nothing.

Tarja leaned toward Peer, who was taking in Diana with eager eyes, and said something with a laugh he appeared to enjoy. He turned toward her and responded in kind. She snuggled. Peer caught me looking and returned my gaze with an acknowledging smile, like a college frat brother spotted with the homecoming queen.

Across the aisle sat Crystal Hernandez. Daughter of Cuban refugees, she'd worked her way through the SNS ranks until landing the plum assignment covering Derek's Everest ascent, where she'd stumbled. Perhaps this expedition was about redemption.

Next to her was Rusty Landon, the cameraman. A former Marine who'd served in the first Gulf War, he was steady in tight spots and utterly fearless on the mountain. Rusty's eyes danced from Peer, to Crystal, to Tarja, then back again with merriment.

This isn't an expedition, I thought. *It's a goddamn carnival road show.*

THREE

You are drawn by the ghosts of all those
giants who have gone before you. Mallory,
Irvine, Hillary, Tenzing! Their spirit calls out
to you! You experience their presence every
step of the trek, every inch of the trek!
    —Quentin Stern, www.AbandonedonEverest.com

At Thyangboche, I watched the helicopter lift from the ground with a great shudder amid a billowing cloud of vermilion dust. To the north was the massive Buddhist monastery—the largest and most imposing in the region—while to the south lay the supporting village bordered by trees just coming to life after the long winter. Scattered in a lazy line was our gear, offloaded by the Sherpas onto the edge of the primitive landing pad that the Nepalese military had built to support air operations against the intermittent Maoist insurgency.

From here also was a panoramic view of the Himalayan mountains—my first since returning to Nepal. Ahead, demanding attention, was a sharp point of rock, the 22,400-feet-tall Ama Dablam, while more than a mile above it rose the mammoth Everest itself.

I looked again at Everest and noted, not for the first time, that it was unlike any other mountain I'd ever climbed. Most closely resembled Ama Dablam, sharp projections jutting above the surrounding land.

I'd raced up them when I could, Alpine-style, working with crampon, hammer, and rope, scaling challenging walls of stone and ice. Once on top, there would be those few minutes of elation and rest, followed by a rapid descent. There were exceptions, but such had usually been my experience.

Everest, by comparison, was a ponderous mass, more like an enormous three-sided pyramid than a mountain rising above its sisters. From its crest, I could see the familiar icy plume, like a pale banner streaming high above. You didn't conquer Everest with a rush, you lay siege like a mediaeval army assaulting a castle, planning—hoping—to exploit a weakness in order to triumph before time ran out and everything turned against you.

Dawa joined me for a moment. "Sagarmatha," he said, looking up at the mountain. The Mother Goddess, as it was known to the Sherpas. They had worshiped her from afar before the British came. Now they dared to surmount her, but did so with respect and a great measure of awe. This expedition would merely be a job for them—one that paid well, of course—but above Base Camp, on the flanks of the mother goddess, the climb became a religious experience for the Sherpa. All they really asked of the Westerners, beyond their pay, was a show of respect.

Tarja coughed the deep hack that is so familiar to all high-altitude climbers. It turned your throat so raw that you could scarcely swallow and at its worst, it broke ribs. At nearly 13,000 feet, the Westerners were already commenting on the thin air. Kathmandu lay at a relatively benign 4,500 feet and we'd had no intervening time period for the climbers to acclimatize. Our blood oxygen content was already so low that if we'd been at sea level, an emergency room doctor would place us on oxygen. From this point on, our bodies would begin building hemoglobin to carry more oxygen to our brains and vital body organs.

We'd experience side effects as well. The headaches would begin, in time producing a searing pain that some would find unbearable, described by most like a spike driven through the center of your skull. At Camp Three, Derek had told me the year before that he'd thought his head was going to explode. There would be bouts of nausea and increasing overall weakness. The sense of well-being all of us had known just a short time ago would vanish, replaced by a pervasive sense of affliction accompanied by depression, fear, and—occasionally—paranoia.

For the Sherpas, of course, this was home. They'd been born and spent their lives at this altitude. Their lungs and hearts were adapted to it by the many generations their people had claimed the region as their own. It did not come without a price. From what I'd seen before, there were no old Sherpas. But in their youth, they were vigorous and hearty, driven by pride or poverty to seemingly superhuman efforts though at enormous personal cost.

Contact with the West had come with a full measure of trouble, but also with enormous benefits. Clinics now dotted their land, bringing medical care never before possible. The better-off Sherpa, lives improved by the money that came from expeditions like this one, were able to move to the city and give their children the prospect of an improved life. But here in their traditional lands both promiscuity and alcoholism were rampant.

We were still standing at the patch of dirt used by the helicopter when a tall, rather elegant man in worn brown trousers, hiking boots, and a yellow parka approached, nodding in greeting. Beside him was a much shorter, weather-beaten Sherpa, also smiling warmly. Both men were deeply tanned, their skin weathered two shades of bronze.

"Hello," the Westerner said with a New Zealand accent as the sound of the helicopter faded. "I'm Harlan Hughes, your expedition leader. This is Zhiku, the head of the Sherpas on the team. Welcome to the Himalayas." A few in the group answered quietly, others merely waved or gestured in acknowledgment.

Harlan moved easily along the line, shaking hands and extending personal greetings to each of us, followed by Zhiku who did the same. Harlan then gathered us around and explained that our quarters were not far away. "We'll be here a few days to allow you to adjust to the altitude. I advise you all to visit the monastery and ask the *Rinpoche* for his blessing. We can use all the good karma we can get where we're going and the Sherpas will approve of our showing him respect."

With that, he flashed a light smile and walked easily away with Zhiku beside him.

I lifted my bag and ambled the short distance to the village and the hostel where we would live during our stay. This was not a tourist destination and quarters were primitive. I stooped to enter, as all the structures in this part of the world seemed constructed for a smaller stature. The dark interior was buzzing with flies and an unpleasant odor carried me back two centuries. Not long before, the room had been lit by candlelight or lamps burning yak butter. The darkened walls and ceiling were smudged with the smoke and the stink was all but overwhelming.

I found my assigned room to be dirty as well. Tiny shapes scurried about, vanishing when I entered the room. I decided to sleep in a bag. The toilet, I knew, would be a smelly squat down the hall. I'd expected no better.

Calvin knocked on my door then entered. "Luxurious, huh?" At forty-one, the expedition doctor was a calm, reasoned man. He was a climbing purist who'd devoted the best years of his life to studying the effects of high altitude on the human body. His published findings constituted the bible for expedition doctors. Divorced at least three times, he was resigned to his fate.

Of all those the previous year, and in this I included Tarja, Calvin had been closest to Derek. We had first met the year before, when we'd all been climbing the 22,800-foot Aconcagua in Argentina and had formed a comfortable relationship.

"We've seen worse," I said.

"That we have, that we have. Did you notice the lovebirds?"

I grunted. "I'm certain she'll appear suitably distraught on camera. Why's Peer here? After last year, I thought we'd seen the last of him."

"I don't know," Calvin said, "but I intend to find out."

"Why are *you* here, Cal? I thought you'd had enough." I hadn't asked, but I'd heard that Calvin had lost some toes the previous year.

His smile was whimsical. "I always say that. I've come to try to find Derek. It's always seemed pretty cold to just leave the dead where they lie. We don't do that anywhere else, certainly not in what is at its core a sport. What about you? You seemed to mean it on that flight to Bangkok."

I grimaced. "Yes. I'm as surprised as anyone to find myself here." I told him briefly about the center and how I'd been maneuvered.

Calvin nodded. "How'd it go with the old man?"

"Awkward. The worst hour of my life." Changing the subject, I said, "What about the others? I never expected to see them all again, certainly not in one spot—not *here* of all places, and not so soon. Did you notice that every surviving climber from last year is here? There's a camera, so I suppose we know the attraction for the widow."

"Maybe. I don't know it for a fact, but Derek was not just the only son. He was the only child and in line to inherit the entire $10 billion, or whatever ghastly amount the old man's looted all these years. There was no prenup. I've heard that has something to do with it."

"Isn't the new Mrs. Sodoc pregnant?"

"So I read. I wouldn't want to be her and around the widow with sharp instruments. What do you say we have a drink? I'm of the opinion that staying drunk is the best way to handle these lower heights."

We set off for the bar as I laughed. Only a high altitude expert would consider Thyangboche to be a "lower height."

⌁⌁⌁

The hostel dining room served as the bar and most of the climbers were already crowded at various tables, their talk and laughter filling the room. Much of their gear had simply been tossed against the nearest wall so they'd yet to even see their rooms. Tarja was smoking, as was someone else I couldn't see, and a blue haze hung in the air. The flies didn't seem to care.

Calvin picked a corner spot where Harlan and Zhiku were in conversation.

"Hope you don't mind the company," he said amiably. "Quarters are a bit tight in here."

"Not at all," the New Zealander said. "We're both looking forward to getting to know everyone. This is all quite sudden, for us as well as for you."

"How did this happen so fast?" I asked. "I was surprised to learn this one was ready to go."

Launching an expedition of this scale required enormous preparation. It was necessary to obtain a permit from the Nepalese government, hire quality guides who were always in demand, ferry the essential equipment and supplies in from outside, secure housing along the trek, and much more. Given the weather for most of the year, the snail-like pace at which the bureaucracy worked and the on-again-off-again rebel insurgency, it took at least two years for any single expedition to position itself for the four- to six-week approach march and climb window the weather usually permitted.

Calvin gestured toward the bar, holding up four fingers to order the Nepalese-brewed Carlsbad beers.

"It's no secret. I don't run my own show," Harlan said. "I work for—actually, am a minor partner in—Extreme Mountain Adventures out of Sydney. This expedition's been on the drawing board for three years. Everything was set and in place, but for another group. Four weeks ago, Mr. Sodoc paid $3 million to buy the exclusive use of it. EMA turned a very healthy profit by accepting. I received a fax informing me that those with whom I've been working these many months would not be going—at least, not with us and not this year. I was to greet an entirely new team." He didn't sound pleased about it.

"What about the permit? Doesn't it name the expedition members?"

"Your Mr. Sodoc has pull with the government here apparently. It hasn't been a problem."

Calvin grimaced. "He's scarcely 'our Mr. Sodoc.'"

"Who were the others?" I asked.

"Some very angry Koreans. Nice people. Two very experienced climbers were running it. We won't see their business again."

"Yes, very mad people, I must say," Zhiku said with a soft smile. The Sherpa appeared to be nearly forty years, old but I guessed his true age at twenty-seven or twenty-eight. Life in the mountains was hard. To hold his position as chief Sherpa, he would be a remarkable climber and a natural leader. The next few years would be the height of his career and establish his reputation among his people—if he survived.

"Have either of you summited previously?" Calvin asked as the beers arrived.

"I've been to the top four times," Harlan said, "though those days are now behind me, I'm sorry to say. I'll likely be staying behind at Advanced Base Camp. This will be Zhiku's third summit." Harlan finished the beer he'd been working and took a sip of the fresh one placed in front of him. "You two both knew Reggie, I take it?"

"Yes," Calvin said. "I've known him for some years. We'd climbed previously."

"And you, Mr. Devlon?" Harlan asked.

"I met Derek and Calvin on Aconcagua in South America about two years ago now. Reggie contacted me last year about joining the expedition. Then Derek called and wouldn't take no for an answer."

"I take it you and Reggie were friends?" Calvin said to Harlan.

"Mates, yes. We started climbing as a pair in New Zealand. We first summited Everest together, in fact. With Zhiku's uncle, actually. I was supposed to join him in South America, but work intervened. A nasty business there."

"Yes," I said as Calvin looked away, "very nasty in the end. What do you think of this expedition?"

Harlan paused before answering. "I can't say I care for it much. Zhiku and I were just discussing it."

The head guide looked up as he spoke. "Very bad. Sherpas don't want to climb. They say leave the dead."

"Sherpa don't like much of anything that brings them in contact with dead bodies. And there's been bad feeling on the mountain for some time," Harlan said. "As for this," he gestured toward the film crew, "you either climb or make pictures—there really isn't a place for both in the Death Zone."

"And just what is that?" Tom Bauman said as he gestured for permission to take a place at the head of the table. "Sounds like someone's idea of a bad dream." He grinned. "This is my first time and I wasn't able to bone up before leaving on such short notice. But I'm told I'm in good hands."

Harlan looked to Calvin. "You're the expert, I believe."

"The Death Zone is that area above 26,000 feet or 8,000 meters. It's the part of the mountain after you leave Camp Four."

"What's so special about it, besides it's cold and windy?" Tom asked.

"To begin with, you inhale just one-third the oxygen as at sea level. If you could be taken suddenly from the beach into the Death Zone, you'd die within minutes. You looked out the window of your jet flying here?"

"Sure."

"A commercial jet flies at the same altitude as the summit of Everest. Think about it. Consider just stepping out on that wing, if such a thing was possible. Everest is so high that the jet stream actually strikes it. When it was first pushed up, it altered the climate in Central and South America by diverting it. We aren't designed to survive at such altitudes. It's not natural for us. Our species evolved on the plains of Africa and for most of humanity's existence, nearly everyone has lived close to the ocean or at elevations not much above sea level. Our bodies are adapted to life there, not the mountains. Once you step into the Death Zone, the most accurate way of putting it is to say that you are dying. If you stayed up there without oxygen, you'd be dead within hours, certainly a few days. It's true even for the experts, even for those acclimatized, even for Zhiku here. We simply aren't meant to be there and can exist on the summit for only a short time. It's like being on another planet."

"Which reminds me," I said, "why were we brought so high up by helicopter? That seems a bit sudden. We started out a lot lower before. What's the rush? We're at more than 12,000 feet already."

"Those were my instructions from the home office," Harlan said. "Someone wants to be certain we're the first team on the mountain— even if we face some bad weather on the approach and when we first make Base Camp. We're now ahead of the other expeditions and I'll make certain it stays that way from here out. In fact, none of them is even scheduled to leave Kathmandu for days yet."

"Why shouldn't we have taken a helicopter here?" Tom asked. "I don't look forward to all that walking."

"You're in the wrong place, then." Calvin said with a smile. "We've come up pretty fast. Typically you don't want to start the approach hike above 10,000 feet. Even then, you set a leisurely pace while your body adjusts. We're pushing the envelope a bit this way. How long are we staying here?" he asked Harlan.

"I'm planning for three days. If no one comes down seriously ill during that time, we leave for Pheriche on the morning of the fourth day."

"So what if the air is thin up high? I thought the big problem was the cold. We'll be on gas when we summit, right?" Tom said, referencing the use of oxygen on the summit climb.

"Yes," Harlan said.

"So … what's the problem?" Tom repeated.

"The problem is," Calvin said, "that gas at that elevation only restores your oxygen level to that of 20,000 feet, about half what you are accustomed to. Canned air also lacks humidity and you'll be breathing through your mouth, so your throat turns dry and raw when you use it. Worse, even though you'll be inhaling additional oxygen, you'll instinctively feel as if you're choking. The lack of oxygen and the mask itself give that sensation, especially when you sleep. Without thinking, you'll remove the mask to get more air, but that will only make your situation worse. And all this assumes no problem with the regulator. They are prone to freezing up and the controls aren't meant for gloved, half-frozen hands and fingers."

"Okay," Tom said a bit sober. "What's it like?"

Calvin made a face. "Your movements will be slow and you'll have little feeling in your feet or hands. All of the equipment you depend on will be difficult to use, not just the tanks. But worst of all will be your lack of judgment. Your thinking will deteriorate to that of a child. That's the real danger. You stop making good decisions and you are so close to the edge that almost anything—bad luck, bad weather, a broken bit of equipment—can do you in."

"There's something else," Harlan said. "I've not read any papers on it, but I've seen it. Up high, really high, it is so difficult and your mental functions decline so significantly that teamwork breaks down. An attitude of 'every man for himself' takes over. Climbers find it very easy to walk past the dying with scarcely a glance. If you get in trouble, you can't be certain of help. If you sit or lie down and refuse to get up, you can be absolutely certain you'll be left to die.

"In the disaster year of 1996, when the IMAX team and others pulled out all the stops to try to save those climbers trapped in the Death Zone, a South African team refused any help, even so much as the loan of a single radio. Twelve climbers died. That's how it gets," Harlan said.

"It sounds pretty cold-blooded," Tom said somberly.

"It is. It's a cold-blooded business we're in—right, Zhiku?" Harlan said.

The Sherpa nodded in agreement. "Yes, many people die up there. Many. Even Sherpa."

"His uncle's dead, the man I first summited with," Harlan said. "The best guide there was, maybe ever. Killed two years ago in the Ice Flow just above Base Camp on a routine effort setting a path through the ice-cliffs. Caught in an avalanche. We all must accept that certain perils are beyond our control. We step on seemingly solid ice and fall to our death. We tie ropes to crampons that appear set, but give when needed. We totter near a precipice and fall. It's happened to the greatest. Death is a climbing partner of every one of us up there. Which brings me to my question, gentlemen. What happened to Reggie last year?"

⌒⌒⌒

Reginald Mahl had been the expedition leader the previous year. Gregarious and relentlessly professional, Derek had selected him because he was the most experienced Everest guide in the business. I remembered the man and his gentle ways fondly.

"I don't know for certain," Calvin said. "The day he died I'd moved up to Camp Four to position myself for help if needed and I made no attempt to summit. You know how it is. Climbers exhaust themselves getting to the top, they stumble back, barely able to stay on their feet. I wanted to be able to move to Camp Five if they couldn't make Camp Four before dark. Reggie was on the summit team. Scott, you were up there."

I nodded. "I was on top around noon and could see the thunderheads below. Though we all set out at about the same time, Peer, Dawa, Dorji, and I were the first up from our expedition that day. The rest of the summit group had spread out on the ascent. On the descent, the storm hit while others were on top and still others were climbing.

"Dawa and I elected to separate when we lost Dorji. Dawa stayed to try and find him. The conditions were very bad. Responding to a distress call, I found Derek on the shelf just above the Hillary Step, where he'd dropped out of the climb. He'd sheltered against some rocks and was already in trouble

"I never saw another climber after that. I don't know what happened to Reggie. He'd been with Derek earlier and Derek was in no shape to tell me how they separated. I'm sorry, Harlan."

He gave me a hard look. "Reggie was twice the climber and three times the man I am. *Something* happened up there. You got down. So did that Norwegian climber. Hell, even the cameraman made it back. So why not Reggie?"

"I don't know. If I had to guess, I'd say Reggie refused to abandon a client in trouble. You should ask Dawa. Rusty was up there, as you say; the head Sherpa, whose name I've forgotten, and Peer. Maybe one of them saw Reggie and can tell you something. I just know that he wasn't with Derek and that I didn't encounter him on the way down."

"I've already talked with Dawa, Tsongba, and the red-headed fellow. The cameraman says he last saw Reggie below him, near the Hillary Step, and that he was moving steadily up. That was earlier, obviously. This is the first chance I've had to talk to Peer. How could you miss Reggie—or the others coming down from the summit to help, for that matter?"

"It was the blizzard," I said. "I could hardly see my own gloves. I was all but frozen myself once I stopped climbing."

There was a long pause and then Zhiku said, "Dorji died that day. Other Sherpa with other teams also. Very bad. Very bad."

"Tsongba lost both feet," Harlan said. "That will not happen this year." He gave me a fixed look then said to all, "No one on this expedition is going to die."

Zhiku gave him a tender look. "Sagarmatha decides, Harlan. Not us."

⌒⌒⌒

Dinner was a yak meat stew. I recalled it with no special affection, but this wasn't bad. The climbing team was crowded into the dining room, the air ripe with the smell of tobacco, boiled meat, exotic spices, vegetables, and beer. The Sherpas were served elsewhere; in that way, at least, not much had changed since the days of the White Man's Burden. Calvin and I found ourselves with Crystal and Rusty.

Though no one had ever told me, I was quite certain Rusty, who wore a New York Yankee baseball cap atop his brilliant red hair, had carried a torch for Crystal the previous year. If so, it seemed to have passed. But there was no denying Crystal's appeal. A fit, attractive woman with dark angry features, she looked more Spanish than Cuban to me. Whatever she was ethnically, she certainly liked her drink. She was nearly finished with the bottle of brandy she'd been working on when we sat down.

"What's the plan, Crystal?" Calvin asked. "Are you doing the same as last year?"

She gave him an unpleasant look. "Last year was a homage to a great climber and man. This," she said dismissively, "is a publicity stunt." She poured herself another shot of brandy.

Rusty set his beer down and said brightly, "Did you see the piece on last year's climb?"

I had not. I had avoided all references to the disaster. In all, sixteen climbers died on Everest in a single thirty-six-hour time span, the worst debacle in climbing history. Four of the deaths had been on our team. The other twelve had been divided between an Italian and a Japanese expedition. The two countries had nearly broken diplomatic relations in the furor over which team had refused help to the other.

"I watched it," Calvin said mildly. "Difficult, but you two did a nice job with it."

Crystal grunted in acknowledgment. "How's your foot, Doc?" she asked.

"As good as can be expected."

"How much did you lose?"

"Two small toes on my right foot. It gives me trouble from time to time, especially when in the cold."

"So why are you here, Cal?" Rusty asked. "It's going to be colder than shit up there, especially since we're leaving so early in the season, which is, in my humble opinion, a very bad idea. It's likely to rain and snow the entire trek. I don't even want to think about how miserable this is going to get."

Calvin stared at him. "I'm here to get my friend down. I'm here to see Derek buried."

Crystal burst into tears and rushed from the room, knocking against a number of others who turned to look.

"Did I say something?" Calvin said.

"No. She's still pretty torn up about everything. I tried to talk her out of coming and thought I had, but the company insisted on the same crew as last year."

"What is it you're doing here, exactly?" Calvin asked.

"They've sent the chipper, famously courageous anchor along and she's going to do pieces on the approach march. I guess the company's got two plans here. The first is to build Diana up for her big morning show, which we hear is launching in the fall. The other is to cover the memorial service for Derek. Piece of cake." He saluted us with his beer and took a long pull.

"Assuming we can locate his body—and nobody else dies in the effort," I said.

"Finding him shouldn't be a problem," Rusty said. "You were with him."

"Yes, I was with him. It turned out that I was the last to leave the area of the summit that season and the last off the shelf. But who knows if he'll still be there or if we can even manage to get him down. We have no idea how violent the storms were this winter. He could have been blown into Tibet for all we know or—like Mallory—he could be frozen into a block of ice and impossible to get out. There's more than one reason why the dead are still up there."

"But you know where he was, right?" Rusty said.

I licked my lips. "There was a blizzard, if you recall. Winds well in excess of 100 miles per hour. Yes, I think I know where we were, but in those conditions, my recollection can't be entirely trusted. My perception at the time may not have been accurate."

"You sound as if you're making excuses, Scott. I don't remember you that way last year," Rusty said.

"I was a different man last year."

Calvin nodded. "We all were."

Rusty shrugged and grinned. "It won't matter if we find him or not. We'll film the climb for the recovery. If you guys can't locate him, we'll still have a memorial service at Base Camp. It's all decided. Hell, I figure they'll take our film stock and make a special out of the climb itself. Everest is hot right now, especially after all those dead climbers last year. Have you been to any of the blogs? They're just a deathwatch. A bunch of ghouls."

I winced and shook my head to stop him. Calvin looked in pain.

"Sorry, Doc."

"Are you summiting this year?" I asked to change the subject.

"You bet," Rusty said.

"Where were you when you turned back? I don't think I ever heard," I asked.

"On the Summit Ridge. You passed me coming down."

"Did I? I couldn't see much of anything in that whiteout. That was tough, turning back when you were so close."

"Ah, hell. The camera was giving me fits, I couldn't feel my toes or nose, the weather sucked—I kept thinking I was going to get blown off the mountain—and we had to find Derek, right? No choice. He was a nice enough guy, but more importantly, the boss' son, so what are you going to do? But I'd like to bag it this time, that's for sure." He rubbed his temples. "Anybody else got a headache?"

"Mine's started too," Calvin said. "Everyone will have one soon enough. Welcome back to Everest."

Throughout the meal, Tarja, at the table next to theirs, had been smoking and coughing relentlessly. Now she hacked as if her lungs would burst. Once calm, she turned in her place and said, "Guess this is it for the ciggies, right, Doc?"

"You should make it permanent."

She made a face and turned back to Peer sitting across from her.

Crystal rejoined us. "Sorry about that. It still comes and goes."

"So ..." Rusty said, "anyone here read the book, besides me?"

"I've read it," Calvin said. I shook my head. Crystal glared at Rusty. "It's a real piece of work," he said. "This Quentin Stern guy used to work for SNS before going to the *National Inquisitor*. I never met him. He knocked the book out in record time. I heard it's now on Amazon's bestseller list. What did you think, Cal?"

Calvin shrugged. "Most of the parts I had experience with were accurate enough. The author added his own tone and insinuations. There are an awful lot of nasty stories though. Very unpleasant. I didn't pick up on any of the ego and other stuff he writes about.

"I can't comment on what happened up top that day. I wasn't there. You'd know better than me. But I don't believe Derek was abandoned. I don't think any of you up there would have turned your back on him as long as there was any hope and you had the ability to help. The Death Zone is a tough place, requiring tough decisions. Everyone who set out to summit that day knew the risks. And I was with him until that last day. It was just very bad luck in a place that has no mercy. And he had no business making the effort when he did."

Rusty frowned. "Stern is merciless to me. He practically accuses me of wanting to see Derek dead. He hinted that I used to be some kind of CIA assassin. He gives credit to Peer for getting Tsongba down alive. He all but accuses you of murder, Scott. He says you left Derek for dead when he could have been saved, that the rest of us were out to save our own necks. I'm not trying to pick on you, but we all know you were the last to see Derek."

"Give him a break, okay?" Crystal said. "We all feel like hell about what happened, especially Scott. Anyway, Derek wasn't the only one to die that day. Just the most famous."

Calvin spoke. "I can tell you that watching someone die is a terrible experience. You never really get used to it. If it's a friend, there's always a sense of guilt—the feeling that you could have done something. Lower on the mountain, Scott could almost have carried Derek down single-handed. But where they were—at over 28,000 feet, in those conditions—it wasn't humanly possible. You remember Phurba Sherpa? It took a dozen climbers and Sherpa to get him from Camp Three to Camp Two and that was in good conditions. I'm of the opinion that if all of you on the summit had managed to find Derek, even with plenty of daylight left, you could not have brought him safely down. You just couldn't. And more of you would have died in the attempt. To place all this on Scott is simply … reckless and irresponsible."

"Hell, I'm not saying there's anything to this!" Rusty said. "I was up there, remember? I know what it was like—and I'm no hero. I didn't rescue anybody. I count myself lucky to be off the top alive and with all my fingers and toes." Crystal gave him a look. "Sorry, Doc," Rusty added. "I didn't mean that."

"Tell us about the book, Cal. We might as well hear it," Crystal said, extracting a fresh bottle of brandy from her coat pocket.

⌒⌒⌒

"*Abandoned on Everest* is like picking up one of those supermarket rags while standing in line," Rusty said. "As I mentioned, it has a nasty attitude and attributes bad motives to almost everyone on the climb. 'Pals' and 'friends' who don't want their names used are constantly sourced and the book suggests intimate knowledge of things most of us who were there knew little, if anything, about."

"Someone must have talked to this guy Stern," Crystal said.

"Yes," Calvin agreed, "clearly he had sources—or a source, at least."

"Rusty, what do you think?" she asked.

"Yeah, someone's been talking, but I think he made all that stuff up about the last day on top."

"What does he say happened?" she asked.

"Come on, Crissie; it's crap, I'm telling you. I was there. I almost died! He makes it sound like we were out for a nature hike, but were so fixed on getting to the top that we didn't care who died. He says we walked by dying people. He says Scott refused Derek's plea for help and that the rest of us were too selfish to stop and lend a hand."

"I don't believe that," Crystal said.

"And you shouldn't. It was hell up there, absolute hell. We were virtually blind from the storm. I personally never saw anyone lying in the snow. I can't say I was in any shape to help if I had, but I didn't pass anyone needing help. I never saw Reggie or the dead Sherpa. I reached Peer and Tsongba on the South Summit Ridge; I don't know how Peer got him down the Step alone, but he did. The guy deserves a medal for that." He stopped and licked his lips. "I'm getting another brew. Anyone else?"

Tarja laughed loudly beside them and Crystal gave the back of her head a nasty look.

"You might as well know the rest," Calvin said. "Are you certain you haven't read the book?"

"I haven't, I told you. Until tonight I didn't even know Rusty had read it." She seemed to brace herself. "So what else does it say?"

Calvin appeared genuinely uncomfortable. "That tone I mentioned. Stern describes the approach march and Base Camp as a ... as a sort of Peyton Place. Plenty of sexual intrigue, jealously, that sort of thing."

Her face turned to stone. "Any names?"

"I'm afraid so. You're named, Tarja, Peer, and Derek."

"What's he say?"

"He wrote about that Paris model Tarja brought with her in Katmandu. He says Derek only married her because she said she was pregnant. That you were carrying on with someone on the Italian team, as well as a few others, that in those last days you were sleeping with Derek, that Tarja was sleeping with Peer, who was paid to resume his affair with Tarja."

She closed her eyes. "That sucks."

"Stern writes that you shouldn't have been there, that you and Derek had been lovers in New York and he'd dropped you for Tarja. He says that the sexual misconduct of so many led to poor planning and decision making, and that's why people died."

Rusty rejoined them.

Crystal said, "At least he got that part right."

"I don't understand," I said. "Things were not ideal up there by any means, but that's not what I saw."

"Well, you don't know very much then, do you?" Crystal said. "Derek was sick, remember? He'd been coughing his lungs up. He had a broken rib. The only reason—I mean the *only* reason—he tried to climb that damn mountain that day was to prove he was a better man than Peer!"

"Why would he want to do that? No one questioned Derek's manhood—and this mountain hasn't seen many climbers better than Peer," Calvin said.

Crystal gave him a piercing look. "Because Peer was banging his wife and the stupid son-of-a-bitch thought climbing that goddamn mountain would get her back!"

FOUR

*Historically, Everest has been conquered by friends.
And when those climbing scarcely knew one another at
departure, by summit day, they were fast friends. But
this wasn't just any expedition, and no one on it became
friends—unless you count sleeping bag partners!*
—Quentin Stern, www.AbandonedonEverest.com

As Crystal stormed out, Tom said, "I guess that confirms a few details," Tom said.

Tarja left, coughing again, and a moment later, Diana came in. I watched as a grinning Peer moved to join her across the crowded room. She smiled politely at him as he sat. I'd seen her flash the same smile on camera a thousand times. I turned my attention to my table. "It didn't need confirming. It was common knowledge. Cal, do you think that's true? That Derek went up to win Tarja back from Peer?"

Calvin considered it. "If he did, he never said anything to me about it."

"That's what Crystal told me last year," Rusty said, "on the return flight. She cried all the way."

Tarja Sodoc had been born Tarja Koivisto, the oldest daughter of a Finnish emigrant who worked as a professor at a small New England liberal arts college. Beautiful and athletic, she'd been the star since childhood. At eighteen, she'd made the U. S. Olympic Team, competing in Nordic sports, and trained for a time, but never competed internationally. The following year her maternal grandmother passed and left the young beauty $75,000. Tarja immediately dropped off the team and moved to Manhattan, where she revealed an entirely new and unexpected side.

The consensus was that she'd sought out an aging and impoverished scion of New York society named Carlton Vanderhoff who'd taken her under his wing. Openly gay and a "must invite" to any function that mattered, companion to any number of rich widows, Tarja had reportedly paid him $30,000 for introductions to very rich men.

The campaign had been relentless. One of Sodoc's tabloids had written that her patron had gone so far as to require her to sleep with a friend, who'd reported back that she was below average in performance. Carlton placed her on a steady diet of porn DVDs with orders to mimic the pros if she really meant to land a rich husband.

A few months into the campaign, Tarja attended a party with Carlton and met Lewis Scarbrough, one of New York's best-known real estate developers—the man Donald Trump had reportedly patterned his own career after. In his sixties, still married to his first wife, Scarbrough was known to be on the prowl. Reasonably fit and not unattractive, but enormously wealthy, he was a magnet for beautiful women. His wife of thirty years was reportedly determined to remain Mrs. Scarbrough—no matter what her husband did.

Scarbrough had responded to Tarja's attention; within days, they were lovers. Carlton turned his attention to publicizing the affair and, for the next two years, Tarja was the stuff of tabloids. Publicly branded "The Other Woman"—not that she cared—she was famous for nothing so much as being famous. She landed several endorsements and even sold a memoir, *Getting It*, though both the reviews and sales were dismal.

Scarbrough grew uncomfortable with all of the attention—or, more likely, tired of Tarja. Following Trump's lead, he'd acquired rights to a beauty pageant—Miss Teenage North America, the lesser known of the franchises—and, at that point, lowered the age of his interests. Tarja was publicly humiliated when the tenacious Mrs.

Scarbrough gave a national televised Sunday afternoon interview about her life and suggested that her husband's former mistress was a bit "long in the tooth" while denying the rumors of his involvement with the latest Miss Teenage NA.

Tarja had reportedly squeezed a settlement from Scarbrough and then left New York for good. She'd been connected to a trio of European playboys before hitting her stride in her campaign to climb the Seven Summits, as the highest mountain on each of the continents was known. Her combination of beauty, athleticism, and daring was irresistible to certain media, egged on by her publicist. It was during one such climb that she'd met Derek Sodoc. And the media had gone into ecstasy.

⁓⁓⁓

We idly explored the village the next day. Calvin and I encountered Tom, wandering about alone. We three located a worn wooden bench and sat against the rock wall of a hut watching Everest's peak in the distance. There was only room for two on the bench so Tom sat in the dirt, his back braced against the wall. We silently watched the newly budding trees, a flight of birds winging in formation across the flank of the nearby mountain, wisps of smoke rising from scattered huts until taken away by a higher breeze, and the fading sun.

"Tom," I said after a bit, "you're new to this, really the only new Westerner on this expedition. Why is that?"

"I can't say. I've done some business with Michael Sodoc these last years. It was big time for me, small for him, but I found problems with our partners on the first project and brought them to his attention. I don't think losing the money bothered him, but it spared him some embarrassment, and he was grateful. Since then, he's had me consult on deals outside of New York, places where he can't keep a close eye on things. We work well together and he trusts me. Sodoc contacted me not long after the book came out. He was pretty upset."

"Don't tell me he believed all that?" Calvin said. "Of all people, he should know better."

"I don't know what he believed. It was his only son. He had questions. His grief had eased a bit and he wanted to know what really happened. Mostly I think he just wanted to talk to someone about it. He called back a few days later and asked me to join this recovery effort. He's paying my expenses. That's all I know."

I considered that. "What's the point of all this?" I asked.

"To see his son buried," Calvin said. "That's why I'm here."

"If this is just a recovery effort to pay respects," I said, "why are all the other climbers here? All you'd need is a team of skilled Sherpa. Why'd he press Tarja to come? Why do we have the same camera crew? Or any camera crew for that matter?"

Calvin shrugged. Tom said nothing at first and then asked, "What's the story with you, Scott?" I told him, omitting the threat to destroy me, as I had when telling the story previously.

"Sounds like Michael wants the same group up again," Tom said. "If what Crystal said last night is true, he's pressured Tarja to come. What about the other guy—Peter something?"

"Peer," I said. "He's a world-class Alpine climber—one of the best. He's almost a rock star in Europe. Last year, he was along for European ratings. I have no idea what he's doing here now, except for the obvious."

Tom hesitated and then spoke again. "I might know something about what's going on." We both looked at him. "I think Michael wants to know how and why his son died. I think he's got it in his head that if he gets the same group together, the truth is more likely to come out."

"So you're an investigator—is that it?" Calvin said.

"Not me. I'm just along for the ride. But …"

"But what?" I said.

Tom cocked his head. "I think your answer's on that helicopter. That's my guess."

⌐┌┌

At the dirt landing pad, the helicopter from the day before was slowly descending. A billowing cloud of reddish dust erupted from below, scattering bits of paper and other trash far and wide. The pilot, I noticed, was scanning the countryside alternately with the landing pad as if concerned about what he might see. With the inclusion of the Maoists in the government, the insurgency was supposed to be over, but apparently was not. Other climbers, including Crystal and Rusty, had come out to watch Rusty working feverishly with a stout black suitcase to extract a camera.

The Russian helicopter hesitated before settling on the ground, easing its weight onto the wheels. He cut the engine and all we could hear were the blades slicing the air as they slowed. The door facing us slid open and a crewman in orange coveralls jumped to the ground, pulled out a step, and stood aside.

Two men with light bags emerged. One was Nepalese, though a bit tall, perhaps forty years old. His hard, dark eyes seemed to take in everything at once as he moved lightly off then away from the craft with a certain athletic grace. The other was a slight man in his late twenties with an insolent grin spread across his face. He stumbled as he touched the rocky ground, but quickly righted himself, stepping deftly away from the craft.

Calvin squinted to take a closer look. "Who are they?"

"The older one is Gody Tshering," Tom said. "He's Michael Sodoc's head of security. I've met him a time or two. I don't know the other one."

Rusty hurried over empty handed. "Do you know who that guy is?" he said eagerly. "That's Quentin Stern—the writer! I saw him on television." Rusty all but rubbed his hands in excitement. "This is going to get really, really good." He rushed back to the camera case and, by the time the men had reached them, had it lifted onto his right shoulder and began recording, moving in that awkward, intrusive way of the media everywhere.

Tom stepped forward and shook Gody's hand. "Good to see you again." He introduced Calvin and me, then pointed out Rusty—still busy recording—and Crystal a few feet away.

Stern hesitated. Tom approached him with an affable smile and extended his hand. "I'm Tom Bauman," he said.

The man took his hand briefly. "Quentin Stern." He glanced elaborately about, stopping with a direct stare at Rusty's lens. "Quite a party you've got here, isn't it?" He was a bit shorter than average, slender like a rock star, and wore blue-tinted wire-framed glasses. His features were sharp with a sallow complexion. For a moment, he was hesitant. He glanced at Gody and strode off toward the village without another word.

Crystal watched his retreating back as she approached us. "Rusty says that's the asshole who wrote the book."

"So we hear," Calvin said. "This is Gody Tshering, Mr. Sodoc's head of security. He'll be joining us."

Crystal eyed him skeptically. "What the hell do we need a security guy for?"

"With respect, miss," Gody said softly. "I am Nepalese. I speak the language and know the country. I am also a former colonel in the Nepalese army. Given the times, I might just be the most important asset to this expedition. Excuse me."

We watched him walk toward the village.

"What the hell is going on?" Crystal demanded.

"I don't know," Rusty said, lowering his camera, "but shit, what a story." He grabbed the case and hurried after Gody. Crystal waited a moment before stalking off behind him.

"Is that who you meant earlier?" Calvin said.

Tom nodded. "That's the man."

"So this is like one of the English set piece mysteries, where all the suspects are gathered in one place while the detective solves the murder?" I said.

"Something like that," Tom said a bit sheepishly.

"Just a minute," Calvin said. "No one says Derek was murdered."

Tom raised his eyebrows. "Not yet they haven't. But the day's young. I'm going for a drink. Anybody care to join me?"

FIVE

The approach to the mother of all mountains leads
trekkers through an ancient kingdom, rich with tradition
and a historical culture Westerners are rapidly destroying.
This cult of the mountain has at its core an uncaring desire
to debase what it does not understand, all in the childish
pursuit of standing on the highest point on earth, to be king
of the mountain if only for a few brief minutes.
  —Quentin Stern, www.AbandonedonEverest.com

Over the next two days, I occupied myself primarily with watching the Sherpas organize the approach march. Most were wearing some form of traditional dress mixed with Western attire. The other climbers spent equally lazy days, taking in the sun when available, moving about as little as possible as we all acclimated to the altitude.

The expedition was broken into distinct groupings. There were the climbers—Westerners for the most part with the exception of Gody. Then there were the Sherpa guides, followed by the Sherpa porters. Last were the yak herders, one for each animal. Without the Sherpas, it was universally held, no Westerner would ever have stood on the summit. In all, the expedition had more than thirty people, which was about average, though there was a string of yak with herders trailing us, bearing replacement supplies. We wouldn't see them until after we reached Base Camp. Some of the early British expeditions had hundreds on them, and even now the large commercial expeditions had well over a hundred in all.

Twice I tried to speak privately with Diana, but she was a media sensation and I found it impossible for more than a moment or two. When she wasn't being mobbed, Crystal had her standing against picturesque backdrops or walking in thought as Rusty filmed bits that would be spliced into later stories. She seemed thrilled to be here, more relaxed than when I'd last seen her on television. The speculation over the cancellation of her anchor position had gone on for more than a year. It must have been a relief for it to finally be over. And she seemed genuinely happy to see me.

I settled into quiet days away from my filthy room, increasingly bundled against a front of dark, boiling clouds that moved in the afternoon of the second day. Dawa joined me when his schedule permitted and we spoke of life away from climbing, avoiding any discussion of the previous expedition's disaster.

When the first Westerners had summited without supplemental oxygen in 1978, the Sherpa guides had demanded a government investigation since they believed until then that only a Sherpa could climb Everest without the aid of oxygen. They had been chagrined when the climb was confirmed, as were several others in subsequent years, but clung to the correct belief that they were superior climbers at high altitude. This, despite their general malnutrition, a wide range of debilitating diseases, and the persistence of worms and other maladies all but unknown in the West.

The Sherpas had assumed their dominance in Everest climbing in 1921, when the British relied exclusively on them during the reconnaissance of the region and the mountain. The British had been denied first claim to both the North and South Poles before World War I and now sought for themselves the conquest of what was then known as the Third Pole, the highest point on the planet. It was considered a goal of national prestige and was an effort to return normalcy to a nation devastated by the losses of the recent war.

The region comprising Nepal—the country through which this latest expedition would make its way to Everest—was desperately impoverished and had always been volatile. It was no less so now. Ethnically, it was composed of groups from India, Burma, and Mongolia via Tibet, peoples forced into a largely inhospitable region by war and all manner of desperation. Most were either Buddhist or Hindu—or more likely a distinctive Nepalese fusion of both. Superstition-driven, religious practice dependent very much on holy men, shrines, and animal sacrifice. In the Kathmandu Valley alone, there are more than 2,700 religious shrines.

The slaughter of the goat at the airport was typical. Yaks and goats were routinely sacrificed for many reasons throughout Nepal. When aircraft experienced difficulties, such sacrifices were offered to the Hindu sky god, Akash Bhairab. Such practices were so routine that Nepal Airlines regularly issued euphemistic press releases that a certain "snag has now been fixed" when in fact, two goats were slaughtered on the tarmac in view of the passengers.

Nepal has more than one hundred distinct castes and ethnic groups, with four major language groups. The 150,000 Sherpa make up less than 1% of the total population, despite their fame in the Western world. Traditionally, they subsisted on agriculture, herding, and trade.

For generations, a single family had ruled Nepal, occupying the prime minister position as a hereditary right, retaining the king as a figurehead. A revolt in 1951, supported by India, led to the king assuming direct power. That changed again in 1991 with forced modest constitutional reform. Five years later, Maoist insurgents backed by China launched a civil war that killed more than 13,000. Between them and the Nepalese army's attacks, entire villages—even valleys—had been destroyed.

In 2001, the heir apparent Crown Prince massacred the royal family at a celebration in retaliation for the king's refusal to grant him the bride of his choice, a massacre in which he died as well. The throne was assumed by the king's ambitious brother, who ruled the nation as a dictator. A popular rumor speculated that the massacre had been staged to reach this end and the Nepalese viewed the new king with distrust.

Under his rule, the national situation deteriorated. Three years later, the insurgents were so powerful that they'd laid siege to the

Kathmandu Valley for a time. After the siege was lifted, the House of Representatives was able to regain some power. Eventually elements of the Maoists formed a political party and managed a coalition that removed the king from power, but the situation remained tenuous.

Twenty-first-century technology was scattered about the nation, but lacked any sustaining infrastructure. The overwhelming majority of Nepalese, especially the Sherpa, lived an existence no different from that of three hundred years earlier. And though tens of thousands of Westerners had tramped through the country in pursuit of climbing's Holy Grail, only the tiniest minority of the Sherpas benefited from it. But the relatively small sums these guides and porters received for their labor were a king's ransom and assured them and their families a higher level of existence that others could only imagine. A Sherpa position on any climb was highly coveted and Sherpas were prepared, literally, to work themselves to death if they were fortunate enough to receive one.

Whether it was the lack of quarters or preference, the expedition Sherpas set up a small camp of their making on the edge of the village. They clustered together in a ragtag group, apart from the climbers. Given the squalid conditions within the village itself, I suspected that this was one reason why Sherpas tended to remain hearty even as I watched some of my fellow climbers become ill.

The Sherpa have been in Nepal for five hundred years. They tended to live in the foothills and up the slopes of the Himalayas and, though accepted as one of the many groups in Nepal, they practiced their own customs and remained apart from the majority. Their life was hard, deprived, and generally short.

The defrocking of a living goddess two years before was just one example of the distinctiveness of Nepal culture. It remained a subject of much contention among all Nepalese, especially the Sherpa as it struck so close to home. The living goddess, known as the Kumari, was the focus of a form of local virgin worship originating in India more than two thousand years before. The Kumari was believed to be the bodily incarnation of the fierce goddess Taleju from the time of her selection and preparation until the moment of her first menstruation, when the goddess fled her body. It was then that a new Kumari was selected from a large number of four-year-old girls put forward by their various clans and families within the clans.

The physical requirements to become a goddess were demanding, from the shape of the child's neck and body to her eyelashes and skin—even the sound of her voice. Dainty hands and feet, black hair and eyes, well-recessed sexual organs, and a full set of teeth were all mandatory and determined by an inspection conducted by five senior Buddhist Vajracharya priests and an astrologer. But the prospective goddess was required to have more than the look.

Given that a ferocious goddess would occupy her body, she must also possess a suitable temperament. The most striking of the tests consisted of the four-year-old being required to enter alone a darkened courtyard filled with the grotesque heads of numerous recently sacrificed animals. On the edge of the darkness, masked men posing as demons danced in a manner intended to frighten her. If she survived this final test, she was pronounced chosen and was suitably anointed and purified.

Thereafter, the Kumari lived in a palace, where docile servants fulfilled her every need. Her feet never again touched the ground. She was borne aloft on a sedan chair on those rare occasions that she left the palace. Typically, suitors called on the girl seated on a gilded lion throne to obtain a blessing and the Kumari's every action was analyzed to decide if the request had been granted. Should she cry or laugh aloud, it meant serious illness or even death for the suitor. Trembling meant imprisonment. Merely picking at her food during the audience was interpreted to signify financial loss. The best response of all—one for which the young goddess was carefully selected—was impassive silence. It alone was auspicious. Her power was considered so great that a mere glance was sufficient to bestow good fortune and those along her path when carried beyond the palace were known to swoon should she meet their eye.

There were several Kumaris selected throughout Nepal and they brought great honor both to the clan and to the specific family from which they came. The most important to the nation as a whole was the Royal Kumari, who lived in the royal palace in Kathmandu. She was always dressed in red, wore her hair in a topknot, and bore upon her forehead a painted "fire eye" that symbolized her special powers of perception. Once each year, during the Indra Jatra, she entered the most ancient section of Kathmandu on three consecutive days, riding about in a garish three-tiered chariot while the teeming throng paid homage. On the third day, the king greeted her and publicly kissed her feet to obtain her benediction.

Five years before, the Sherpas had been thrilled when one of their own was selected as Kumari for their region of eastern Nepal. Porters about to depart on expeditions called on her for blessing. Then, nearly two years ago, a Western news team had flown the Kumari to Bangkok to film a series of interviews in support of a documentary that was about to be released. When she'd returned, the priests announced she was defiled and no longer Kumari. They then proceeded to select another from a different demographic group altogether.

The Sherpa were angry and humiliated. There had been riots and the army was summoned to restore order. A few months later, the disaster on Everest unfolded, resulting in the death of the chief Sherpa, his replacement's loss of feet, and the deaths of others. The Sherpa commonly held the defrocking of the living goddess to be the cause and Dawa told me that it was the reason that there remained so much uneasiness over this year's climb.

"The omens are very bad, Scott," he said one afternoon. "My own family doesn't want me to go this year." Dawa had two small children.

"Perhaps you shouldn't, my friend," I said. "If you don't feel right about this, you should stay home."

Dawa gave me that sly smile Sherpas were known for as he rubbed his fingers together in the universal sign for money. "It is necessary."

～～～～

The third night in Thyangboche I met outside with Diana—having pulled her away from Peer, who seemed determined to monopolize her every moment. The front had moved through earlier that evening and the sky was black, filled with luminescent stars, the air bitterly cold. We found a private place on the edge of the hostel and sheltered against a wall to block the light, but freezing, breeze. From inside, we could hear the tinkling of bottles, voices, and occasional laughter. She took my face with her hand and kissed me tenderly on the lips.

"Sorry to be such a stranger, soldier. This being a celebrity is really not all it's cracked up to be. Hold me, I'm cold." I took her in my arms, inhaled the familiar fragrance of her hair, and relaxed. How many times had I dreamed of sitting just like this with Diana again? "I was told you'd be here," she said, "but it still caught me by surprise seeing you like that."

"No more than my seeing you. How long has it been?"

"More than two years. It's hard to believe." Two Nepalese walked by, holding their jackets tight against the cold. "Why did we stop seeing each other?"

"You became rich and famous. Only the jet set was good enough."

"Jet set," she said, nudging me. "No one's used that word in decades. Besides, it's not the case. I've been true to you."

"You have?" I said.

"Sure. Of course, I haven't had time for a social life and you should have seen the creeps who wanted to date the evening anchor. The truth be told—and it rarely is in the news business—I'm glad it's over. It was never a good fit. And if I was still in New York, I wouldn't be here with you."

"Why *are* you here?" I asked.

"You first."

I told her the story. "But that's only a part of it," I added, having considered my motives at greater length. "I need to be here, to do this."

Diana looked up at me. "I read about last year. I tried to reach you several times, but you never called back. You can't blame yourself for what happened, Scott. I know you. You did everything you could."

I didn't answer for a long time. "I just wish that were true."

Diana Maurasi had always wanted to be a television reporter. Some of her earliest memories she'd told me were of sitting in front of the television set and watching the weather lady point to the big map. She'd loved the idea of always showing off, of having everybody watching her. At the small liberal arts college she'd attended in Vermont, she'd raised her sights from the nightly weather. She worked on the campus newspaper and then at a local television station after graduation. She'd been promoted to local anchor and, two years later, was selected as the Los Angeles reporter for one of the big three local television stations owned by Michael Sodoc. The following year, she'd caught his eye when she'd interviewed him and was soon hired away to the SNS national bureau in New York. From there, she was assigned to Jerusalem. Her rise had been meteoric; during our months of greatest intimacy, she'd confessed that she'd sacrificed everything for her career, missing her own father's funeral because she was working a story. Her first misstep had been the anchor chair.

"Are you going to tell me about it?" she said.

I considered my answer. "Derek was in pain the day before the summit attempt. Cal told him not to even try, to go back down to Base Camp and recoup his strength, but Derek wouldn't hear of it. The weather window appeared open and there was no telling how long it would stay that way.

"The day before he died, nine of us with four Sherpas moved in two mixed groups from Camp Four on the South Col to Camp Five. We tried to rest there a few hours on oxygen, but it was miserable. It wasn't snowing, but it was so, so cold and there was a wind pummeling the tents, making such a drumbeat it was impossible to nod off.

"We were to set out for the summit at midnight. Derek was slow getting up and very late preparing to leave. Reggie, the leader, told Dawa, another of the Sherpa, Peer, and me to go ahead. There was some practical reason for that. There'd been a bad storm earlier and we were the first up after it. There was some concern as to whether the lines would still be in place. And there would likely be snow to be cleared along the route."

"So what happened?"

"The way was open, it turned out, and the ropes were all in place. We only made a few improvements here and there. For a summit day, we made remarkably good time and reached the top just before noon."

"Congratulations."

"I guess."

"What's the problem?"

"I shouldn't have been there. The whole point was to get Derek to the top. I wasn't even supposed to make the attempt to summit. I'd never planned to go above Camp Three, in fact. But we'd lost the head Sherpa a few days before and another of the Sherpas was struck with edema, and others had to take him down to Base Camp to be helicoptered out. We were shorthanded, so Reggie asked me to go up to help. I just ended up going all the way to the summit."

"I still don't get it," Diana said.

"Peer and I knew that by the time we reached the Summit Ridge, the way was clear to the top. Our job was to get Derek and Rusty up there so they could record what they'd come for. We should have waited, or even gone back down to lend Derek a hand. We could see him, Reggie, Rusty, the others moving slowly."

"So why didn't you, if it was such a big deal?"

"Peer had gone on alone. The Sherpa with us—I forget his name, he died later that day—was young. He'd never summited before, and summiting is a career-maker for Sherpas. Dawa didn't want him to go alone and objected when I said I'd wait for them. He was probably right. You stay warm up there by moving. If I'd just waited, I'd have really frozen up. Still, I could have moved toward the group coming up. Instead … instead I decided to go for it with them. I convinced myself we'd summit early, go back down, meet Derek, and then help out if needed."

"That sounds okay."

I snorted in disgust. "It was crap. The kind of thing you do when you're talking yourself into something. I'd seen climbers come back from the summit. Once you've made it to the top, you're in no condition to help anyone. You're exhausted, dehydrated, and cold to the bone. Climbers in that shape are lucky to stand upright without assistance. I was fooling myself. Hell, one in four climbers who get to that point *die* on the way down." I closed my eyes against the memory. "Anyway, it was harder reaching the top than I'd expected, even with the way as relatively clear as it was. Dawa spotted the thunderheads once we were up and we knew we were in trouble. That storm swept in without warning, as they will. It was a boiling black cauldron below. I'd never seen or experienced anything like it. There were flashes of lightning and thunderclaps that grew in intensity. We started back down immediately."

I didn't say anything for a long moment before I spoke again. "It was a nightmare after that."

"Tell me," she whispered.

"It's a jumble pretty much, Diana. I guess Reggie—who was primarily concerned with getting Derek to the top, since that's what he'd been hired to do—had been trying to get him to turn back all morning. Derek had one of those climber coughs and his condition just kept getting worse. Reggie, who was one hell of a climber, had slipped at one point and broken his hand, so I heard. You have to wonder if he was distracted shepherding Derek. He was in great pain and the hand was utterly useless; but worse, he couldn't grip the rope properly or safely. The two Sherpas with them were working as much to keep him going as they were Derek, who still refused to quit. Even before the storm hit, Rusty and a Sherpa had gone ahead toward the summit. I don't know what that was all about. Rusty was there to film Derek."

"I still don't see what it is you feel so badly about. It sounds as if the entire situation was deteriorating. Bad decisions, worse weather."

"Sure. Chalk it up to bad luck. That's the easy way. After we were all separated ..."

"There you are!" It was Peer. "I've been looking for you two! It's time to join the party. Come on. We're all waiting for the return of the star!"

⌐⌐⌐

Inside was much warmer, the lingering haze gone as the smokers had given the habit up for the duration. The dingy room was ripe with the smell of alcohol and the pungent evening meal. Before Crystal was her ubiquitous bottle of brandy, from which she pulled shots at a steady pace, not bothering with a glass, her face aglow, and a damp sheen on her skin. When she spotted Diana, she cast a look of contempt her way. Peer bundled Diana off to a crowded table, leaving no room for me, which I took as no accident.

Instead, I ordered a beer, scanned the room, and joined Gody, sitting alone. I reintroduced myself as I sat.

"I know who you are, Mr. Devlon," Gody said with the mixed Nepalese and British accent of the educated class. He had the characteristic dark features of the region, but only a slightly Mongolian look, appearing more Indian in heritage. His eyes were black, nearly luminescent pools that I found impossible to read. Though Gody was nursing a drink, he sat with military bearing. He seemed in every way a very controlled man.

"Someone told me that you are Mr. Sodoc's head of security."

"For him personally, not the company."

"You're from Nepal, I take, from what you said earlier."

Gody gave nothing away as he spoke. "Yes. This is my country. I've been gone a long time."

Gody Tshering was a Gurkha, born in one of that region's most destitute families. One of nine children, he was the oldest of the three who lived to puberty. Brave, obedient, and stoic—the very qualities that had made the Gurkha the darling of the British Army in India—he was taken at the age of fourteen to be educated for service in the army. He proved intelligent and adaptable, and rose rapidly once enlisted. A subaltern at the outbreak of the Maoist insurgency, he proved his worth in battle and was rapidly promoted through a series of field commands. Shortly after making colonel, he was placed in charge of offensive operations in eastern Nepal and commanded units responsible for a notorious cleansing campaign in one of its obscure valleys. Not long thereafter, the Maoists raided his own village in retaliation and murdered his family, including his young wife and infant son.

But the true turning point in Gody's life came the following year when the heir apparent allegedly murdered the royal family and killed himself. The king's brother took the throne and assumed dictatorial power. Gody and the clique of officers with whom he was associated had been loyal to the dead king and at odds with his ambitious brother. In the subsequent housecleaning, he was too low to be killed, but had no choice but to flee the country.

With the recommendation of the army chief of staff, he obtained a security position with the Sultan of Brunei. Such efforts were common on behalf of discarded officers, as no one knew for certain which side would next be on top and which would need assistance. Those lucky enough to survive the purging were helped.

Located on the island of Borneo in Southeast Asia and ruled by a Sultan whose title had passed down through the same dynasty since the fifteenth century, Brunei was enormously rich from its oil and natural gas fields. It was a lucrative region for security specialists since the country had been under an Internal Security Act since a rebellion in the early 1960s.

Within months, Gody had demonstrated his ability and was made part of the Sultan's private security staff. He remained apart from the other security personal, fiercely loyal to the Sultan, and was trusted absolutely. He lived in Spartan quarters not far from the Sultan's private residence and took his meals in quiet corner of the mess. Once each week, he called on a house reserved for senior, unmarried officials and spent the night with one of the Western "models" regularly recruited for private parties. Otherwise, he appeared to be a man without passion, lacking all emotion.

Five years earlier, Michael Sodoc had spent a week with the Sultan finalizing a business deal when he casually mentioned his respect for his host's excellent security staff. A week later, Gody found himself in New York and in the employ of Sodoc. There he was no less trusted.

"Are you a climber?" I asked.

There was that sly Nepalese smile. "I try to stay fit. In my childhood, I played in the hills near my village. I did some mountaineering in the army. Climbing is in our blood."

Laughter erupted not far away. Our table seemed to rock slightly and the room fell silent. A moment later, there was a distant rumble, like thunder but different.

"What was that?" a woman's voice asked.

"Earthquake and avalanche," someone said. "They are common up here."

Slowly the room filled again with nervous laughter and conversation. "Forgive me for being blunt," I said, "but may I ask why you are with the expedition?"

Gody raised his eyebrows. "Mr. Sodoc wants to be certain that his son's body is recovered and treated with the respect he is due." The man took a sip of his drink. At this rate, it would take him until dawn to finish it.

"And that's all?"

He eyed me evenly before answering. "Mr. Sodoc also wants to know what really happened."

"I'm not following you." The background noise had vanished for me.

"Perhaps the young Mr. Sodoc was, in fact, abandoned to his death, as the book says. It would be tantamount to murder, wouldn't it?"

"What are you saying? Who would want to kill Derek? Everyone liked him."

"There are many reasons to kill someone and it isn't always necessary to actually do it. You can lead someone astray, place them where they are beyond hope, and then leave them to their death. I've seen it, I assure you."

"That's what Sodoc thinks?"

"Such a man doesn't share his thoughts with me. But you ask who would do such a thing?" Gody leaned forward on the small table. "Peer was sleeping with that woman, wasn't he? Jealous lovers have killed husbands before."

I glanced at the laughing Peer nearby. The idea was absurd.

"Or perhaps Tarja persuaded him to do it. It would not have been difficult in the circumstances. The storm presented the perfect opportunity. All of that money she'd married was about to vanish if Derek lived long enough to annul the marriage. Perhaps she told him she'd split it."

I shook my head. "You're wrong."

"And there's Rusty. Surely you've considered all of this before. It isn't difficult once you consider the possibilities."

"I don't believe it."

Gody pressed on. "I understand that Rusty and Crystal were once a couple and then Derek took her away. Again, you see, sex, jealously. They are powerful reasons to kill. With Derek out of the way, Rusty could hope to get his woman back."

"You don't know him like I do."

Gody smiled and I shivered. "I know men. I know what they are capable of. What we are *all* capable of doing."

"You're forgetting I was there. Neither of them killed Derek. I was with him until the end."

Again he eyed me steadily. "Were you? I wonder. In such conditions, would you really have remained until the very end? If it's true, then, of course, there is you to consider."

"Why would I want Derek dead? That's insane!"

Gody sipped his drink a final time. "If you say so." He rose. "There is plenty of time to consider the alternatives. I'm sure not all of them are yet apparent. It's been a pleasure speaking with you. I know we will talk again."

No sooner was Gody gone than Tom slipped into his place. "So what's the scoop? That's the most that guy's talked since he got here."

I took a long pull on my drink as I watched Gody retreat from the room.

"You okay?" Tom asked.

"Yeah, just peachy."

Crystal laughed drunkenly across the room. Tom's eyes lingered, then he looked up, spotted Peer and Diana with others, then back to me. "I'd say Peer's moving in on your girl."

"She's not my girl."

"Could have fooled me."

The door opened and a wave of frigid air rolled in. Rusty shouted, "Shut the goddamn door!"

"Sorry," Calvin said, spotted us, waved, and ordered a drink from the bar before joining us. "How are you gentlemen tonight?"

"Good," Tom said. "What have you been up to?"

"Doctoring. Seems half the team has some form of stomach ailment."

"That's no surprise," I said, "given what we're eating and conditions here."

Tom gestured toward the others. "I think they're self-medicating." We laughed.

"So much for the antibiotics I gave them." Calvin took a long swig of beer, set his can down, and said, "How are you feeling, Tom?"

"All right. Short of breath. I woke up last night thinking someone had a pillow over my face."

I laughed. "Get used to it. It only gets worse."

The door opened again and in stepped Quentin Stern.

"Shut the goddamn door!" Rusty bellowed, this time with malice.

Stern left it open longer than necessary, only partially closing it as he moved to the bar. Peer stood up and shut it properly without gesture or comment.

Since arriving so dramatically in camp the day before, Stern had kept largely to himself. He'd been the subject of much discussion the night before and throughout the day. Crystal, for one, was frothing.

Harlan had been chatting with Diana, but now moved to a table with two open seats and was joined by Stern once he had his drink. The pair lowered heads and spoke quietly, Stern glancing about every few moments as if he knew a secret no one else in the room shared. For all his cockiness though, he seemed ill at ease, like a man expecting something very unpleasant to happen at any moment.

"What's that about?" Tom asked. "And why is he here, anyway? Michael must hate the guy after the book. He's the last man on earth I expected to see on this expedition."

"Is he on the climb?" I asked. "Or just snooping around?"

"He's apparently a climber," Calvin said. "I asked Harlan about it earlier. As he understands it, Stern bought his way onto the expedition after Sodoc came on the scene. I guess he acquired it so quickly that Sodoc's people failed to dot all the I's and cross the T's. Extreme Mountain Adventures in Sydney sold Stern a slot. Harlan's not very happy about it. He expects trouble."

"Trouble?" Tom said, looking over at Crystal and then at the smirking Stern. "Hell, someone could be killed up there."

SIX

It is the nature of such climbs that among the climbers
develops an air of congeniality. Respect is the rule among
those who seek the greatest prize of mountaineering. So when
friendship turns to suspicion, it is inevitable there will be trouble.
—Quentin Stern, www.AbandonedonEverest.com

"How'd everyone meet?" Tom asked to change the subject. "In South America, wasn't it?"

"That's right," I said. "Just over two years ago when we climbed Aconcagua. I first met Calvin, Reggie, and Derek at the hotel in Penitentes Village."

Calvin stirred in his chair.

At 22,841 feet, Cerro Aconcagua is the highest peak in South America, one of the seven continental summits, and the highest mountain in the world outside the Himalaya range. South of the equater, it is located in a region of Argentina that includes a number of challenging peaks. The area is quite popular with climbers, especially as the Argentine summer comes during the Northern Hemisphere winter, when closer climbing opportunities are limited. Professional guides from throughout the world often spend their winter guiding amateurs to its summit. It is the most frequently attempted high-altitude climb in the world and, during a normal season, some four thousand permits are issued.

The climb itself is not considered especially demanding, with no technical climbing at all, though it requires very strenuous hiking up steep grades that can turn away all but the most determined amateur. A peculiarity of the earth's geography, however, causes the approach to the summit to be more difficult than the altitude suggests. An irregularity to the earth's crust, accentuated by the centrifugal force of the earth's rotation, creates a bulge. While the elevation above sea level is measured as less than that of Everest, the mountain's summit is more than one mile beyond the perfect sphere of the globe. Vegetation on Everest, as one measure, extends to 5,000 meters, while on Aconcagua it ends at 3,500 meters. The atmosphere there is harsh, cold, and with greater oxygen depletion than a similar height elsewhere. Though climbers rarely sustain serious injuries, high-altitude sickness and sudden death are far more common than on peaks of a similar elevation.

Because of the perceived ease of the climb, many try it who should not make the attempt, not understanding how harsh the climate can be or how dangerous the high altitude. In all, one hundred climbers have perished in the attempt, most succumbing to Acute Mountain Sickness, AMS, or the more serious High Altitude Cerebral Edema, HACE.

Aconcagua had been the last real peak I climbed before starting my new position at the center. Time off thereafter would be at a premium and I had no desire to spend it in the cold and snow nursing the inevitable cuts and injuries that plagued every climb of a serious nature. It was toward the end of our time together and Diana, who'd rock-climbed with me on weekends, had made the suggestion. I booked our places well in advance, but by the scheduled date, Diana had started her new job in New York. The telephone conversation in which she apologized for not going had been the last time we'd talked until three days ago.

In the end, I'd simply gone on alone. I reasoned that I'd be with a party of climbers and decided I'd hurt no less climbing the damn mountain than if I'd stayed home licking my emotional wounds.

I flew to Buenos Aires, then on to Mendoza—the wine center of Argentina. Across the rolling land, above the green vineyards, rose the majestic Andes, the first time I'd seen them. The two and a half hour ride from Mendoza to the Andes was along a narrow winding road chiseled from the hard surface, snaking through narrow canyons and across rugged ridges. Away from the expanse of vineyards, it was a barren, inhospitable land.

In the foothills, I joined my expedition at the picturesque village of Penitentes, the marshaling site for most Aconcagua ascents. I checked in and was given a room at the Hotel Ayelen along with the rest of the climbers. It was there and then that I first met Derek Sodoc.

Described in magazines, newspapers, and on television as an "international adventurer," Derek was about as famous as possible without being a film star. His father's worldwide media conglomerate routinely covered his son's latest exploits. If it wasn't actually scaling a lofty peak, there was the television special covering it or programs about his preparation. His cable series *High Adventure!* aired to consistently good reviews and ratings. Handsome and well spoken, when he was not filming or on an expedition, he was a frequent guest at international seminars.

I spotted Derek and Calvin sitting at a table beside the hotel bar. As I was alone, the affable Derek soon waved me over to join them. I knew Derek by sight, of course. Over six feet tall, trim and fit, Derek was very much the figure of a professional climber. He had sweeping light brown hair and bright grey eyes. He smiled frequently and broadly, his teeth all but glittering.

I had never met someone so rich before. I knew that Derek had lived a life of privilege almost from birth, yet in most ways, he appeared unaffected by his birthright. I soon came to see a great deal to admire in the man. He insisted on carrying his own weight, for one. He was also an engaged listener with that special knack of making you believe that you and what you had to say were the most important things in the world to him. Though Derek had certainly met many famous people, he was not a name-dropper. And, of course, he had selected a life in which being rich and famous was of little help. He still had to scale the cliffs with the same skill and strength as any climber, and conquered every mountain he summited one weary step after the other.

Certain aspects of his nature, however, were less pleasant. Though Derek was a keen listener and formed what appeared to be fast friendships, he cast them off as readily as they were made. He also carried an air of entitlement that was difficult to pin down, but pervasive. That first night, for example, he'd left the table as if to use the restroom and never returned. Calvin and I had paid the tab. Derek seemed oblivious to money, often at the expense of those around him, who were constantly paying his bills without compensation. On other occasions, though, he could be quite lavish. After the Aconcagua summit, he'd presented each of us with a new Rolex watch.

The bond between Calvin and Derek was apparent from the first. They'd climbed before and had developed a close relationship that was quite common among mountaineers—even those who found themselves at odds on flat land. Calvin was a traditionalist when it came to climbing, holding to the Hillary school that climbers should do as much as possible themselves and not rely on others to clear the way for them. Derek agreed, but only to a point.

"There are times it makes no sense," he said that first night as he ogled a lovely dark-eyed Argentine woman across the room. "You must respect your local guides. They know things only someone who was spent a lifetime on a certain mountain can possibly know. That knowledge has come at the cost of many lives. You ignore them and go your own way foolishly. There's also the issue of access. Here we fly to within ten days or two weeks of the summit. That's a pretty short approach trek, just enough to allow time to acclimatize. We're sleeping in a hotel tonight. In a day or two, we'll be at a camp set up for us. You aren't arguing we should carry it all on our backs, are you, Cal?"

Calvin laughed. "I suppose not. Nor do I believe we should walk here from Buenos Aires. I'm just saying you should set your own pitons, string your own rope, clear your own path through the fresh snow, set up your own tent, and cook your own meals."

Derek laughed with good nature as he gestured for another round of drinks.

"And what about Everest?" I asked. "An expedition there is like an invading army. You must carry it all with you and for each climber there are three or four others. Every climber who summits has two Sherpas, perhaps more, who made it possible. Even Hillary went up with a Sherpa."

"Only a fool climbs alone," Derek said. "That's no problem. But he has a point, Cal. What about all the support for Everest?"

"Well," Calvin said almost sheepishly, "I'm against it. With all respect to Hillary, I don't even think we should use oxygen. You do it naturally or you don't do it."

Derek laughed. "We'll put you to the test, my friend."

"What does that mean?"

"This summer, I'm off to Nepal to set up a climb for next year. We'll see what you think about oxygen when you're gasping to breathe at 27,000 feet. Hell, Aconcagua is tough enough."

We spent the next day in the village itself, waiting for the last of the expedition to arrive. Climbers with other expeditions were arriving in pairs and groups. There were perhaps a hundred setting off for the summit at different times and with diverse intentions. Some were quite serious about summiting, while others were clearly on a lark, intending to turn back at the first sign of difficulty.

The crew filming international adventurer Derek Sodoc was Argentinean and the lovely woman from the bar the previous night turned out to be Maria Sabato, who would be handling sound for the three-person crew. She was apparently related to the producer and this was her first assignment.

Penitentes is a ski resort and January is the offseason. The climbers who gathered here and set off from it each year were most welcome and the shops, bars, and restaurants accommodated them. Derek showered young Maria with the full glow of his personality and, like a budding flower first receiving direct sunlight, she basked in his attention. I was certain that she was in love before we set out for Confluencia, though I had not the slightest doubt that she was nothing more than the mountain equivalent of a shipboard romance to Derek. It was heartbreaking to watch and I hoped I was wrong in my assessment.

It was a morning hike of no great difficulty to Confluencia, where we formed a line and entered a small house to obtain individual passes from a jovial ranger for the national park in which Aconcagua was located. Our gear had been trucked ahead and wranglers loaded it onto mules to be portaged to the Plaza de Mulas, where we would camp the next night.

Following a zigzag trail the next morning, we reached the gorge of the Rio Horcones by noon. Then we dropped down to the river itself and traversed a small footbridge. There, at 11,000 feet, was a permanent camp. Having moved so quickly from relative sea level, where I lived, I felt the effects of the reduced oxygen content acutely. I had lost my usual hearty appetite and was feeling nauseated.

Not everyone was so affected, as is typically the case. Age or conditioning didn't matter, how often you'd climbed or how high; for reasons not yet understood, some people were more significantly affected by the diminished oxygen content and air pressure. And those not troubled on one climb could find themselves in serious, even life-threatening, shape on the next.

I was certain that Maria and Derek were not especially bothered, as I was persuaded they'd became lovers that night. I was equally certain by then that she'd been a virgin. The light in her eyes was unmistakable and she followed her man around like a puppy. Watching them together made it difficult to keep Diana out of my thoughts.

In camp at Confluencia, the air was crisp and quite cool at night, but the days spent beneath direct sunlight were invigorating. The local staff was efficient, the food well above average, and the evening wine quite good. The mules were off to the side, downwind most of the night and braying until fed, at which point, they'd fallen silent. Not counting the film crew or the teamsters, eight climbers were on the expedition, along with three guides and another five to tend camp, cook, clean up, and see to our needs. The expedition leader was a young sturdy mountaineer named Raul.

Rounding out the climbers were an attractive German couple and two lighthearted Brazilian men. Only the woman spoke sufficiently fluent English for communication. I was never able to reliably determine the German couple's relationship. They might have been friends, siblings, or lovers.

I hiked with Reggie Maul, a New Zealand-based Everest guide. As part of the acclimatization process, Raul directed us to follow a path toward a nearby glacier at 13,500 feet from which we'd have a commanding view of the south side of Aconcagua. The mountain, I found, was imposing—if not exactly impressive. It resembled a slab of dirty ice cream, I'd thought, expressing my disappointment to Reggie.

"I wouldn't judge too quickly," the quiet man said. "I've heard tales. She can be a bitch near the top. The weather can be quite severe and, even at this time of year, the temperature often plunges below freezing with little warning. Don't let the lack of technical difficulty fool you. We'll be very high and high-altitude climbing is inherently dangerous."

Reggie was perhaps forty-five with the face of a man who'd spent his life in the sun. There'd been a loss in his family he never discussed, but the consequence was a measure of sadness about him. His instinct and skill as a climber were readily apparent—even on a modest hiking trail. He moved with a natural fluidity that I envied.

As for Aconcagua, I took Reggie at his word though I remained unconvinced. Lacking sheer cliffs to scale, with no treacherous ice flows to cross, I didn't see the challenge—except for some hard walking in thin air on summit day. Diana had laughingly picked the peak, saying she thought it the most she could manage and have it still sound impressive. In bed, she'd looked at me with her camera face and intoned, "The highest mountain outside the Himalayas." I'd laughed and she'd made a face. "How about this one: 'The highest peak in the Southern Hemisphere.'"

"That's only marginally better," I'd allowed.

"I'll work on it."

"Are you really an Everest guide?" I asked Reggie as we returned to camp. The day's hike had only taken four hours. The body has a peculiar reaction to relatively short periods in reduced oxygen. For the next several days, even after returning to a lower altitude, it feverishly produced red corpuscles to carry more oxygen, apparently anticipating a return to the low-oxygen conditions. This meant that even short hikes such as this put the body into supercharge mode and were the key to climbing successfully at high altitude.

"I summited with a friend some years ago. We've both got expedition companies now."

"It must be exciting, tackling the greatest mountain in the world every year."

"Oh, it has its good points. I don't think I'm cut out for office life, anyway. I make a fair living these days, but I'm away from home too much. And I'm starting to lose my enthusiasm for the high altitudes. Another three years or so and I'll have enough to buy a place we've got our eye on. It will be time to leave the peaks to the young men."

We'd walked in silence. Then I asked, "Is Derek serious about Everest?"

"I should say so. He's already climbed three of the Seven Summits. This will be number four. After that he's got Kilimanjaro in Africa and Vinson in Antarctica—neither of which is especially difficult. All that will leave is the big one. He's going to Nepal in a few months and wants me to come along, so I'd say he's already making plans."

Returning, we encountered Derek and Calvin in heated discussion on their way to the glacier. We exchanged brief greetings in passing. Further down, we met the rest of the climbers joined by the three smiling Argentinean guides. They, at least, were in good spirits.

The campsite at Confluencia was pleasantly situated and Raul's team was efficient. They put up fresh tents, replacing the old ones left behind. Humberto, the producer, posed Derek by a campfire that night and asked him a series of neutral questions while Maria held a boom microphone and soaked in every word. They disappeared into Derek's tent not much later, to Humberto's manifest displeasure. It developed that he was her uncle and the two of them had quarreled at the glacier earlier.

The next day the team made the more demanding thirty-kilometer hike, ending in a steep climb to the Plaza de Mulas at 13,977 feet, located due west of Aconcagua. We were above the tree line by now and the landscape had turned desolate. The weather was presenting its best face, though, so the day was bright, the sky nearly absent clouds, and there was little wind. Conditions were warm and I hiked in a plaid shirt and shorts, as did the Germans, who apparently were experienced Alpine climbers. The Brazilians struggled a bit the last mile into camp, which I also found a challenge.

Certain aspects of the climb were bizarre. Along the way, we'd encountered scores of climbers who seemed unprepared for what lay ahead. I assumed—hoped—that the amateurs would turn back before getting into trouble. The bizarre part was that not far from Plaza de Mulas was a hotel, complete with showers, bar, and restaurant. There climbers could rent needed equipment, even clothing for the remainder of the climb.

Instead of staying at the hotel, we remained at the staging area some distance from the hotel. We pitched tents and set up camp. Here our mules were to be left behind. From this point on, each climber or porter would carry on his or her back everything we'd need to the summit and back.

The following day was designated for rest. I was feeling no better and remained in camp, as did the Brazilians, who were clearly struggling while putting on a brave face. Derek and Maria, accompanied by the Germans and Calvin, hiked to the hotel and took lunch at the restaurant, spent a few hours in the bar, then returned shortly before sunset. Maria and her uncle had another argument that night.

The next day was an acclimatization hike of about four hours, this time to the Bonete Peak at 16,340 feet. The trail led past the hotel, then climbed in a series of switchbacks to the summit. There, Calvin and I had a commanding view of Aconcagua that included the route we'd take for the ascent. From where we stood, it did not look especially demanding.

This day was cold on the ascent, though with only moderate wind. The sky remained largely clear with fluffy cumulus clouds and a brilliant sun. Behind us some distance, we could see Derek and Maria followed by a glum Humberto and his assistant, Jesus. Before they arrived, Calvin and I began the two-hour descent.

After passing Derek and the others, Calvin asked, "Feeling any better?"

"I am. Not fit, but not so ill. Is that," he said indicating with a gesture that I took to mean Derek, Maria, and Humberto, "anything we should worry about?"

Calvin paused and then said, "I don't think so. Humberto looks ready to kill Derek, I'll admit. Well, go for the innocent and bad things can happen. I warned him. I can't see it being a problem on the climb though."

The following day, we portaged equipment to Canada Camp. The guides and porters made two trips, as did Humberto and Jesus. Over largely flat terrain, it was not especially demanding, except for the altitude and, by nightfall, I was myself. That night was awkward; Humberto had decided to stop speaking to his niece. Derek carried on as if he had no concerns.

Following a day of rest, shortly after dawn, the real climbing was scheduled to begin. We planned a long hike to Nido de Condores; at 17,710 feet, it was a middle station and usually designated as Camp Two on climbs. Remnants of abandoned tents were pulled down and set aside, then new ones erected. This was the last point at which we'd have creature comforts.

That night, Raul gathered the climbers with news. "There is a front over the Pacific moving toward us," he told us. "It is a big storm and will bring heavy snow and wind."

"When will it reach us?" Reggie asked.

"Two or three days at the earliest, four or five at the latest."

"What do you recommend?" Derek asked.

"We have one more day of climbing to reach Berlin Camp. From there, we'll make the summit attempt. We are scheduled for another day of acclimatization here, though, and it is risky to press on without it. The safest course is go back to the hotel at Plaza de Mulas and wait out the storm. In a week or so, we will know conditions and can consider resuming the climb."

Derek looked to Humberto. "What will that do to our schedule?"

The man shrugged. "We will stay until we've filmed. Waiting is not a problem for us."

"Anyone else?" Derek asked.

The Brazilians, who it turned out were brothers, expressed their desire to turn back, all the way to Mendoza. One of them had struggled the last two days, while the other had serious blisters.

The German couple consulted and the woman spoke, "We are for going on, Alpine style. Fast up, fast back. If we go to Berlin camp tomorrow, summit the day after, then retreat straight to the hotel, we have time before there is trouble." Her companion nodded.

"Reggie? Cal?" Derek asked.

"It's been my experience to always play it safe in these situations," Reggie said quietly. "Weather at these altitudes is very dangerous and we shouldn't risk anything. The mountain will still be there." Calvin nodded.

Derek gave it some thought. "All right, Raul, here it is then. I'm scheduled to be in Paris to give a speech in eight days. I can't wait. So we'll do it the way the Germans suggest. Up and back—fast. Okay?"

"You're the boss," Raul said. "Just so long as nobody gets sick, I think we can do it."

That night, Raul divided the expedition into two teams. One consisted of the Brazilians, a porter, and a guide who were going back down. The other team would press on up the mountain the next morning for Berlin camp. There the porters would remain while the rest of us attempted the summit the next day, if all went well.

It did not.

The next morning, the temperature fell to freezing. Though the sky remained clear, a swift wind blew from the west. The ascent to Berlin camp, at 19,690 feet, took half a day of steep climbing and more than one struggled with the effort. Situated on a very small plateau, the site was exposed to the full force of the wind—though it had a few huts, nothing more than wood walls with tent roofs that offered better shelter than a tent. With sunset, it turned bitterly cold.

That night, Maria became ill.

Derek summoned Calvin at two in the morning. He said that Maria had complained of fatigue all day, had lost her appetite, had forced down a meal thinking it would help, and then had thrown up her dinner. Since then, she'd been unable to sleep at all. Calvin ducked into the tent as Humberto paced outside. Five minutes later, Calvin emerged looking distressed.

"She is very sick," Calvin said. "Her coordination is gone and she isn't thinking clearly. She's got HACE. We need to get her down as quickly as we can."

Humberto shouted to his crew to get ready.

"Just a minute," Derek said. "We're summiting in the morning, Humberto. I need you and your crew. I didn't come up here not to get the shot for the show."

"But, *señor*, she is my sister's daughter. I must take care of her."

"I didn't tell you to bring someone who couldn't hack it. You should have brought someone with more experience."

Humberto could scarcely contain himself. "Until this moment, *señor*, you have expressed no dissatisfaction with my niece."

Derek ignored him. "We're setting off at dawn as planned. One of the porters can handle sound if you can't, understand? Raul will see to Maria. She'll be in good hands. Do you hear that, Raul?" The man nodded. "You take good care of her."

Derek instructed that Maria be moved to her own tent, "So I can get some rest," then turned in. An hour later, three porters and one of the two remaining guides left in the darkness with Maria, whom they carried in an improvised litter made with a sleeping bag. At night, it was difficult going. As they set out, the young woman was mumbling to herself and dry heaving.

"Is that wise? She sounds pretty sick," I asked Reggie. "That's steep going. Wouldn't it be better to wait for light?"

Reggie shook his head. "No. Even a few hundred feet can make all the difference with HACE. She could die if she stays here. They're right to go now. And this is their mountain. They know the way."

I was unable to sleep after that and hunkered close to the fire with Calvin and Reggie, talking quietly, until it was time to prepare for the ascent. As first light gathered, Derek joined us for a hot climber's breakfast, clearly eager to be on his way.

"What's the weather report, Raul?" Derek said as he gathered his gear.

"Bad. The storm is moving very fast and hits sometime today."

"Then let's haul ass," Derek said with a grin. "I've got a mountain to climb. And a show to film!"

SEVEN

*No longer must the world await dispatches from remote
regions. With modern communication, it is now possible to
have images, video, sound, and the latest information almost
as it happens. Now the public sees reality, no longer spoon-fed
to them by publicists, and reality is truth, truth the rich and
famous often don't want you to know.*
—Quentin Stern, www.AbandonedonEverest.com

In the dining room in Thyangboche, Harlan rose after just a few
minutes with Stern, glanced about, and left. Crystal tried to rise, but
Rusty held her down by placing a hand on her shoulder. Stern, spotting us, grinned, picked up his drink, and joined us without invitation.

"You don't look as hostile as the rest," he said. I'd never met anyone
who wore blue-tinted glasses; they made him look very strange
indeed. "Shit, it's cold up here. I guess I'll be living in all my clothes
these coming weeks and months. I hear bathing is the first victim
of high-altitude climbing." He toasted us and took a long pull of his
beer. Stern had a challenging edge, like an open invitation to a fight.
I suspected that he wasn't often disappointed.

"So," Stern said, "what's the scoop?" His smile was gratuitous.

"You tell us," Calvin said. "You're the reporter."

"Hey! It's *author* now. Everybody read my bestseller?" He looked at me. "You must have, Scotty. Got a comment? I'll be sure to include it in my next book."

"Is that why you're here? Sucking around for another book?" Tom asked.

Stern looked uneasy for moment before his brashness took over. "Why else? We've all got our reasons. It's certainly not for the mountain air. Have you taken a real look at this shithole? These people are filthy. Shangri-La, my ass. But hell, how could I not come? All the living players returning for another bout with the old lady. Talk about your high adventure." He laughed and then looked back toward the others. "What a story. Take Tarja, screwing her way up the mountain. She's even brought along the stud again. I heard she's being pressured to make this climb. Anybody hear about that?"

"We wouldn't know," Calvin said.

Stern shrugged. "It's pretty common knowledge, I'd say."

"Let me ask you something," Calvin said. "Where'd you get all that crap you wrote?"

"Crap?" Stern said in mock surprise. "I had sources. I can't help how people act. It's my job to write about it the way I see it."

"You weren't there," Calvin said. "You didn't *see* anything."

Stern held up a hand in self-defense. "You don't have to be 'there' to know what happened. I had my sources, like I said. I trust them. Anyway, it's not my fault."

"What's that mean?" Tom asked.

Stern leaned forward as if confiding a secret. "It's my editor. She didn't think what I wrote was hot enough, you know?" He gestured like a boxer. "She punched it up a bit." He laughed nervously and finished his drink. He glanced at me as he extended his hand. "No hard feelings, all right? I didn't mean anything by it." He said the last with a lewd wink.

I ignored him.

"All right then," Stern said shrugging. "I didn't think it would be that easy. But you should be nice to me anyway. Never get the writer pissed—you know what I'm saying? So what's the story here?

Everybody on a pilgrimage to find the great adventurer Derek Sodoc encased in a block of ice?"

"Watch your mouth," Calvin said. "Just shut up or I'll shut it for you."

"Hey, hey! Take it easy here. Just a bit of literary license. No offense. Anybody want another drink? No? Suit yourself." Stern went to the bar, brushing against several others in the crowded room on the way.

"Don't let him get to you," Tom said. "That's his stock in trade—how he gets people to say and do things they regret so he can write about it. When he was a boy, he likely pulled the wings off flies just for fun."

"He better watch himself—that's all I've got to say." Calvin stood and left the room, a blast of frigid air sweeping in before he closed the door.

"Where'd the big guy go?" Stern said as he returned with a fresh drink a few moments later. He pushed his tinted glasses up to the ridge of his nose. "You know, if he didn't like the book, he's going to hate the blog."

"What blog?" I asked.

"'Abandoned on Everest.' The book's a Web site now and I've got a blog going on it. Hits are through the roof, I'm pleased to say. If I told you how many followers I've got on Twitter, you'd think I was bragging." He wiggled in his seat with delight.

"Now? You mean *right* now?" Tom asked.

"Yeah. That's what I was doing this afternoon. Making sure the uplink worked, posting my first piece on the blog. Good stuff. It'll form the backbone of the next book." He grinned. "You gotta love technology."

"What's your blog about?" I asked.

"I'm posting my thoughts and observations as we go. A few photos here and there. When I've got time and am in the mood, I answer questions on the forum. Everest is hot right now, in case you didn't know. They've cleaned up NASCAR to the point where it's pretty tough to get killed. They make us wear seatbelts in cars and helmets on motorcycles—everywhere we go anymore is padded and safe, safe, safe. Think about how often someone going on a so-called adventure actually dies? Almost never. You go up the Amazon River now in luxury, sipping champagne as you watch the rustic natives in their splendid squalor. Filth, lice, rats. Disgusting." He shivered.

"Everest is the last place where the foolhardy are genuinely at risk," he said. "Anywhere from five to ten or more die up there every year. Look at last season: Derek Sodoc, one of the luckiest and richest bastards in the world, decided to knock off the big one so he could complete his set." He lifted his hands and counted fingers as he made his points. "He had the best guide, the latest technology, great communication gear. So what happened? The guide gets killed, all that technology didn't mean shit in the end, the radios failed and, from what you say, the great international adventurer froze to death!"

Stern took a pull on his beer. "Nothing can protect you from nature or bad decisions or just bad luck when you're in the Death Zone. Hell, from what I hear, the Sherpa think some mountain god did it. And *that's* its appeal! It's the last place on earth people go knowing they just might get killed. You gotta love it, and the public's eating this shit up!"

"You say your lies came from your editor? Is that your story?" Tom said.

"And I'm sticking to it." Stern was clearly enjoying himself.

"In other words, you're hiding behind a woman's skirt," Tom said.

Stern looked stung. "I wouldn't put it like that."

"And just who are these 'sources' you used? Don't tell me you plan to hide behind them as well?" Tom said.

Stern smirked. "It's just a book! You know how it is."

Behind them, Crystal staggered to her feet, staring blurry-eyed at Stern. She shook off Rusty's hand and moved uneasily toward their table.

"Uh oh," Tom said looking up. "Here comes trouble."

Stern turned in his seat to look just as Crystal arrived and dropped into an open seat. "Wha' the hell," she said, learning forward almost against Stern. "What kin' of shit did you write, asshole? Why you trash me? What'd you say about dear 'ol Derek, huh? Huh?"

"Hello, Crissie. I don't think this is the time to talk, do you?" Stern said, pulling back from her.

"Why'd you say all tha'? I'm no slut. An' he was a good guy, really good, better than you!"

"I'm sure he was a fine fellow."

"It's that bitch," Crystal said looking over her shoulder toward Tarja. "She's a bitch, cold, cold, cold. She made him do it, really. And why'd you say stuff abou' me? I ne'er did you any bad thing."

"Lighten up, Crissie babe," Stern said. "The book'll do your sex life good. Just give it some time."

"Come on," Tom said standing as he waved the nearby Rusty to them. "Time for bed." The two men nearly lifted the woman to her feet.

"Let's go, Crissie," Rusty said. "Time for beddy-bye." He all but carried her toward the rooms.

Stern pulled a small digital camera from his pocket and snapped three quick shots. He looked at us and grinned.

Tom stood up. "You're a real shit, Stern. Stay away from me. You understand?"

Stern pulled a reporter's notebook from his inside jacket pocket and flipped it open. "I'll quote you on that." He looked at him over his tinted glasses. "Are you threatening me?"

"Try me and see," Tom said and walked off, going outside, slamming the door behind me.

Stern smiled and set the notebook down. "These are real sensitive types, you know? Not at all like I thought mountain climbers would be."

I learned forward and said, "Just so we're clear here. You don't have permission to quote me—about anything—understand?"

"Hey! What did I do?" Stern said as I left him alone at the table.

～～～

Outside, I cleared my mind. Stern was a pest and troublemaker; it was Gody who stayed with me. Could Sodoc really believe someone had murdered his son? The idea was preposterous. Still, what explanation was there for the effort and expense he'd gone through to get everyone from last year's climb on this expedition? Looking at it from Gody's perspective, it now all made perfect sense.

Tom was on the lee side of the building, sheltering against the steady, frigid wind coming down from the nearby ice and snow.

"You'll freeze out here," I said.

"Quarters are pretty tight and my room's filthy."

I drew a deep breath and let it out slowly. "We're setting off tomorrow. Things will improve once we're on the trek. Everyone will be too tired to fight or get drunk."

"I guess. I'm worried about Crystal."

"Me too. She didn't drink like that last year. Don't let him get under your skin. I've had you pegged as the stable one on this climb."

"It's not him, not really," he said. "It's the whole expedition. It's ill advised. I don't have a good feeling about it. I read it was a harsh winter up there. Who knows what we'll find?"

"That seems to be the majority opinion."

We stood in silence for a while before Tom said, "You know, Michael asked me to come last year. He told me he thought Derek was pushing too hard. He'd heard about what happened on Aconcagua. He was afraid if his only son took that kind of a risk on Everest, he'd die. But I couldn't make it. Business. Anyway, he heard you'd be there—and Calvin. Between the two of you, he thought Derek would be all right."

"I didn't think Mr. Sodoc ever heard of me."

Tom gave me a long look. "Oh, he knew all about you. Believe me." After a moment he said, "So what happened in South America?"

⌁⌁⌁

On Aconcagua, we set out even as threatening clouds boiled in from the Pacific, heavy with moisture. In addition to me, it was Derek, Calvin, the German couple, Humberto, Jesus the cameraman, and the final guide, a quiet Argentine named Felix. The last three divided the sound and camera equipment among them. Humberto took the time to show Felix how to run the camera, "Just in case." All of us were mummified against the elements in colorful high-altitude jumpsuits.

Aconcagua was typically conquered in the kind of Alpine-style assault we were planning: up in a flash, down even faster, though more often from a point a bit higher up the slope, at Independencia Refuge. On this day, the first hour proved the warmest. After that, the air turned bitterly cold. By noon, the temperature had fallen below zero and every one of us was chilled to the bone. Struggling in the thin air, we stopped every few steps to gasp.

When we reached El Portequelo del Viento, the wind was approaching gale force. We stopped briefly, but were exposed, and the German couple insisted we keep moving. "We will freeze if we stop," the woman shouted over the wind.

Felix agreed, having climbed the mountain previously. We set out and soon faced the Canaleta, 1,000 feet of unstable scree that was the final obstacle before the gentle summit approach ridge. This was the point at which most climbers turned back—even though in good weather, it could be surmounted with an hour's heavy climbing.

By this time, the storm had struck in force and conditions were rapidly deteriorating. The snow was all but blinding and bit into flesh at certain points—even with the protective clothing. With the howling wind, it was difficult to hear and, with dry mouths and sore throats, it was a strain to speak, let alone shout.

Raul called an exposed huddle before the ascent. "Do we go on?" he asked Derek.

"Of course," he answered. "I didn't come this far to turn back. The storm can't last like this."

"It can last, Derek," Raul shouted. "It can go on like this for days. And the snow hasn't really started yet."

"We're almost there," the German woman shouted. "Let's go. We can't stop now!" Derek nodded and we set out, tackling the obstacle in a line.

I've climbed many screes, but this was the most difficult I'd ever encountered. The footing was uncertain and, from time to time, a furious gust of wind all but knocked me over. For every three steps I took up, I slipped back two. We stretched out in an irregular, staggered line—those carrying equipment soon bringing up the rear. The usual one-hour climb took more than two and each of us arrived at the high col exhausted, cold, and weary to the bone.

The Germans were leading the way by now, having proved very strong climbers. I looked back repeatedly and realized that Derek was struggling. Though he was a solid climber and certainly motivated, from what I had seen, Derek was not the most gifted mountaineer.

The unreported truth of it, however, was that none of the Seven Summits, including this one or even Everest, required extraordinary climbing skills. Success came from preparation, determination, and just enough luck to manage it.

I sucked in gobs of thin air and gathered myself for the final push. Derek arrived in a bit, taking hardly a moment to rest, inhaling a few sharp breaths. Spotting the Germans, he set out after them, as if in a footrace to reach the top. Calvin, who'd fared much better, matched him step for step. I waited for the film crew to be certain none of them was in trouble. They each arrived, breathing heavily. "Go on!" Humberto shouted, his face a white mask of encrusted snow. "We're right behind you." The man looked exhausted, near his end.

The heavy snow began shortly after noon, about thirty minutes from the summit. The climbing was not that difficult at this point, but with gale force winds and limited visibility, the going was very, very tough. I lost sight of the film crew behind us and of those climbing ahead. As often happened in such conditions, every climber labored in isolation.

And then I was on the summit.

I'd never conquered a mountain before with less sense of triumph. I felt as if I was a survivor. The moment I reached the Germans, Calvin and I clustered in a dark mass in the snow on top, my thoughts turned to the descent. We were out here in the open—at the mercy of the increasingly deadly elements. We all needed to get off this mountain before people started to die.

Derek looked terrible, standing like a ghost in the storm, his face covered with snow and ice, his lips chafed and bleeding. He was struggling for every breath and his words came out in forced clusters. "Where is … the film … crew?" he asked as I reached them.

"Right behind me, I think. I lost sight of them."

Raul shouted, "We can't stay here long, Derek. We need to get moving."

"I'm not … leaving without … my shot," Derek answered.

A few feet away, Calvin finished taking a photo of the Germans, though I couldn't help but wonder what it would prove. No one would see anything but snow around them. The picture could have been taken anywhere.

"They're going back down," Calvin said when he joined the huddle. "Derek, we need to go. I'll take a photo of you."

"No. The film ... crew." Derek hacked repeatedly, half bending over, as if trying to heave up his guts.

We stood shivering in the fierce wind. I monitored the time on my watch, telling myself I should join the Germans and get moving. Calvin was clearly going to stay with Derek. Raul stared in the direction from which the film crew would come and I sensed he would not leave his client.

Finally, at the very moment I had decided to set out, a shadowy image emerged from the blinding snow. It was Felix with the camera. Neither Humberto nor Jesus was with him. "Where are the others?" Raul shouted.

"I don't know," Felix answered. "They were in front of me after the scree. I lost sight of them. They didn't reach you yet?"

"No!"

Derek stood against Felix. "You take the shot. We'll do it without sound. I'll dub it in the studio. Let's do this now." Derek moved a few feet, looking left, then right, seeking a suitable backdrop, though it made no difference. He stood in a white fury. He finally turned with his back to the wind as Felix fumbled with the camera. When he lifted it to his shoulder and turned the lens toward Derek, the adventurer began to speak.

I could not hear him over the howling wind. Derek spoke for about one minute, then slashed his gloved hand across his throat and stepped forward. Felix lowered the camera, bent over, and pushed it awkwardly into its case.

We huddled again and Raul shouted, "We need to leave now! We'll pick up the others along the ridge on the way to the scree!" Without comment, the group set out, Raul taking the lead, me holding back to bring up the rear. I knew from experience that at this stage, with their thinking clouded, exhausted, and cold to the core, climbers could simply sit down in the snow to rest and remain there until they died. Stopping was easy; moving took every bit of willpower a climber possessed.

We did not pass Humberto or Jesus.

The wind shifted and, in the descent along the ridge to the scree, we were forced to walk directly into it. For a time, I could only see Calvin who was immediately in front of me. After an hour, I could make out two figures walking side by side. The pair slowed and I soon caught them. Calvin had his mouth pressed to Derek's ear and was urging him on. Derek shook his head slowly, snow falling from his hood, then his knees bent and he went down, Calvin unable to hold him erect.

"What's wrong?" I asked.

"He says he can't go on," Calvin said.

I bent down. "Get up, Derek! You have to get up. If you sit here, you will die!"

Derek was squatting on his haunches, his feet and knees in the snow, his arms dropped listlessly to his sides. His eyes were closed and he sucked air in labored breaths.

Calvin pulled at him. "Stand up, Derek! Stand!"

But Derek remained as he was—a statue in the furious snow.

I moved to Calvin. "We have to pull him up. We have to get him moving. Now! Either that or we leave him!"

Calvin shook his head at the unthinkable. "Let's get him to his feet."

Moving one to each side of Derek, we awkwardly slipped a forearm under Derek's armpits and then, on the count of three, lifted him to his feet, turned into the storm, and began to drag him toward the scree. Every few minutes, we stopped. Calvin shouted at Derek to walk, to help us. Finally, after several excruciating minutes, I felt some relief in my burning arm. Derek was holding his own weight and slowly he began to move his feet. Like a blind drunk, he staggered forward, Calvin and I each to one side, holding him erect. At the scree, we stopped. Derek wove back and forth, but remained on his feet.

"How do we get him down?" Calvin asked.

"We rope. One in front, one behind pulling back. Slowly. It won't be easy, but we can do it."

It took an hour to descend the thousand feet, slipping, falling, and cursing the entire way. But toward the bottom, Derek came to life and began to help. By the time we reached El Portezuelo del Viento, he was able to walk without our assistance.

The storm had not abated; if anything, the snow was even more furious. The air was just a trifle richer here, the hike down slightly less daunting than the climb up, so we were able to keep moving. On the Alpine ascent from Berlin Camp, we'd passed a traditional staging area for an attempt on the summit. This was the old ruined shelter, Independencia Refuge, at 20,506 feet. Within its walls was slight respite.

Derek was coming around slowly. Calvin was able to pour a bit of water into his mouth. All of us were dehydrated and exhausted.

"How much time?" Calvin asked. Among experienced climbers late in the day, the question had only one meaning.

I pressed my watch nearly to my eyes to read the dial. "About one hour to dark," I said. "We need to get moving."

In a normal descent, it was an hour from the refuge to the huts at Berlin Camp. For us, darkness fell as we continued down, still fighting the storm with every step. Night came without warning. We stopped while Calvin extracted a headlamp and fixed it about his hood. We set out—following his light into the blinding storm—until finally we spotted a pulsating cold, white glow in the darkness.

Raul had set a flashing beacon to guide us in. We followed it, staggering into the startled camp. "Get Derek inside," Calvin ordered. "I need to check him."

Raul and one of the porters led Derek to the hut in the best condition where he collapsed atop a sleeping bag. Raul came out and joined me in another hut as I drank the hot tea I'd been given. "Where are Humberto and Jesus?" he asked. "Felix arrived two hours ago. He's asleep."

"We don't know," I said. "We never saw them once we topped the scree. They were behind us. They aren't here?"

"No—and if they aren't here," Raul said with great emotion, "they are dead in this storm."

I didn't answer. What could I say? Derek, Calvin, and I had come as close to death as I ever hoped to be. It was the first time that I'd experienced a loss on a climb. Until the storm struck, I hadn't even considered the possibility. I'd never before felt so drained and so cut off from my own life. "The Germans? Where are they?" I asked.

"Gone. They had enough daylight to reach El Nido de Condores, so they set out. The storm is less savage the lower you go, so I think they made it. They are very strong."

Calvin joined us. "I gave Derek something to put him to sleep. I don't see any major damage and he's not disoriented, so I think he'll recover." He looked at me. "Thank you for helping. If you'd left us, we'd both have died up there."

I found my sleeping bag in one of the huts, lay down, and passed out. The storm raged all night, beating against the hut walls and wiping the tent roof incessantly, but I heard nothing. My sleep was black and deep.

By noon the next day, the storm eased and we were all able to hike down to El Nido de Condores. Derek was distant, but moved unassisted. There we spent a restless night before descending to the hotel at the Plaza de Mulas. By now, Derek was much improved, though in very poor shape.

The hotel was filled with climbers—seated and reclining everywhere—seeking shelter from the storm. There was nervous laughter and murmurs. It was as if they'd survived a disaster at sea. Stories of hardship and danger were exchanged like lunchroom gossip. After seeing Derek to a room, Calvin joined Felix, Raul, and me in the restaurant. "Nothing permanent," Calvin said. "He just needs to be warm and to rest."

"Like us," Felix said, toasting us with his brandy.

"Any word on Maria?" I asked.

"The manager says she was here for one day and was much recovered," Raul said. "She was able to hike out."

"That's good news," Calvin said.

"And the German couple?" I asked.

"They moved through yesterday," Calvin said. "I doubt we'll see them again unless we run into them in Mendoza."

I didn't see Derek after that, not until Everest. Everyone except Calvin and Derek left the next morning and, three days later, I was back home in the States. My Rolex arrived by mail. Engraved on the back was "Aconcagua. Friends for life. Derek." Four months after that, I saw the climb portrayed on *High Adventure!* Derek looked like the walking dead on the summit. Maria was cut from every camp scene. I wasn't surprised. I'd heard by then that she'd died during a botched abortion, which is illegal in Argentina. I also left the girl out of the story in my telling to Tom.

EIGHT

Without beasts of burden, there would be no conquest of Everest.
The British at first used small Mongolian ponies, but over the years,
the yak has emerged as the second preferred conveyer of every necessity and
every luxury needed to an expedition. The first choice is, of course, the backs
of the Sherpa themselves. The poorer they are, the more desperate, the more
they are compelled to carry until finally they are broken and discarded. But
unlike the yaks, they are not eaten, merely abandoned.
　　　　　　　—Quentin Stern, www.AbandonedonEverest.com

The Sherpa were gathered about the supplies as they prepared to load the yaks early the next morning. There was none of the teasing and jokes I recalled from the previous year. Instead, the mood was solemn, the Sherpa looking grim and unhappy.

I remained overwhelmed by the mountain of luggage and equipment required for an Everest expedition. But the reality was that almost everything we'd need—from food to personal necessities—had to be carried atop a yak and eventually portaged on the back of a Sherpa—and to a lesser extent by team members—to where it would be needed.

The Sherpas were scrambling about, herding the two dozen or so yaks into position, and breaking the supplies into parcels that could be conveniently packed. Zhiku ran the show and his team worked long, demanding hours, as did all expedition Sherpas. As an experienced and senior climbing Sherpa, Dawa was spared the more grueling manual labor, but did his part. He was popular with the others and greatly respected.

The yaks made a peculiar grunt as the Sherpas carefully placed loads on them. The creatures are alert and mischievous, requiring the constant attention of special herders who spend their lives with them. The animals are, surprisingly, easily spooked and on occasion fall to their deaths. When that happened, the Sherpas would gather up the carcass and butcher it to feed the expedition over the next several days.

Yaks are shaggy with long tails and dark hair wrapped about them, hanging like a monk's cloak almost to the ground. Weighing a solid 2,000 pounds, they stand between three and four feet tall and are most noteworthy for their vile smell. They are indigenous to the region and can be found in the wild between 10,000 and 18,000 feet, where they graze on native grasses and lichen, with an occasional plant mixed in.

The Sherpas use them for everything—as beasts of burden, for milk, cheese, and finally for dinner—on our expedition. They walked at an easy gait that did not tax the climbers and their every move was accompanied by music from the tinkle of the bells tied about their hairy necks, their recurring belches, and the passing of unpleasant gas.

Rusty was moving up and down the line, taking shots of the Sherpas almost like a tourist. He was working alone and Crystal was nowhere to be seen. I observed once again how light his camera was, how small compared to those I'd seen before. The digital age had arrived in full to Everest. This particular camera was the size of a large breadbox with a very wide lens.

Others on the expedition approached in hiking gear, sporting small backpacks that contained little more than an extra sweater, snacks, and a water bottle. Stern ambled out shortly before departure, snapped several stills, and then moved to the head of the line where he joined Harlan. Crystal was the last to make it, her face red, wearing very dark, wraparound sunglasses.

Harlan gathered us before departure. The air was sharp and clean, the sky above clear except for a scattering of fleecy clouds with no threat of rain or snow.

"The pace for the next few days will be easy," he said. "You'll have plenty of time to stretch your legs and break in any new boots or other equipment you've brought along. Primarily this is an acclimatization hike—though it is, of course, necessary to portage our supplies to the mountain. If you develop any symptoms of altitude sickness, even minor ones, be certain to call them to the attention of Doc here. He's an expert and can keep you alive. Disregarding symptoms can be fatal."

"Does a hangover count?" Stern said with a cockeyed grin. No one reacted.

"If the headache persists," Harlan said, "yes, it does count. Any other comments or questions? None? All right. We'll hike about six hours each day. There will be plenty of stops and starts as the line crosses streams or we negotiate a narrow bit of trail, so be patient. It's all part of the whole. We'll be going through some lovely country these first days, so take the time to enjoy, snap a few photos." At that, Stern lifted his digital camera and took a photo of the group.

"How long to the next village?" Tom asked.

"We'll camp out five nights. The next village is Pheriche. We'll only be there a single night."

"What about the weather?" Tarja said. "Aren't we leaving early in the season?"

"We are—and I don't mind saying I'm concerned about the weather. Those of you who were here previously under perfect conditions know this part of the expedition is not unpleasant in the least, but if a front moves in, as they will this early in the season, we could be in for some rough going. But there's a reason we're leaving now and not in a few weeks. For the success of this expedition, it is essential that we be first to Base Camp. It might mean a bit of rough weather, especially after we get there, but we must stake our claim and clear a path through the Ice Flow so it is ours. That way we control access."

"Why is that?" Tarja asked.

"At the end of the climbing season last year, in which a handful of you were the last up there, some of the most violent storms in Everest history struck. The climbs scheduled for last fall were canceled even before reaching Base Camp. The result is no one knows conditions above. I've examined recent satellite photos and don't like what I saw. We expect the worst. Clearing a path will almost certainly be grueling work."

"Sounds like we should let someone else do it for us," Peer said.

"That's not possible," Harlan said.

"Why not?" Peer asked. "I've been on climbs where it's customary. Take last year, for example."

When Harlan hesitated, Gody spoke. "Because it's important that we be the first to Mr. Sodoc's body."

No one spoke for a moment until Stern, who I noticed never looked directly at Gody, glanced around as if what he was about to say was obvious and said, "Why?"

This time Gody was silent. Finally, Harlan answered. "It just is. Nothing else? Then let's go." Harlan gave a whistle and the first yak was prodded into motion and led off toward the distant mountains. Slowly, the rest of us set out in turn, the line unfolding like a vast accordion.

Though the bulk of our gear was atop the yaks, we were followed by a string of Sherpa porters, most carrying a load as heavy as that on the animals. Sun-darkened and wiry, they set out with steady determination.

The meandering trail led us past clumps of birch and juniper, bubbling streams, enormous boulders backed by lovely gardens of stone, and the occasional roaring white waterfall. In brilliant and temperate weather, it was easy to understand why so many Western writers were enamored of this region.

The climbers spread in a haphazard line, walking with and among the yaks, each typically joining another, the pairings selected as much by happenstance as choice. For long periods, we fell silent, as if in a trance, then someone would speak and conversation would resume. The yaks belched, the bells tinkled, an occasional breeze rustled about us, and the sounds of boots and hoofs on the trail made a pleasant thwapping sound that was hypnotic.

The most compelling view was always the jagged line of peaks, cast as they were against the brilliant blue sky. It was like the child's rhyme about the bear going over the mountain. Every time you thought you had the scope of the Himalayas, you turned another corner and discovered new peaks, a fresh horizon. It was always breathtaking.

In the distance was the imposing south face of Lhotse, some 1,000 feet lower than Everest. Our objective just peeked from behind it—a black ominous pyramid—a ghostly plume trailing off from the summit.

I was with Harlan and Tom that first morning, glad to be on the move at last. Though I'd always enjoyed scaling rock walls and reaching the summit of peaks, it was this—hiking toward the goal, the camaraderie of the approach march, the anticipation—that I'd always most enjoyed.

The New Zealander employed a wooden walking stick as he moved easily along the trail, in a gait not unlike that of Reggie the year before. He was answering a question from Tom. "In general, you can say there are two ways to attack a mountain. In one, you go up fast with no more than you need to carry on your back. You reach the top, you take a photo if that's what you want, and then you get the hell down as fast and safely as you can."

"The Alpine style, right?" Tom said. "I've heard about it."

"Precisely, and so called because for the challenging—though by Himalayan standards modest—peaks of Europe, that is the best way to do it. There are rarely places to set up camp on those mountains. You can only walk so far. After that, you must scale rock, cross crevasses. If you are skilled, you can reach the summit and return in a single day in most cases. It's thrilling and requires a measure of technical skill, though that is declining in these times."

"What do you mean? The mountains aren't any lower, are they?"

"Well, take ice axes for example. Hillary conquered Everest with an ice ax no modern climber would touch. Today, they are light, made from titanium, have a curve to them, and teeth to grip the ice and hard snow in ways Hillary could only dream about. Take crampons. Mallory and Irvine died up there wearing hobnailed boots, for God's sake. By the time Tenzing and Hillary came along, they had crampons—steel spikes—to attach to their boots. But the forward spikes on those crampons went straight down like the rest, so he and Tenzing were forced to use an ax to cut a spot for each step all the way to the top. Just imagine the effort it took. Today, the two forward spikes stick out so we can punch them into the snow, and with the new light axes you can practically crawl your way up steep inclines. It takes a lot less effort."

Harlan stopped and squinted toward the sun. "And there's more. The first thing my Sherpas do is clear the path. They set ladders, cut trails, string line, and plant anchors. These amateurs who pay me to get them to the top are attached to a line all the way. A blind man could find his way up, and if you slip, the line saves you."

"That seems wise."

"Of course it is. You'd be a madman not to use all the security possible. And with the kind of climber we have today, it's essential—or even more would die than already do. But the safer we make it, the more climbers come who shouldn't be here. And that brings with it a whole new set of problems. But you were asking about techniques. After the Alpine approach, there is the siege. That's what we're doing here."

"How does that work?"

"The British basically invented it. When they first set their eye on Everest in 1903, this region of the world was even more inhospitable than it is today. It was a monumental effort simply to get to the base of the mountain itself. Initially, they could only approach from Tibet, through China. As it turned out—though they didn't know it—that was the toughest, most technically challenging route. The Kingdom of Nepal was closed to outsiders, though, so they had no choice.

"Two events coincided to change it all. First, the communists invaded Tibet and shut that route down. At the same time, there was a revolt in Nepal—backed by India and not a coincidence—that opened the country up. That's what made this approach possible and led to the first summit.

"What we do is what you see. We bring in absolutely everything we will use on the expedition. We hire locals and we portage it all up in stages. It turns out we Westerners need to acclimatize so it works out for the best. We go from village to village, stopping and resting as needed. Once at Base Camp, we in essence do the same thing, only we create our own little villages up the mountain. We clear a trail, erect shelter, stockpile supplies. We then tackle the summit in waves.

"Mallory and Irvine basically tried an Alpine climb the day they died. They significantly underestimated what lay ahead of them and paid for it with their lives. Hillary and Tenzing only made it first because two climbers three days before them turned back in sight of the summit. One of their oxygen regulators malfunctioned. We'd have two different names in the history book but for some bad manufacturing. But that's the way of this business. Luck has as much to do with success as planning and skill."

"I heard Dawa say that the mountain decides who climbs her." Harlan laughed. "He's got that right."

At that moment, the line came to a stop again. We drew deep breaths—even at these relatively lower altitudes—and were glad for the delays. Tom looked up to Everest. "It's snowy up there," he said. "It's going to be tough going for someone."

Harlan glanced at the icy plume blowing like a banner from the peak. "Snow on the mountain is always bad for climbers. It means avalanches—and avalanches kill far more often than do falls. But that's not snow, not like you think. No, this starts in the morning when the first rays of sun strike the snow on the Kangshung Face up there. It heats that area like an amphitheater and the moisture rises until it meets the frigid jet stream, where it is condensed into the plume. It's the same principle as contrails from a jet. It's possible to judge the wind at the summit from the length of the plume."

Tom watched the distant peak for a moment. "Can you tell anything from the looks of it right now?"

Harlan squinted as he looked. "Today would be a very bad day to be up there."

～～～

Allowing time for loading and unloading, a lunch break, and the plodding pace of the yak meant that we were in actual motion less than the six hours Harlan had indicated. Night came quickly at these altitudes, so the New Zealander ordered each day's stop by mid-afternoon. At designated camping sites, the Sherpas erected tents, started fires from dried yak dung, boiled water, and prepared dinner.

There was very little for the rest of us to do beyond observe, comment, and disappear for a nature call. Dinner was taken at dusk on folding chairs beside one of two campfires typically set out for us. The Sherpa had a separate camp for themselves beside the belching yak.

Diana, who'd walked with Crystal most of the first day, took a place with Harlan and me and said, "It's really beautiful up here, isn't it?"

"Yes, lovely away from the city and villages." The air was clear with a night chill just beginning, small puffs of moisture appearing as we spoke.

"I've been thinking about Thyangboche. I wonder why they live in such squalid conditions?" she asked.

"Who can say? It's just the way it is," I said.

Harlan set his tin plate on the ground and leaned back in the chair. "But it's closer to the real Tibet for these people than all the majesty. Try to say that in your reports, will you?"

"What do you mean?" she asked.

"This is no paradise. It's a cold, grim world here and the people live hardscrabble lives. When you struggle to simply exist, to put even meager food in your belly, when you live in such a harsh place, personal hygiene is a much lower priority than it is in easier climes."

"Why doesn't the government do something?" she asked.

Harlan laughed. "The government. Let me tell you about the government, but don't put my name to it. This kingdom is desperately poor. You can't imagine. The Sherpas up here in the foothills are largely protected, but lower down, young girls are routinely kidnapped and sold into prostitution in India. I'm talking girls, you understand, eight, nine, ten years old. It's been going on for hundreds of years and nothing we can do will put a stop to it. The Indians believe that women from these parts are especially sensual."

Diana glanced at the two women in the Sherpa camp who'd been carrying a load all day. Weather beaten, calloused, they were scarcely objects of sexual desire. "You're not serious."

"I am, though I can't explain it." He drew a pipe from his jacket pocket. "Any objections? I can smoke with the Sherpa if it's a bother." He waved the pipe toward the other camp.

"No," Diana said, "my grandfather smoked a pipe. I love the smell."

Harlan took a moment to pack the pipe and lit it with a burning stick from the fire, the flame casting a warm glow across his chiseled face. He drew a puff then said, "It's really the government that's the problem, you see. This region, I suspect, is filthy rich with minerals, but they permit no exploration. They put almost nothing into infrastructure. They really don't want outsiders here. We're tolerated, not welcomed. And they are surrounded by traditional enemies. This is an especially difficult time. The unpopular king was removed from power, but the communists are now part of the government. No one knows what that's going to mean in the long run. The fighting was supposed to end, but the guerilla war just goes on and on. People have died by the thousands and there's no end in sight. The prisons are full, young men are forced into the army, and the population is taxed to death. It's a cruel place, young lady—far crueler than you can imagine. The old ways, at least, gave them a measure of stability, but those are under assault from radio, from television, from us."

"Us?" Diana said. "We're no threat. We just want to help."

Harlan laughed. "Help. You see those two women over there? You glanced at them a bit ago. They're names are Laki and Ongmu. Neither is twenty-five years old yet, but they look forty. They and their extended families depend on these expeditions to live. Take Laki. With her husband dead, she has no choice. She's fortunate to be in Zhiku's clan so he gave her a place out of sympathy, but she's not an experienced porter. This is going to be very, very difficult for her. But I've seen worse, much worse. I've seen young women, no more than girls, with a baby wrapped to their bosom, carrying loads on their back that would break a fit Western man. I've seen them push until their hearts literally give out. I've seen them, too many of them, simply lie down and die, apologizing as they do." He puffed at his pipe. It had gone out and he relit as Diana said, "How do they do it?"

"With guts. Because they are a hardy people. Most of all they do it because they have to. They might die on this mountain, but they'll die giving it their all. They have enormous pride and it's a shame culture. Fear of shame keeps them from admitting defeat. My point, though, is that this is their way. If you talked to those women about women's rights, about education, about standing up for themselves, they'd have absolutely no idea what you meant."

"You mean they *want* this kind of a life?"

"No, they're like everyone else in most ways. They'd like an easier life, one that isn't so demanding. They'd like to be healthy, to live to an old age, and to see their families do well. But this is the way their world is. They can't see it being any different. They're Buddhists, you understand. They believe in karma. They've lived before and today this is their lot. When they die, they'll come back as someone or something else. It's all very fatalistic."

"So they tough it out?" I said.

"What choice have they? It's just as well they believe they get another shot at life. This one's so miserable as it is." He smoked in silence for a while.

"But the mountain must help?" Diana said finally. "Look at all the money for just this one expedition. People are drawn here from all over the world. It must make a difference."

"Oh, it does, it does. The lives of many hundreds—perhaps a few thousand—Sherpas are better because of expeditions. But there's a price, there always is. The old ways are disappearing. Not that all of them are worth keeping, but along with plenty of bad, a lot of good is vanishing as well. Young men all want to be like Zhiku or Dawa, men of respect, honored climbers and leaders. They ignore the traditional ways of making a living and focus all of their efforts on climbing. During the off-season, they train constantly, to the neglect of their families and traditional occupations. Most of them never make more than a modest living as porters, some die, others suffer frostbite or injuries that cripple them for life causing them to be a burden on their families."

"You make it sound terrible."

"Do I? I suppose it is, in a way. But men have always been drawn to Everest and to these mountains. The Sherpas understand us, better I think than we do, because they share the same fascination for the mountain. These expeditions made it possible for them to do what they'd always dreamed of doing."

"I thought they worshipped the mountain?" Diana asked.

"They do, but not like you think. It's more like a special place, a place where the gods live and work their will on man if he misbehaves. They can go there, just so they show the proper respect. The

Sherpa are glad enough to climb the mountain. It means as much to them as it does to any of us. The Sherpa who manage it are big men in their village and they are a very macho group. That's what gets a lot of them killed. They also think they are tougher than us. They're right, of course, they are, but in certain situations, we're all the same up there. But the Sherpa always think they've got the edge on us, even when they don't. And that's cost more than a few of them their lives." His pipe was out again. This time he tapped the ashes against a stone on the ground before continuing.

"It started with the India Trigonometrical Survey in the nineteenth century. They spotted Everest from hundreds of miles away. The region was inhospitable though and climbing the highest point on the planet had to remain a dream for a century. The British lost both the Poles and they weren't about to let this prize slip from their grasp. In all, it took fifteen expeditions and claimed the lives of twenty-four men before Hillary and Tenzing knocked it off. Tenzing had been on a Swiss expedition the previous year and nearly made it to the top. The Brits were scared to death that they'd get beaten again.

"Until Dick Bass climbed the beast in 1985, only very skilled climbers made the attempt. The mountain was just too daunting, the region too remote, and the cost too prohibitive, for more than a couple of dozen climbers to have made it. By the time Bass managed it—with lots of help—every approach had been tried and conquered. He was the first, you see, to climb the Seven Summits—and that made him a celebrity. In the process, he turned climbing Everest—or it along with each of the Seven Summits—into a sport for rich adventurers. It's become a cottage industry and every year more and more rich men and women, take a couple of months out of their lives to make the attempt. More than a few die trying."

"I read there are as many as a hundred expeditions each year."

"That sounds high. If you're talking about major expeditions, the number is far less. Still, some two hundred climbers summit every year and the number is growing almost geometrically. Half of those, mind you, are Sherpas, sent to get the rich to the top."

"Since it's been conquered so many times, what's the point?" Diana asked.

Harlan laughed. "It's about bragging rights. One bloke climbed it so he could brag to his pub mates that he'd done it. It's gotten ridiculous. Now it's the fastest to the top, oldest to climb, the youngest to climb—which, by the way, is fifteen years old. It's a game, a dangerous one, but still a game. And a lot of the dead up there have been the Sherpas paid to help the amateurs who have no business trying it."

"Is it really easier than it used to be?" she asked.

"You still get up there one step at a time and for anyone it's an impressive accomplishment. But it's nothing like it was when Hillary and Tenzing did it, just the two of them roped together, cutting each step in the snow and ice. They had no radio and no knowledge of the route. Every turn was a discovery. Today, the route is well established. Oxygen bottles are lighter and more efficient. All of the equipment is far superior than it was and getting better every year. And communications are so much better. All of my climbers and Sherpa will have radios. If you wanted, pretty lady, you could broadcast from the summit."

"First, I'd have to climb it," Diana said with a quick smile and a fast look before she averted my gaze.

"There is that. But with the right equipment, a Sherpa to pull you along if necessary, the anchored line right to the summit, ladders for the steps, any reasonably fit and very determined adult can do it—with the right weather window and luck."

"And that's what's getting so many people killed?" I said.

"Yes. The technology and organization make it easier and easier to climb the mountain. But in the end, the weather kills—that and bad judgment at the wrong time—or just plain bad luck."

"Yet you still guide people to the top," Diana said.

"Yes, I do. I tell myself that if I didn't, someone less capable would. And I know that's true. But sometimes I'm not very proud of it. I tell my climbers, just like I'm going to tell all of you, that it doesn't count if you don't get down alive. And I don't pay these Sherpas to die for you. They've got strict orders. Once a climber will no longer listen to reason, they leave him or her. No questions asked."

No one spoke for a while. A gust of chilled air swept across the camp. "So what do old summiteers do afterward?" I asked.

"They lecture or guide. They write books. Hillary built clinics all over these mountains. They worshiped the man. The rest just go back to being a doctor or whatever it was they did before. They are often seen as wise. They've been to the high mountain, like Moses, and must possess knowledge." He stared at the ground for a moment, adding, "But most of them, like me, just keep coming back."

NINE

When the bloom is off the rose, when the lovely days of hiking turn into cold, wet days of slogging, when the specter of death greets you at every turn of the trail, you know more is at stake than your reputation. The overriding question becomes: will I get down alive?
—Quentin Stern, www.AbandonedonEverest.com

"I've got a blister," Stern complained as he wiggled his boot off to the side while still walking. He hopped on the other foot for a moment and nearly fell. He'd ended up with me that morning, explaining that no one else would hike with him.

Since leaving Thyangboche, Stern had managed to offend nearly everyone on the expedition, taking unwelcome photographs, intruding on private conversations, openly taking notes, and generally being a nuisance. It seemed to me that the man relished collecting enemies.

It was a cold, windy day, heavily overcast, with the lingering threat of rain or snow. The once vibrant colors of the land were now hues of gray. I had worn an extra sweater beneath my coat, but even then, I was often chilled.

"This is really remote, you know?" Stern said. "You have no idea what it's really like until you get here. My daughter thinks this is just another trip."

"You have a daughter?"

"Sure—and a pit bull ex-wife. But Samantha is my world now. She's seven. Here." He dug in his jacket and produced a photograph of a smiling and seemingly very happy young girl who looked nothing like Stern.

We walked in silence for a while as I listened to the tinkle of the yak bells. "How'd you come to write your quickie book?" I asked.

"My editor at the paper knew I'd worked for SNS before and, when the story came his way, he gave it to me."

"Lucky break."

Stern laughed. "It was like joining the *Inquisitor*. It's a much better deal—makes the *National Enquirer* look like the *New York Times*."

"No issues with the truth then?"

Stern smirked. "We don't tell lies—we just write about the irrelevant or prurient. And what's the truth? After Pearl Harbor, every newspaper in America wrote about the great defeat in the Pacific while in Japan they were trumpeting the great victory."

"So it's all relative in your mind?"

"My mind? Shit, it's the way of the world. You should have talked to me when I called. I always protect my sources."

Until that moment, I had forgotten that Stern had in fact called, leaving a voicemail. "It was a bad time," I said.

"Snooze you lose, but I was fair about it. So, tell me. What really did happen that day?"

In the distance, we heard the muted rumble of another avalanche. The snow about us was heavy and wet. We heard at least three every day. The Sherpa, I'd noticed, were getting more and more spooked by the restless mountains.

"Glad we aren't close to that," Stern said.

We walked a bit without speaking before I answered. "Maybe if you climb to the shelf above Hillary Step and get trapped in a blizzard, you'll have some idea of what happened."

"Me? Not hardly. I'm sticking to Base Camp. That's as close to God as I ever expect to get."

We hiked a time before I said, "I'd say that Sodoc is pretty pissed with you."

You'd have thought I hit him with a club. He stumbled and blanched in the same instant. When he recovered, he said, "You talked to him?" His voice quivered.

"Yes, we met." I didn't volunteer that Stern's name had not come up.

Stern licked his lips. "What did he say about me?"

"Oh, this and that. You aren't worried are you?" I couldn't help myself.

His head jerked rapidly side to side. "Me? Why should I be worried?"

〰〰〰

The noon break came after a light drizzle. The winter weather pattern still clung to the mountains, so intervals of good weather were certain to be short-lived. Soon, the pattern would move northward and a brief window of relatively temperate weather would prevail over the Himalayas and Everest before the onslaught of the summer monsoon and heavy snow. That was what we were aiming for.

A wide patch of blue suddenly appeared as the line came to halt. There was no suitable area for noon camp, so the Sherpa started fires along the line, placing battered pots out to boil water for tea.

As they made preparations, Stern went to one of the yaks and removed a tube. From it, he extracted a roll that he laid on the ground off the trail, spreading it like a new carpet. It was covered with rectangular sections of solar cells.

Stern looked up at me with a grin. "My power supply. This stuff is just great." From his own backpack, he removed the very latest tablet PC. He plugged it into the solar carpet with a short cord. "It charges directly. I don't need to carry a separate power pack. The computer weighs less than two pounds. Pretty neat, huh?"

"What are you doing with that?"

"I'm just recharging right now. I filed a report last night and the battery's a bit down."

"A report?"

"Right. I've got a small sat phone that charges from the same blanket. I link to it and shoot my stuff to a satellite and from there to the home office. It's just the roll, the sat phone, a digital camera for stills, and a bit of video, and the tablet PC. Amazing."

"What report?"

"The blog. I'm updating it every few days. Once we're at Base Camp, I'll upload morning and afternoon. I'll be able to keep the charging going all day you see. Digital photos take some time to upload so I'm not sending too many of those right now. I'll be able to send plenty once we reach Base Camp."

"You can do this all the way to the mountain?"

"Sure. Hell, you can do it from anywhere now. Absolutely anywhere. No place on earth is safe from a *National Inquisitor* investigative journalist." Stern laughed.

One of the camp Sherpas approached with two bowls of hot food. Lunch consisted of rice, some greens with bits of canned fish intermixed. I took mine. Stern said, "Forget it. Give that slop to the yaks." The Sherpa moved down the line as Stern pulled a PowerBar from his jacket. "I've got a month's supply of these in case the food doesn't improve."

"It'll be pretty good at Base Camp."

"That's good news. Part of the rich living the good life?"

"We're all starting to lose our appetite. It's one of the symptoms of being at these altitudes. As I understand it, the body no longer has enough oxygen to properly support the digestive process so it tells us to stop eating by killing hunger."

"Is that right? What a diet. Kind of expensive, though. So they cook good grub to stimulate you?"

"That's the idea. It's easier to force yourself to eat if the food's appealing. The early expeditions brought gourmet dishes along, hoping it would encourage an appetite. That really didn't work and it's costly. Now they just cook quality meals."

Stern pulled out a notepad and wrote. "I'll have to write a piece about that. How's this: 'Luxury meals as Sherpas die.'"

"You're a real piece of work, Stern."

I moved up the line, leaving him to join Crystal and Rusty. The first day out had been tough, but she'd not been drinking on the trail and seemed her old self. "What's the weasel up to?" she asked.

"He's got a solar recharging setup for his sat phone and a tiny PC. He's recharging while the sun's out."

"That's all he brought?" Rusty said with a bit of envy. "Our stuff's on two yaks. I've got a video camera and some digital cameras for still shots, a power source, and several solar blankets for recharging. We've each got a sat phone. On top of that, there's the tripod and editing equipment. Plus the tents for it all. But we can do a lot more than he can. I tested it all back home. It's slicker than last year."

"Are you using the camera I saw back at the village on the mountain?" I asked.

"That's it. It's shoulder-mounted, but that's really just for steadying it and the viewfinder. Even with the mic, it weighs less than twenty pounds. Nothing to it. The real problem is the cold. It's only been approved to freezing."

"It'll get a lot colder than that on top," I said.

"I put it in my freezer at home for two days and gave it a try. Piece of cake."

"What's he been up to?" Crystal asked, staring down the line at Stern.

"Blogging, he says," I answered. "He plans to do it twice daily once we reach Base Camp."

"The little shit! He accused me of being the camp whore! You should be pissed too, Rusty. He called you an assassin. Someone should do something about all those pictures he's taking."

"It's a free country," Rusty said.

"No, it's not," she snapped, glaring at him. "This is Nepal. They put you in prison if you don't bow to the king or sacrifice to the right god. His equipment should have an accident, Rusty."

"Hey, Crissie! Let it go. He's a jerk, but he's just doing his job. You want to sabotage his operation, you're welcome to try."

"It's business, Rusty. That guy's in competition with us, get it? And he was fired from SNS for fudging his resume. He's got an ax to grind. We're just grist for his mill."

"You need to spend some time with the guy, Crissie," Rusty said. "He doesn't need an ax. He was born a jerk."

Just then, Harlan called out from the front. "Five minutes! Eat up!"

"I'm taking a leak," Rusty said as he moved off into the stunted shrubbery.

"Men," Crystal said with disgust. "You get all the breaks. Not a decent bush in sight."

⌐⌐⌐⌐

As the Sherpa set up camp that night, I watched them go about their business. They unloaded the yaks and then herded them together to munch whatever they could find. In camp, they were fed, but on the trail, they were expected to forage for food. The Sherpa carefully separated from the packs what we needed for the night, before methodically erecting tents and setting out camp chairs.

Dawa spoke to me one night and our conversation turned to the porters. "These people come from my valley. They are all from my clan." This was how a team was typically selected, so nothing was unusual in that. "Zhiku is trying to help as many as he can. There was trouble, you understand. Perhaps you heard."

"No."

"The army came. There was much killing."

Yes, the army. In 2000, the year before the massacre of the royal family, the valley with his people and those of Zhiku had been raided by the Nepalese army. An air assault had been followed by an army sweep of their remote village. They had been hunting a Maoist unit operating in the region. I'd heard a little of it the previous year, but not in this detail.

"Many people killed," Dawa said. "Villages destroyed. Very bad."

"You were there?"

"No, but heard later about it. It went on for more than a week. Women were raped, children murdered. It was terrible."

"Yes, I understand."

"They have rebuilt, but things are very bad. They need this." He looked up. "Bad weather, I think," he said to change the subject. "Snow tonight."

"It's too early in the season to be out like this," I said. "We should not have left for at least another two weeks."

"Zhiku says this is what the boss wants, so we do it."

"Yeah, we do it. How are your people? I don't see many familiar faces from last year."

"Few wanted to come with us. Very bad omens. Just Dawa comes." He looked at the Sherpas setting camp up, making fires. "You know about the women?"

"Not much. No husbands, I heard."

"Laki, yes. That one." He pointed with his lips in the polite Sherpa way. Laki was a small woman, just five feet tall and very thin—even with her bulky mountain clothing. Her impassive face gave nothing away as she worked. "Dorji was her husband."

Dorji. How could I forget Dorji? Lighthearted and more open than most Sherpa, the climb the year before had been his first as a guide and a tremendous opportunity for him to make his Everest career. He'd portaged to Base Camp twice before, but that was the first time he'd been trusted to work on the peak. It had been Dorji who'd wanted to summit that last day and it was for Dorji that Dawa had gone ahead with me deciding to join them and give up my wait for Derek. Dorji became lost in the blinding storm on the descent and was not seen again.

"She seems awfully small to be a porter," I said.

"Too small. I told Zhiku not to bring her, but what can he do? Her husband was his friend. Her parents are dead. No man will have her with two children. On this trip, she makes enough to support herself for five years or to buy a small shop she can live on. Zhiku wants to help her."

"And if she dies?"

"She only goes to Base Camp. She won't die. He is watching her closely."

"What about the other?"

"That is Ongmu. She has done this before. She is favorite girlfriend."

I smiled. "Who?"

Dawa smiled slyly. "Zhiku. In the village, his wife watches too close. Up here …"

I smiled. "The others?"

"That one is Daiza." He was indicating a stout, young Sherpa carrying a very heavy load. "He is good guide. His wife is pregnant. Her belly is way out here." Dawa held my hand out from my stomach and laughed.

"What about those two?" I had seen the pair from the first day, always working together, walking together, and wondered about them.

"That is Gametup and Chepal."

"Don't I know Chepal?"

"Yes, he was a climbing Sherpa with us last year."

"Are they brothers?"

Dawa looked around. "The war. They fought together."

"With the army?"

Dawa shook his head. "The other army." He meant the Maoist insurgents. "Say nothing. That man who came in later with the red man, Gody, he is army."

"Not now. He used to be though."

Dawa shook his head again. "They are always the same. Those people never change. Be careful of him."

～～～

That night during , Rusty joined Crystal, Diana, and me. "Bad news, boss," he said.

"Now what?" Crystal said.

"Stern's been blogging like he said. New York wants us to file daily reports."

Crystal made a face. "You're kidding, right? We *can't* file yet. They agreed to give us until Base Camp. We explained all of this before we left New York."

"That's what the message said."

"Stern's got what? A dinky PC, a solar rug, a sat phone, and a couple of little cameras. He can file a piece for his shitty blog in a second. It takes you an hour to off load and set up. And we've got high-def video of Diana here that takes half an hour to upload. Plus they want sound and it's a bitch out here." She glared at no one in particular and said, "I'll take care of it." She stomped off into the darkness.

That night, it snowed, blanketing the ground with a light white powder. The morning was frigid with a brisk chilling wind. After a short breakfast, Harlan gave the order to set off and kept the expedition moving to warm everyone. We skipped the usual lunch break, but at the customary hour encountered one of the occasional ramshackle teahouses that dotted the route and most climbers bought a mug of hot, sweet tea and biscuits.

Though this region was inhospitable, it was not unpopulated. Along and near the trail were crude huts made of rocks, even caves with clusters of dirty-faced Sherpa living primitive, squalid lives. In the near distance were occasional small villages clinging to the sides of sheer mountain slopes or atop steep escarpments. More than once each day, we passed religious monuments, tattered prayer flags flapping in the breeze.

Throughout the day, the sky was heavily overcast, the rolling clouds so low that it seemed I could touch them. A somber mood settled on the expedition as it trudged in silence except for the grunts of the yak, their tinkling bells, and the intermittent coughing of a few of the climbers.

We snaked our way through mist-filled depressions and tiny valleys. We forded freezing streams of racing water, passed beside steep rock walls, slipping on wet stones, or tramping through mud almost continuously. At mid-afternoon, the trail entered a narrow and uncertain place as we passed a spot where it had been carved from the side of a steep incline. The line slowed appreciably as both yak and man tentatively made their way.

"Careful now!" Peer called. "This is very slippery."

A few moments later, I was about to cross the treacherous section of the trail when I heard a scream in front. The yak reared in panic, its handler pulling away so as not to be pawed while yanking on the tether to regain control of the animal. When the beast failed to respond, he moved near to its side to calm the creature. It suddenly emitted another sound, much like a human scream, lost its balance, and tumbled from the trail, taking the shrieking Sherpa with it. The two bounced and rolled down the steep incline.

I immediately went off the trail, sliding and running down the sheer slope. The Sherpa shouted to one another and then a few began cautiously making their way toward the yak and fallen handler. The distance was not that far, but the side of the incline was quite steep so the yak had rolled several times before coming to the stop, its load mostly flipping off and about in the process. The animal had pinned its handler at least once during the tumbling; the man now lay motion-less not far from the beast.

He was still breathing when I reached him. His head was cocked to the side at a grotesque angle, his mouth formed into a grimace. I knelt, but before I could decide what to do, heard a protracted release of air from the man. Then nothing. He was dead.

The nearby yak clawed its way to its feet, briefly attempted to climb the steep embankment, and then stopped, making very un-yak-like sounds as several Sherpas approached. Two joined me beside the man and, a moment later, cries of lament passed up to and along the trail.

The dead Sherpa was young, smaller than average. His clothes were filthy. His hands were heavily calloused. I looked at his feet. He was wearing canvas tennis shoes. No wonder he'd fallen.

For the next fifteen minutes, the Sherpa scrambled to recover the supplies, which they passed and carried up to the trail. A handler reached the yak, calmed it, and then moved the animal tentatively along the incline in a path parallel to the trail to a point where they would merge. The animal seemed to move normally, a development I found remarkable.

Two of the Sherpas helped me pull the body up to the narrow trail. Harlan had passed along a blanket, in which I wrapped the dead Sherpa.

I considered my options. The space was too cramped to do any-thing else, so I lifted the body onto my shoulder fireman-style. No yak could carry him as well as the supplies already loaded. I had to be very careful, since the trail was narrow and wet. I moved slowly, taking the passage with great patience.

Once clear of the trail, Zhiku was waiting. He ordered supplies shifted and the body laid across one of the yak, but the creature refused the load and went to its knees. Prodding did no good. Finally, Zhiku ordered a stretcher constructed and two of the Sherpa to carry the body to the next village.

I stood to the side, exhausted. A Sherpa, Chepal if I recalled cor-rectly, met my eye as he placed part of the reassigned load on his yak. "Bad," he said shaking his head. "The mountain not want us." Ahead,

Harlan called out and the line moved forward. A few minutes later, a steady, frigid drizzle began.

I remembered this portion of the approach from the previous year. The weather had been splendid. Derek had been jovial, regaling the nightly encampments with stories. Tarja, the new, beautiful wife, had hung on every word. It was later, at Base Camp, when it all fell apart. The expedition had been lighthearted, excessively so in retrospect, overconfident as it turned out.

⌁⌁⌁

Late that afternoon, we entered Pheriche, a gloomy village strung along an unnamed stream swirling over grey rocks. It held a medical clinic run by Western volunteers, the only real medical care for the Sherpa for a hundred miles.

Harlan gathered us into a warm teahouse for an afternoon meal. The fire here was also dried yak dung, hotter than one of wood, but with its own unpleasant smell. As we ate, he stood and said, "I've looked about, and conditions are better here than they've been in years past. Given the state of the weather, we're going to hold in place at least two nights, so I suggest you plan to sleep indoors. More snow is expected.

"The risk of infection or bacterial contamination will be higher and none of us wants to get sick, so be certain to take the usual precautions." He told us where to find the hostel that would provide beds. "Finally, the dead Sherpa, Kima, will be cremated just before dark. I've known him since he was a child—him and his family. This is a great tragedy. It would be nice if all of you would attend."

Afterward, Calvin looked me up. We tossed our gear into a room and watched preparations for the funeral. Stern was everywhere with his camera. Rusty had set his on a tripod and was quietly filming the activity. Crystal walked over and said, "We had to pay to film. They seem to think Stern's with us, so they're letting him as well. What a shit."

The dead Sherpa was wrapped in a shroud of white cloth. A frame had been constructed and he was placed on it. A local holy man reverently cut a lock of the young man's hair and presented it to Zhiku to give to his family. As dusk fell, several young village men beat on drums, one rattled a cymbal, and another blew on a conch shell, the sound echoing forlornly off the mountains. The holy man recited verses from memory. At last, someone set the fire. It was dark by the time the flames had turned to embers.

At dinner, no one seemed much in the mood to talk, so I turned in early. Toward midnight, I awakened, scratching. Calvin was sitting up, grimacing. "Lice."

It was snowing the next morning as we walked to the teahouse for breakfast. Harlan approached and said, "Have you seen Gody?"

"No. Not last night after dinner or this morning. Why?" I asked.

"No one's seen him. I don't think he slept in the village."

I stared at the bleak landscape. "Where'd he go?"

"That's what I'd like to know," Harlan said as he marched off.

After breakfast, Calvin and I set out for the clinic. "I want to meet with the medical staff here," Calvin explained. "They probably know more about high-altitude sickness than any group in the world."

Heavy, wet flakes dropped like small stones in the still air, muffling every sound. As we walked, all we could hear was our breathing and the gentle flop of each boot on the ground.

The clinic was the best building in the village, constructed of large rocks with a rusted metal roof. It was manned by three Westerners—a doctor from Oregon named Lisa and two nurses, one from Australia, the other from Switzerland. Lisa and Calvin were old friends from the previous year. I spotted Calvin's tome on high altitude illnesses on her bookshelf.

"How's your foot?" she asked. Perhaps forty years old, she was tall and rangy with a warm smile, large white teeth, and a gregarious manner.

"Hurts in the cold," he said.

"Then don't go in the cold." She sat us in wooden chairs and requested tea from a young Sherpa assistant. "Seriously, Cal, what are you doing up here again? You don't need to be on another mountain climb. That was a bad business with the Sherpa. This is a dangerous place."

Calvin told her about the expedition.

"I've heard. We get the BBC broadcast each night. I suppose it stands to reason that one of the world's richest men would want his son to be the only one recovered from up there. How many do you think will die in the attempt?"

"None, we hope." Changing the subject he said, "The village seems smaller than I recall."

She nodded. "A lot of the people have moved out. There was fighting not far from here last year. There's talk of more fighting once winter lifts. The people were frightened and moved away. I don't know if they'll ever come back."

"There won't be any fighting on Everest," I said.

"Not there, no. The mountain doesn't need guns to kill. But not so far from here, back the way you just came. Now let's take a look at your foot," she said to Calvin, "you were limping as you walked in." As Lisa removed Calvin's boot, she said, "How are the expedition members?"

"As far as I know, the Sherpa are fine. You might talk to Zhiku about that, though. The climbers are in pretty good condition. Tarja—you remember her?—has a nagging cough. And Tom—this is his first time up—is developing one. I think we got lice last night."

"Bedbugs. They've been a problem all winter. I've got a powder for you. Don't let me forget. Now let's see your foot."

<hr />

Outside in the snow, the Sherpa were gathered near their camp. I wandered over as Calvin had his foot tended and began discussing developments in high-altitude sickness. A few feet from the Sherpa was a yak, tethered to a pole, making its peculiar grunting sound. "What's going on?" I asked Dawa.

"The yak hurt his leg yesterday and it is no good now. Zhiku says we should kill it for the meat, but no one will do it. They say we should sacrifice the yak and turn back. This no good. Zhiku will not give in," Dawa said. "He says we are not going back and that anyone who does will not be paid. He wants someone to kill it."

I'd seen this before. As Buddhists strongly influenced by Hinduism, the Sherpa believed in reincarnation. This yak might well be one of their passed relatives. Or it might disapprove of whoever slaughtered it in this life and seek revenge when reborn. Either way, killing it was a bad situation. Sherpa much preferred that a Westerner do the killing. Let him face the consequences. They were happy to enjoy the meat afterward; they just didn't want to make any mistakes by doing the killing.

"You do it, Scott," Dawa said with his sly smile. "It will be dinner tonight. The Sherpa will be very happy with you."

"Not me. I'm not cutting any throats today. Anyway, I thought they wanted the animal sacrificed."

Dawa shrugged. "They do now. Once they smell the cooked meat …"

Peer, Tarja, and Gody approached followed by Stern carrying a camera in his hand. I explained the dilemma. Tarja teased Peer. "You do it." She coughed, turning her face to the side.

Peer grinned. "I'm a lover, not a killer."

"Someone do it," Stern said. "It'll be a great picture."

Gody drew a knife from somewhere on his person. It was a kukri, the traditional inwardly curved blade of the Gurkha. Stern jumped then moved back noticeably. "These people are superstitious peasants," Gody said. Then he spoke in a native language and the crowd parted. Stern moved to the side of the gathering and, keeping his distance, knelt down, and began recording. Gody approached the yak, glanced at Stern, then with a quick clean slash, cut the animal's throat. It fell forward onto its knees with a loud grunt, sounding almost like a moan. It held still for a moment as hot blood rushed into the cold air with a cloud of steam, then struck the snow to form a crimson pool. The animal toppled to the side and two Sherpas descended on it with knives, all smiles.

Stern moved instinctively forward to catch every bit of the bloody business with his camera. Gody fixed the little man with a glare. I thought Stern would faint. He lowered the camera and melted into the crowd.

The knife was gone as Gody walked by me. "They are an ignorant people."

⌁⌁⌁

The snow lightened that afternoon and the day turned bitterly cold. At the hostel, I dosed myself and my sleeping bag with the brown powder Lisa had given us. Calvin did the same, saying nothing about his foot. Afterward we went into the dining area where Rusty, Diana, and Crystal were busy setting up a shot.

"This sucks," Crystal said.

"They want a feed today," Rusty said testily as he disconnected a microphone cable from his camera.

"You should have filmed him dragging the guy up the hill. We could use that. Now we'll have to take a segment from the file we recorded earlier," Crystal said.

"They won't know the difference—or what we missed," Rusty said.

I approached Diana. "What's up?"

"Problems with the power supply. We didn't expect to file this soon, so Rusty wasn't bothering to keep it charged. It's a nuisance to unpack and repack all that gear. Crystal says a video he took of you trying to save the Sherpa appeared on television. She's pretty mad that Rusty couldn't get his camera out in time." She leaned close to him and spoke quietly. "You've been avoiding me, soldier."

"The trail is nowhere for a social life."

"Do I have bad breath or something? You haven't walked with me yet."

It was true. I had been avoiding her. Since arriving, she had asked me more than once about the previous year, about what really happened on the summit. She should have known by now that was the last thing I wanted to talk about. I couldn't help wondering why a reporter, an employee of Michael Sodoc, would be pressing me so hard on a subject I was reticent to discuss if she were truly my friend.

"We'll catch up tonight," I promised as Crystal cursed and stomped out of the room.

<hr />

That afternoon, Calvin asked each of the climbers to report to the clinic, where he'd arranged to have our blood tested. The expedition was now at 14,000 feet—and from here on, regular blood draws were essential to be certain we were properly acclimatizing. Any climber slow to build the vital red blood cells essential to carrying oxygen risked suffering extreme hypoxia and succumbing to any of a variety of lethal ailments.

The problem was that the higher we climbed, the lower the air pressure. By the time we reached Base Camp, at 18,000 feet, the air pressure would be half of what it was at sea level and that translated into half the number of available oxygen molecules. As a consequence, every breath drew just half the oxygen the body was accustomed to. Even now, the air had significantly fewer O's, as they were called.

The effects were easy to see. Even standing still, we tended to pant like dogs on a hot day. Pulling the Sherpa's body up to the trail had nearly done me in. Everyone was already suffering from a loss of appetite. Strength and stamina would now begin to fall steadily. Headaches were nearly universal, though they would become much worse before this was over. With chronic sore throats, no one was drinking enough. Dehydration was already a concern and would be more so if the weather turned, as it often did, and the days became bright and relatively warm in climbing attire.

The body's response to a diminished supply of oxygen was to create more red blood cells so there were more of them to carry oxygen. It was like a line of porters, each carrying a load to a certain point. If each porter carried a lighter load, more porters were needed to keep the same delivered amount.

Even though our red blood cells would increase, there was a limit to what the body could do. Base Camp was still 11,000 feet below the summit—and even at that relatively lower altitude, the bloodstream was unable to provide the body with the amount of oxygen it was designed to receive and was required for sound health. The higher the human body rose, even with acclimatization, the worse the effects. Nevertheless, the production of cells at this point on the expedition was essential; if the body failed to produce enough of the vital corpuscles, too quick an ascent could turn deadly.

Lisa and her assistants drew the blood while Calvin examined a smear under their microscope. No one received exact results from him, merely a "Looks good," or "Not bad." If he viewed a bad sample, he didn't say anything. Because the Sherpa were from the region, they were not tested.

When finished, Calvin gave us each a small bottle of baby aspirin and directed us to begin taking one every day. "Why?" Tom asked.

"To reduce the likelihood you'll have a stroke," was the sobering answer.

In addition—and for reasons I didn't understand, but were more likely the result of observation than what he saw in the microscope—Calvin placed several climbers on Diamox. This is a fairly common diuretic often used to treat glaucoma. In recent years, it's been employed more frequently as a prophylactic against high-altitude sickness. It had the effect, in most cases, of speeding the acclimatization process. Among those given the medicine was Harlan, which only served to emphasize the ultimate reality of high altitude climbing: it didn't matter how often you'd been there, HACE could take anyone, anytime.

TEN

*Tarja Sodoc was an odd bride. Preoccupied with her looks,
behaving daily as a prima donna, she demanded camera time.
Whenever the great adventurer gave an interview, Tarja could
be counted on to hang on his arm, her chest jutting to maxi-
mum, that "come hither" look in her misty eyes.*
—Quentin Stern, www.AbandonedonEverest.com

Overnight, the weather cleared. Blue skies meant very cold temperatures that morning and we bundled against the elements. The Sherpa
did what they did every day; they wore all their clothing. If they were
cold, they were cold. There was grumbling this morning and I saw
Zhiku meeting with Harlan, who shook his head over and over.

"What's going on?" I asked Dawa.

"The Sherpa want to turn back. They say this is very bad karma.
A yak dead, a Sherpa. Boss say we go on."

The expedition set out an hour later—moving slowly—in a
somber mood. The Sherpas chanted as they left the village, the string
of prayer flags set up over the dead man's mound fluttering in the
breeze. Today I hiked with Dawa, who was not in a mood to talk. It
was just as well; neither was I.

In the triumphant Everest expedition of 1953, Edmund Hillary
had sought out the renowned Sherpa guide, Tenzing Norgay. The

previous season, Tenzing and the Swiss climber he was guiding had nearly conquered Everest. They had spent a miserable night bivouacked near the summit and then only just failed to make it. Hillary had correctly decided that Tenzing was the most experienced and knowledgeable Sherpa on Everest and had actively sought his company during the long approach march. It had served him well on summit day, when, after another miserable bivouac not far below the peak, they'd overcome every obstacle that would have thwarted lesser men and made it to the top.

The previous year, I had no such thoughts when I'd found myself hiking so often with Dawa. I had no intention of summiting, but knew that Dawa had and I found myself wanting to learn what it was like. We formed a strong and lasting bond.

On the trek last year, we had encountered a steady stream of yak caravans and Sherpa porters carrying the seemingly endless stream of supplies required for so many people. When we'd arrived, we'd been just one of more than a dozen expeditions, albeit the most famous. A crew from Canal TV in France had been filming another expedition and I had spotted a reporter from a national television news program in the United States. The idyllic conditions of the approach that year had largely continued at Base Camp, though a zoo-like state of affairs soon developed. Several expeditions were already on site when we arrived, ready to begin the staging climbs to the summit. The Sodoc Foundation Everest expedition was anticipated since the publicity campaign had been worldwide. Climbers from nearly every European nation—along with a large contingent from Korea and Japan—all gawked as the celebrities hiked into camp. I'd never seen anything like it.

Tarja's tabloid reputation had proceeded her, as had word of her recent marriage to the heir. The presence of professional cameras and the film team had only increased the celebrity aspect of the expedition. The first tent erected had been for media use and Crystal had started filing gushing reports almost at once.

Within days of our arrival, five other expeditions arrived. In all there were nearly two thousand people of all types at Base Camp and the area resembled a carnival site, with some four hundred tents set up haphazardly amid all the clutter and debris from previous years. Three and a half miles above sea level and situated at the foot of the Khumbu Glacier, residents tended to treat the ad hoc village with an excessive degree of normality.

The reality, however, was that everyone was at some risk simply by being there. The escarpments above the camp were draped with hanging ice, which produced enormous avalanches that roared nearby at all hours of the day or night. These were not a danger *per se*, except when climbers ventured there for training and acclimatization climbs, but they should have been a reminder of the danger we were in. And for all the talk of crevasses, cliffs, and death from oxygen deprivation, one-third of all climbers who perished did so from falling snow and ice.

Each of the expeditions could be identified by its distinct Buddhist prayer pole and the radiating lines of colored prayer flags anchored beneath mounds of rock. Tents were scattered haphazardly among the larger rocks and slabs of ice wherever there was a flat space. Brightly colored four-person tents marked either climbers or staff. The larger, dark-colored tents were used for storage and cooking. Off to the side were the ubiquitous small brown toilet tents or open squats.

After dark, climbers bundled and mingled, freely drinking from small bottles or smoking strong marijuana bought in Kathmandu as they chatted and flirted, music blaring across the natural amphitheater that housed Base Camp. A general party atmosphere prevailed. It was then that Derek and Tarja's marriage had openly begun to disintegrate.

━━━━

We resumed the next day under a steady drizzle. The yak plodded along the muddy trail unconcerned. The Westerners complained at each stop while the Sherpa suffered without comment. I was miserable.

The second night out, the rain finally eased, then stopped. Shortly after sunset, the sky broke clear, displaying a vast canopy of brilliant stars set against black velvet. The adverse effects of our stay in Pheriche had been apparent throughout the day—much worse than at any time since we'd set out. Peer had a racking cough, while Diana's was much worse. Tarja had developed the runs and I'd seen her squatting off the side of the trail more than once, joined occasionally by Tom, who met my eye at such moments with a sheepish smile. Calvin was walking with a pronounced limp, though he said nothing about it.

That night, we camped on a small rise nestled between two steep cliffs. Harlan gave orders for a more elaborate meal—probably to lift our morale—and the Sherpa took the time to erect the cooking tent before setting to it. They placed folding chairs about a single bright fire. It was cold and we climbers were swaddled in thick clothing as we sat about it. Few had anything to say. We were all very, very tired and wet to the core.

As dinner was served, Crystal emerged from the media tent she'd ordered erected in an exceptionally lighthearted mood. "You have to love technology," she said as she sat and accepted a plate of food. Her face was more alive than it had been in days.

Stern joined us with his typical smug expression. Rusty arrived a few minutes later and took a chair beside me, looking like the cat who'd swallowed the canary. Gody sat silently—as was his custom—in the shadows just beyond the flickering light of the fire. Tom was nearest the darkness and an impromptu privy. Across from us, Peer was taking turns hacking along with Tarja. Calvin looked drained of energy and I wondered if he'd be able to continue. I'd rarely seen him so exhausted.

No one said much as we ate. I had to force my food down, knowing that my body needed the nutrition and energy. Tarja scarcely touched her meal. The others picked at their plates.

I suppose Rusty couldn't contain himself any longer. "Tarja," he said as Crystal all but giggled, fixing her eyes on the woman. "I was on the Internet a bit ago and saw you there."

"Yes?" she said. "What's your point? I'm sure there are thousands of pictures of me on the Internet."

"Not like this, trust me. I think Stern here took it earlier today. You're squatting down, taking care of business."

For a moment, Tarja didn't appear to get his meaning, then her head snapped to Stern. "Is this true? You took a picture of me like that and posted it?"

Stern shrugged. "Why not? You were only doing what comes naturally." He laughed, looking at the rest of us for approval.

Tarja stood up. "That's disgusting. We should have some decency toward one another in these conditions." She threw her plate of food in his face.

Rusty reached into his jacket, drew out a still camera, and snapped a flash shot of Stern, wiping the goo off his face and clothes. "I'll post this in a bit," Rusty said.

"Screw you!" Stern countered as he stood. "To hell with you all!" With that, he marched off into the dark toward the Sherpa camp.

"What are you laughing at?" Tarja demanded of Peer, who was grinning.

"Stern, of course. What do you think?"

"You're a bastard, you know?" Tarja stomped off and disappeared into her tent.

Harlan stood, sighed, and said, "You must forgive my candor, but many of you here need to grow up. This is not a lark we are on."

～～～

That night, I bedded in a two-person tent with Calvin, but sleep wouldn't come to either of us. Outside, the wind whipped at the tent while the rain returned in sheets. We were cold and too exhausted to nod off. We spoke in whispers for some time about what we'd been doing since the disaster the previous year. There was a long moment of silence—and though I thought he might have fallen asleep—I said, "Why this devotion to Derek, Cal? I don't understand it. I've never understood it."

"He should receive a proper burial."

"I can't see why. He lies up there with some of the greatest athletes in history. I can't think of a better place for him to be."

"His father asked me. I couldn't say no."

"Why is that? I saw you today, limping along. You shouldn't be up here. You've had your time at the high altitudes. You need to know when to stop."

I thought he'd fallen asleep, so much time passed before he spoke again. "Let me tell you about me and Derek. I met him when he was at Princeton. We were members of the same rock-climbing club. It's a year-round sport in that part of the country. We were scaling the Gray

Matterhorn, a name someone made up for a nasty wall of rock. The stone was soft and you had to proceed with great care. There'd been some falls, even a recent death. A group of us were supposed to climb it, but when the weather turned foul, everyone backed out except us.

"Until that day, we didn't know each other all that well. I was pretty shy and he was the son of one of the world's richest and most powerful men. He was a star, everything I wasn't. I guess each of us was looking for the other to give an excuse not to climb. When that didn't happen, we went ahead. We roped together and set out, taking it very slowly."

"Don't tell me he saved your life?"

"In manner of speaking, but not the way you mean. I'm about two years older than Derek. In the years we've been friends, I've usually felt like an older brother. I think he felt the same way about me. He'd had a pretty lonely childhood. His mother's suicide hurt him deeply. He hid behind that false self-assurance and bravado, but inside he was very injured, very angry, and very needy. I know he struggled with it, but it proved a lethal combination in the end. His father's a real bastard when you get right down to it."

"So what happened?"

"It was a miserable day. It had rained all the night before and the rock was slippery. Once we set out, it started raining again. I don't know why we kept going, except we were young and stupid. We were climbing without helmets, being certain we'd live forever.

"A bit over halfway up, Derek set a piton. As he pulled himself up, it gave way. It all happened so fast, I don't recall any details. I heard him shout and, before I could react, he fell past me. I instinctively hugged the rock and braced myself. His weight hit full force and I was certain we were both going to die, but I had my boots on a shallow precipice and my piton held. I hung on for my life and managed to hold him for the longest time. I thought my arms would fall off; my shoulder was raw from where rope burned across it and I was certain I'd dislocated it.

"Derek had slammed his head against the rock and was stunned. I don't know what I'd have done if he hadn't come to his senses. I kept calling down to him without an answer. I was straining on the rope, trying to figure out what to do if he was really knocked out. I doubt my piton would have held the two of us indefinitely. At some point, I was either going to have to cut him loose and kill him or my strength would give out and we'd both fall to our deaths.

"After what seemed an eternity, I could feel him start to move below me. He must have found a small ridge or crack to rest a boot on because the pressure eased just a bit, then I heard his hammer as he drove in another piton. Finally, the pressure was off. And a minute later, he was climbing again, passed me, and eventually all the way to the top."

"He finished the climb?" I asked.

"It was amazing. He was bleeding almost the entire distance. He never said a word. He just worked methodically. I took him to the hospital after we'd rappelled down and they kept him overnight with a concussion. He told me later that he really didn't remember finishing the climb. He'd done it on instinct."

"So you saved his life."

"I suppose. Or after he fell and recovered, he saved mine. I couldn't have stayed that way indefinitely."

"What's the word they use? You two bonded."

"You could say that."

"I can see the devotion you've shown, I guess."

"No, you don't understand. I wasn't attending Princeton. I was from nearby Rock Hill, where my dad worked as an airplane mechanic. I'd dropped out of community college when an engine fell on his arm and he couldn't work like that any longer. They kept him on in the office, but the drop in pay was just too much. I had to give up my dream of being a doctor."

I understood. "Then you saved Derek's life."

"That's right. His dad put me through college, then medical school. It turned my life around—even more than it does for most doctors because I went into practice without debt. I was able to support my parents almost at once. It's made all the difference. I felt that I owed Derek a great deal; I owe his father everything. So if he wants me to help bring Derek back down, I'll do my best. And if my foot hurts a little, so be it."

We set out the next morning in a determined mood. We wanted nothing more than to reach Base Camp and bring an end to the ceaseless trek through rain and snow, the path never so treacherous. We often slowed to a crawl then, toward mid-afternoon, the rain eased slightly. It was a relief to be out from under the spigot. Occasional clear patches presented a view that was panoramic, the landscape swathed in low-lying clouds, the rocks dripping water.

As we crossed a level rise in the land between a narrow divide bordered by steep cliffs, the line came to an unexpected stop. I looked and could see ahead the signs of a recent avalanche. I felt sick as I moved up the column and reached Harlan who was standing with Zhiku, transfixed by the sight before them.

"Wasn't there a settlement here?" I asked.

"Yes," Harlan said quietly. "Not much more than a teahouse and a few huts, but perhaps thirty people in all. It must be recent; there was no word at Pheriche."

The entire wall behind the village had given way, nearly blocking the divide. I could see nothing of what had been here the year before. "Are there survivors?"

Zhiku shook his head. "Not in the village. It is gone completely. Perhaps someone was away. If so, and they are still alive, they will come to us, if they can."

It certainly looked recent, but, in this part of the world, natural catastrophes a hundred years old often looked as if they'd happened the day before.

Dawa approached and in his quiet way began arguing vehemently with Zhiku, soon joined by Chepal and Gametup, the most experienced climbing Sherpas after them. This went on for some minutes. I asked Harlan what it was about.

"They want to turn back. They say this is a terrible omen—that we aren't meant to be up here. Dawa is almost insistent."

"They may have a point. At the least, we're clearly too early in the season to be moving though this region to Base Camp."

Harlan sighed. "We've had a run of bad luck, that's certainly true. The long-term weather forecast was favorable, but it turned out to be shite." He looked again at the remains of the avalanche. "There's nowhere to hole up and wait. And I have my orders."

As the argument continued, the other Sherpa built a small mound, set up prayer flags, and performed a devotion. Finally, we set out again. The guides selected a new course that skirted the freshly moved mountain. Dawa dropped back in the line and hiked a bit with me.

"The Sherpa are angry," he said. "They do not want to go on. Talk to him, Scott. This is very, very bad. I have tried to tell him we should not continue, but he will not listen."

"We've had some bad luck, Dawa," I said. "But that's all. These things happen."

He shook his head. "Not like this. Never before like this." He became pensive and said, "They say it is the goddess. This is happening because of our great shame."

⌁⌁⌁

We set camp at sunset, the site of the catastrophe still visible behind us. All the talk was of the poor souls buried beneath a mountain of rock, not that anyone was in much of a mood to talk. The Sherpa were genuinely spooked by events. They kept even more apart than usual and spoke in hushed voices, eyeing the Westerners with suspicion.

The next morning was overcast, but the storm had passed for now. The reality of what we'd seen the previous day settled over the entire expedition like a pall. After the traditional light breakfast of sweet tea and flat bread, we set out. The trail remained slippery where there were rocks, but muddy otherwise. All life had by this time been left behind, tragically so in at least one case. There were no longer settlements or the occasional teahouse. Vegetation was reduced to patches of lichen.

The vistas, however, were dazzling. The air was clear at this altitude and remained mercifully still. The yaks plodded at their own pace, grunting from time to time, and we advanced to the sound of their tinkling bells. I felt as if I was on a distant planet, far from the world I knew.

I watched the two women Sherpa with great interest, especially Laki now that I knew who her husband had been. Across her forehead was a supporting strap she used to lift and balance her eighty-pound load. I was carrying no more than ten pounds in my light pack and found it a burden. She was a small, hard woman and the load was very difficult for her, I could see, especially as she weighed no more than a hundred pounds herself.

The air continued to grow thin and was more frequently a problem for all of us. Fortunately, we forded many steams because of the rain and had time to recover before pushing on.

We stopped in line for a lunch of soup and the local bread. When we resumed, I encountered Peer, who was standing to the side and fell in step with me. "Not so pleasant as last year, is it?" he said.

"No. It's been pretty miserable. I guess that's the price of moving to Base Camp so early. And an entire village gone—just like that."

"It happens in Norway sometimes," he said. "Though not so often anymore. It is what comes from living in the mountains."

"Why are you here, Peer?" I asked. "You and Derek were hardly friends."

"Me? I'm being paid. Aren't we all?"

That brought me up for a moment. Paid. Sodoc had covered my expenses, as I knew he had Calvin's, but paid? "I don't think so."

Peer looked surprised. "Really? You should have asked for money. He was ready to give it."

"Why?"

"I have no idea. I assumed you knew. The story I heard makes no sense to me."

"I was told we're here to recover Derek's body."

Peer scoffed. "I didn't know Sodoc had a religion other than money. It is the same with all Jews. Then why is Gody here? And Tom? You seem friendly with him."

"I know nothing more. Really. And I don't think Sodoc's a Jew."

Peer eyed me skeptically. "Bank on it. So, what happened last year? You never told me. You were in a big hurry to get away."

"We all were, Peer."

"That's fair."

"What happened to you that last day?"

"I was on the ridge near the Summit when the storm hit. Then I heard Derek's radio call for help and went looking for him. I heard you found him."

"That's right. No one else came to help, though, and I couldn't get him down alone. Where were you?"

"Me? Fighting for my life, my friend. It was very bad up there. You know what it was like."

"I had radio contact for over an hour before we finally lost communication. We were practically on the path from the shelf to the Summit. I saw no one."

"My friend, I probably walked within ten feet of you without us seeing each other."

"Did you look? You knew when you were at the Hillary Step. You knew we were there."

Peer glared. "Don't accuse me!" We walked in silence for several long minutes. "Anyway, I stumbled across Tsongba, half frozen. I took him down the Step. I didn't stand around waiting for help." He leaned over and coughed.

***

The next day we passed slowly through Lobuche, the most disgusting and vile place I've ever seen—and I've stayed in some real hellholes. Garbage and excrement were simply tossed out of the squalid huts and, despite recent snow, the smell was overpowering. A single dirty hostel served meals, but Harlan cautioned us all to take nothing from it. "I've arranged to pass through the place at midday. Touch nothing."

His words were ignored. The line slowed to a crawl and then stopped as Sherpa set down their loads to take tea. They were joined by Stern, Tarja, and Peer—who claimed he was immune to diseases in such places. Tom, Calvin, Gody, and I kept moving and stopped outside the town where we waited for the expedition to resume. Diana and the film crew remained on the far side.

For all that, the village did not appear hospitable. The windows were shuttered and the usual gathering of Sherpa had not appeared to welcome or even to watch us. I caught sight of an old woman—old for a Sherpa, at least—and she stared at us like a witch placing a curse.

Half an hour after we stopped, Dawa joined us.

"What's going on?" Tom asked.

"Eating, drinking. The Sherpa are saying prayers."

"Again?" Tom said.

"Oh yes. Much bad in this. The women say they heard ghosts last night. All want to turn back, but Zhiku won't let them. These people say we bring them bad luck."

We now learned about the disaster we'd seen. The avalanche had apparently taken place three days earlier. They'd heard the low rumble even at this distance. Sherpa had gone to see and returned later with a four-year-old girl—the lone survivor. The entire village had been spooked since. They'd put our expedition together with the vanished village and blamed us.

"Tell me, Dawa," Tom asked. "Why is this village–and some others—so dirty?"

Dawa looked toward the huts. "These are ignorant people up here. Life is hard. They do not understand that dirt means sickness. This is the way it has always been."

"I guess they are immune to it," Tom said.

"Yes," Dawa agreed after a fashion. "The ones who don't die aren't sick too often."

⌐⌐⌐⌐

We were approaching 18,000 feet and I was increasingly exhausted. My lungs were starting to burn from constant effort and my body ached from the uncertain ground. I welcomed arriving in Base Camp, where we would rest; the higher camps were set up before beginning the search for Derek.

That night, Crystal summoned me to her media tent. I found Calvin and Tom already there, looking very unhappy.

"I want you people to see this," she said. Rusty was slumped on a camp chair. A laptop lay open on a table and was online. "How long, Rusty?" Crystal asked.

"We're good for a bit. I need to recharge after tonight, though. The batteries are getting down."

"Take a look," Crystal said. "This is the Abandoned on Everest Web site. Go ahead and check it out, Scott. I'd like your opinion."

I sat on a camp chair and took a look. Calvin and Tom leaned over my shoulders. The Web site itself was a standard one promoting a book. There were reviews—all favorable of course—and a photo of Stern that I thought was a mistake—but I suppose that's an author's privilege.

"Go to the blog," Crystal said.

I clicked. Across the top was the windy peak of Everest in faded blue set against a white background. The rest of the mountain trailed down the page, disappearing eventually in artistic wisps. In the middle of the page were dated entries, many by Stern, others by a commentator named Elsa who was associated with the publisher, probably the publicist for the book. At each entry was a link for comments by visitors. Every Stern entry I saw had at least twenty. You could click on the link to view them.

"Read some. Then check out the photos he's been filing." Crystal dropped into a seat and began gnawing on a thumbnail.

One entry from Elsa read: Quentin and the expedition are now passing through a treacherous region on their way to Base Camp. Unusually violent storms caused by global climate change have made the trail all but impassable. Quentin is pressing on, though most of the rest want to turn back.

I suppose that was one version of what was taking place. Another, this one by Stern, read: Tarja Sodoc continues to be the spoiled prima donna she has always been, treating everyone about her as if they were her personal servants. Her intimate relations with one of the climbers are quite open, so open that no one comments on the propriety of a widow engaging in such behavior while on a trek to recover her late, heroic husband's body.

One of the comments by browsers read: She's a fox! Can't Quentin get a pix of her taking a shower? That would be awesome. If she wants to f**k me to death that would be real cool!

Stern's most recent entry read: The poorly paid Sherpa continue to labor under extraordinary loads. Most of the burden is placed on the small backs of the women who struggle to keep up. This expedition is conditioned upon the exploitation and abuse of the powerless. It is heartbreaking to witness. Today we passed the site where once was a peaceful Sherpa village. It was obliterated by an avalanche brought on by deforestation. I cannot but help question the price these kindly people pay for positioning themselves to sell us a mug of tea so they can exist. In this case, their kindliness killed them.

"Now go to the photos," Crystal prompted from her chair.

The photo page was divided into short film clips that Stern had taken with his digital camera, along with more traditional stills. Two of the clips caught my eye. One was of me struggling with the Sherpa to bring up the body of the dead yak herdsman to the trail. Next to it was a short clip of the cremation. He'd caught Tarja and Peer, looking anything but respectful. Another clip was a slow pan of the buried village, or to be more precise, of the fresh rock that covered it. The most grotesque was that of Gody slicing the yak's throat. Stern had moved in for a close-up of the gore.

The stills, I must admit, were quite professional. Stern had a knack for composition and storytelling in a single frame. One was of Laki, collapsed during a break, the exhaustion and strain written across every line of her weathered face. The other woman, Ongmu, lay beside her, resting against her equally heavy load, looking no less exhausted.

There were stills of us fording streams and passing across muddy flats, along with close-ups of yaks and Sherpa of all kinds in various poses performing the wide range of tasks that were part of their job. There were also stills of us about the fires. One showed Gody standing to the side of the group, the look on his face very unpleasant. At that moment, he was clearly a man you didn't want to cross. There was one of me talking to Calvin intently about something and Cal grimacing in pain. And, of course, there was Tarja squatting off the side of the trail, unaware she was being photographed.

The last was the most deplorable. I hadn't realized that the man had been snapping so many pictures. I knew from the year before that the closer we came to Base Camp, the more casual would be our attitude toward modesty. With the primitive living conditions and the intestinal ailments most or all of us would suffer, body functions were rarely private. It was understood that everyone just looked the other way. Stern was violating the most basic rule of an Everest expedition.

Crystal caught my eye. "I've told Rusty I want one of Stern taking a crap."

"That will be lovely," Tom said.

"And what will we do with it, Crissie?" Rusty asked. "Our Web site won't post it."

"Try YouTube. They'll post anything. It's time we brought him down a peg or two."

Calvin leaned in for a closer look. "This is a really bad idea. I don't think Stern realizes how easy it is to settle scores up here if someone has a mind to."

<center>~~~</center>

The next day was clear, the sun possessing that unnatural quality you get at high altitude. By late morning, we reached another of the countless streams. Crystal, Rusty, and Diana had set up a dramatic shot beside the rushing current. Rusty had most of his gear out, including several solar cell blankets. As I passed, Diana caught my eye and winked.

This crossing was routine, if slow and cautious. As I reached the other side, however, there was a sudden shout. Everyone turned to look.

One of the porters had collapsed. Calvin was already there when I arrived. It was Laki. Zhiku and Dawa rushed up as others gathered around.

The young woman had swooned and was unconscious. As Calvin checked for symptoms, he was asking about her health. "Headache last night," Zhiku said. "She said she could go on. She knows we are close to Base Camp. I was watching her carefully."

Harlan had joined us by now. "How is she?"

"I'm not sure yet," Calvin answered as he took her pulse, inserting the armband to take her blood pressure. "Go ahead, Zhiku."

"She has been very tired and feeling weak."

"Anything else?"

Dawa spoke. "Last night she did not sleep. She told me she was worried about her daughter. She had a bad dream the night before that her daughter is very sick."

The entire expedition had come to a halt. Harlan moved along the line telling the porters to drop their loads and for everyone to rest. "Calvin has the situation in hand," he called out. "Stay where you are."

Calvin took Laki's temperature. A moment later, Stern arrived with his camera. "Get him away from her!" Calvin snapped.

Stern lifted his camera just as Gody—who'd I'd not seen before— stepped over and knocked it aside. "This is not the time. Get back to your place."

Stern looked at the man with sudden apprehension. Raising his arms in mock surrender, he retreated, saying, "No problem. No problem." Stern moved back along the line.

I looked back at Laki who was out cold. It was impossible to accept that she was in her early twenties. She appeared at least twenty years older. She had dainty hands and the smallest feet I've ever seen on an adult.

Calvin straightened up and spoke quietly to Harlan and Zhiku, but I could hear. "She's suffering from Acute Mountain Sickness, possibly HACE." The second was High Altitude Cerebral Edema and was fatal if not treated.

"That cannot be," Zhiku said. "She is a Sherpa."

"It can be, my friend. She is not really fit for this and is very worn down. Not all Sherpa are immune to HACE."

"But not here. We are very low yet," Zhiku said.

"I think there's some brain swelling."

"We should reach Base Camp tomorrow. Is she all right until then?"

"No. She should stay here with two Sherpa. I'm putting her on Diamox, which should help. Once she's recovered enough to walk, they must take her back to the clinic in Pheriche. If she recovers, she can stay and help out there until we return. If not, the nurses will get her back down."

The treatment for all high-altitude ailments was the same. Descend into thicker air. There were medicines and procedures for when you were in thin air, but the only real cure was a lower altitude.

Fifteen minutes later, we moved out, leaving Laki and two Sherpa behind.

～～～

That night, the rain returned. It began as a wet snow, but soon turned into a downpour. By first light, I was shivering in my sleeping bag. Some of the rain had managed to dampen it and my body heat had steadily drained away.

A Sherpa handed mugs of hot tea into the tent. Calvin and I drank as we complained. His night had been no better—though his ailment had been his right foot. "Amputated toes," he allowed, "hurt like hell."

We dressed and set out in the continuing rain for breakfast, which was being served under an expanse of blue plastic. Tom, Peer, Gody, Tarja, and Crystal were already there with Crystal standing apart. Harlan joined us. "Base Camp today," he announced, "barring major trouble."

"Why's it raining?" Tom asked. "Shouldn't it be snowing at this elevation?"

Peer laughed. "You sound as if you miss it."

"It's warm air above," Harlan said. "Don't worry. You'll have your fill of snow before we're finished. Ten minutes."

I can't say it was the worst hiking of my life. I've had too many bad ones to rank them, but that day is very high on the list. Besides the icy temperature and slippery footing were the numerous rushing torrents we were forced to cross. I could recall scarcely more than a handful from the previous year, but now they sprang from the nearby elevations in clusters. What ground there was had been soaked by the earlier storms and now the water simply rushed down the mountainsides. It was miserable and treacherous going.

Toward mid-afternoon, the line came to still another halt, this one lasting much longer than any previous ones. Word passed from climber to climber and a murmur arose from the Sherpa. Peer moved back along the line. "What's the delay?" I asked.

"They are taking it slowly. The footbridge was swept away over the winter. Zhiku thinks we can cross without wasting a day or two restringing it. They are rigging rope for us to hook to." He scanned along the line as if searching for something, then said, "Anyone want Tarja? I've had enough of her endless complaining and bitching." Peer didn't look like a happy man.

"No takers here," Calvin said.

Peer sighed. "I should know better than to waste my time with an American woman. They are so provincial."

"What did you do? Make a pass at Crystal?" Calvin asked.

"Please. I have some taste." Peer loitered with us a few minutes before moving back in the direction from which he'd come.

Half an hour later, we'd crawled to the raging stream the expedition was crossing. It gave me pause. Two ropes had been strung over it and, one by one, climbers and Sherpa were making their careful way across some twenty feet of rushing white water. As we came in view, Tarja had just reached the other side. Say what you would about her, she was a steady and reliable climber compared to some Westerners. The Sherpa on the far side had set up a stove and was serving tea to each climber as they emerged from the freezing water. Tarja took hers without looking back.

Peer set out next. He moved steadily across, making it look simple, the water boiling up to his knees, but giving him no pause.

Next was a Sherpa burdened with his full load. I imagined there'd been some talk about that. Halving the load would have made the crossing less treacherous, but would have required two trips. Knowing my Sherpas, they'd taken the macho approach. It seemed to me that the heavy load worked to the Sherpa's advantage, though I could see balance against the surging water was a problem. Once he made it to the other side, the next Sherpa set out.

This one was a bit smaller than the first and, because of that, his load appeared disproportionately larger. He was hesitant as he moved, advancing a few feet, stopping—which is never a good idea when fording rushing water—then taking a few cautious steps. Zhiku, who was on my side of the current, shouted at him. The Sherpa looked at him and nodded in understanding, taking his attention away from his footing, and at that moment fell.

One second he was standing erect and the next he was in the water, though hooked to the ropes. There was shouting on my side and a flurry of action on the opposing. The water built up against the man, forming an enormous pulsating berm that pressed against him with ever-greater force.

Peer was already hooked back up to the rope and started out for the man, just as Dawa had from my side. But before they could reach him, his line gave and he was swept away. Without a second's thought, Peer disconnected himself and plunged into the raging water after him.

I'd never known a Sherpa who could swim. They simply had no opportunities to learn. I'd seen one other man lose footing on such a crossing and he'd gone down like a stone. We never recovered his body.

This poor fellow still had his eighty-pound pack strapped to his body. He was rolling over and over, pushed along by the violent stream. Peer was doing a sort of Australian crawl as he went after the man.

The stream made a slow turn toward my side before rushing away into the steep valley to join a nameless seasonal river. I dropped my pack and bolted cross-country toward the water, adjusting my course to intercept the Sherpa. I heard voices behind me, but not what they said.

It was insanity. The footing was impossible. I slipped and nearly fell several times, my arms flailing like a windmill as I fought to keep my balance. Somehow I managed it and reached the water at almost the instant the Sherpa swept into view.

I had just one chance. I stepped into the raging current, leaned over, and grabbed. My hand caught the strap of his pack and his body swung behind me, threatening to pull me after him. I was bracing myself, considering releasing him to keep from going down, when the strap snapped. I fell backward, nearly losing my footing as the Sherpa was carried away toward the torrential river and certain death.

I looked to my left and saw Peer, no longer trying to reach the man, instead swimming frantically toward my side of the stream. In his hiking clothes and boots, he wasn't going to make it. Just as he reached me, I seized his soaked jacket and hung onto him for his life. I could feel myself going over and realized I'd have to release him or die with him.

I felt arms behind me and the two of us managed to get Peer to shore where we collapsed beside Tom, who'd come to our rescue.

The Sherpa swarmed around us in equal parts admiration for what we'd attempted and in shock at what had just happened. Stern was there, his camera hard at it. Harlan knelt down beside us. "Good job. Too bad about the Sherpa."

"Maybe we can—" Peer said.

"There's nothing we can do," Harlan said. "He was already drowning when you reached him. He's long dead. I doubt we'll ever find his body."

Peer placed his hand on my arm. "Thank you, my friend. I don't think I would have made it."

"You were crazy to go in like that with all your clothes on," I said.

"Yes! Crazy. I didn't think." I believed him.

Once we had our breath, Harlan asked if we thought we could still cross the torrent that had caused the trouble and move out. "It's the only way you won't freeze without us setting up camp."

We agreed to get moving. At the water's edge, Peer said, "Christ. I already crossed this damn thing once today."

I grinned. "Twice—if you count swimming."

Someone broke out blankets once we were on the other side and threw them across our shoulders, but it did little good. We resumed the march, the route now passing up and down over stretches of scattered rock for several miles before descending downhill. We passed among boulders and walked atop cinders and gravel. Frigid water coursed through each depression and I was forced to cross those stretches, which caused me to shiver uncontrollably.

If I've had a colder hike, I don't know when. Within the first hour, I'd lost all feeling in my feet. As I was considering telling Harlan we had to stop, we straggled into Base Camp, more closely resembling a band of survivors than conquering heroes.

Diana was waiting as I hobbled to where the camp was already being erected. "You crazy fool. You crazy fool," she said again as she took me in her arms.

ELEVEN

More than a dozen major expeditions were scattered about Base Camp, twice that number of smaller outfits. For many of the climbers, men as well as women, this was a time to party, the immediacy of danger and the possibility of death serving as the ultimate aphrodisiac.
— Quentin Stern, www.AbandonedonEverest.com

That night it snowed and kept snowing, spreading a heavy white carpet across the terrain. Not far away was the recurring rumble of avalanche after avalanche as the wet, unstable snow collapsed under its own weight.

At first light, with a snow coming down in heavy flakes, the Sherpa migrated to the existing rock prayer mound. The mound grew each climbing season with the addition of more stones and prayer flags. Carved or painted on the rocks were names: some commonly known to climbers, others known only to family and friends, of the many, many dead about and above us.

I watched as the Sherpa, now wearing bright Gore-Tex parkas, respectfully raised the tattered flags tied to lines on the ground and once again set them in place. The Sherpa next made an altar on the mound and lit sprigs of juniper incense. To this they added bits of food, some beer, and tea, along with a sweet cake. You can never be certain what the gods want, so they try to cover the spread. They added bright new flags with the names of those who'd died since we'd set out. Afterward, they spread prayer rugs and made their benedictions while a handful of Westerners paid respects by kneeling or simply looking on. This time there were no cameras.

This was known as a Puja ceremony and one of the Sherpa, Gametup, who'd spent two years in a monastery, led the others in prayer chants. Sherpa will not climb absent such a ceremony, as there are many gods to placate and they are everywhere—in the forest, in water, the soil, even the very air we breathe. It was essential to pay attention to them. It was even better to find some way to make them happy.

The Sherpa also believe that there are ghosts all about and it is best to avoid them if at all possible since they wish us no good. This is why they have an aversion to the dead and find climbing the summit a difficult spiritual undertaking. As is the case with all religions, in my experience, they have their worship shortcuts and, for many Sherpa, their religious practice is inseparable from mere superstition.

Laid before the altar were ice axes, crampons, and harnesses, there to receive the approval and presumed blessing of the gods. It was a means for asking for safe passage to the mother god above.

The praying finished, the Sherpa passed around milk tea, soon followed by whiskey and chang, a strong regional drink. Alcohol is an important component of the Puja. Dawa approached and handed Tom, Calvin, and me a can each of beer, this time San Miguel, which had been picked up in Namche and portaged here. Much like an alcoholic who gets going with a stiff morning pick-me-up, Crystal took the whiskey and drank with gusto. I sipped the beer and felt its kick almost at once. The effects of alcohol at altitude are enhanced.

The Sherpa became a bit high as they moved to the next part of the ceremony, which consisted primarily of chants as they tossed rice grain onto the mound and the altar. Before long, the scene degenerated into a sort of food fight. Tom expressed some surprise at the turn of events.

"They want the gods to be happy," Calvin explained, "so the idea is to turn this into a party and hope the gods join in. It's the opposite of disrespect. I think they are really afraid of going up this year. What do you think, Scott?"

"It sure looks that way."

As the party wound down, Harlan was understandably in a somber and nasty mood. He gave orders to set the camp right despite conditions. He'd yielded to pressure to leave too early for reasons that had nothing to do with climbing Everest and, as is often the case in life, others had paid the price. Two Sherpa dead, one of them critically ill on the approach march, and the most deadly part of the expedition still lay ahead.

To Westerners, the dead were faceless and anonymous. But Harlan had known them and their families for at least a decade. Each had been handpicked based on clan and family connections as well as experience. To us, they were strangers; to Harlan, the dead were friends.

The drinking continued throughout the day even as the snow fell. It was the first time since we'd set out that the divide between Sherpa and Westerner broke down so completely and that at least seemed to me a good sign.

Perhaps it was the liquor or maybe we were paying the price for loitering in Lobuche because diarrhea became the scourge of the camp starting that night. Stern was finally taken sick and lost his enthusiasm for photographing squatting people when a number of them surrounded him in the act, snapping pictures constantly.

I'd managed to avoid catching anything, unlike the previous year, until my plunge into the icy water and the forced march while freezing cold. That first morning, I awoke with a fever and struggled with illness all day—even at the Puja. Shortly after sunset, Diana ordered bed rest for me and set herself up as my personal nurse. I fell asleep that first night to the sounds of the party outside.

For the next three days, as disease and gloom settled over the expedition, I remember very little of what took place. I burned with fever and was tormented by persistent nightmares, some repeats of actual occurrences, others of events I hoped never to experience in life. Diana stayed throughout it, calming me, keeping me hydrated, and muttering reassuring words. Outside, the snow fell, deadening all sound and at times it seemed to me it was just the two of us, cut off from the universe.

When my bout had largely passed, I emerged from the tent, tired and drained. Crystal immediately grabbed Diana, saying something about not playing Florence Nightingale, and dragged her off to film a piece since the snow had finally stopped and the enormous sky above was a startling azure. I wobbled to a camp chair where a smiling Bawu, our camp cook, served me my first real meal in days.

Situated at the approach to the Khumbu Glacier, Base Camp is located in a natural amphitheater that had the tendency to overemphasize benign weather under clear skies. So even with the snow in the still air and bright sun, I soon became warm and removed my jacket. Careless climbers were often unprepared for the frigid reality only a short distance away. Open to the southwest, on sunny afternoons, there was typically little wind and climbers could, and did, sit outside wearing T-shirts. But once the sun set, the temperature plummeted into the teens.

When you are first on the scene at the start of a season, Base Camp is like what's left after the swap meet is over. The amount of debris scattered about was amazing. Even with the fresh blanket of snow, I could still see expanses of discarded oxygen bottles piled in such a way as to resemble an auto junkyard along with a small forest of collapsed tents and their aluminum frames. At its peak, twice each year during the climbing windows, Base Camp was the largest village in the region and climbers were no more meticulous about their garbage and discards than were the Sherpa.

Even here at Base Camp, ice walls loomed all about and, with them, the threat of avalanches. The crashing of ice and snow was continual, a constant reminder of what could happen in an unlucky second, without warning if you were within reach.

Now that the snow had lifted, Zhiku set his best climbers to the dangerous task of creating a passageway through the Ice Flow immediately above. From this point on, every climber moving above Base Camp was issued a radio and was required to make periodic checks with Harlan, who turned his tent into a communication center. He'd sit outside when the weather allowed, monitoring anyone in the Ice Flow. He set up his telescope to observe the mountain above and, in time, would use it to chart the course of climbers setting up the higher camps. This, and making the crucial decisions, would be his primary role from this point on, though once Camp Two was in place, he'd relocate to it. Zhiku assumed direct responsibility for anyone actually on the mountain.

As I knew from experience, a radio network was better in theory than in practice. The old analog radios that had been standard on Everest for the last decade were notoriously unreliable and you never counted on them working when you needed them. The new digital radios weren't much better, as their signal was too easily obscured. They were often interrupted by heavy snow, which I'd discovered that last day the year before. Worse were the batteries—they simply wouldn't function in the extreme cold found in the Death Zone or during the most violent storms.

This meant that climbs were safer because we had radios, as in most conditions they worked. The steady stream of information to Harlan made planning and organizing much more efficient. But it also meant that in the most crucial moments, when communication meant the difference between life and death, you could be certain your radio would fail you.

As for the Ice Flow, no climber who had summited and returned to it with his life intact considered himself truly safe until he'd traversed that final stretch. For all the talk and the reality of the summit, more climbers died each year navigating this nasty, ever-shifting body of ice than ever did higher up. The process of carving a route through the Ice Flow would consume many days and have to be redone as long as we were here, as portions collapsed or were covered by fallen walls of ice. The fresh snow made it even more dangerous than usual and I didn't envy the Sherpa at work up there.

The Ice Flow was a chameleon, transforming into a new manifestation not just with each season, but also frequently within the season itself. Footpaths were carved along stretches of sheer ice, metal ladders were laid to create bridges were snow bridges failed—often after a path had been established—and ladders were set in place as needed to allow climbers to reach the next level like you'd climb onto the roof of your house to clean off the leaves. Knowing how to climb ladders with crampons was an essential skill to safely navigate the Ice Flow. That's what passed for mountaineering in the twenty-first century.

That first morning out of my sick bed, as I was visiting with Calvin, Harlan made a point to inquire about my health.

"Weak, but okay. Just need some rest," I said.

He patted me on the back. "That was a good show before. But you're lucky to be alive. I don't advise taking such risks, no matter who is in jeopardy. As many people perish up here trying to save others as otherwise."

"How is Peer?"

"Fine. He's sturdy as a horse."

I asked about the route-clearing taking place above.

"It's going to be tough—worse than I've ever seen before. There's lots of fresh, heavy snow. It's very unstable."

"Maybe you should wait," I suggested, but Harlan merely shook his head.

"Is there any word on the other teams?" I asked. Harlan had a small laptop with which he monitored weather. He also had a sat phone I'd seen him use to call Kathmandu.

"Three have left the capital and are already at Thyangboche. They're ready to set out any day."

"So they're six days or so back?" Calvin asked.

Harlan nodded. "Or less—depending on how fit they are and the weather, of course."

"How long do you estimate it will take to establish the high camps?" I asked.

Once the Sherpa had carved a route through the Ice Flow, they would set up Camp One just above it at 19,500 feet. All of the Sherpa except the yak herdsmen would then begin the arduous task of ferrying supplies there. Weather permitting, this was a process that would continue every daylight hour until our mission was complete.

Each of the high camps was traditionally positioned a half day's climb apart. Westerners with almost no burden took at least the full four hours, sometimes as much as eight if sickness or bad weather intervened. The Sherpa, on the other hand, could typically carry fifty pounds between camps in the four hours. They'd return the same day to spend the night below before repeating the process. Without a load, they could descend very rapidly. In fact, they were under instruction to return as far as Base Camp except in extraordinary circumstances or with special permission. Harlan didn't want them consuming supplies carried at such effort above the Ice Flow.

Though everything we'd brought with us to Base Camp had been carefully considered, supplies here were relatively abundant. Nothing, however, went higher unless it was essential. The effort and risk associated with raising every pound of gear—even a hundred feet in elevation—made them precious.

Camp Two was in the Western Cwm at just over 21,000 feet and was also known as Advanced Base Camp. It was the last place on the mountain with amenities. Here, a cook and Sherpa would still see to our needs.

Four hours above it, at 24,400, feet was Camp Three, and from there on you did your own cooking, your own everything. Camp Four was located at 26,000 feet, at the demarcation of what has come to be known, quite accurately, as the Death Zone. Above there, the body began to succumb, and no one but the dying spent any time longer than essential.

Camp Five wasn't really a camp at all, but a very primitive bivouac on a patch of slanting snow. It was windy and miserable. If conditions permitted, climbers passed it on the descent from the summit, since Camp Four was only an hour or two further on going downhill, but on the ascent, it was necessary to spend a final few hours resting there on oxygen before setting out at midnight for the summit.

Harlan pursed his lips in thought. "Once we are through the Ice Flow, weather permitting, we should have the camps in place in about twenty days."

I thought that schedule optimistic. The Sherpas would have to carry on their backs at least six hundred pounds of food above Base Camp, some fifty sleeping bags, about forty tents, along with rope, kitchen equipment, and, of course, supplemental oxygen tanks. It was an enormous—and treacherous—undertaking. We'd had no luck so far and I didn't expect it to improve.

"So you're saying that in just under three weeks, we can begin the search," Calvin said.

"That's about right," the New Zealander allowed.

"The other expeditions will have arrived by then," Tom pointed out.

"Yes. But we'll control passage through the Ice Flow."

The Ice Flow is a two-and-a-half-mile river of ice slowly flowing down a draw toward Base Camp, easing downward some three or four feet a day. In the afternoon, when the temperature has risen, the ice softens and the entire Ice Flow moans and creaks as if it were alive. To describe it as frightening doesn't even approach the fear the ice passage instills in even the most seasoned climber.

The ice walls towered overhead like tottering skyscrapers. The walls loomed over us at unnatural angles, looking as if they could crash down on us any second. The crevasses were not always wide, but they were consistently deep. Light entered the chasm, turned blue, and then dissolved into the darkness. It was as if you passed over a Viking hell of ice, snow, and cold.

The snow bridges we used most often to cross these crevasses gave no sense of security, as they routinely collapsed without warning. Here your skill meant nothing. You were utterly in the hands of fate and being tied to the line stretched for your safety was no guarantor of your life.

Every season, the Ice Flow is renewed at a higher source. It is fed by winter storms and summer monsoons, only to vanish over a precipice near Base Camp. It was a creature of eternal life, endlessly born above only to die in a great crashing of ice below. More than once, the fall of ice had awakened me from the light sleep that was normal at these altitudes.

Behind us was the rumble of another avalanche, this one louder than most. We all turned to look. It seemed to me an appropriate end to the discussion. I raised my eyes to Everest to check the plume, which grew throughout the day. Watching that great hulk, gazing at the peak, was instinctive. It was, after all, why we were here.

With clear weather, Stern and Rusty spread their solar blankets and recharged batteries. Crystal and Stern were busy filing reports, Stern twice a day. Crystal set up various shots with Diana, uploaded video, and made preparations for a live feed. They spent a lot of time on the sat phone, engaged in long, expensive conversations.

The evolving camp grew more elaborate. The single biggest tent was for cooking and contained the dining room as well. It was here that Harlan held his periodic briefings. The second-largest tent was that of SNS, with the corporate logo prominently displayed on both sides of its roof. Stern had a flag with the *National Inquisitor* logo on it that he erected outside his little tent. One night, Tom showed me the video story that Stern had uploaded to his Web site comparing the two operations. I had to admit it was pretty funny.

As work on the route through the Ice Flow continued, I spent my afternoons lazing in the sun, working on my recovery, often joined by Tom and Calvin. Stern took to calling us the Three Musketeers and we gave up waving him away whenever he loitered with his camera. Diana joined us when she was free and Rusty dropped by from time to time. Harlan and Dawa made it a point to visit as well. Peer and Tarja remained apart. Gody especially was a stranger to us all. We men talked about the mountain while it seemed to me that Diana avoided the subject.

Behind us, I knew, stretched a steady stream of herdsmen with teams of yaks, beginning in Kathmandu. They were bringing fresh food for Base Camp and feed for the yaks. The first would start to arrive any day. As I say, the logistics of an Everest expedition are all but overwhelming. If from start to finish, the expedition was underway or on site as long as two months, something I found very likely, we'd consume some 13,000 pounds of food in all. When a herdsman and his yak arrived, he'd leave the next day with a fresh yak in tow to hold the number at Base Camp stable.

Our cook, Bawu, was genial, all smiles. Dawa told me he'd been head cook on more than twenty expeditions of all nationalities. I could easily see why. Our food was tasty, hot, and nourishing. We were served some version of eggs and potatoes with every meal, it seemed, but Bawu was creative in the mix and that was not all he prepared. He'd constructed an oven and, though Sherpa do not bake as we know it, he managed bread—which failed to rise much at this elevation—pizza, and cakes, all of which were a great hit.

None of this should give the impression that we were gorging ourselves. Everyone—even the Sherpa to a milder degree—suffered from headaches, nagging nausea, and a lack of appetite. Though the smell of a well-cooked meal could tempt, I found it difficult to consume a single plateful. The previous year, I'd lost nearly thirty pounds in six weeks. I was on pace to do the same again—especially because once I moved above the Ice Flow, I knew my appetite would simply vanish.

My third day back in the land of the living, after our major meal which was served at midday, Tom quizzed Calvin about the Sherpa and the mountain. "They are so much better than us, it's phenomenal," Calvin said.

"In what way?" Tom asked.

"In every way. It isn't just that they are acclimatized to higher elevations, they are a remarkably fit race, and the men are driven to be very good at this. Not long ago, a Sherpa speed-climbed Everest. You heard me right. Starting from here, at 18,000 feet, he climbed to the top of the world then back to this very place in just under seventeen hours—and without supplemental oxygen."

"That's amazing."

"It's superhuman is what it is. A standard expedition gives its climbers something like six weeks to cover the same course. And that's with a Sherpa guide for every climber, staging camps along the way, a secure line, and oxygen. We aren't even in the same league with these guys."

"I saw that woman a few days ago. She'd collapsed on the trail," Tom said.

"Yes. Malnutrition, exhaustion from the strain. She had a baby just five months ago, you know. And she's too small for this. I don't know why she came along."

"Money is my guess," Tom said.

"Yes, money, of course. A climbing Sherpa," Calvin explained, "is a superstar among his own people. He is not only the richest man in his village; he has the greatest respect and the most wives."

"Wives?"

"Oh yes. Dawa. How many wives do you have?"

Dawa smiled sheepishly. "Only three. They are sisters, so I climb a lot."

We all laughed.

"Tell Tom here how you started out."

"I was kitchen boy before with Bawu. I washed dishes and carried load. I was lucky. After only one year, I came to here, but still just washed dishes and cleaned up. Reggie like me and paid for me to go to climbing school."

"That cost a fortune," Calvin interjected. "Something like $100. Go on."

"Three years ago, I work up there," Dawa said, pointing toward the summit, "cutting trail, setting up camp, carrying oxygen. Two years ago, I summit for first time. Big deal. Get two more wives, but my wife make me take sisters." Dawa grinned as he shook his head. "Not good thing."

"Now Dawa is king of his village, right?"

"Not king, but big man." He mockingly puffed out his chest. "But big responsibility too."

"How many do you support?"

"Many, many."

"And if you couldn't climb?"

Dawa only shook his head as if it was something impossible to consider.

There was more to his story, but it was personal. His first wife had lost her first baby and as a result was infertile. She wanted him to marry her sisters since they had no husbands and to produce the child she could not. It had complicated his family life and he now preferred to be away as much as he could.

"I'm planning on moving up to Advanced Base Camp," Calvin said. "It depends on my foot and the weather. But if you're serious about going any higher, Tom, I suggest you go to the mound and take some time to read the names carved there. Many of them were great climbers—greater than any of us will ever be—and they're up here somewhere." He gestured toward Everest.

Tom lifted his eyes and said nothing.

‿‿‿

The next day, while the usual group of climbers was busy elsewhere, Tarja sought me out. I was lazing in a chair, facing the early afternoon sun, and sipping a beer to keep up my weight—at least that was my excuse—when the beauty sat beside me.

I must say that the approach march and now the time at Base Camp were doing nothing to diminish her looks. Unlike Crystal, who'd still worn makeup almost to Base Camp, Tarja had remained clean-scrubbed since we'd set out. Bathing had been a problem for all of us, but you'd never know it by her. She'd stopped wearing her contact however. The one eye was her customary pale blue, the other a nearly tan brown. I had no idea where to focus when I looked at her.

She inquired as to my health and made small talk by heaping scorn on Stern. "He's a worm," she said.

"You won't get any argument from me on that," I said. I'd read his most recent blog entry early in the day and knew she wouldn't like it.

"Did you know that he wrote I got the clap last year? And he hinted I'm some kind of lesbian. How he could take a simple, innocent friendship with Yvette and turn it into dirt?" She placed a finger to her eye, but I saw no tear.

"Some men are intrigued by the idea, I suppose."

"Why does Sodoc want him here? Surely you know," she asked.

"Sodoc? I don't think he wants him here. He wrote the book—remember? I'd say Stern is about as unpopular with Sodoc as you can get."

"Stern all but called me an Everest whore."

I wasn't going anywhere near that. Tarja and I had been only casually acquainted the year before. I couldn't do anything for her, so she had no reason to make me her friend. And she could not have helped but notice my disapproval of her affair with Peer. She certainly wasn't trying to make friends now—even if she was making nice.

"What can I do for you?" I asked.

The direct question caught her by surprise, and she hesitated. Finally, she said, "I don't know if you've followed what Sodoc's been doing to me since last year."

"I haven't. Frankly, I wasn't aware he'd done anything to you."

She rolled her eyes. "The stories I could tell. He's made my life hell!"

"There's a rumor he's fighting your inheritance," I allowed. Stern would have been proud of me.

I could see the wheels working in her head. She decided not to lash out at me. "That's true. Derek didn't want a prenup." I'd heard it the other way around. "I told him it would be best. I didn't want his money. I told him if we didn't do a prenup, his father would think I was a gold digger." Now there was a novel thought. "But he insisted we just go ahead. I'd never met anyone like him before." She said the last a bit breathlessly, pausing for my reaction.

I knew Tarja too well to be drawn to her. She might as well have been pitching her wares to stone.

"He was special in his way, I must admit."

She suddenly seemed misty-eyed. I say "seemed" because with Tarja you just never knew. "He thought the world of you."

"I doubt that."

"No, it's true. He often spoke of you with awe. He never talked about South America, but I took it that something happened there that bonded the two of you. Someday I hope you'll tell me. All I have of Derek are memories."

This really was a Stern interview. "Is there something you want?" I asked.

"Tell Sodoc to let me go home. Please."

"Sodoc? I don't have any pull with him."

She eyed me skeptically. "Of course you do. He knows how close you were to Derek." "Close" was not the word I'd have used. "And he met with you personally—that's what I heard. No one else here did. He must value your opinion."

"I don't know who met with him and who didn't. He saw me, I think, because I was the last person with Derek the day he died. And because Stern's book said I'd abandoned him when he could still have been saved."

"No one who knows you could say that."

This was getting to be a bit much. "I can't help you with Sodoc. We're not friends. Just leave the expedition if that's what you want. No one's keeping you here. You can go back with any of the Sherpa herders returning after a supply drop."

She laid her hand on my forearm. "After the memorial service on the family estate on Long Island"—I'd heard about it, but hadn't gone—"Sodoc called me into his office. He told me he blamed me for everything that happened to Derek. He told me he knew I'd been carrying on—those were his very words—with Peer and I'd never see a penny of Derek's money. He called me a lot of very nasty names." I was certain she'd heard them all before. "Then he set about destroying me with his media empire."

I recalled nothing like that—not that I'd been paying particular attention. "In what way?"

"Every job my publicist has lined up for me has fallen out. I can't even buy a spot on television or in a magazine."

"Why do you want to? What difference does it make?"

"It's my career—one I've worked damn hard to establish. Maybe you don't understand, but being a celebrity—being famous—is a job in itself. People want to meet you—have you promote their products—and they'll pay you for it. I'm no different than a movie star or a best-selling novelist."

"I guess." Given the level of acting and writing I'd been exposed to in recent years, I had to admit she had a point.

"Anyway, I wanted to work, to put all this"—she waved her hand lightly at Everest—"behind me. I told Sodoc I didn't want Derek's fortune. But when he blocked my every effort to make a living, I had to file for it."

That was a story with more than one side, I was certain.

"A few weeks ago, I got a call. He'd stand aside if I came on this expedition. So here I am." She turned her head and coughed lightly.

"What are you supposed to do here?"

"I have no idea. His agent just told me that if I came, Sodoc would withdraw his objection to my claiming Derek's estate." Sodoc had been generous with his only son over the years. His estate was worth upward of $100 million, I'd read—not counting a sizable percentage of SNS stock that Sodoc would have to buy back. He'd given up a lot to get her here. And he didn't impress me as a man who gave up a lot without expecting to get something of great value out of it. My conversation with Gody flashed through my mind. She'd have to be alive to collect.

"What's the point in your coming?" I asked.

"He didn't tell you?"

"We aren't friends," I repeated. "I had no idea who would be here until I arrived."

I finished my beer and considered getting a little hammered that rest of the afternoon. It was very pleasant in the afternoon sun and I knew from experience that there would be few days like this from here on out. "I think we're here to be punished," I heard her say quietly.

"Punished? For what?"

"For killing Derek."

"Nobody killed Derek."

She snorted. "Tell that to his father. I think he blames us all and wants every one of us punished. That's the only way I can explain everyone being here. You don't know him like I do. He hates me and he's very vicious. There are stories—" She stopped herself.

I cleared my throat. "I understand you're to be interviewed for the memorial service. They want you here as the widow."

"Then why aren't they interviewing me? I've suggested several really good story lines to Crystal. She just smirks and tells me to behave myself. And why send her if they want a story? They know she hates me. At least talk to Tom," she said. "Please. I just want what's mine and to leave here. Something is very wrong."

"Tom? What's he got to do with anything?"

She gave me a strange look. My eyes bounced from the brown to the blue, then back again. "I've seen how you two get along. Tom works for Sodoc. He's his man here." She seemed to make up her mind about something. She stood up. "Forget it, all right? Forget I said anything to you."

⌒⌒⌒

As the Sherpa labored in the Ice Flow, the camp settled into a routine. Harlan could be seen outside his tent throughout the day talking on his sat phone or tracking weather patterns on his laptop. He paid a subscription for some of the world's most exclusive weather predictions—and still shook his head in amazement at how often they got it wrong.

The problem was Everest itself. This region of the Himalayas created its own microclimate. While benign weather here at Base Camp could be one consequence, so could sudden violent and lethal storms not far above us. Climbers died every year having spent most of the day in so-called summit weather—only to be caught in a storm that enveloped them within minutes of creation.

Harlan organized training and conditioning climbs on the nearby rock and ice walls, even within the beginning of the Ice Flow itself. Everyone, except perhaps Peer, needed to become reconditioned to walking and climbing with crampons. While they are essential on snow and ice, they are awkward when you must traverse rock. They also tended to create wear on your foot at unusual places and we needed time to develop calluses. The effort served as well to speed our acclimatization.

We needed no encouragement. Staring at the Ice Flow every day, watching the exhausted Sherpa return from working it, and seeing Everest above us like an ominous pyramid, was motivation enough. We were rigged to harnesses with ascenders, fitted crampons to our high-altitude boots, and forayed into the lower Ice Flow or along the nearby mountains to practice. Tom found it difficult and frequently tangled in his line. Tarja, who had largely recovered from her cough once Calvin began administering antibiotics, found her skill returning rapidly. Peer served as instructor, as he was easily the most gifted climber. My ability returned with my strength, but I was never expert on ice and snow, only adequate—though on Everest, that is enough.

Stern, true to his word, did not practice and made it clear that he was never leaving Base Camp. He loitered about, camera in hand, smarting off, and filming, but had by now become like a recurring rash, a known irritant to be ignored. Even his blog entries, sensational as they remained, no longer bothered anyone. In some ways, I pitied him standing alone at night after dinner.

Crystal, Rusty, and even Diana had been practicing. I wasn't surprised with the first two, having seen them higher up previously and knowing their ability, but Diana caught me unaware. I'd hiked with her often enough and scaled a few rock walls with her to know her skill level. She'd clearly had instruction and taken time to practice.

After seeing her that first day, I approached following dinner and asked what her plans were.

"I don't know for sure," she said. "I doubt I'll be leaving here, but I want to be ready to move up if my boss wants it."

"The Ice Flow is dangerous."

"Everything's dangerous according to you, soldier. Once the path is clear and the higher camps are in place, if the weather permits, I might go up to Advance Base Camp for some shots. We'll see. How about you? How high are you signed on for?"

That was an excellent question and I'd given it considerable thought. The Sherpa were the men to find Derek. I could give them the detailed instructions about where we last were–but there was that question about just where I'd left Derek. "I may have to return to the Hillary Step," I said.

"Oh, Scott, no. You can just tell Zhiku and Dawa where you were. That should do it."

"I'll suggest that initially, of course, and they may find him on the first attempt, but things were uncertain up there and this was a very violent winter. I have in my mind where we were, but I became disoriented on the way back. I was lucky to find the route."

Diana gave me a very strange look. "They're counting on you, Scott. We all are."

I nodded. "Your climbing skills are much improved, I noticed."

"That's me," she said with her award-winning grin. "A natural." She learned forward. "Let me ask you something. Have you ever tried high-altitude sex?"

I must have looked surprised.

"Neither have I. From the way Tarja and Peer are going at it, though, I'd say it's a good thing. It will help with the acclimatization. Why don't you drop by my tent after dinner and we'll see what's what."

Work on the passage through the Ice Flow proceeded slowly. What could take as little as four days stretched beyond, with no end in sight. The fresh snow created dangerous conditions and masked others. Avalanches occurred every few minutes. The typically confident Sherpa arrived back in camp toward dark looking high-strung and exhausted.

I asked Harlan what he thought he was doing. "Why all the rush? We had rain not that far from here. That snow up there is heavy and unstable. Give it a week or two to settle down. You're going to get someone killed, pushing like this."

His look was steely. "I have my instructions, Scott. Stay out of this. The Sherpa know what they're doing."

I almost answered that he'd killed two Sherpa getting here, but held my tongue.

Then a week into the trailblazing, another Sherpa was killed. While cutting steps in ice, he was buried in an avalanche. Harlan took to his tent that night. We didn't see him for two days.

The morning after the Sherpa's death, someone placed a fresh flag on the memorial mound beside the camp. Every Sherpa attended the service, kneeling on prayer rugs and uttering prayers. I was shocked to see Laki there, looking like death.

"What's she doing here?" I asked Calvin.

He scanned the gathering and then looked as shocked as I felt. "I have no idea. I thought she'd gone down. I need to talk with Zhiku about this."

Gody stalked the camp, or so it seemed to me, unwelcome everywhere he went. The Sherpa distrusted the man and wanted nothing to do with him. Gametup and Chepal, who took turns in the Ice Flow, often stood to the side staring at him in a peculiar and unpleasant way. The Westerners simply didn't care for his standoffish manner, vague condescension, and tendency to remain apart.

After the memorial service, he approached Harlan. "I'd like to work the Ice Flow," he said.

"I don't think that's such a good idea."

"You can use the help and I'm sick of staying here. I understand they are nearly through. Just another day and they'll have a trail cleared so you can start establishing Camp One. The Sherpa are frightened. Can't you tell? Only two of them are even willing to work up there right now. You can use me."

"I wasn't aware that you knew your way around ice and snow so well."

"I've done my share. During one campaign, the Maoists retreated to high elevations. I ordered an assault against them. We cut many passageways through ice and snow just like the Ice Flow. I'll join them in the morning and we can get moving." With disgust he added, "At this pace, it will take the entire season to find the body."

⌐⌐⌐

Calvin had set up a clinic in the dining tent. Even the usually hardy Sherpa had suffered on the very difficult approach trek and were in need of attention. Several asked to be placed on Diamox. From this point on, even they would struggle with acclimatization and they wanted every advantage.

We Western climbers were, of course, in much worse condition. Twisted ankles and blisters were the least of it. Everyone suffered from the lack of oxygen and the many adverse symptoms associated with it.

We all had headaches and nausea, even the Sherpa. Deep breaths helped because the true cause of our maladies was not an actual ailment, but the lack of oxygen. Should any of us lay down atop our sleeping bag with a bottle of oxygen, we'd have felt restored within moments. Our body would have returned to normal in almost no time. Our illness was self-induced.

"I've never seen so many problems on a climb before," Calvin confided.

Laki was the most serious patient he had. "Why is she here?" I asked.

"Stubbornness, from what I was told. She refused to move down. She thought she wouldn't be paid, since that's the usual price for turning back. Zhiku should have made it clear that she'd still get her salary. Regardless, once she could walk again, she rejoined us."

"How is she?"

"She recovered a bit, but has no business being here. I'm talking to Harlan and Zhiku to insist that the next porter take her down at once."

Over dinner, Harlan told Calvin he'd ordered Laki to descend the next morning. I understood that he'd argued with Zhiku for not seeing to it the first time.

Afterward, I joined Diana in her tent—as I had for the last few nights. I felt conspicuous about it, since everyone knew what was going on. The Sherpa often stood near Tarja's tent and made sounds mimicking sex whenever Peer joined her, all with grins and laughter.

Peer didn't mind, but once Tarja had stormed out of her tent, scream-ing at the men—who'd only laughed all the harder at her display.

But the Sherpa left Diana and me alone. I didn't know why and didn't ask. Afterward, wondering again if the effort was really worth the pleasure, I heard a commotion outside.

"What is it?" she asked in the dark.

"I'll go see."

She pulled at my sleeve. "Come back, Scott."

I dressed, spotted a gathering at the Sherpa camp, and joined it. Calvin was furious and making his anger known. Harlan looked hangdog and defensive.

"What's going on?" I asked Tom.

"That Sherpa woman is in trouble."

"Laki?"

"That's the one. I saw her for a moment. Horrible. Her eyes were all bugged out. Cal tried a shot of dexamethasone, but it doesn't seem to be working."

Dexamethasone was the drug of last resort in such a situation. It was an anti-inflammatory steroid that in certain situations was a lifesaver. That it wasn't working was very bad news.

I went into the clinic. Calvin was still arguing with Harlan, who was making no attempt to explain himself. Laki lay nearby and looked dreadful. To see a snapshot of someone suffering from HACE with edema, you cannot imagine what you are actually looking at. Such a photo might even look funny, with the eyes bugging out in an unnatural way. What was taking place was that her brain was swell-ing and there was nowhere for it to go except through the openings that held her eyes.

Laki was panting like a dog in summer. Her face was gaunt. She looked at me for help and I had none to give. She knew that she was in trouble and was very, very frightened. You didn't have to be a doctor to know that she was at the end of her rope.

Tom joined me. He glanced at her, grimaced, and turned to me. "Calvin said she's got to be carried down now. The shot doesn't seem to be helping. Harlan told him that the woman is already dead and he won't risk the Sherpa in the dark."

Harlan was right. A few minutes later, Laki stopped breathing. Calvin worked to revive her, but it was hopeless. He finally gave up and stalked off as angry as I've ever seen him. The Sherpa who had been nearby moved away, not wishing to come in contact with her ghost. Someone pulled a blanket over the woman's face, frozen in horror.

Outside, Dawa approached, shaking his head.

"I'm sorry, my friend," I said.

"Yes. Now her baby has no parents. Very bad. Too many die, Scott. Too many. Sagarmatha doesn't want us here. Not this year. We should go back. Talk to Harlan, Scott. Tell him. We must turn back or many, many more will die."

TWELVE

*An irony of the great mountain is that the most dangerous
portion of the climb was the Ice Flow, an ever-changing
deadly river of ice. Its sheer white canyons spike terror into
the heart of even the most intrepid climber.*
—Quentin Stern, www.AbandonedonEverest.com

The day after Laki's death, the Sherpa prepared yet another burial
service. Watching them go about it, I could tell they were dispirited.
I'd heard a rumor that Harlan refused to confirm that he'd been
compelled to increase their pay to keep them on the expedition. Dawa
told me stories from the Sherpa camp about men and the surviving
woman seeing ghosts walking among them. One of the climbing
Sherpa working in the Ice Flow was now refusing to enter it again,
claiming he'd seen the ghost of the Sherpa who'd been swept away
telling him to turn back. It seemed to me that most of the Sherpa
now looked at us Westerners with suspicion and distrust.

At this elevation, we had nothing to burn except the gas for our
stoves, so it was not possible to consume Laki's body. The Sherpa
covered her in stone, not far from the mound. She was not the first
to die at Base Camp, so she was not the first to be buried in such a
fashion. Other semi-rectangular piles of rock stood beside hers. If

we managed to get Derek's body down this far, that would likely be his fate.

I joined in paying my respects. Calvin was still angry that she'd not been made to return. He had unpleasant words with Harlan before the service. From where I observed, the New Zealander appeared to offer no defense for what had happened. As Calvin explained it later, Harlan had thought the woman had been taken back down the mountain. He'd been shocked to learn that she was in camp. He and Zhiku had a falling out over it—one from which they would never recover.

The Sherpa believed that the deaths we'd suffered so far occurred because Westerners had defiled their goddess. That was also how they explained the previous year's disaster. That was as good an explanation as any.

⌐⌐⌐

The next morning. I joined Harlan, Peer, and Tom at the foot of the Ice Flow for more practice. Shortly before we set out, Gody left camp with Chepal and a climbing Sherpa I didn't know by name. I was surprised since Chepal had always worked with Gametup. Maybe he was the one who'd seen the ghost in the canyon of the Ice Flow.

Once we reached the flow, our little party—wearing helmets and body harnesses—stopped to don crampons. The long steel spikes were fitted to our high-altitude climbing boots, just as I used to put roller skates on when I was a child. They're awkward to walk in—even across thick snow and ice. In loose snow, I'd always found them a hindrance. But for what we had to do, they were indispensable. Once equipped, we set out the short distance to the mouth of the glacier.

The passage was all but carved one foot at a time. Short pathways were cleared in the still-soft snow and steps were chopped out along ice walls, which had to be taken very, very carefully. The crevasses that lacked a snow bridge were traversed atop aluminum ladders. More than one was often necessary, so several were lashed together. Such a bridge bent like a bow from your weight, bouncing beneath, as you carefully placed your crampons on each step and held on with your hands for dear life. It took steely nerves not to look down but to concentrate on each movement of your body. In all, some sixty ladders were used. It was graceless and a bit silly, but that was how you crossed the chasms.

Walls of ice and snow were also scaled by ladder. I never approached one without a sense of guilt, recalling how it was done before climbers were too proud for such devices. But I always took the ladder, grateful that it was there.

Today, however, that was all ahead of me. I had only to work here at the entrance to the Ice Flow, to practice my basic skills and restore some of my dormant self-confidence. As it was, we were not all that far from the previous day's reversal. I could see where Gody and the two Sherpa were working their way around a fresh crevasse, the Sherpa taking the lead, Gody lingering back, expanding the steps they carved, widening the passageway. I didn't envy any of them.

At the first ice ridge, Harlan indicated that this was the place. Peer unraveled the orange nylon rope he carried across his body. With his ice ax and the forward thrust crampons on his boots, he rapidly made his way some fifty feet up the nearly vertical ridge. It would have been more impressive to an amateur, but I was impressed enough. A ridge was not like a sheet of glass, despite its appearance to the untrained eye. There were small shelves, crevasses, and outcroppings that made his course easier than it might seem, and the ice itself was forgiving. Still, he moved like a spider up a wall with a grace I'd rarely seen in any climber.

Once on top, he tossed down the rope and then secured it where he was.

Harlan gestured to me. "You first."

I clipped onto the rope, grasped the ascender firmly with my gloved hand, swung out, and planted my spikes into the ice. I walked and hauled myself up the face with only a few missteps, electing not to use my new ice ax since it was never really needed. *Not bad*, I thought for the first time in a year as I gulped air. At sea level, such a climb was nothing. Up here, it sapped my strength and left me breathless.

"You're a natural," Peer said with a grin as I unhooked from the line. "Okay, Tom. Let's see what you've got."

From here, I could see into the Ice Flow more easily. Gody was now in the middle between the two Sherpa, making his way across a snow bridge. The first Sherpa moved beyond my sight as I watched. They were on a different channel so I didn't hear them on their radio—not that they'd have much to say. What needed doing was evident to any experienced Everest climber.

Tom started moving very slowly up the face. I could hear Harlan speaking softly to him—the words unintelligible, but the tone reassuring. After the first ten feet, Tom got his legs and began moving more strongly.

"He's not bad," Peer allowed. "You never know about a climber until you see them with crampons, ice ax, and line going up a face."

I glanced toward the men in the Ice Flow. Now Gody was out of sight, leaving just the final Sherpa to cross the snow bridge. Below Tom was suddenly floundering. He'd managed to tangle himself in the line and, in his effort to free himself, lost his footing. He was swinging back and forth, cursing like a sailor while Peer laughed. "Set your feet, Tom!" he shouted. "Set your feet!"

Harlan moved to the side to see more clearly, but if he said anything, I couldn't hear it.

Tom cleared his ice ax to the side and then reached at the wall with his hand to stop his pendulum swing, but it only caused him to start spinning. Finally, he managed to grip the wall with his ax and stop himself; he swung out, set his boots in the ice, and began straightening the line. Within a minute, he was working his way toward us.

I glanced up. The sky was a faded azure with streaking clouds racing across. I could hear Tom grunting as he approached the edge. Peer leaned forward, gave him a hand, and effortlessly pulled him to us.

"Sorry about that," Tom said, struggling to catch his breath. I slapped him on the back.

"You recovered well," Peer allowed, "That's what's important."

I'd lost sight of Gody and the two Sherpa who were back in view a bit further along in the passage. The walls of ice towered over them, one looking as if it would topple any moment. I drew deep breaths, feeling the energy course through me as I did. Tom was hunched over at his waist, trying to catch his breath.

In the near distance, I looked again at the three in the Ice Flow when, without warning, a section they were on fell away with one of the men atop it. A moment later, I heard the rumble from the collapse and then the shouting.

Peer and Tom both looked. We could see Gody leaning back, pulling hard on his line. The Sherpa on the other side of the new chasm had no line from what I could see. Sherpa often worked not tied by line when they thought it would speed things along. It was up to Gody.

Peer leaned down and called to Harlan. "Snow bridge gave! One man went with it, but is on a line!"

I doubted Harlan could see the scene from where he was. This was just as well. Gody suddenly flopped backward into the snow and, even from where I was, I could tell the line had given. The man in the crevasse had fallen to his death.

Peer looked at us. "I'm going to help if I can. Follow me down and then return to camp."

He disappeared over the side as Tom and I watched the remaining Sherpa and Gody. They were shouting across the new crevasse, but I couldn't make out their words. Only the anger.

〜〜〜

As Tom and I returned to camp, we speculated, but had no answers. I told him I was certain that Gody had survived and that one of the two Sherpa was dead. That was all I could say.

We'd turned our radios to the channel they'd been using, but the transmissions from Harlan, Peer, Gody, and the remaining Sherpa were choppy and not especially informative. The snippets I caught were distraught and emotional. Not far from the camp, we passed Zhiku and three Sherpa moving rapidly toward the Ice Flow, their faces grim. None of them greeted us or met our eyes.

Diana was there as we entered camp. "What happened?" she asked. I told her what I'd seen. "You say the line broke? But how's that possible? This is nine-thousand-pound test rope."

She had a point. The thought had crossed my mind. The days when you climbed mountains with hemp were long past. The new continuous-drawn nylon yarn ropes were light and incredibly strong. They were not overly elastic and were resistant to fracturing against rough rock. In fact, wear should not even have been an issue with Gody's rope since we'd not used climbing rope until the Ice Flow.

Rusty joined us. "You say the rope snapped? I don't believe it."

"That's what it looked like to me. I was some distance away though. Gody will likely know more when we talk to him. Have you heard anything on the radios?"

"Not much," Rusty said, shrugging. "We really don't get many transmissions from inside the Ice Flow. I think they're trying to get the other Sherpa back. He was caught on the wrong side when the snow bridge gave."

Crystal reached us and wanted to know everything. I let Tom tell it. When he finished, she turned to Rusty and said, "Can you get a camera up there? How long do you think they'll be?" The last was addressed to me.

"I can't say. They have to get the man back to this side of the crevasse and they'll likely spend some time seeing if they can safely recover the body of the man who fell—though that's unlikely. Still, they'll do what they can."

"Rusty, take a camera and one of the guides and head up there. Maybe you'll get them bringing a body back. If not, try to get the scene of the effort or at the least the rescue party returning from the tragedy. You know what I'm looking for."

That's really the way she talked. Everything was a production piece to her. "Don't you think these people hate us enough already?"

"Just do it!" she snapped. Rusty gave her a look I couldn't comprehend and then set out for his equipment.

"What's this about the rope?" Tom asked.

"A single strand of our rope can handle ten men—let alone one," Diana said. "I can't imagine it just snapped."

"Is it a story?" Crystal asked sharply.

"Give it a rest, Crissie. For once, just let it go," Diana said.

A grim-faced Bawu had brought us large mugs of sweet hot tea, the same every climber received after returning from higher up. Tom and I sipped as we made our way to the dining tent to remove our climbing gear and rest. Rusty set out a few minutes later with one of the Sherpa. Crystal and Diana speculated about what could have happened.

"That's four dead," Crystal said. "My God, what a disaster. And we haven't even really set a foot on Everest. If this keeps up, they'll have to send down for more Sherpa."

"Assuming any would join us," I said.

Shortly after dark, the climbers straggled into Base Camp. Zhiku led the way, looking depressed and angry. None of the Sherpa was Chepal, so he was the one who'd died. Gametup was waiting and spoke quietly to Zhiku. Harlan brought up the rear with Gody. Crystal descended on him with questions, but Gody just shook his head and refused to talk. I noticed that no one offered him tea. Within moments, he was in his tent for the night.

Crystal went up to Harlan. "What happened?"

"I have no comment," he said.

Crystal laughed. "I'm not asking for a statement."

He looked at her sharply. "Of course you are. That's why you're here, isn't it?"

"I have a right to know."

"Perhaps. Let's just say the line broke and leave it at that. Another very brave man is dead."

"Come on, Harlan. These ropes don't just break."

"That's what happened. Now leave me alone. I have a very hard message to convey to someone's wife and children."

⌇⌇⌇

That night, Dawa sought me out and gestured me to join him away from the others.

"How are your people?" I asked.

"Bad," he said. "Most want to leave, but Zhiku say we must stay. I don't know … maybe some will go, I think."

"It's been tough, I'll admit. I wouldn't blame anyone for going back at this point."

"What about you? Will you stay?"

"Yes. I'm going up to do what I can."

He considered that a bit. "Be careful."

"Always."

"Stay away from Gody," he added quietly.

"What do you mean?"

"There is trouble with him." Dawa told me what had been brewing in the Sherpa camp for days now. "Gametup and Chepal, they fight him before."

"Fight? I don't understand."

"Gody led army who killed our people. Chepal said last night that Gody was there. Today he is dead when on line with Gody."

I considered that for a long minute. Gody had massacred the valley home of our Sherpa? It seemed incredible. From what I knew, Sherpa were not a forgiving people, but then Gody didn't strike me as one either.

The wind stirred and, despite my insulated clothing, I felt a sudden chill.

—⌁⌁⌁—

The next day was yet another memorial service. Afterward, I watched as Diana filed a report of the death, standing with the mouth of the Ice Flow as her backdrop. Crystal and Rusty worked on the edit for two hours and uploaded it just before lunch.

Following the memorial service, every available Sherpa turned out for the Ice Flow. Zhiku had given orders to clear the passageway. Apparently, he'd convinced them that things would improve higher up.

Gody missed breakfast and the memorial service, but arrived for lunch. I joined him. "Want to talk about it?" I asked.

He didn't look as if he'd slept a wink. "There is nothing to talk about. I understand you saw it."

"Yes, after a fashion, but I don't understand what I saw."

Gody looked directly at me. "I can add nothing. The snow bridge gave way. The Sherpa was on line with me. It snapped and he fell. That is all."

I drank coffee and said, "I'd like to see your line."

Gody smiled coldly. "You would? Go to the crevasse. You will find it down there. I lost it when we tried to recover the body. Now let me eat in peace."

THIRTEEN

Bodies litter the summit like so much confetti. Climbers move steadily past the dead, and often the dying, oblivious that this could be their fate in a few short hours. The Sherpa believe it is this disrespect for the ghosts of the dead that kills so many.
　　　　—Quentin Stern, www.AbandonedonEverest.com

The next day, we were through the Ice Flow and the process of setting up Camp One began. I took a seat with Tom and Calvin—the Three Musketeers back in our favorite position—and observed the steady stream of supplies pouring toward the first of the staging camps. The weather had turned again and today was clear, windless, and almost balmy. Rest was a vital part of the acclimatization process since it places an enormous strain on the body. If we weren't climbing, Calvin expected us to be at leisure.

"Peer seems eager to get on with this," Tom commented. Peer had gone to Camp One just after breakfast. We were expecting him back before dark, since the camp wouldn't be functioning for another two or three days. We'd all noticed that he'd sat away from the Nordic beauty that morning during breakfast and she'd made a point to ignore him.

"It was a long hike to here," Calvin allowed. "It tests even the best relationship."

I drew a deep breath to fight off a momentary sensation of suffocation. "I don't think Crystal has filmed a segment with her yet. I wonder when she goes into her grieving widow routine."

"I noticed her laughing it up with Rusty last night," Tom said. "Maybe she's working on it."

"That might be why she and Peer aren't getting along," Calvin suggested.

"I don't think so. He was looking to get rid of her just last week, remember?" I said.

We sipped tea, sucked air, and discussed turning to beer at lunch. None of us would be moving to Camp One for another two or three days and there'd be no beer above Base Camp. We speculated about the death the day before. I'd told them what Dawa said.

"Do you really think Gody killed him?" Tom asked. Such things didn't happen in his world. They didn't happen in mine, for that matter.

Calvin shrugged. "Without the line, we can't know what happened. But murder seems extreme."

"How do you just lose line like that?" I asked.

Calvin shook his head and then said, "It's possible he killed him, I suppose, but it doesn't make much sense. Gody would surely have known that Chepal had said something to the others. What was he to gain from eliminating him? And that assumes he'd even consider something so drastic. He strikes me as a man who can take care of himself."

We mentally chewed that for a bit. I said, "I heard this morning that Gametup wants to kill Gody, but Zhiku says no."

"You're kidding," Tom said.

"Don't let their mild manner fool you," Calvin said. "These people know how to settle a score." He let that sink in as another team of Sherpa bearing fifty-pound loads set out. Zhiku was sending them up in relays. If the weather held, each team would go up and back twice today. They were pressing hard to manage it. Zhiku was of the apparent belief that busy porters don't have time for mischief.

I spotted Tarja striding across the camp with a smile, making a bee-line for Rusty. Crystal and Diana were off scouting for another shot.

"Do you think there's anything to this karma business?" Tom asked. "I keep thinking about all the deaths so far and can't help but wonder."

"I don't know. We have a saying, don't we? What goes around, comes around. Another: You get what you ask for," I said. "I think to some degree it's universal."

"'You reap what you sow,' is the way the Bible puts it," Calvin added.

"Dawa says it's this goddess business," I said. "It's put a hex on this expedition just like it did last year's."

"Maybe if that's what they believe, they make all the bad happen subconsciously," Tom suggested.

"You don't cause a mountain to engulf a village," I said. "Or a snow bridge to collapse."

"Or a yak to panic," Calvin said. "Still—"

"What?" Tom said.

"We don't know everything," Calvin said. "For some time, the West has been in the grip of the scientific age. If you can't measure it, something doesn't exist."

"What's your point?" I asked.

"Before the Geiger counter, you really couldn't measure radioactivity, but it still existed. It killed Madam Curie. It was just as real before you could measure it. What else exists that we haven't found a way to measure yet?"

"So you think there might be something to this karma business?" Tom said.

"I'm saying we shouldn't dismiss it. It's a pretty universal human concept, in one form or another. The Sherpa have just honed it a bit finer than most."

Tom started to speak. I caught his eyes and shook my head to silence him.

After a bit, Calvin continued. "I've been thinking. After Aconcagua I came to Nepal with Derek. Did you know that, Scott?"

"I think so. I recall some mention of it last year. I thought it was a scouting mission for the expedition."

"It was. Then Derek got a call. SNS wanted to do a show on the Nepal living goddess, the Kumari. I don't know if the show was already being planned and they wanted to take advantage of Derek being here or if his being here gave them the idea. Anyway, we located the priests who handled the goddess and Derek pitched the idea. It was unusual, to say the least, but they agreed to let her be filmed in Kathmandu, for a price. They did a lot of consulting with other priests to make sure it was okay. Derek just thought they were trying to increase the fee. But there was some kind of problem at the studio, something about a rival Kumari the film crew revered, and they wouldn't work with the Sherpa goddess. So Derek flew her and her family to Bangkok to film."

"Did he clear that with the priests?" I asked.

"I don't know. I think so. We had priests with us and her usual chaperones. Derek said it was no problem, just more expensive."

"So what happened?" Tom asked.

"Nothing, at first. The filming went fine and we brought the girl back to Kathmandu like we were supposed to. But once she got home, the priests for the other goddesses in Nepal started raising hell, claiming she'd left the sacred area and was no longer the living Kumari. Derek was disgusted by it all. He said they'd asked for a payoff and he'd refused. He had his story. It was quite a stink and she was defrocked, if that's the word for it."

"The Sherpa blame all this bad luck on that," I pointed out.

"That's my point. Think about last year. Derek's dead, I lost some toes, Reggie died, Tsongba lost his feet, all the others died, and now look at the deaths so far this year. It makes you wonder, that's all. It makes you wonder."

Two days later, I set out for Camp One with Diana, Rusty, and Crystal. Harlan had suggested that two Sherpa go with us, but Rusty had talked him out of it. They needed to get the camps set up before another expedition arrived and, now that the passageway was clear, we could do it without help. Harlan had agreed, but this would be the last time we'd climb without Sherpa.

It was part of our acclimatization. We'd reach camp about noon, if all went well, spend an hour or two, and then come back to Base Camp for the night.

It was a brilliant day and I felt the heat as soon as we entered the first canyon in the Ice Flow. I'd cautioned Crystal to avoid stopping us to set up shots since crossing this glacier the first time was challenging enough and we didn't want any unforced delays. She'd told Rusty to film what he could—and with Rusty, that was a great deal.

Bizarre as it seems, there were places from here to Camp Four at 26,000 feet that lent themselves to unusual and extraordinary heat. If the sky was clear, as it was this day, the air still, and the weather pattern benign, relative temperatures could soar. I knew that this was going to be one of those days as we crawled across our first ladder bridge. It wasn't very graceful and I wasn't surprised that Rusty kept his cameras tucked away.

On the opposite side, as we waited for Rusty to bring up the rear, Diana complained, "I'm getting hot."

"We should all open up our clothing and vent. If that doesn't help, start putting ice under your helmet directly on your cap."

"Why not just take off the high-altitude jumpsuit?" she asked.

"It's not worth it. We'd have to climb out of the harness, then put it back on, and adjust it for our reduced size. Then we'd have to carry the suit. Worse, this weather can turn in an instant and you'd have to climb right back into it. Welcome to Everest."

The Sherpa managed this climb in two hours—even with a load. From point to point, it was a bit over four miles, though all the twists and turns of the passageway made it longer. The rise in elevation was 2,000 feet, about average for each camp. We were not yet on oxygen, though, and every strain left us breathless. We sounded like four struggling nags pulling a heavy load uphill.

The passageway consisted of a trail marked in snow with a periodically anchored line to which we hooked ourselves. There would be sections spanning pitched ice where each step was hacked for us by ice ax. Sometimes lines were in place, sometimes not, depending on the length and whether a proper spot to anchor was available where needed. If there was no line, we hooked to each other Alpine style. There were ladders up cliffs, ladders laid across crevasses, and finally the always-uncertain snow bridges.

Three hours into the climb, we stopped again to catch our breath. This was the first time through the Ice Flow for Diana and she said, "Am I the only one scared to death in here?"

It wasn't just the snow bridges or bouncing ladder bridges; the ice walls were enormous, rising as high as two- and three-story buildings. It would take almost nothing for one to give way. The Ice Flow was always unsettling, but today, with the warm weather, it was even more so, moaning and creaking constantly.

"We're all scared shitless," Rusty said. "This isn't very glamorous and it's deadly as hell if you have bad luck."

I checked my altimeter watch and read 19,156 feet. We weren't far from Camp One. Ahead of us, though, was a precarious pathway carved one step at a time across a face of angled ice. I didn't like the looks of it. The morning sun had been beating on it for at least an hour and the ice had a mirror-like sheen that spelled trouble. Beneath us, the shiny ice disappeared into murky blue before dissolving into a black void.

"You first," I told Rusty, who understood what I had in mind. We re-roped to place Diana between us, as there was no line across the face of the ice.

Rusty made his way steadily to the other side, which I estimated at just over twenty feet. Diana gave me a forlorn look, bit her lower lip, and then started across, using her ice ax to secure her balance, placing each spiked boot carefully in the carved step, and cursing under her breath whenever something didn't go perfectly.

The problem was that she was moving too slowly. I'd noticed this earlier on a shorter crossing and had mentioned it to her to no effect. It's hard to explain, but you must set a certain pace to keep your balance. It was like riding a bicycle. If you move too slowly, it's hard to stay upright. So it was here. She needed to be in a faster, more secure rhythm. As it was, her uncertainty was affecting her footing.

There was no use calling out to her since it would only break her concentration. I could see Rusty was watching carefully; he had subtly turned his body and set his crampons deeper into the snow in case of a fall. I did the same. Crystal sensed something and, for once, shut up.

Just past the halfway point, I heard Diana curse again, more loudly than before. She paused and then fell.

I thought I was prepared, but the fall caught me by surprise. Diana screamed. Crystal, behind me, shouted her name.

Both Rusty and I gave a bit under the force of her weight, but held. She bounced once—I could feel the strain lighten for an instant— then settled down. Rusty and I pulled against her. Crystal shouted, "Diana! Diana! Are you all right?"

She was stunned—emotionally more than physically— she'd not struck anything in the fall and we were all wearing helmets. She placed her hands on the rope that held her from falling to her death. "I'm okay," she called up, sounding very frightened.

"Use your ax and plant your crampons!" Rusty shouted. "You need to start working up the ice."

It took a long minute since she was not in the most convenient position, but she located her ice ax, which was connected to her wrist by a loop. On her third swing, she planted it in the ice wall, stabilized herself, and then dug into the ice with her boots. Slowly, she started as we eased her way with the rope.

"Toward me!" Rusty shouted. "Head to me!"

Diana angled his way and, a few minutes later, took his hand as he lifted her onto the passageway.

I gave everyone a few minutes to settle down and then crossed. The Sherpa had done a good job and the steps were carefully cut. Still, I could see the problem for someone not used to this. I made a mental note to suggest that the steps be expanded and the time taken to find a way to stretch a line.

Crystal came up the rear without incident and went straight to Diana. Rusty approached. "Camp One's just ahead. You can see it when we turn the next corner."

We set out a few minutes later and arrived at Camp One at noon. A Sherpa had a pot on for lunch. I led Diana to a camp chair where she collapsed, shaking violently from head to toe.

⌒⌒⌒

"Did you hear the report?" Stern said as he greeted us at Base Camp four hours later. He was wearing his usual electric blue parka with a red bandana along with his blue-tinted glasses. Like all the men, he was no longer shaving, though in his case, his facial hair was an unhealthy looking patchwork. He was excited about something and it didn't appear to be good news. Stern struck me as one who was always first to tell anyone something bad.

"Of course not," Rusty said. "We've been in the Ice Flow."

Stern didn't care about the answer. He was just eager to give the juicy details. "The rebels have resumed their offense. We're cut off up here!"

As Harlan explained it at a gathering in the dining tent an hour later, the Maoists had launched an attack well below us, but disrupting the route to Base Camp. The expeditions that had been on their way had turned back for Kathmandu.

"How long is this going to last?" Crystal asked.

"I can't say," he allowed.

"What's the history?" Diana said. "Do these attacks last days, weeks, months?"

"It varies. I wasn't expecting anything this early in the season or as high up as they are. Both are very unusual. I wouldn't want to hazard a guess."

"I read that they besieged the capital for months a few years ago," Tom said.

"That's true," Harlan answered.

"Aren't they part of the government now?" Tom asked.

"Not this group."

"Exactly where is the attack?" I asked.

"At Thyangboche, against the military camp there."

That was odd. The military presence was so slight in Thyangboche that an attack struck me as pointless. But with insurgents, you just never knew. Some group may have decided to stop the expeditions to economically hurt Nepal and this region in particular. Or it might just have been a raid for supplies.

"We'll press on," Harlan said, "and leave it to the army to clear them out. I expect they'll make it a priority. This is bad publicity. Now I want to update you all on our progress," the New Zealander said. "Camp One is now in place and ready for use. Camp Two is also set up. Once the search is about to begin, I'll relocate and manage affairs from there with the telescope and radio. I'll have a clear view to Hillary Step as well as radio contact. In general, it's three days from ABC to the Step where the search will be concentrated, the last of that is on oxygen so we need to do this smart. Our supplies are not limitless. I'm intending to use Sherpa primarily for the actual search, since they can go without oxygen for extended periods—even in the Death Zone."

"Is Scott going to Hillary Step?" Diana asked.

"That depends. It was a very violent winter up there. I'm asking him to move up to Advanced Base Camp at Camp Two to be on standby. I anticipate the description he'll give the Sherpa should serve, but if not, we may need for him to go up as well. Is that acceptable, Scott?"

"Yes. I want to do what I can to help."

"Good then."

"We're filming this, right?" Rusty asked.

"Of course," Harlan said with resignation. "You will move up with the Sherpa to film the search. Crystal, how high do you plan to climb?"

"No higher than ABC—most likely with Diana. We'll be filing reports from there. One of the Sherpa can help Rusty with his gear."

Harlan continued. "Derek's body is primary, of course, but others died up there last year as well. It's long past time we started showing proper respect to the dead. In my view, the Sherpa have that part of this right. In particular, I'm asking the search party to be on the alert for Reggie's body. We can be certain he died near Derek."

"But Scott says he never saw Reggie. How do you explain that?" Stern asked.

"Quentin, put your notepad away and stop acting like a nasty reporter. I don't have to explain anything. There was a blizzard. Reggie could have fallen off a cliff or into a crevasse;—he could have collapsed just feet from Derek and by the time Scott arrived been nothing more than a mound of snow. He might have tried to go down for help once the radios were out and he's along the route somewhere. I'm just asking the searchers to be on the lookout for him, that's all."

"You aren't going to attempt to carry him down?" Gody said. It was the first time he'd spoken in one of these meetings. "That is not what Mr. Sodoc is paying you to do."

"No. It will take a heroic effort to get Derek's body down, let alone two. No, I'm hoping Reggie can be located, perhaps some personal effects recovered for his wife and children, covered if feasible, and a brief Anglican service read over him. I don't believe that is asking for too much."

"Are you taking Derek's body out by heli?" Stern asked.

"That's up to his father," Harlan answered. "But I'm under the impression there is to be a service here at Base Camp." He looked to Crystal. "That's correct, isn't it?"

"That's the plan," she said.

"I'm going up," Peer announced.

"Yes, of course, Peer," Harlan said. "I wouldn't dream of wasting your skill and courage. As I say, though the Sherpa will be primarily responsible for the search, many more of you may well participate—especially if we have no initial success. We will do this in waves, teams departing one day apart until the body is recovered. Calvin, are you keeping your clinic here or moving up?"

"Once the searchers have set out I plan to move to ABC and will work from there. I'd like to be as close as I can."

"How's the foot?"

"It hurts like a son-of-a-bitch." People laughed in sympathy.

"How long will the search last?" I asked.

"I can't say at this point. The body is very likely covered—unless he is lying where the wind can sweep him clean. A few days, I hope, perhaps a week. We can sustain an effort up to a month, weather permitting, and I'm prepared to do just that."

"What about the Maoists?" Stern asked.

"They are of no concern to us. We are self-contained. Their intervention has assured the privacy we need to do this, so in that instance they've been a service to us. Any questions? Good, then. Scott, I'd like you, Peer, and Rusty to plan on moving to ABC in two days with two Sherpa. Once you are at ABC, Scott will brief the search party who will already be in place. I'd like them to set out the next morning. Let's hope for a quick success. Crystal, you and Diana, plan to move out the day after Peer, Rusty, and Scott if the weather holds."

After Harlan left, the buzz was about our being cut off, though no one seemed especially concerned. The idea of insurgents storming us with AK-47's struck us all as ludicrous.

"The greatest threat," Calvin said, "is that our ongoing resupply will come to an end. That means no fresh produce or fruit. Otherwise, we've got enough here to last two months. Of course, anyone needing evacuation is going to be in trouble."

"We can always start killing yak if food runs low," Crystal suggested with a laugh.

"And if all else fails," Tarja said, "They can helicopter us out."

"Helicopter? They can fly one to here?" Tom asked.

"Weren't you listening earlier?" Stern sneered.

"Oh yes," Peer answered. "They can and have. It's one of the reasons Everest expeditions have no respect among real climbers. But this is their limit. And with the insurgents, they might not want to risk one."

Crystal was talking to Tarja. That was a sight. When she finished, Tarja said loudly, "It's about damn time." Apparently the grieving widow was going to get her next round of fifteen minutes.

⌁⌁⌁

After breakfast, Crystal summoned me to the SNS tent. "Look at this," she said, indicating a laptop.

It was more of the same from Stern. Prominent was an especially unflattering photo of Tarja. Nothing new there.

"Do you see what I see?" Crystal asked.

I scanned the page. "I guess not."

"Look at the sponsors. The big ones are Alpine equipment companies."

"So?"

"Peer is spokesman for at least two of them. Take a look at his jacket. He's wearing patches for the others. I don't know why I didn't notice this earlier."

"You're saying there's a connection?"

"I think so. I think Peer and Stern are on the same team."

"What's that?" Tarja said as she entered. Crystal explained. Our beauty was all freshly made up. Must look your best when you're the grieving widow. I gave her my seat. "That f%&#g bastard!" she said a moment later. "He's the one all along." Then the photos and lurid commentary caught her eye. She shot to her feet and stormed out, shouting, "I've had it with that little shit! Stern! Where the hell are you?"

He was at his tent some fifty feet away. He came out, blinked in the sunlight, spotted Tarja storming toward him, and then started backing away from her as quickly as he could.

Crystal had come out and was grinning at the prospect. She'd stirred the pot and produced the result she was after. The rest of the Westerners and the Sherpa in camp were all drawn to the commotion.

"What's up?" Stern shouted at Tarja, who was closing ground fast.

She called him a name and then broke into a trot. I experienced an instant of sympathy for the weasel. No grown man wants to turn tail and run from a woman. Besides, where could he run? We could not have been more isolated if we'd been on the South Pole.

I could see him consider flight and then he stopped backpedaling and raised his arms into a defensive position. He'd evidently decided what this was about. "It's not personal, Tarja. Come on. It's good publicity! You normally eat this stuff up."

Without missing a step, she scooped up a rock the size of her fist. Stern's eyes turned wide. When she raised her arm, he bolted.

Somewhere, Tarja had practiced because she caught him squarely in the back of the head. Stern stumbled, threw his hand to his head, staggered to keep balance, then continued away from her, running unsteadily like a drunk—with Tarja in hot pursuit.

I glanced toward the Sherpa who were greatly amused at what they were witnessing. They weren't alone. Stern hadn't made a friend since joining the expedition.

"With luck, she'll kill him," Crystal said with malice.

Rusty joined us. He looked at me and rolled his eyes. In the distance, I could hear Stern shouting at Tarja, begging her to stop. His hand was soaked and blood was streaming down his neck. She seemed satisfied to keep her distance as she ignored his entreaties and continued chucking rocks at him. With his hand to the back of his head, he now faced her and tried to dodge the missiles coming his way, mostly—though not entirely—with success.

Calvin responded to the commotion, went out, and persuaded Tarja to stop. She was panting by then, exhausted from the effort. Afterward, he took Stern to the clinic and treated him. Tarja continued to rage the rest of the day—much to the camp's amusement.

FOURTEEN

*Death comes cheaply on Everest. Even when you sleep, death
can find you in the form of a rushing wall of snow and ice.
There is really no rest in this place, no respite from the peril in
which we found ourselves, every hour of every day and night.*
    —Quentin Stern, www.AbandonedonEverest.com

As we waited for our turn to move above the Ice Flow, Tom and I
discussed everything that came to mind and were joined by Calvin
when he wasn't drawing blood or administering drugs. We'd monitor
the BBC world broadcast with a handheld radio Tom had brought
along and often heard a report on the status of our expedition. The
Sodoc publicity machine was in full gear. We were, we learned, on a
grand adventure.

In all, upward of three dozen of us were at the foot of Everest, if
you counted the herders. Between six and ten of the Sherpa were now
at the higher camps and every Sherpa not tending to the yak spent
the days portaging supplies up. The mountain groaned and the ice
beneath us creaked throughout the day—even here at Base Camp.
Tom took to counting the number of avalanches we heard or saw
each day, but became depressed with their regularity.

The contrast between Base Camp this year and the previous one
was as remarkable as that between day and night. The year before, this

had been a bustling impromptu village, a veritable United Nations with flags of many countries snapping in the wind.

In stark contrast to that ensemble, a ghost town stretched before me. The winter, violent wind, and incessant storms had taken a toll on the abandoned tents and discarded paraphernalia. Mangled aluminum poles amid patches of bright fabric dotted the site.

Diana was busy with Crystal and Rusty—either filing live reports or recording segments that could be used later on. Part of Crystal's job was to anticipate what would be needed and to record it while conditions permitted. Rusty told us that SNS ratings were spiking whenever Diana went live and the home office was sending a steady stream of congratulations along with an endless list of requests. The intrepid reporter in search of the body of the world's most renowned adventurer was capturing the public's imagination.

The day after stoning Stern—that was how we liked to think of it—Tarja gave her first on-camera interview. Wearing a pink parka that I'd not seen before, she positioned herself with the memorial mound behind her, the colorful prayer flags, old and new, fluttering in the breeze as Diana interviewed her. The Three Musketeers were on hand to witness the performance and, I must say, she did herself proud. To observe her stoic demeanor, to hear her quivering voice intone her adoration for the fallen hero, you'd never have guessed what a conniving bitch the beauty was—or the true story behind her marriage. She even managed a tear that first day.

Afterward, Diana approached me and said quietly, "I think I'm going to throw up."

"You're the real star. Call her on it."

She shook her head. "Not a chance. The home office has a script and I'm to follow it. She's the grieving widow who just wants to find her lost husband's body so he can be shown the respect he deserves." She caught my look. "This isn't news, Scott—it's show business."

For his part, Stern kept mostly to his tent after the assault. One evening, I overheard him speaking to his daughter on the sat phone, telling her that everything was just fine. To hear that, you'd think he was a normal human being. Calvin said the first rock had nearly killed the man. No one expressed any sympathy. I checked the blog.

He'd certainly toned down the nature of his posts, so it was unlikely that Tarja would slit his throat in his sleep—not that I ruled it out.

Apparently, Crystal's suspicions were true—or true enough for Tarja—because Peer's relationship with her came to an end. The day before we were scheduled to move up to Camp One, Peer joined us as we sat outside the dining tent. It would be Peer, Rusty, and I along with two Sherpa the next morning—if there was no snow that night. We discussed the climb for a bit and the Ice Flow in some detail, as it was an all but endless source of fascination for any climber compelled to navigate it.

Finally, Tom asked the sixty-four dollar question that had been on our minds the last few days. "We take it you're Stern's source in his book?"

Peer laughed. "*A* source, of course. He paid me $10,000. What was I to do? But I told him the truth. The lies in that book are from someone else or he just made them up."

"That book's hurt a lot of people," Tom said.

"Not anything I said. I'm not responsible."

"Tarja didn't seem to take it well," I said.

Peer looked toward her. She was pacing back and forth on the edge of the camp, having an argument with herself. "No. She was already upset with Stern for his blog. She thinks he's out to get her."

It had seemed to me for some time that Stern focused on Tarja far more than on anyone else. Either he didn't like the woman or he had an agenda. "Maybe he is," I said.

"He doesn't tell me," Peer said.

"You two are partners in this?" Tom asked.

"We are being paid by the same companies, yes, but we are not partners."

"But it's in your interest for his blog to do well."

"I suppose."

"So will you be providing him with information from on top this year?" I asked.

Peer had the decency to be embarrassed. "There is a contract, I admit. But I will say nothing that isn't true."

"This is going to be fun," Tom said as he met my eye.

"Perhaps you'd like to visit with your friend," I suggested, indicating Stern's tent.

Peer got the message and stood up. "He's a little shit, you know?" Then he walked off toward Stern's tent muttering about the things you must do in life.

***

The Sherpa were convinced that their fallen goddess was the cause of our calamity, as well as the disaster the previous year. Since every Sherpa at some level is surely related to every other Sherpa, the dishonor was felt acutely. Her defrocking had brought great shame to her specific clan and I was not surprised to learn it was Zhiku's. She was a relative in one way or another to every Sherpa on the climb, this year as last. In fact, I learned, the goddess had been the child of Dawa's brother's widow—in our culture, a niece. It was no wonder that he felt so strongly about what we were doing.

It was Dawa who told me one night between trips up the mountain. "It is a great dishonor to the clan," he said. "Now, with so many more dead this year, they will say we caused it. I hoped we would have a good climb, no deaths, but the gods do not wish it."

"Perhaps the worst is behind us," I said.

"Maybe. Or it is to come. It is no good to bother the dead, Scott. Tell boss Harlan. Their ghost is with them and will cause great trouble if we bother the body."

"Isn't it disrespectful to just leave them?"

He thought about that. "That is true, too. It is maybe why we should not be here at all."

"But you're here."

He shook his head. "I know. I know."

***

We passed through the Ice Flow early the next morning. Peer was eager to be clear of the ice canyons before the sun had time to warm them. Four Sherpa with packs joined us and the passage went without incident.

Camp One, at 19,500 feet, comprised twelve tents. A kitchen had been established and the camp possessed all the amenities of Base Camp. But as we'd already had our acclimatization climb to Camp One, we spent just that one night and moved the next morning to Advanced Base Camp at 21,300 feet, arriving just at noon. There we would remain several days before moving higher.

Perhaps eight tents made up ABC. Here was also a kitchen and I could see the tent that would be the communication center for Harlan—once he made the move—and for Crystal, who would be moving up when the search began.

Tents and a growing volume of supplies were in place above at Camp Three. At 24,400 feet, it was unpleasant—there is no other word for it. Windy, with tents perched precariously on sites carved from ice and stone, it was worse at night than during the day, but always unpleasant. Here, climbers typically prepared their own meals and saw to their personal needs. No one stayed at Camp Three more than a single night unless stranded by a storm.

At 26,000 feet, on the South Col, was Camp Four—a forlorn and grim place that served as the staging area for every summit attempt. Here on the border of the Death Zone, climbers spent their last full night before setting out. A bivouac was established two thousand feet higher up, known euphemistically as Camp Five. On the descent, climbers skipped Camp Five altogether unless they were in desperate shape. Your condition only declined there and it was not uncommon for climbers, exhausted and unable to continue, to simply lie down in one of the tents and die.

Harlan's plan was to organize the search parties at ABC and dispatch them from there. The Sherpa would go straight to Camp Four the next day, a climb well within their abilities—if they were not overly burdened with supplies. They would spend the night there before moving directly to the shelf above the Hillary Step early the next morning. They intended to spend about four hours searching before descending all the way to Camp Three, then down to ABC for a few days' rest, before moving up again. Harlan set up the parties in groups of three and planned to dispatch them one day apart, in waves, weather permitting.

The weather, as always in high-altitude climbing, was the key. When weather made the search impossible or impractical, the searchers would cluster at ABC. Westerners who were less hardy at that altitude might be sent down to Camp One.

Final steps preparatory to the actual search were well under way when we arrived at ABC. The weather turned nasty and I spent most of the next two days in my sleeping bag until Harlan joined us with three Sherpa carrying his gear and set up his communication center. His tent was only slightly larger than the two-person standard tent that the rest of us used, but it was brimming with all sorts of equipment—though the heart of his operation were the two laptops, his radio, the sat phone, and telescope.

That afternoon, even before all his gear was in place, Harlan gathered the first search team and asked me to tell them what I knew about where they might find the body of Derek Sodoc. It seemed to me that a lifetime had passed since I'd first learned of this expedition and, until now, its objective had been largely unspoken. Rusty broke out his camera and I was certain I'd be all over the Internet before morning—if not on the evening news.

It was a grim, overcast afternoon with a chilling wind blowing from below, ripe with moisture and the smell of Nepal. My persistent headache was pounding. Harlan gathered us, using his tent as a sort of shelter from the wind, though it did little good. Zhiku served as interpreter. Dawa was scheduled to come up the next morning. The only other Sherpa I knew by name was Gametup and he was still below. Gody, I understood, would be staying in Base Camp, which was just as well given how the Sherpa felt about him.

"The shelf above Hillary Step is not that far from the actual summit," I said to begin, knowing a number of these Sherpa had not been there before. In fact, at over 28,000 feet, it is only a few hundred feet below the peak at a point where most of the difficult climbing is behind you. "The shelf is separated from the summit by a nasty traverse, then a narrow and treacherous ridge, but you'll have no reason to go there. After hearing Derek's distress call, I descended from the summit. A blizzard engulfed us and it was very difficult going. Dorji, one of the Sherpa with us, became separated in the storm and Dawa went back to find him. I never saw either of them again that day.

"I found Derek sitting down, leaning against a rock formation. It was to my right as I descended, a distance from the route climbers take so he is off the regular path. It took me some time to locate him."

"How far from Hillary Step were you, Scott?" Zhiku asked after translating what I'd said.

"I'm not certain. I wish I could be more accurate. I was disoriented in the blizzard and was moving directly into the wind when I started my descent. I really couldn't see much. I left just before dark and reached the step as night came. I made my way down the line and then followed the wind to Camp Five. I got there around nine o'clock at night."

"You were three hours from above Hillary Step to Camp Five?" Harlan said.

"About that, yes."

"And you lowered yourself down Hillary Step alone—in the dark?"

"Yes."

Zhiku repeated what I said and the Sherpa murmured in admiration. To Zhiku, Harlan said quietly, "I had no idea. That's amazing." Then to me, "What else can you tell them?"

"The last time I saw Derek, he was sitting up, leaning against the rock, as I say. He was wearing a bright orange high-altitude jumpsuit. He was partially sheltered from the wind and, when I descended, I went directly into it as I say so I estimate he was facing southwest, but don't rely on that. I was disoriented up there. Be careful now. Finding him is not worth another life. Too many have died already."

Zhiku translated and spoke at some length to the three climbers. As he finished, the men grinned in unison. "What did he say?" I asked Harlan.

"He probably reminded them of the $1,000 bonus for the man who finds the body."

Rusty was panning the Sherpa's smiling faces and then pointed the lens at me. I stared into the camera with something approaching hate.

⌐⌐⌐⌐

That night, I was violently ill. The intestinal ailments were the scourge of all the climbers—even the Sherpa, to some degree. I had been having trouble keeping anything in my stomach for several days. Harlan called Calvin at Base Camp and he recommended that I stay put and do what I could to keep fluid down and wait it out. Several in Base Camp were similarly stricken and he didn't want to risk anyone getting me back through the Ice Flow.

I slept in bits and pieces, but never satisfactorily. I'd come awake fighting the sensation that I was drowning. Miserable scarcely describes my condition. After two nights and an entire day in my tent, I emerged shaky—only to find another dreary, windy day.

There'd been no snow, so the Sherpa teams had been moving up on schedule. The first was arriving above the Hillary Step that day. I joined Harlan, who was monitoring his two laptops and the radio, wearing a headset and his heavy parka, half of his body inside his sleeping bag. I had a mug of sweet tea and some biscuits and sat forcing it all down as Harlan filled me in.

"Peer went up this morning and is spending the night at Camp Four. He is moving with two Sherpa to the shelf tomorrow to join the search or recovery, depending on what the team discovers today."

Tom had joined us, looking drained. He gave me a wan smile as he took his breakfast, which matched mine.

"Where's the first team?" I asked as I nodded my greeting to Tom.

"They set out in high spirits about two hours ago. They're climbing Hillary Step now. You can see on the screen."

I looked at the larger of the two laptops and saw three separate images, bobbing and weaving as the Sherpa moved up. They were climbing strongly. There was a rumble to our right—I'd heard several since arriving at ABC—and we all craned our necks to look.

"Loose snow," Harlan said. "There's a pack above that I'm concerned about. It shouldn't strike us if it sets loose, but it's damnably close."

I could see what he was talking about. A bank of snow lay above, but to the east and north of our position. When it went—and it would—it would be a sight. Our position so close to such danger was symbolic of the problems faced by all Everest climbers. From this elevation on, suitable campsites were rare and none was perfect. Each presented its own challenges with exposure to weather or safety. ABC was a calculated risk, as were all the camps.

"Boss," I heard over the radio. It sounded like Zhiku, who was with the first search party. "We are on the shelf. Snow and ice heavy in places, but clear in others. We start search now."

Watching the screen, I could not make out where they were. I'd been there just twice. Once on the ascent the previous year when we'd moved through and beyond Hillary Step quickly—or what passes for quickly there—before I'd stopped with Dawa and the lost Sherpa to wait on Rusty, Derek, and Reggie. My return had been in the midst of the blizzard. I had only the sketchiest recollections of the shelf.

Tom and I spoke quietly so as not to distract Harlan, but it turned out that his story was much like mine—if not as extreme. He'd not been well since arriving at Advanced Base Camp, but unlike me, he'd managed to stay ambulatory.

"How's it been here?" I asked.

"Busy. Yesterday and this morning, the teams set out. A third team is arriving around noon today and will leave tomorrow. Another is coming up and, by the day after, the team up there now will be here to rest. If the weather holds, they'll cover a lot of ground in the search area. If they haven't already found the body."

By three that afternoon, it was clear that there'd be no locating Derek's body this day. The team had worked a grid—to the extent that such a thing was possible—and called their progress down to Harlan and the team that would resume the search the next day who were monitoring the radio broadcast. They set out back down, aiming to leapfrog beyond Camp Four where the next search team was waiting—since resting is hardly the word for it—to spend the night at Camp Three. They'd join us at ABC the next day before noon.

"Not bad," Harlan said. "It went smoothly, which is saying a lot for something as complicated as this."

"Any word on Reggie's body?" I asked.

He shook his head. "I'm not optimistic on that front. There is no reward for finding him. I'm counting on the Westerners to keep an eye out."

⌐⌐⌐

Rusty arrived unexpectedly with the new Sherpa team. He'd been assigned a Sherpa named Kusang to carry his extra gear. I'd seen him with the other Sherpa and he was, if anything, quieter. I was pleased to see Dawa heading up the three-man searching party. He greeted me with his usual sly smile and then moved off to unload his pack.

Nothing was wasted at ABC, so even the rescue team that would spend the night before moving up to Camp Four the next morning portaged fifty pounds of supplies apiece up to us. They'd take what they'd need with them to the next camp as well. This consisted primarily of the three oxygen bottles each would use the next day when they went to the shelf.

"Moving up or working from here?" Tom asked Rusty.

"This is plenty for now," Rusty said, pushing his goggles back and breathing deep in the thin air. "Crissie wants some shots from ABC to fill in Diana's voiceovers." He scanned the camp. "I'd forgotten how miserable it is up here."

Harlan looked over at him. "Welcome to Club Med."

Rusty shifted his eyes to the view. "I guess it's got some redeeming qualities."

The search proved equally fruitless the following day. As the team left the shelf, I heard Peer talking to Harlan. "Scott will need to come up. We've looked everywhere with no results. We need to next dig in the snow and chop at the ice. We have to know the precise location to succeed. Tell him."

Harlan looked up at me. "I heard," I said.

"Can you set out tomorrow?"

"Sure. Tomorrow."

∿∿∿

That night, sleep evaded me totally. I'd known for a year, I suppose, that it would come to this. I'd certainly known since meeting Sodoc in New York. If there is anything in life I've learned, it's that you can never really walk away from certain decisions. The good ones don't linger with a positive effect as long as we'd like; the bad ones never go away.

I must have nodded off because the vibration awoke me with a start some time after midnight. Every seasoned high-altitude climber sleeps with part of him attuned to such a moment. I knew at once what it was. The roar of crashing snow followed the vibration. I scrambled out of the tent in time to see the avalanche Harlan had feared racing very near us. The New Zealander was out, shouting for everyone to get out of our tents and waving for us to move away from the torrent of snow and ice.

As soon as the snow stopped moving, Tom and I rushed to the edge of the avalanche. We could hear the wall of snow still plunging below us. The Sherpa had been located on that side of ABC and one of their two tents had been carried away. Dawa ran up, having just escaped being carried off.

"The tent is there, Scott!" he shouted pointing some distance below in the tumult of the avalanche.

Some in the camp rushed off to try to find the two Sherpa who'd been asleep. I doubted they'd do much good without the proper footing or equipment. We hurried back to the tents, where Tom and I climbed into our boots with crampons, put on our warmest jackets, fitted lights to our heads, grabbed our ice axes, and set out.

We did so in a quandary. Men trapped beneath snow in an avalanche haven't long to live, so every second counts. But without the right gear, it might not be possible to reach them—let alone get them out alive.

As I feared, those who'd set out in that first enthusiastic rush had not reached the location of the tent, which under the light of a full moon could just be discerned as a dark disheveled shape against the white snow. Lacking proper footing, the men had slipped and fallen repeatedly. Only Dawa, who must have been sleeping in his boots, had made it to the spot where he was furiously digging with his bare hands.

When Tom and I reached him, we threw ourselves into the task, joined only a moment later by Reggie, who'd also taken the time to equip himself properly. In fact, he arrived with two small folding shovels. He handed me one and the two of us dug rapidly, widening our site as we did. Only a portion of the crumpled tent was visible; we could not be entirely certain that it was even the one with the men. Some supplies had been swept away as well. Dawa was moving behind me on all fours, searching for some sign. Tom was matching him on the other side.

All climbers are taught the same technique in the event that they are caught in an avalanche. Place one hand across your mouth, to keep the snow away, so that when you come to stop, you have a small space in which you can breathe for a precious few minutes. Extend your other arm away from you, trying to reach upward with it, to mark your place above or as high in the snow as you can. That was what Tom and Dawa were searching for.

Reggie and I worked our way down around the tent, hoping the men were still within it. If that was the case, we had a good chance of finding them alive—should they be located in time. Dawa and Tom had worked themselves through a complete circle, having found no sign of the men. Others were joining us now, having put on their hiking boots. Flashing light spilled across the chaotic scene.

I was exhausted and Reggie was slowing down as well. The effort to dig was more than either of us could endure for long. Rusty was one of those who'd reached us. "I'll take it," he said to Reggie and started digging the moment he got the shovel.

A minute later, I struck something. "Here," I gasped, so exhausted that I thought I'd keel over. "Something." I collapsed onto the snow. My lungs were burning like cold fire. My arms ached almost beyond bearing.

Dawa, two other Sherpa, and Reggie started working with their bare hands, yanking at the tent, and tossing handfuls of snow aside as rapidly as they could. Someone spoke in Sherpa and the men began working feverishly. In a moment, they'd uncovered one body. They pulled him out and spread him on the snow. The man was dead. They started digging again. A few moments later, they had the other man, hoping for a miracle, but he was dead as well.

Later, when I had the strength to move my light, I caught the face of one of the men who had yet to be covered. It was Kusang, who'd come up with Rusty just that day. As the Sherpa would not touch their friends, we zipped the men into their sleeping bags—a largely effortless task since each had died in one—and dragged them up to Advanced Base Camp. Shortly before dawn, exhaustion drove us back to our own bags and tents.

FIFTEEN

*At very high altitude, climbers resemble the Pillsbury dough-
boy in their jumpsuits. They waddle about awkwardly, unable
to move freely, as much a prisoner of their attire as anything.
Anywhere else, it would be amusing. Here it is just one more
reminder of our bizarre existence.*
                    —Quentin Stern, www.AbandonedonEverest.com

I moved up to Camp Four the next morning, joined by Dawa and
one of the climbing Sherpa whose name I did not ask for. As it had
been in combat, I was weary of learning the names of men who'd
only be dead soon enough.

Before we set out, there'd been an argument about what to do with
the dead. Harlan decided to wait for Zhiku to deal with it when he
came down, so the bodies were laid off to the side away from the potties. Each would take at least six Sherpa to lower down the mountain.

The climb to Camp Four was not especially difficult for the Sherpa,
but it exhausted me. I'd take two steps, stop to suck air, hack, and then
take two more. To reach Camp Three, we ascended the half-mile-long
Lhotse Face—the steepest exposed section on Everest. Here was blue
ice slick as glass, over which I trod with enormous caution. More than
one skilled climber had made an error when moving his clip from
one section of line to another and fallen to his death.

Along the way, we passed the body of a dead climber. From his—or her—gear I estimated it had lain here since the 1980s, more than twenty years. The clothing was still bright and, from a short distance, you might think that someone climbing with you had simply lain down to rest. There'd be more bodies from now on—those I'd see, such as this one, and others that would be covered by the barest layer of snow and would seem to be simply a pile of white. The greatest number would be buried too deeply for me to know they'd ever existed.

We passed through Camp Three, taking only the time to drink tea before setting out again. We encountered the first search team descending at this point, looking glum and disappointed. The next section was very steep and, since we were not on oxygen, it was exhausting. At times, I seriously considered turning back. More than once, I sat in the snow, near my end, and had to be coaxed to my feet by Dawa.

I wondered on occasion what the Sherpa really thought of us Westerners, what they said about us among themselves. I'd never seen a Sherpa squat down in the snow to be pulled to his feet by another, though I had witnessed more than one simply keel over and die from exhaustion. Finally, we reached Camp Four, situated just below the Death Zone. Peer came out to greet us with a wide grin.

"What are you doing here?" I asked. He was supposed to be resting in Camp Three after spending the previous day with a search team above Hillary Step. I'd not seen him earlier, but assumed he was within one of the tents.

"I'm going back up with you tomorrow. I'm tired of sitting on my ass." He grinned, his lips chapped and cracked from the dry air, his cheeks burnished a ruby red.

"Does Harlan know?" I gasped as I struggled to catch my breath.

"I told him. What can he do? Refuse my help? Here, let me take your pack."

That evening passed as unpleasantly as I'd expected, warmed only by Peer's constant good cheer. Dawa was oddly withdrawn—even a bit distant—and spent the evening with the other Sherpa in quiet conversation. Their unease was pervasive by now.

There were few clouds that night and the stars stood out against a jet-black canvas. Peer regaled me with stories of his teenage climbs in Norway. I almost forgave him for talking to Stern and betraying Derek with Tarja. He was a hard man to dislike—especially in such a hostile environment, where courage and good cheer have enormous value.

It is common these days for climbers preparing to summit to sleep on oxygen at Camp Four. To stretch our supplies, and since he was using Sherpas primarily for the search, Harlan had made the decision to forgo that luxury. We'd do it the old-fashioned way, which meant I awoke repeatedly that night, gasping for air. Even Peer, with whom I shared the tent, struggled. Neither of us slept more than an hour the entire miserable night.

Before dawn, I forced myself to eat a hot breakfast, some kind of sweet porridge that nearly gagged me. My throat ached so badly that every swallow was painful. I did my best with the tea, drinking two full mugs, but even that was less than thirty ounces—a pitiful amount given my chronic dehydration. Though we usually prepared our own meals here, Peer had persuaded the Sherpa and Dawa to cook for us. This was not a question of luxury so much as of effort. Cooking in these conditions was exhausting and I think he could see how weary I was already.

As we donned our oxygen equipment, Peer said, "I'm sorry to ask you to do this. I just want to get this part over with. We need a better idea of where to look."

I nodded. I'd not had much choice in this and just wanted it done with. Harlan's voice popped in my ear. Gone were the days of crackling and faded voices. These were the very latest in digital radios. They either worked or they didn't. The sound was perfect or did not exist. Someone's idea of a bad joke.

"How's it going?" he asked.

"Good," Peer answered. "We will set out on time."

"Weather should be fine," Harlan said in my earpiece. "There will be some wind, but no snow. It will be cold, however, so keep moving."

Peer acknowledged the report and then turned the valve for me. The tank was mounted on my back and the control was difficult to reach.

The exquisite elixir of oxygen flowed into my body. I'd forgotten what it was like not to gasp like a fish out of water and not feel suffocated every minute. Within moments, I was revitalized—even though I was receiving only half the oxygen I would at sea level, an amount about equal to what was available at Camp One. Here at 26,000 feet, it was nectar. Energy coursed through me.

Dawa and the other Sherpa were ready, also now on oxygen, grimly eager to set out, no doubt thinking of the reward. I heard Diana's voice in my ear, sounding nervous and worried. Apparently, she was going to monitor our day. "Be careful what you say, guys. We're recording down here. I expect today will go out for the morning news shows."

"We wouldn't want to cause any ladies to blush," Peer said with a hearty laugh. "Not unless I'm there to enjoy it."

With Peer, perhaps Europe's greatest Alpine climber, and me, the last man to see Derek Sodoc alive, the man accused in a national bestseller of abandoning him to his death, I suppose it was too big a story not to be broadcast. I should have been prepared, but the idea of celebrity caught me by surprise—though in the desolation and isolation of the Death Zone, it was impossible to accept that any such world existed.

Following final adjustments and shortly after sunrise, we set out, joined by Dawa and the other Sherpa. We planned to climb to the shelf above the Hillary Step and spend three to four hours searching before returning to Camp Three—if I was still on my feet by then.

As long ago as 1938, the noted British explorer and mountaineer Eric Shipton wrote that true climbing is not possible above 25,000 feet. If ahead of us was genuinely technical climbing of the kind that Peer had mastered as a near child, it is unlikely that Everest would have been conquered as soon as it was. The best we could manage, even with oxygen, was to plod our way up a few steps at a time.

We were swaddled in the latest high-tech climbing gear. Our high-altitude suits were tested to near Mars-like conditions, our climbing boots were the very latest, and my new ice ax was light, strong, and efficiently designed. I wore a mouth microphone and a tiny camera mounted on my head. And I was cold to the bone—even with the extraordinary effort climbing the final 2,500 vertical feet to the Hillary Step entailed.

At this elevation, climbing Everest is about endurance, about disregarding pain and discomfort, and about ignoring that voice that every climber is trained to honor—the one that screams, "Turn back! You're going to die!"

I'd manage two steps, stop to breathe three times, then two steps again, and so on. The idea was to establish a mindless rhythm. I was connected to the line, two Sherpa were ahead to break any trail that needed breaking, and Peer was behind to make certain that I didn't fall over and resign myself to death.

My throat was so painful that every gulp of air was excruciating. My lips were parched, split, and bleeding. A water line was beside my mouth, but I took no moisture. I just moved steadily like one of those mindless robots you used to see in department stores at Christmas.

It took two hours of this hell to reach Camp Five. Someone had taken the time to erect a fresh tent and supply it for use in an emergency. One of the collapsed older tents was round with a body I recalled from the previous year. I knew for a fact that there were at least half a dozen other dead within fifteen feet of where the Sherpa had erected this tent. We scarcely paused before pressing on, taking just enough time for Peer to call in a progress report.

"Good job," Harlan said.

"How are you?" Diana asked, meaning me.

"All right," I answered.

I still didn't drink, though I cautioned myself repeatedly that I must. I hadn't the energy and exhaustion suppressed my thirst. We moved steadily up the mountain face, grinding it out one step at a time, to the area known as the Balcony at 27,600 feet. There, we paused for a few moments and took in the majestic view. From here, you could see the five highest peaks in the world.

Beyond the Balcony was a ridge that on summit day often held the first traffic jam. As climbers were no longer moving, their core body temperature began to drop to dangerous levels; their feet, hands, and face grew numb. But, for us, a path through thigh-deep snow had been cut by the two previous search parties. Dawa and the Sherpa widened the path on occasion, though there was no real need.

Then we were at the South Summit, 28,704 feet officially. From here, all that stood between you and the conquest of Everest was Hillary Step—the slippery traverse just beyond that could plunge the unwary into the plains of Tibet—and then the ridge to the peak mound. And, of course, all you had to do then was get down.

We stopped a few moments at the South Summit. The sky was the vivid blue typical of such elevations. Below us, in the valleys among lesser peaks, floated dots of clouds.

"South summit," Peer said into the microphone.

"Brilliant pictures, boys, just brilliant," Harlan said.

"Glad to please," Peer answered as we set out.

There had been a steady breeze since we'd left that morning. It made staying warm very difficult as it stripped away any body heat that we produced from our effort. From here on, the wind increased in intensity, causing me to turn my face away. I was so cold that I felt myself shudder when I stopped to suck air between steps.

Twenty minutes later, we reached the Hillary Step. When Tenzing and Hillary arrived at this point, having taken the same route we were following, no man had ever been here before. They'd come this way, hacking each step in the snow and ice—a grueling, exhausting ordeal. Every few feet, they traded places to rotate the labor.

Hillary, being the more skilled climber, had tackled this forty-foot face of rock alone. He'd managed to wedge himself between a wall of ice and rock, using it to make his slow way to the top. He always made light of it, but the achievement was remarkable. On the shelf, he'd secured his hemp rope and then tossed it down for Tenzing to join him.

Before us, the line was already rigged and secured. I'd dreaded this moment since setting out. Though not a perpendicular cliff, Hillary Step is still a very steep pitch. It was the most demanding and exhausting part of the day. I clipped onto the rope, steeled myself, and started up. I heard Peer in my ear. "This is Scott. He's moving up Hillary Step now." Play by play. I had to assume I was on camera. For just an exhausted second, I considered trying to make a finger gesture, but it was impossible.

Little snow clung to the face, so I struggled against bare rock. I required the security of the line more than once and, about halfway up, I was tempted to stop in an attempt to get my breath, but knew how counterproductive that would be. If I stopped, it would just be that much more difficult to get moving again.

My lungs burned a familiar fire. The dry air coming from the tank was like sandpaper across my aching throat. The only part of my body that didn't hurt was numb from cold and I couldn't be certain it would respond to my command or not have to be cut away from my body by Calvin once I was down from here.

After an indeterminate period, I found myself above the pitch. I was so tired as I cleared myself from the line, I thought about just lying down. Then Peer joined me. The summit was forty-five minutes to an hour more, but this was enough for me.

We stood unmoving for some minutes, sucking air. This was the second time in three days that Peer had been here. It was a remarkable achievement.

To my shock, the scene about me was as alien as if I'd never been there before. That last afternoon, in the blizzard, I'd formed an impression of the place that was blazed in my mind, but bore virtually no resemblance to what I was now seeing. No wonder they'd not found Derek's body. My directions must have been meaningless to the searchers. Still, this shelf on which we stood seemed an impossibly small place on which to lose a body.

"Look at me," Peer said.

I turned my head.

"Point your head," he said. "Get the shot."

I understood and pretended I was a cameraman. Peer removed his mask, lifted his goggles and grinned at the camera mounted on my head, then gave a thumbs-up. In my ear, I heard, "Good shot, Scott. Great."

Peer moved his mask and goggles back in place and then turned toward the scene before us. "Where is he?" he asked. "Can you tell?"

To my surprise, the top of the Step was quite narrow, with a white overflowing crown of snow rising precariously above us at a slight overhang. No sane person would remain where we stood a moment longer than necessary. I scanned the scene before working slowly left to right, ending at the edge of the mountain where the traverse starts, leading to the Summit Ridge. The passage from the traverse to the line going down the pitch was so narrow it seemed impossible that Derek and I could have been here and not encountered anyone coming to help. In bright sunlight, the area looked very restricted. My own story made no sense to me.

I had an image of a scene that placed Derek to my left against one of the rocks or rock walls. That was how I'd described it to the Sherpa, but such a place didn't exist. Instead, the ground sloped off to my left, leading to oblivion. Directly ahead was a single rock the size of an SUV and the place most like what I recalled.

"Over there," I said, gesturing with my left arm toward the wall of rock. We four set out awkwardly that way.

Elsewhere, the search would have taken just a few minutes, but in these conditions, we were at it an hour. There were awkward patches of considerable ice and scattered mounds of snow. The bitterly cold wind raced across our exposed position with growing intensity. We worked haphazardly at first, hoping to stumble on a body by sheer numbers, but after that failed, Peer organized us into a line, arm's length apart, then inched us forward, moving right to left from the traverse opening to the point where the shelf we occupied dropped off significantly and dangerously. Nothing.

"They searched this already," Dawa said. "I think his body was blown away over the winter. It was very bad up here."

He had a point. Two teams had already searched this small shelf with no results. Winds in excess of 150 miles an hour had been recorded on Everest's summit over the years. That would be enough to sweep this area clean of any human body.

"I think he's right," I said.

"We've come a long way and at great cost," Harlan said into our ears. "Keep looking. Are you certain you have the area right, Scott?"

In fact, I was not. Logic told me that this place we'd searched *had* to be the location, but my memory said it was wrong. I'd returned down the Step, moving into the storm—yet Derek and I had been partially shielded from the wind, which I recalled had come from my left when I sat down beside him. The problem was that there was no place like that here.

"Could you have been further along?" Peer asked.

I was very tempted to throw up my hands in surrender and admit to any possibility. If I did, the search would move along the dangerous traverse to the point where it met the Summit Ridge, but I knew that we'd not been there. I'd separated from Dawa near the end of the ridge when he'd turned back to find Dorji and distinctly recalled making the traverse. No, Derek had been in this place.

"It was here," I said. "On this shelf."

We stood unmoving—the only sounds were our own ragged breaths as we drew in oxygen and the wind whipping our bodies. I moved toward the traverse and then turned toward the pitch and the line down. I was certain that Derek had been to my right. It seemed to me that I'd followed these rocks until I'd encountered him. Peculiarly, he'd been easier to find in a blinding storm than he was today in brilliant sunlight.

I moved along the rock, attempting to replicate my path from the year before. It was difficult going, especially since there was so little snow and ice beneath me and the fierce wind battered us. There were two or three tight places in the rock where we could possibly have been, but they were too small, too exposed, and there was no body in any of them. Finally, I reached the steep decline and stopped. There was a sharp belly to it and it was not possible to see its end from here—though I had a climber's sense that it did not go far. The rock I'd been following curved back on itself here and was lost to view.

Dawa was behind me and touched my shoulder. "Not here, Scott. It is too steep with much loose rock. Very dangerous."

He was right. The scree before me was treacherous—and it looked nothing like what I remembered. I turned back.

"What do you think?" Peer said.

I was speechless. What could I think? "Dawa is right. His body was blown off this winter."

Harlan was monitoring us. "You have another hour, perhaps more. Keep searching."

With reluctance, we returned to the task. Mounds of snow turned to ice were scattered about and I saw the problem that the two earlier teams had faced. Chopping into that ice would be daunting and no one wanted to do it without some expectation of what they would find. The wind was relentless. The sky was now covered with high, fast-moving clouds and had turned grey.

Peer, Dawa, and the Sherpa tackled each ice mound with the points of their ice axes—stabbing into them repeatedly, hacking away with the pick—in a futile attempt to determine if something was frozen inside. I was too exhausted, too cold, and too uncertain to join in. Instead, I scanned the shelf again, hoping somehow to jog my memory, to fix on something that would make sense of this jigsaw.

We were down to ninety minutes of oxygen and reaching our turnaround point when the Sherpa called out. We hobbled over to see what he'd found.

"What is it?" Harlan asked.

Peer was at the mound and stabbed with his ice ax. "There's something here," he said. He lowered himself awkwardly to his knees and then shouted, "It's a body!"

SIXTEEN

In his bright orange high altitude climbing suit,
Derek was easily spotted high above in even the most
deadly of places. He was a fearless climber.
　　　　　—Quentin Stern, www.AbandonedonEverest.com

I suppose a reporter would say that the news flashed around the world. Diana came into our ears using that evening news voice she'd perfected, so I assumed this bit of the search was going to be used. For all I knew, we were going out live.

The four of us soon looked like those Old West movies where you see men driving spikes for the railroad. We set up a rhythm so that we each had a clear shot, but we were all so tired and clumsy that we still managed to strike on top of each other's ice axes. I stopped every few strokes to draw air into my ragged lungs and then resumed the excavation. Finally, Peer signaled for us to stop.

He dropped again to his knees, gesturing at me to keep my camera focused on him as he cleared away the bits of ice that we'd hacked lose. "I see a high-altitude jumpsuit," he said as if to an audience. I'd have been very surprised if he didn't, since no one went to these altitudes without one. Still, it made good drama.

"I see …" He scraped away some more ice, stopped, and straightened. "Blue. It's blue. You can confirm Derek's was orange, can't you, Scott?"

It was theater. Peer knew as well as I did that Derek had been the only one in the expedition wearing an orange jumpsuit. Crystal had insisted on it so he could be easily picked out against the white snow in distant shots.

"Orange, yes," I croaked, trying to remember who'd been in blue. Reggie. Reggie had worn a blue suit.

"Is it Reggie?" Harlan asked as if reading my mind.

"I can't say," Peer answered and got clumsily to his feet. "We need to clear more ice." He took a swing with his ax and we joined in. After a few minutes, he told us to stop and knelt again, clearing bits of ice with his gloved hands. He touched a red muffler. Reggie's wife had knitted it for him.

"It's Reggie," Peer said. "I can see his red muffler."

"Mark the spot for a service later," Harlan said. He had earlier announced that if anyone's body other than Derek's were found, services would be performed only after the search was abandoned. Until we found Derek, the hunt for him was priority.

Dawa spoke. "We should go back now. It is getting late."

I looked at my watch and was surprised to see that it was already four in the afternoon. We'd agreed to call off the search at this time.

Peer nodded. He reached into a pocket and produced a bright red dye. With the wind, his task was difficult, but we three formed a wall. On his knees, Peer managed to spread enough of the dye to mark the place—if it didn't snow and cover it. He then removed an electronic marker from a pocket and inserted it into the hole we'd created and covered it with ice. It would emit a homing beacon for several days, unless the batteries became too cold to function, which I was certain would happen. Finally, he rose, stood back, and—like the skilled mountaineer he was—took in the scene so he could recall it again. Satisfied, he said, "The place is marked and I can return to it if necessary. We're heading back down."

To say I was tired would be pointless. I just wanted to turn away from here and descend—but something was pulling at me, teasing with my mind and memory. I moved again the few feet toward the scree and stood staring. Peer joined me. "We should go, Scott."

"Yes."

"What is it?" he asked.

"Nothing," I said finally. The scene was no different from a fresh look. "Nothing." I turned toward the line that would take us down Hillary Step.

But Peer detected something in my manner. He gestured toward the Sherpa. "We'll check it out," he said. Then, for the audience, "There is a spot Scott thinks might be right. It has not been searched because it is treacherous. We will search regardless."

He and the Sherpa connected to one another, then Peer handed me the line, which I hooked to myself and passed to Dawa, who did the same. We found good footing for our crampons and braced ourselves as the two men started cautiously down, the stiff wind pushing them forward.

The incline was not so steep as to be impossible to navigate, but it was an area that went nowhere and one where you'd not venture, if you knew where you were. The scree was exposed and unstable, as deadly a piece of terrain as existed on the mountain. But the more I watched Peer and the Sherpa descend into it, the more I began to think this may very well have been the place—and if it was, it explained everything.

If this had been where I was, thinking myself closer to where I now stood, no wonder I'd never encountered anyone coming down to help. We'd been well off to the side and down—possibly even along where the rock turned back. I'd been moving away only twenty feet or so to not lose contact with Derek, but also because I was certain that placed me on the route to Hillary Step. In fact, if we'd been anywhere near here, I'd not gone nearly far enough, let alone in the right direction. Those coming down could have moved right by me seeing nothing——and had.

In my ear, I could hear Peer and the Sherpa grunting in effort, the sound of their heavy breathing, as they worked cautiously down, angling toward the rocks to our right. Dawa and I steadily fed line to them.

The area had been swept clear of snow, except at the base of the rocks or within the crevasses between them, where it was piled thick.

Because of the slight bow, it was not possible to see where it came to an end. It took nearly ten minutes for them to move down along the rock. Once there, Peer leaned against the stone with his left hand as he poked at each cache of snow and ice, working meticulously to the right then to the left.

"We must go," Dawa said. "It is late."

The Sherpa was joining in and the two men made steady, if slow, progress in their search. They had moved uncomfortably far from us and we could no longer see the lower part of their bodies. The line we were feeding was nearly at an end. Soon they'd round the rock and be cut from our sight altogether.

"Careful," I said. "You must be close to the edge. Peer, I don't recall being that far over. And if I was moving up that scree, I'd certainly remember it. This is a waste of time—and dangerous."

A moment later, I heard the Sherpa exclaim in triumph. He didn't speak English, but it was clear that he'd found something. Peer moved toward him as Dawa said to me, "He says he's found a body in orange."

"What is that?" Diana said. Apparently she was still monitoring.

"We've found something," Peer said. He was nearly to the Sherpa, whom I could see moving in excitement. If he was right, the reward was his.

"Scott," Diana said, "can you see anything?"

"No, they're just below a bow in the scree. I can't see the ground from here."

Then I heard, "It's him! It's Derek, Scott! We've found him!"

At that moment, there was a horrible scream as the Sherpa went over the edge.

⚡⚡⚡

Nearly two hours later, we entered Camp Five and exchanged our depleted oxygen bottles for fresh ones. None of us had been in any condition to discuss the tragedy earlier. I'd know soon enough why the Sherpa had not been fastened to Peer in such a dangerous place.

Immediately after the tragedy, Peer had composed himself and then made his way back to us. He'd told Diana that the Sherpa had leaned over the edge on his knees in an effort to lift the body, lost his balance, and—before he could gather himself—he'd simply gone off the shelf, falling thousands of feet. There was no hope of recovering his body.

It was nearly dark as we set out for Camp Four, but it wasn't far now. Peer turned our air controls to full and we breathed a richer mix than we had going up, when keeping air as long as possible was vital. We weren't going to finish these bottles before reaching Camp Four and speed mattered with approaching darkness.

It's difficult to put into words, but climbing is more secure than descending. When you climb, your body leans forward so that the force of gravity keeps your weight over your boots. You can also see more clearly where you step. When you descend, your weight is slightly back, off center, and your feet are difficult to see. Picture climbing stairs, then walking down them and you get the point. I suspect most people fall when descending a staircase. That's how it is on mountains—especially on Everest—and I was terrified with every step.

Peer brought up the rear to make sure I didn't do anything foolish or to save me if I did. We made our way with lights mounted to our foreheads, like coal miners of old—or perhaps of today, for all I know. They cast a stark white light that seemed to glow in the darkness—the snow and ice sparkling like glitter at a ball in its intensity.

It was nearly seven when we reached Camp Four, where I all but collapsed. I sat in the snow and took the cup of hot tea I was given. I'd had no feeling from my knees down since above Camp Five. I could no longer talk. We'd been on the move with no rest for nineteen hours and I could not recall ever being so tired. I crawled into one of the tents where a Sherpa helped me into a sleeping bag. He adjusted my gas mask so I could receive the full flow and, for the first time in weeks, I fell into a deep black sleep.

⌁⌁⌁

A hot breakfast waited for us shortly after dawn, but I could not eat. I managed some liquid—hardly more than a few ounces—and was relieved when Peer said we should set out before the sun warmed the ice and snow. Diana and Crystal called up questions during breakfast, but Peer put them off. We'd see them soon enough, he said.

Unburdened now by oxygen tanks and going downhill in increasingly rich air, we made good progress and were in Camp Three by mid-morning. The recovery team heading up was already here. Harlan had moved quickly. I counted eight in all. Digging Derek out of the ice, rigging him to be carried and, and, lowering him down Hillary Step and below was a formidable task. I wasn't certain even eight experienced Sherpa could manage it. I'd seen more than a dozen struggling to lowering a body from Camp Three to Camp Two the previous year.

The team was led by Zhiku, who looked grim with the loss of still another friend and member of his clan. He and Peer spoke at length about where Derek's body was to be found. I overheard some of it and it made no sense to me—none at all.

"He's hanging from a cliff," Peer said to Zhiku. "Follow the rock into the scree and you'll find him over the edge. He's tangled in a line and hanging mostly free, though part of him is frozen into the snowpack."

As they set out, we wished them well. The sky was ashen. There was less wind than the day before and it was not as cold, which made an enormous difference. We rested a bit more and then resumed our descent. Just over an hour later, we were at Advanced Base Camp, where Harlan greeted us with a grim smile, pumping hands all around. Behind him, Rusty filmed away with Diana standing beside him. I could see Calvin further back.

"God bless you all," Harlan said. "Good job. I'm sorry, Dawa, so very sorry for your loss."

"It is the mountain," Dawa answered quietly and with resignation. "It was his time."

Diana stepped up, gave us all a hug, and then asked Peer if he was up for a few questions. Do bees like honey? Peer nodded sagely with more than a hint of sadness. He knew his part. I moved off to Calvin.

"You look like hell," he said by way of greeting.

"I feel it," I croaked.

"Let me look at that throat." I opened my mouth as if I was at the dentist's office and he peered in. "As I feared. You've got strep. I'm putting you on a different, and much stronger, antibiotic. Get some rest. This isn't something to take lightly—not in your condition."

"How do you feel?" Harlan asked from behind me.

"Okay," I managed.

"You should go to Base Camp today if you can manage it," he said. "The weather is good. You can be there well before dark. If you aren't up to it, spend the night at Camp One and go down in the morning."

"I should make it." I shook my head and gestured at my throat. "Can't talk."

After Peer's somber interview, we were served a meal that smelled wonderful. I managed a few swallows of soup, but the pain wasn't worth it. Crystal and Rusty remained apart from us, very busy, and I assumed that it had something to do with the uplink for their feed. Diana approached me and spoke lightly for a time. As we prepared to leave, she hugged me fiercely.

"Take care," she said. "Careful in the Ice Flow, okay? And don't worry about me. I'll be fine. Really."

I can only say that—given my condition—her words and manner did not have the impact that they would have had at another time. When she turned away, there was a finality—a certain resignation in her body—that I should have recognized, but did not.

An hour after arriving, we set out again and reached Camp One in just over an hour, the going becoming easier and easier. The passage was well marked and the air increasingly rich to our adapted bodies. Here, we encountered a heavily laden party of five moving up. Every climbing Sherpa, and some who'd been volunteered for the effort, was now in motion up the mountain.

"What's that?" I managed to say.

Peer shrugged. "Recovery, I'd say. What else?"

We soon entered the Ice Flow. The towering walls were no less threatening and the aluminum ladders down and across each crevasse were as difficult to navigate as ever, but we were inured to danger by now. We were careful and made steady progress, ignoring the occasional tremor in the ice. Two hours later, we emerged just above Base Camp.

Peer turned to me and grinned. "I think we'll live now."

Compared to before, Base Camp seemed deserted. Bawu and a kitchen helper remained behind, as did Stern, Tarja, Tom, and

Gody—all of whom I could see. I spotted just one herder with the yaks. The camp, however, had been significantly stripped of supplies.

"I guess it's over," I said to Dawa, who had been very quiet on the descent. I knew he was at least distantly related to the Sherpa who'd plunged to his death; they might have even been good friends.

"No, Scott. It is not yet finished." With his lips, in Sherpa fashion, he gestured down the long valley into the distance. I couldn't see anything out of the ordinary, but in a moment, I heard it.

"What is that?" Peer asked.

Now we could all see the massive Russian Mi-17 helicopter and hear with increasing vigor the distinctive thwap of its beating rotor. We reached Base Camp in time to watch the helicopter lower itself to the ground not far away, near the memorial mound.

I knew. I want to say that now—regardless of all that was to follow. I knew when I saw the helicopter who would step out, so it came as no surprise to me.

Michael Sodoc.

SEVENTEEN

Like captains of sailing ships, the Sherpa believe a woman on the mountain is bad luck. Watching Tarja strut her stuff, flirt with every man who could advance her career, and lean her breasts against an arm when she wanted something, was a gagging experience. As tension with her husband rose, she elected not to sleep alone—assuming sleep was what she was up to.
—Quentin Stern, www.AbandonedonEverest.com

Gody, of course, stepped forward to deliver his report. The pair stood unmoving beneath the revolving rotor as it slowed.

Stern had his camera out and was filming with great enthusiasm and a wicked grin. Tarja approached us and said, "Why is that SOB here?"

She didn't look good—and that was a first. She was getting a wild stare in her eyes as well as letting her personal appearance slip. I'd seen something like it before in combat.

Tom arrived with her. "You guys look like shit; well, Scott does, anyway. Any thoughts on the big guy being here?"

Tarja glared at him. "As if you don't know." Her eyes appeared to be giving him a hex. I understood why, in former times, such women were considered to be witches.

"Hey! I had no idea the man was coming."

Tarja snorted. "You'll be sucking his dick before dark."

Tom looked as if he was going to respond, but said nothing, just looking at her in stunned disbelief.

"He must be here for his son," Peer said. "Perhaps he has more heart than people say."

Tarja laughed, the sound coming out as sharp bark. "This is bad. Very bad." She turned and walked away, saying over her shoulder, "None of you know him like I do."

The Great One and Gody now approached us, the Nepalese face utterly blank. The truest sign this was no publicity stunt was Rusty's absence. He was up the mountain, waiting on the recovery.

Sodoc's considerable luggage was being offloaded, so the man planned to be here for more than a few hours. In a bright yellow parka and a Sherpa-style hat, he looked enormous, if a little silly. His dark eyes were as cold as I recalled. He shook hands around, appearing fit and ready for a fight. He ignored Dawa who drifted away as he spoke.

"Good to see you, Tom," Sodoc said. "We'll talk later." He turned to us. "I take it you two just came down."

"Yes. We arrived as you did," Peer said.

Sodoc scanned us both in more detail. "I see you finally remembered where you left my son," he said to me.

I could scarcely speak. "It looked different," I managed to say.

"Scott needs to go to bed. Any illness at these elevations is dangerous," Peer said in my defense.

"Go," Sodoc said, though from his tone, I took him to mean, "Go to hell." "Derek's body will be here in another day or two." Then he gave me a look I hope never to see again.

～～～

I downed a round of pills, found my tent, and crawled in, but exhausted as I was, sleep did not come. It might have been the daylight pouring in, but it was instead the events of the last three days, the memories they invoked, and the unexpected sight of Sodoc.

The expedition the previous year had set out with great fanfare amid high expectations. Our approach trek had more closely resembled a Mardi Gras procession than anything associated with serious mountaineering. Sherpa living along the route had turned out in droves to observe the spectacle. The international media had clustered at Phakding, from where we set out on foot, to cover the gala.

Tarja had secured a contract with a bridal magazine and, for several days, posed for glamour shots: the woman who'd landed the world's most eligible bachelor. Even after our departure, camera crews remained with us nearly to Base Camp. Tarja basked in the attention, clinging to Derek's side whenever the cameras were directed at him.

It might have been a traveling circus, but this was to be Derek Sodoc's conquest of the last of the Seven Summits. No expense was spared to make certain that it would not only succeed, but would be accomplished with worldwide acclaim and a certain style. I was, frankly, delighted to be a part of it. I'd never climbed in the Himalayas before and, in my ignorance, was utterly unprepared for the reality we were all soon to face. I actually believed that with advanced weather reporting, state-of-the-art communications and climbing equipment, and the knowledge we'd gained from so many decades here that we would not face any obstacle we could not overcome.

It was a delightful spring in the foothills. Every bit of arable land was terraced and under cultivation. Strings of prayer flags stretched across the hillsides. Dirty-faced children ran laughing to see us, hands extended. At each pass, we encountered walls of carved stone standing sentinel. The trek was only marred by the abject poverty and filth we saw in the villages and settlements along the route.

Tarja and Derek had been married just four months and they were in the transition from honeymoon to reality. It was no rockier, but not easier, than others I'd witnessed. Occasionally, I saw them off to themselves and the conversations were intense. Tarja didn't seem to be getting her way about something.

It was good to see Calvin again. I made no mention of Maria Sabato, though this was the first time we'd seen each other since her death the year before. Crystal was younger that season, more lively and fun loving. I didn't recall that she drank much at all. Covering Derek Sodoc's summit triumph was a tremendous opportunity for her and for Rusty, and they both took it very seriously. With digital cameras, sat phones, and uplinks, this was a new kind of reporting and they were inventing the rules as they went along.

There was no reporter with the expedition on that climb; Derek did his own reporting and voiceovers. Because his equipment was digital and lacked the restriction imposed by carrying so much film, Rusty shot hours every day. I'd see him and Crystal at night, their media tent aglow in the darkness, poring over what Hollywood would call the dailies, deleting scenes they wouldn't need or hadn't worked. By the time we reached Base Camp, they were uploading pieces daily, usually featuring an interview with the intrepid Derek Sodoc.

Peer, I learned, had come along for his appeal to the European audience. He was a virtual rock star there and had been well paid to serve as Derek's assistant. He was unchanged since then, a skilled mountaineer, a bit full of himself, but not unpleasantly so, a good companion. There'd been no snake like Stern to spoil our lovely garden.

As expedition doctor, Calvin was very busy; that expedition had been considerably larger than was this one. I'd gotten to know Dawa quite well and hoped to have him as my guide above Base Camp.

I was undecided just how far up the mountain I'd go. I was reasonably certain I'd spend at least a night at Advanced Base Camp at 21,300 feet. It was possible that I'd make a day hike up to Camp Three at 24,400 feet, which would be the highest point I'd ever climbed, but if so, I was certain I'd come back down the same day. My attitude was to wait and see.

Each day of the approach, Everest loomed nearer and a sense of excitement and expectation pervaded the expedition. All eyes turned to the massive pyramid towering above us and a sensation that I can only describe as a sort of fever began to consume us. As we neared Base Camp, every climber was talking as if summiting was in the cards. I was no different.

Reggie was as amiable as ever. This was, I learned, his fifth season as an Everest guide. The tragedy in his past, I heard, had been the death of his oldest daughter when climbing with him in New Zealand. He'd never fully recovered. He had taken lessons from the 1996 disaster and the many deaths since very much to heart. Reggie considered it his mission to get those who were to summit up and down alive and in one piece. The plan I heard was for Tarja and Derek to summit together, but that changed later on.

Gyurme was head of the Sherpa. He was much like Zhiku, which I suppose is no surprise. Sherpa respond to a certain style of leadership and prerequisite climbing skill so their leaders would logically be similar. He did an efficient job and his subsequent death in the Ice Flow came as a great shock to everyone, though it was a place where skill and experience counted for very little. The Sherpa believed that the gods decided who lived and who died. I didn't believe that yet.

Gyurme was, of course, only the first of many deaths that deadly year. I don't like speaking poorly of the dead and the truth is that, for all his faults, I liked Derek very much. He was, in most ways, more a man's man than one on whom a woman could depend. Women served one purpose in his life and—except for climbing mountains—the conquest of every reasonably attractive female within striking distance was his relentless goal. This could be seen as sad—even tragic—but he accepted the occasional reproof with such good humor and self-depreciation, while not crowing at his triumphs, that from a man's perspective, it all seemed harmless enough. The women certainly didn't seem to mind, having acquired bragging rights. In fact, watching events unfold, I was often confused about who was pursuing whom.

I observed his reasonably discreet liaisons from the time I arrived. Initially, I'd been shocked that a man so recently wed—and to such a beauty—would engage in such behavior, but I've also seen it in other men. For some, marriage and the prospect of cheating is an enormous aphrodisiac; I suspected that was the case here. I'd not recalled him being quite so randy in South America, but he'd been preoccupied with Maria and we'd not been there long.

It had started, I thought, with the Italian expedition that advanced to Base Camp with us. I dismissed the incident initially because the woman had been aggressive in going after him and, to my knowledge, it was just that one night. Only later did I learn that he and Crystal had resumed their affair in Kathmandu before I arrived, having been heavily involved earlier when he'd gone to New York to plan the filming of the expedition. This had taken place only a month before his sudden marriage to Tarja.

I say "from a man's perspective" because Tarja saw it quite differently, which only stands to reason. I saw the change in her along with the realization. Initially, she'd been unaware what her husband was up to, but eventually his excuses for being absent on the march became transparent. She took to stalking him and finally caught him emerging from a tent, still fastening his trousers.

There'd been a scene. Predictably, she'd gone after the woman first, telling her to leave her husband alone. There'd been a fight, pulling of hair, and things thrown. That woman was part of a Japanese film crew covering the expedition, and the price for peace was Derek telling them that they'd have to turn back. They weren't very happy about it and I imagine that the tryst did the woman's career no good.

The irony was that, from what I'd been told, Tarja had carried on shamelessly in Kathmandu with a French model, leaving little doubt to onlookers about the nature of their relationship. I'd not seen any of it and I didn't assume Derek took exception since I've known men who do not consider women having sex with women to be infidelity. Still, it struck me as odd behavior for a newlywed.

We reached Base Camp without further incident and it was there, at the foot of the Khumbu Glacier, that it began to come apart. The Sherpa blamed the incident with their goddess—but as I say, that was later.

Base Camp was a zoo when we arrived. More than a dozen major expeditions were already in place and at least three dozen smaller ones were as well. We paraded through camp and set up our tents on the side closest to the Ice Flow, one that had been previously marked and held for us.

Those first days were a media frenzy, as everyone wanted a photograph with the great Derek Sodoc and he was generally agreeable. There were a fair number of young, fit women so Tarja stayed very close to him, as if tethered to his side, a role I'm certain was new and humiliating. The SNS crew filmed pieces for a daily feed and stored others to be used in upcoming shows. It was a busy schedule unrelated to climbing the mountain.

While this was going on, Reggie set about moving supplies to the staging camps and had an acclimatization schedule for us all to follow. It went reasonably well, the only unsettled event being Gyurme's death the third day after we arrived. An earlier Korean expedition had already cleared the passageway through the Ice Flow, but it remained as dangerous as ever. That day, we were moving supplies to Camp One and he'd been caught in an avalanche and killed. Tsongba, the second in command of the Sherpa, took over and it seemed to me that the transition was seamless.

The primary problem faced by the Sodoc expedition was obvious—even for an Everest novice such as myself. There were too many climbers for just one route up—and a limited window of opportunity. Derek was the richest, the most famous, and he was committed to getting to the summit. Everyone knew it—and nobody not connected to our expedition cared. They wanted to summit as well. For many of the climbers with the smaller expeditions, this was a once-in-a-lifetime opportunity. They would not be back—whether they succeeded or not. Those climbers who'd paid the big expeditions expected to summit and the expedition leaders knew that future clients depended on achieving success. No one was going to step aside for Derek—no matter how rich or famous he was.

Reggie met with the expedition leaders to work out a schedule, but for the most part, it wasn't followed. Teams would agree to one thing, and then decide to do something else based on their own changed circumstances or the weather. The situation caused some consternation, but in the end, we just bullied our way up, making no friends in the process. Since we controlled SNS coverage of the climb, the world saw the face that Crystal elected to present.

The real trouble began after Derek and Calvin had been to ABC for a night. We'd had a brief period of recurring inclement fronts followed by glorious summit weather and a number of climbers scurried to move up the mountain while they could.

Our situation was a bit more complicated, since summiting wasn't our only concern. Crystal and Rusty were filming for more than one show. The ratings were high for the news programs and they were under constant pressure to produce more clips. No one had ever filmed so extensively at such extreme altitudes and they struggled with the logistics of the challenge as well as the demands of New York producers.

It was now that our next bit of bad luck struck. A Sherpa named Phurba came down with HACE while at Camp Three. From ABC, Calvin gave orders by radio. The Sherpa was placed in a sleeping bag; a dozen Sherpa carried and slid him in the dark to ABC, where Calvin was waiting to administer drugs. At dawn, the same dozen men struggled to return him to Base Camp, an effort that took the entire day. The effort delayed any summit attempt and we had angry calls from New York. Derek decided to return to Base Camp. Phurba, fortunately, recovered over the next few days.

On his return from ABC, in the relatively rich air of Base Camp, Derek was feeling his oats. I've described the Sherpa women, but there are exceptions. One was tending the herd of yak that grew with each new expedition. Bright faced and smiling, she had given her favors to more than one man on the trek. She expected a gift for time spent with her, but to describe her as the camp whore would be going too far. She was just free with herself and expected to be paid for what the men wanted.

After dinner, Derek excused himself to use one of the portable potties and was gone perhaps one minute longer than Tarja thought he should be. She stalked off after him.

Derek wasn't being very subtle. He'd gone to the Sherpa woman; she'd dropped her drawers and bent over as he humped away, getting what we called a "quickie" in college. They were scarcely concealed by the yak and a boulder. Tarja caught him at the moment of orgasm.

Derek tried to laugh it off, but Tarja was furious. I think that the last straw for her wasn't this latest infidelity, recurring as it was, but rather his cheating with what she called a "stinking, filthy little gook." If he'd jumped another Westerner, they would have had a fight, but she'd have accepted it. This was unthinkable and intolerable. He'd demeaned her in everyone's eyes.

I saw Peer ducking into her tent an hour later.

They had been lovers during her days as an Alpine competitor. For both of them it had been as casual as sex can ever be, and I'll say this for Peer: he respected her status as a married woman until Tarja invited him to her sleeping bag. He'd never even hinted that he'd known Tarja previously—let alone the fact that they had been lovers.

It was one thing for the great Derek Sodoc to screw anything that moved. Such behavior in a handsome, young, wealthy, famous man was expected. It was quite another to be publicly cuckolded. Word spread across Base Camp within moments and you could tell by the way that others looked at Derek that something profound had taken place.

I don't believe anything like this had ever happened to him before— at least not publicly. When it came to women, he set the rules; they played the game and took the penalties. I had only to recall Maria to know that. This was very different and you could see the effect it had on him. Tarja was his wife. Had she screwed Peer on a public beach, her behavior could not have been more brazen.

I don't know what I expected—a fistfight, an argument, or Tarja sporting a black eye like some Italian bride. What happened was nothing. Derek sulked. He used another tent without comment while Peer spent as much time with Tarja as his schedule permitted. As for her, she behaved as if nothing of importance was taking place—and perhaps to her it was not.

A few days later, Crystal and Derek resumed their affair.

The mountain gods passed judgment, my Sherpa friends would say, and decided that the good days were behind us. Now we experienced equipment failures, increasing bouts of illness, and scheduling difficulties with New York. Derek wasn't his consummate self on camera and I heard his father had called on the sat phone to express concern over the quality of the programming coming from the mountain.

The weather also turned erratic. The other expeditions, with schedules and concerns of their own or perhaps wanting to escape what was clearly our bad karma, set out in spurts, depending on circumstances, and Reggie was faced with the increasingly daunting task of putting Derek on top of the world—ideally during East Coast prime time.

As first one expedition summited, then another, the pressure grew. The spotlight would only shine with sufficient intensity for so long—then it would of necessity play elsewhere. Derek had to get to the top as quickly as possible.

Despite the considerable difficulties and the sheer logistics of moving not only what was needed to sustain a summit push but to record and transmit that effort from such a remote and forbidding location, Reggie pulled it off. As it developed, two of the major expeditions summited before us and, though this was unwelcome news in New York as there'd been some talk of us being the first up that season, it had the effect of temporarily clearing the route for a few days—except for several small teams that presented only situational problems at choke points.

I don't know the story behind what followed. I know what I saw and can only report what I heard, speculate, or surmise the rest. It may well be that Tarja insisted on summiting with Derek as the original plan called for—or perhaps Derek offered it as an inducement sop. She was still clearly interested in pursuing a career and this would be as important to her as it was to him. Perhaps there were other considerations. I simply don't know. What I do know is that the couple set out together for Advanced Base Camp with fanfare. Their departure was covered live during a special half-hour report following the SNS Evening News. I'm sure it made for great theater.

I followed, joined by Calvin and a Sherpa carrying supplies, with a diminished sense of excitement and a bit of foreboding. Everything that had gone so perfectly for so long was now going very wrong—and you didn't have to be a Sherpa to see it. You couldn't help but feel that bad things were yet to happen. On Everest, that meant death.

The acclimatization climbs were behind everyone hoping to summit or be of assistance at the high camps, so the only delays from here on came about from weather or logistics. That first afternoon at ABC, Reggie called a meeting before dusk to plan the push up the mountain. Derek and Tarja were to be the principal climbers on what was now designated as Team One. They would be accompanied by Tsongba, Reggie, Rusty, and two of the experienced climbing Sherpa—one of whom would carry recording equipment. Crystal was to remain at ABC to monitor the video coming in and to provide the uplinks to New York.

We were not as connected as we would be the following year. Each of us was wired so we could speak to one another, send reports, and call for help. But there were no head-mounted, miniature cameras. Filming the summit attempt was up to Rusty.

Originally, Peer was to be with Team One. Though he'd never summited, he was easily the most able mountaineer on the expedition and his participation assured good European ratings. This was taking place at a time when SNS was engaged in a major expansion in the European Union.

Derek, understandably, vetoed Peer's participation. There was an ugly scene in the media tent over this and Reggie eventually brokered a compromise. Peer would climb with Dawa, Dorji, and me on Team Two. The two teams would climb as separate efforts, though we would set out together each climbing day. From the editing room, a single cohesive team would emerge.

Reggie took me aside to be certain that I understood my role. "I know you want to summit," he said. "Everyone does. But you're going up to help Derek. You can join him if circumstances allow, but I'm depending on you to take care of your friend. We need someone to go with Peer so that what is really going on isn't so apparent. You all need to stay close together to give mutual support. I don't need to tell you that Derek's distracted right now. He's under enormous pressure to do this and I don't trust his judgment. I've seen you in crises before and know I can depend on you."

I told him he could. So it was that I was placed in position to summit. I wanted to, obviously—we all did—but with the difficulties we'd encountered these final days, it had looked less likely. Now I was to be on the summit party and was very pleased when I heard that Dawa would climb with me.

That night, Tarja and Derek had a bitter argument. We were not yet on oxygen and it left them gasping and coughing, but it was clear that there'd be no mutual summit by the formerly happy couple. Reggie met with Peer and me later and told us that Tarja would be returning to Base Camp the next morning.

I admit that none of these theatrics meant much to me. I was consumed with the idea of standing on top of the world. I never expected to be in this position again and intended to make the most of it. As the enormous mountain loomed ever closer, we'd talked of nothing else. Though I'd spent a day at ABC and an afternoon at Camp Three to jumpstart my cell production, that night was very difficult and I hardly slept at all. My head ached as if a nail had been driven into it and I could scarcely control the constant cough from which we all suffered. The wind beat against our tent, creating a drumming sound that made it difficult enough, but most of all was the sensation of suffocating. I'd manage to drop off—only to suddenly come awake convinced I was being smothered.

The next morning was cold. We stood with our backs to the wind like cattle in a storm. The intrepid Rusty had his camera out, recording preparations for the climb to Camp Four. Derek was distracted and unhappy. Crystal was putting her best foot forward—clearly torn between personal loyalty to Derek and her commitment to her job. Even Peer was uncharacteristically distant.

The plan called for Calvin to remain at this camp. As we returned from summit day, he would move up to Camp Four to meet us and provide such medical care as was required. He was checking with each of us to be certain of our final condition, administering pills and words of caution.

The Sherpa distributed breakfast as we buttoned up our high-altitude jumpsuits and rigged our gear. I saw Crystal exchange words with Tarja and then stomp over to talk to Reggie who just grimaced at whatever news she brought.

The sky was a vast canvas of dismal gray. The stiff wind was heavy with moisture gusting up from the canyons below. Clouds and blankets of mist filled the sky below us and it seemed that we were in our own bleak mountain kingdom, cut off from the greater world.

Derek gave an on-camera interview, but conditions weren't suitable and Crystal cut it short. It was just as well. He'd seemed off of his game to me. If I didn't know him better, I'd have said I detected fear in his manner. A few moments later, without his signature jaunty wave, he set out with Team One. Peer joined me with Dorji and Dawa. We gave them a ten-minute head start to diminish the likelihood of delays above and then set out ourselves.

As we did, Tarja joined us. Since it wasn't my place to get involved, I said nothing. No one else spoke to her and Peer appeared unsurprised. He led the way, setting a brutal pace for all of us.

The ice was uncommonly slick and the going was treacherous. As I've said, a line now stretched from Base Camp to the summit. Every hundred feet or so, it was secured; at those points, it was necessary for us to disconnect and then reconnect to the next line. These were potentially deadly moments—if we slipped, we would fall or tumble to our all-but-certain death. At sea level—perhaps in the specialty shop where such equipment is bought—disconnecting and reconnecting is, literally, a snap. Here, in freezing conditions, with a stiff wind and numbed gloved hands, it was often difficult and took as long as a minute. Even then, climbers occasionally missed the line and moved on, believing they were secured when they were not. More than one paid with his or her life as a result.

This was very different from traditional climbing in which each climber was fixed to the others. Before hooking yourself to a stranger, you made certain that he or she was not a dead weight and knew how to climb. If a climber fell, it was possible to take the entire string with them to their deaths. This need to trust one another created the bond that every climber feels for every other. We all needed and relied on each other.

On Everest, there was none of that. It didn't matter if another climber was skilled or not. It had no effect on you. Everyone connected to—and trusted—the all-important line. The result was an attitude of every man for himself—an emotional distance from other climbers that is alien to traditional climbing.

Reminders of our peril lay all along our route. Several times, we passed bodies lying on the ice, some dating back more than twenty years and others as recent as the previous season. I read an article once describing American pilots in World War II. Upon being briefed about the heavy casualties anticipated in that day's raid, each man had looked at the other and thought, *You poor son-of-a-bitch.* So it was for us. Despite the death all around us, no one believed he or she would die.

I was the least skilled of those moving up that day, though I was by now no slouch at this. We made steady—if exhausting—progress.

My lungs burned and I had to force myself to keep hydrated—as we all did—but for Everest, in such conditions, it was a good climbing day. I'd hear an occasional word from someone in my ear, but more often just the heavy breathing or coughing of a climber. No one wasted effort on speech.

We moved through Camp Three, taking time only for the hot tea a Sherpa assigned there for that purpose gave us. No one spoke to or about Tarja. None of us had much to say about anything. We set out twenty minutes after arriving. Despite the wind and cold, we arrived at Camp Four on the South Col on schedule, never having caught up with Team One.

The scene awaiting us was unpleasant. Reggie confronted Tarja before she set foot in the camp. With the gusting wind, I couldn't hear the conversation, but it was obvious enough. She wasn't welcome. Her attempt to stomp off in anger was muted by conditions.

We hunkered down for the rest of daylight—Derek on one side with Rusty, Tarja on the other with Peer—all of us coughing and feeling sorry for ourselves. I was too numb and exhausted to appreciate how awkward it was. Reggie spent time on the sat phone and then announced that the wind was expected to die down overnight. That was the good news. The bad news was an approaching front—though it was not anticipated to reach the summit for another seventy-two hours. That gave us just enough time to get up and down.

Camp Four is a bitter, lonely place. If until this point you've managed to disregard the enormity of what you are about to attempt, it comes home here. I could count with no great effort three bodies around us. One of them lay partially exposed in his abandoned tent—not fifteen feet from where we sat. The camp is on a slope with no cover, so we were fully exposed to the wind. On two sides, the ground dropped off precipitously after only a few feet. It was like sheltering on the edge of a knife.

Even for the great Derek Sodoc, there was no help at Camp Four. We were at the beginning of the Death Zone and here we all saw to our own needs. Dawa and I prepared our tea and meal together, huddled in our tent. Tarja and Peer spent the night together. We slept on oxygen and what little sleep we managed was the last until the push to the top was over.

It was, as predicted, less windy that night. The next morning was not as cold as the day before. With that dawn, we were all but on summit day. We would move up to Camp Five, spend a few hours resting as we breathed oxygen, perhaps nodding off in tents prepared for us and then set out at midnight for the summit. We were scheduled to return to this spot in about thirty hours.

I heard Calvin talking to Derek, futilely arguing that he should descend, that he wasn't in shape for the big push. Calvin, of course, was right. We all knew that soon enough.

I was surprised when an angry—but resigned—Tarja prepared to descend as we gathered our gear to move up. Somehow I'd imagined her bullying her way up with us. I asked Dawa about it. "No Sherpa for her," he said. "If she goes up, she goes alone. She knows she cannot do it. She go down today. It is best. Women here no good. Just trouble."

Before setting out, Tarja spoke to Peer at some length. He glanced at Derek on the other side of the camp and then nodded his head in comprehension. Tarja set out alone for Advanced Base Camp. A Sherpa should have been with her—as was the practice at such elevations—but we had none to spare. No camera recorded her departure. As I prepared to leave, I paused and looked after her, wondering for a moment if she'd die attempting her solitary return to Advanced Base Camp.

EIGHTEEN

You can be rich and famous, handsome as well, and have all the breaks in life. But on Everest, you're just another climber and when it's your time, there's nothing to be done about it— especially when so-called friends, those sycophants and hangers-on who've put you in this predicament, turn their backs and leave you to die.
    —Quentin Stern, www.AbandonedonEverest.com

We set out as two teams, but before long, formed a single straggling line up the mountain.

To describe the next hours is only to be repetitive. We were on oxygen, but it was more of the same agony: two steps, stop, breathe, two more steps. Climbing in the Death Zone—even with oxygen—is more about overcoming misery than it is athletic accomplishment.

Derek was easily visible in his orange jumpsuit and I could see he was laboring. Rusty, even with a camera, had the better of it and was able to stand aside to film a bit and then still manage to catch up with Derek. Reggie, it seemed to me, was shepherding Derek, double-checking his line connection, and offering encouragement.

Still, we moved steadily—if more slowly—than we'd planned and, by mid-afternoon, arrived at Camp Five. This was no more than a layover before the midnight departure for the summit. Reggie used a sat phone to report our status and check the weather. We clustered with him afterward. He shouted to be heard.

"The front is moving as predicted. It's due tomorrow night. Everyone needs to be back in Camp Four before nightfall tomorrow. Understand?"

We did. I glanced at Derek and did not like what I saw. He looked distant and in pain, but Reggie knew better than I did and Derek was primarily his responsibility. That's what I told myself.

"Let's turn in and get some nourishment. Try to sleep. We set out at midnight."

Reggie joined Derek in a tent. Tsongba was with Rusty. Two Sherpa whose names I never learned shared a tent as did Dawa and Dorji. We'd killed our oxygen getting here, but like babies suckling from their bottles, we all settled in with a fresh one to last until we set out in a few hours. I can't say it was pleasant lying in that weather-beaten tent, but compared to every alternative, I wanted nothing so much as to breathe that oxygen and do nothing.

I didn't sleep. I doubt any of us did—except perhaps the Sherpa. I managed to drink a bit of water, but food was beyond me. Peer was unusually distant and I wondered if he was injured in some way. He'd never been this high before and such an altitude can have unexpected consequences for even the most seasoned climber. I asked, but he replied with a dismissive snort.

When leaving home, I'd never expected to be in this position, but here I was a half-day's climb from the summit. It was intoxicating. The plan was now quite simple. The long weeks since leaving Phakding were all directed toward the next few hours.

But that was not why we were here. The objective was to get Derek to the top from where he was to broadcast to the world, the first such live broadcast from Everest. Everything was in place to make it possible. The only obstacles were the weather, which we were assured was cooperating, ourselves—and the mountain gods.

At midnight that last day, the camp began to stir. With great effort, I crawled from the tent and assembled my gear. We all wore headlamps and I was first reminded of miners. The wind had stopped at last and, though it was cold, it was not the bitter, numbing cold we'd experienced previously. Peer and the Sherpa were soon ready, followed by me. Reggie was delayed, working with Derek, who was coughing repeatedly. Finally, he turned to us.

"You go on ahead. No one's been up this far for several days and there was a violent storm here since. Check the lines and make certain they are secured. Peer, lay new line if necessary, and clear the route if needed. We'll follow in a bit." I then saw him remove a sealed syringe of dexamethasone, which I assumed he was going to inject into Derek. Rusty, I saw, was not filming.

Peer, Dawa Dorji, and I set out. Dawa, after Tsongba—the most experienced climber with us—was matched to me, the least experienced on Team Two. Dorji, new to summiting, but otherwise quite skilled, was paired to Peer, the most accomplished climber of the group. Team One followed perhaps half an hour later.

To describe it in this way strips the expedition of all the excitement with which the viewing audience saw it. This was the culmination of a massive media event. Anyone in the world in contact with a television or who surfed the Internet had at least some exposure to what was taking place. Rusty was filming at every opportunity. Crystal was picking it up, giving it a rough edit, and then sending it on. In some cases, entire segments went directly to New York. They filed breathless reports every few minutes. Anyone following it moment by moment—and millions around the world did—would have thought that no one had ever set foot on the top of Everest before.

As for myself, my lamp focused my attention on the splash of light before me, while the surrounding darkness masked the abyss on either side. Even with oxygen, in the thin atmosphere, my mind was no longer properly functioning and I didn't know enough to be terrified. I placed each foot in front of me, one after the other, paused to breathe, and then placed them again. I paid no attention to time. I simply repeated the process again and again until Peer drew up, and said, "We are on the balcony."

I stopped and, a moment later, heard Reggie in my ear. "Good job."

At 27,600 feet, the Balcony offers a commanding view of the highest peaks in the world. Most of the extraordinary photographs you've seen from Everest have been taken from this spot. We saw nothing in the blackness. I turned to look back and could see the bobbing lights of the others below—much farther back than I'd expected. They scarcely seemed to move.

"What do we do?" I asked.

Peer said nothing. He just set out along the narrow ridge toward the South Summit.

⸺⸺⸺

The rising sun found us on the Southeast Ridge. When I reached up to turn off my light, I took a moment to look behind us. If anything, Team One was farther back than they'd been earlier. In the middle, I could see the orange jumpsuit scarcely seeming to move. Reggie had made no mention of trouble, but he wouldn't. Though scrambled to outsiders, our communication was not secure.

The sun brought a welcome increase in temperature. Though my effort since setting out had been demanding, I'd been cold all morning. Now the feeling slowly returned to my feet, hands, and cheeks.

The Southeast Ridge stands at 27,800 feet and is fully exposed on both sides. Nepal was to our left, the barren brown plain of Tibet to our right. There was nothing here to diminish even the slightest breeze and climbers have been blown from this ridge routinely, but at first light, the air was dead calm.

I continued my steady unthinking pace of placing each boot in front of the other, pausing to breathe, and repeating the process. I wasted no effort in worry or concern for what would happen next. All that mattered was that I kept moving. In my ear, I heard breathing and the occasional grunt. No one spoke needlessly. No one had the energy. Every part of me—every cell in my weary body—screamed for me to turn back, but that was a voice I'd learned to ignore, if not silence.

By early morning, we were at the South Summit. Again we stopped and I took the occasion to look back along the route. Through thin clouds and a light mist below, I could see the West Ridge to Pumori and, further across, Cho Oyu—a white peak and the world's sixth-highest mountain. I tried, but from here I couldn't see Team One. I removed my mask and pushed the microphone out of the way.

Without that sweet flow of oxygen, I felt as if I was suffocating. I leaned over toward Peer. "Where are they?"

He shook his head and then, into his microphone, I heard him say, "We're at the South Summit. Shall we wait or press on?"

After a minute, I heard Reggie say, "Move up the Step. We don't want a logjam there." His answer suggested that they were right with us, when in fact they were more than an hour behind.

"We'll meet up on the shelf for the final push," Peer said generously. Once above Hillary Step, I couldn't reasonably see us standing around for long. Every step we took up the mountain made it less likely that we'd be of any help to anyone on Team One. The one justification for our continuing was to clear the route, but so far—except for a powdering of snow—there'd been nothing for Peer to do in that regard. I returned my mask and we stood resting a few moments before setting out.

It was a short distance to the Step where Peer took the lead for the climb. The line was still in place and secure. He fixed his ascender, set his crampons, and then moved up the rock steadily, followed by Dorji and me; Dawa brought up the rear.

I moved with much greater effort than Peer—my crampons slipping on exposed rock more than once—but I steeled myself and concentrated on each movement to get me to the top, where Peer reached down, grabbed my suit, and helped me onto the shelf.

I was exhausted, but I experienced a sensation of triumph inside. I was going to climb Everest. Some part of me shouted in elation. My life would be changed permanently and for the good. Nothing stood between me and the top of the world except the traverse and the short Summit Ridge. In these conditions, I'd be on the peak in an hour or less.

⌐⌐⌐

Our situation was not critical, but remaining stationary was not an option. Maintaining your core body temperature on Everest depends on movement. Stand still long enough and you freeze solid, literally.

We remained in the sun and sheltered as much as we could from what was now a steady wind. Peer called down to Reggie, speaking with great diplomacy, but conveying our reality. We couldn't just wait for them. We needed some sense of when Team One would reach us. We could see them well below, moving at a snail's pace.

Finally, he came to me, removed his mask, and pushed the microphone aside. "I'm going up. I suggest you come with me or start back down. We can't stay here any longer. Something is very wrong with them. They are two or three hours behind us."

I had no thought of descending. I nodded and pointed toward the traverse, indicating my desire to climb. We four set out.

The traverse is a treacherous passageway along the side of the mountain. It is quite steep and the footing is awkward, but the path is well marked and over the decades has been improved. There is also that ubiquitous line on which we all depended for our lives. In good conditions, the passage is not especially demanding, but in certain situations, it can be lethal. There is no mercy if you slip and are not hooked to the line or the line gives way when you fall.

We carefully made our way across the traverse and in half an hour I found myself on the Summit Ridge. I knew from what others had said that you could not actually see the summit from here as a rise obscures the view, but I also knew nothing stood between me and Everest but a half hour hike.

Peer didn't stop long. "I'm going on," he said. "I'm not waiting."

I couldn't blame him. We were no help to Team One here and he'd never summited. His chance was before him and he was going to take it. We, on the other hand, were committed to helping Derek and had a duty to wait. I watched him set out toward the summit.

We gave it fifteen minutes. I called down, but Reggie was no more assuring than he'd been to Peer. After the second call, Dawa leaned toward me and said, "Dorji must summit, Scott. It is important."

There it was. Dorji's career as a guide depended on reaching the top. It was looking increasingly as if something was very wrong with Team One and it was unlikely that they'd summit today. I wasn't even convinced that they'd tackle the Step. I didn't want to refuse the young Sherpa his chance and I didn't want to be left alone.

"We're heading up," I said into my microphone. "We'll meet up on the descent."

As I told Diana, it was crap. Right now, relatively speaking, I was in pretty good shape, but I'd be stretched when coming down. I'd seen other climbers at the end of summit day. They looked like death warmed over. The truth wasn't that I wanted to help Dorji or that I was all that frightened at being left alone on the Summit Ridge. The truth was that I wanted to climb Everest.

We turned away from the traverse and started up the final steps to the summit. I glanced back only once. In the valley beneath us, I could see heavy clouds that had not been there earlier, but I gave them no thought. What was really important was just ahead.

Two regularly used routes lead to the summit. We were approaching from the more popular—the one leading out of Nepal that Hillary and Tenzing had taken to conquer the mountain. The other, more technically challenging route leads from the China side. That approach is every bit as deadly as the one we climbed, perhaps more so.

Despite that, in recent years, it has been taken more and more frequently. For the 2008 Olympics, with all of the tourism that went with it and followed, the Chinese government pushed a paved road through Tibet to its Base Camp. It was meant to be a moneymaker for the country and to assist in the further destruction of Tibetan society.

I was not entirely surprised as we passed over the final rise to spy a small crowd of brightly colored climbers on the summit mound, flags fluttering in the stiff wind, climbers posing for photographs, masks and goggles thrust aside, wide grins on many faces. Among them was Peer.

Spotting us, he waved us over and said, "Glad to see you. Come join the party."

And party it seemed to be. There were perhaps twenty climbers on and about the summit—most of them Asian, but with a smattering of Europeans. I learned later that the teams were from Japan, Korea, and France. For all the smiles and elation, everyone—even Peer—looked exhausted. Some were sitting, while others angled to get their photographs taken on top. They held flags in front of them or on aluminum poles, photographs of loved ones, climbing club banners—even corporate logos. Different things were important to different people. On the ground were scattered the remains of other expeditions, now discarded. Something about the scene was eerie and not quite right.

The one presence the summit fortunately lacked was the dead. They had dotted our passage to this highest point on earth, been clustered—seen and unseen—about our campsites, and scattered along the route, but here were no bodies. I was unaware of anyone actually dying on the summit itself. No matter how tired, no matter how late in the day, every climber at least made the attempt to descend. It was then that they perished if they'd managed to reach the summit without dying. In a childlike stupor, numb from the cold, exhausted, the last of their reserves spent, they walked off a precipice or more likely sat, then lay, in the snow until dead.

We'd done well; it was just noon. The sky directly above was a vast canopy of pale azure common to high altitudes. The sun was extraordinarily bright, intense even through my protecting goggles. I scanned the horizon, attempting to take it all in, and storing memories for later. The view was all I could have imagined.

I removed my camera and handed it to Peer, uncertain if Dawa knew how to take a photograph. The Norwegian grinned and gestured me toward the crowded top. There I took my place, all but leaning against a grinning team having its photograph taken. I removed my mask and lifted my goggles for the picture, squinting against the harsh light, then quickly put them back on when Peer signaled that he was finished. I'd felt myself suffocating without oxygen and, absent the goggles, I'd suffer from snow blindness in a very short period of time. Some of the other climbers foolishly had their goggles off and, in a few hours, would have to be led down the mountain like blind men.

"You take our picture, Scott," Dawa asked. I snapped several of our Sherpas. Dorji was elated, grinning like a schoolboy. As I put the camera away, I spotted Peer not far away, waving jauntily as he set out alone. He'd not said goodbye. Perhaps he understood that we weren't ready to leave just yet and he'd been on top long enough.

You don't really rest on the summit—not even when breathing oxygen—so it's difficult to convey why we lingered. It was the culmination of all these miserable weeks, a crowning achievement for every man and woman here. For Dorji, it meant a new and more profitable future; for me, it would be a photograph on the wall and modest bragging rights. None of us wanted to let go. We all were experiencing a rush of elation—and we knew that only half the effort was over. We still had to get down and, in many ways, descending is just as arduous—and more dangerous—than climbing. No one was in a hurry to get started on that leg.

We joined in the celebration of others, watched a few climbers depart, and greeted an arriving group from Turkey. I took cameras and snapped photographs for others. But the longer I remained, the more difficult it was for me to think rationally. Dangers seemed remote—the here and now very appealing.

After twenty minutes, Dawa said, "We must go, Scott. Look." He pointed with his arm. The dark clouds of just an hour before were now a boiling black cauldron with flashing lightning. Thunder rolled up the mountain and the chatter about us suddenly stopped. The storm was rising toward us rapidly and we knew we were all in peril.

Climbers immediately began organizing themselves for the descent. Several of them would die over the next few hours; in all, seven from the China side died over a two-day period. We three set out within minutes but had not gone twenty feet before the first snow hit, so fast did the storm move. It was light on first contact, almost benign, but we all knew what was coming.

The storm struck with all its fury well before the traverse. The wind was suddenly peaking in gusts of a hundred miles an hour and I had trouble keeping my balance. My body temperature plummeted and I began to shiver. While I could still see the Sherpa, I saw Dorji actually go down to his knees once from a violent gust. The snow flew across us horizontally, obscuring all vision. We were clipped to the line, but in these conditions, moved cautiously forward. I wondered how we'd handle the traverse in this wind.

At the first change from one line to another, I knew that we were in trouble since the next line was simply gone. It had been there on the ascent, but it had vanished in this furious storm. Dorji and Dawa were leading the way and I stumbled on them searching on their hands and knees in the snow for the line. Finally, Dawa stood up and leaned against me to speak. "The line is gone, Scott. We must be very careful."

I tried to recall how many links of line there'd been from the traverse to the summit, but couldn't in my childlike state. Several, it seemed. We pressed forward, anticipating that we'd pick up the line at the next point where it was secured about a hundred feet away.

But we didn't. I don't know if the line was gone or we simply couldn't find it in the whiteout.

Now, perhaps half an hour from the summit, we were all but lost. Only the steep slope on both sides kept us on the Summit Ridge and moving in the right direction. Still, small as the ridge was, in such a blinding storm and in such conditions, it was a big place. Rusty later told me that he passed me there. I have no recollection of it, but I believe him.

Half an hour later, we were in very serious trouble. We'd not found a line. Worse, in our confused state, we'd not thought to hook to one another—a safety precaution that should have been instinctive. I was confused and uncertain. The sense I had, dim as it was, was that I was in great peril and that every step I took increased that peril. *I should stop moving*, I thought.

That was nonsense, of course. If I stopped, I'd die. It was the easy thing to do—and the deadliest.

I lost sight of Dawa and Dorji. It was not difficult in those conditions. If they veered slightly left and I lost sight of them for just a moment and veered slightly to the right, I could lose them for good. Something like that happened. We were probably no more than twenty feet from one another, but we were blind.

You cannot imagine the sense of aloneness in such a situation. I was by myself on the far side of the moon. I've never been more isolated or vulnerable in my life. I stopped and considered what to do. It was all but impossible to clear my mind. For the first time since leaving Base Camp, I had no line to follow. I was utterly on my own—without even the help of the two Sherpa.

I felt a sensation on my shoulder and turned. It was Dawa. "My radio is not working," he shouted. "I cannot see Dorji. I must find him."

I'd been worried about the radios in these conditions. The batteries were tested for cold weather, but we'd had some question if they could continue functioning in the extreme cold of the summit or if the weather turned for the worse. The snow had a tendency to block transmitting and receiving as well. I'd not heard a voice in my ear for some time and my efforts at broadcasting had not been answered.

Now, logic dictated that I tell Dawa not to be a fool. For every dead climber on Everest, there is at least one dead would-be rescuer. The Sherpa are supermen, but they are not invulnerable. As many of them have died up there as all the rest. I should have discouraged him, but I did not. I wasn't thinking—not the way people think at sea level. I just accepted what he said and wished him luck. In a moment, he vanished into the white.

I turned and realized that I had absolutely no idea where I was.

❧❧❧

Ask every survivor of an Everest disaster his story and you'll get a different version of what happened. You can't even be sure that what you remember is what really happened. Your mind is so numb and your thought processes so impeded that memories as often as not are an illusion. The situation is aggravated by hallucinations and phantom images that become commonplace in the Death Zone.

Much of what happened next is a jumble to me. Trying to recall it in a logical, coherent fashion has always escaped me. As for Team One, for the parts I didn't see myself, I have to rely on Rusty, who was there for part of it, and on Tsongba, the sole survivor, and I heard his story only secondhand. I've often wondered how much he really recalled. He lost both feet and most of his right hand along with his nose.

As I learned, the problem with Team One began even before they left Camp Five. Derek's cough had returned with a vengeance and Reggie tried to talk him into descending, with no luck. Later speculation was that he coughed so hard that he broke a rib—not that unusual on Everest—and that accounted for his great difficulty in climbing.

Worse was his state of mind. I've seen it in others, but can't really describe it. Derek was distant, withdrawn, and not himself, but determined to press on. The shot of dexamethasone helped to get him moving, but the effects wore off.

They moved slowly, falling back steadily. Tsongba finally roped his two Sherpa to Derek, essentially to pull him up the mountain. If true, this was insanity so far from the top. Still, Derek wouldn't quit.

They reached Hillary Step about the time that we summited and managed to get Derek up with great effort and another dex shot. In the process, Reggie injured his hand, possibly breaking bones, which are very brittle in such cold. By the time the entire team was at the shelf, Reggie was a one-armed guide.

They argued, Rusty told me, but Derek would not consider turning back. It was do or die—even though someone surely saw the storm boiling up from below. Derek ordered Rusty to go across the traverse with one of the Sherpa to film him reaching the Summit Ridge. At that point, he'd believed himself just half an hour from triumph. Rusty did as he was told, crossed over, and waited at the Summit Ridge. He never saw the rest of the team again and his radio stopped working. Finally, for reasons I can only guess, he began moving toward the summit—apparently with the intention of climbing the mountain—but nearly as soon as he set out, the storm hit.

What happened behind Rusty was disaster. Reggie, working one-handed, attempted to shepherd Derek across the traverse with Tsongba and the remaining Sherpa assisting. But not long into the effort, the line came loose and the Sherpa fell to his death, while Reggie just barely clung to the rope. With extraordinary effort, Tsongba managed to get Reggie and Derek back to the shelf, where they sought shelter from the storm.

The summit attempt was over. Reggie's hand was swollen and he was in agony. He told Tsongba that he was not certain whether he could get down the Hillary Step, but he refused to leave Derek, whose condition had worsened considerably.

Nothing Reggie or Tsongba could say would budge him. Derek hunkered down against the rock and waited for salvation—or death. It was then that Reggie, whose radio still worked, began broadcasting his distress calls, urging all climbers to return to the shelf and help. I heard one of them.

But before I reached the shelf, much more happened. Peer apparently passed Rusty and the Sherpa in the storm. I don't know if they saw each other. In those conditions, other climbers are nothing more than dark shapes, hardly discernible from the phantasms that mock your peripheral vision.

When Peer reached the traverse, he found the line gone. Undaunted, he made his way across—a superb bit of mountaineering. Peer did not see Reggie or Derek. I don't know if he looked for them. Tsongba had apparently decided to descend for help and to retrieve the oxygen bottles stashed at Camp Five. Reggie and Derek would soon need them—without oxygen, they had no hope of salvation.

Instead, in much worse shape than he realized, Tsongba's body succumbed to the effort and cold at the top of the Step. The Sherpa are spare men with little body fat. When the cold finally overwhelms them, it happens quickly. Peer found him there and, with extraordinary courage, manhandled him down the Step.

Reggie, I can only speculate, at some point moved from Derek, perhaps doing what I later did, seeking to intercept help coming down the mountain.

When I arrived and found Derek by chance, I was unaware that Reggie lay dying only a few feet away. I couldn't have done anything for him, but the thought is disconcerting. I was also unaware that Peer had taken Tsongba down and did not see Rusty and his Sherpa when they reached the top of the Step and descended. Below, they met Peer and Tsongba and helped. Once at Camp Five, the Sherpa bravely volunteered to take oxygen to the shelf. He was never seen again.

The deaths of two Sherpa and the serious injury to a third may seem unusual given their greater acclimatization and stamina at high altitude. In fact, it is not unusual at all. They are desired as guides not just for their physical attributes, but also because they are so unselfish with their lives. Peer, a superman on any mountain as far as I'm concerned, made no offer to carry oxygen back out into the storm. He knew that he'd die in the attempt. But the Sherpa could not leave to their deaths two men that he had vowed to help without doing everything possible—even if it meant his own death.

⌒⌒⌒

I was on the Summit Ridge when I heard Reggie's call for help. I walked ten steps in one direction and realized I was approaching the edge. I retraced my steps and walked the other way to the same end. I then moved at a right angle and, after nearly five minutes, realized that I was going up the mountain. Now I oriented myself, trusting the wind. I made my way down, reaching the traverse some time after Peer had crossed.

The absence of the line terrified me even in my dulled state. The wind was so fierce that I could scarcely stand; I was certain that I'd be blown from the traverse, which even in ideal conditions is treacherous enough. But to remain where I was meant death, so I took that first tentative step toward oblivion. The fall to my left was 4,000 feet.

I moved at a snail's pace, carefully positioning each boot, testing its security before fully applying my weight, then moving my leg to place my other boot. I clung to whatever rock or ice was available to maintain my balance. Several times I nearly fell, the wind gusting so forcefully that it all but lifted me up. I suppose somewhere, at some time, I've done more technically challenging climbing, but I know that never in my life have I been in greater peril than I was in that crossing. One mistake was all it would take.

After what seemed a lifetime, I reached the shelf. When I realized the traverse was truly behind me—that I was on level ground again—I nearly wept in relief. I stood unmoving for some time until the creeping cold compelled me to resume. I moved with the rock, snow, and ice to my right.

I can't say that I was actually searching for Derek. The last broadcast I'd received from Reggie reported that they were on the shelf and the shelf is not that big. I sensed that the line down the Step was more to my left, but that area was exposed and what logic I could muster told me they would be sheltered against the rock so I followed its face. I moved awkwardly, feeling my way as you would in the dark. The wind howled and the snow whipped against me.

I nearly stumbled over Derek. He was a pile of white, partially hidden in a crevasse. I realized that it was a climber and bent down to speak to him. I turned on my light, but in the snow, it only created a white glare that was even worse. I extinguished it and placed my face against his.

I was looking at death. Derek's eyes were black, luminous pools. Ice was encrusted across his face in a horrid mask. At some point, he'd foolishly removed his right glove and the wind had stripped it away. Now his forearm and hand were extended awkwardly away from his body, frozen in place. I checked his regulator and saw that he was still receiving a flow of oxygen. It was about three in the afternoon and we each had two hours of oxygen to go. I couldn't tell if he was breathing. In fact, I couldn't tell if he was alive. I shouted repeatedly, but he didn't answer.

Finally, at last, he blinked his eyes once.

Drama was occurring near me, but I saw and knew of none of it. Reggie was dying. Rusty and his Sherpa managed the traverse after me, descending while I was with Derek, but I never saw them. All I could see was the blinding snow; all I could hear was the raging wind. I knew Dawa, Dorji, Rusty, and the Sherpa were coming at some point, so I began to move away from Derek to intercept them. I called out repeatedly, but my radio was no longer working.

On the shelf again the following year, I realized that I'd never moved far enough to intercept anyone coming to help, but I was so disoriented that I hadn't known it. It had seemed to me that I was standing on the passage that they'd have to take to descend.

I began to freeze to death. First I lost the feeling in my lower legs, followed by my hands, and then my cheeks. If this continued, at the least I'd suffer severe frostbite. My lungs burned white fire and my cough had returned with a vengeance. I moved sluggishly as a great numbing lethargy enveloped me.

With no radio, I had no idea if anyone was coming. I knew that Peer had been ahead of me. Tsongba and Reggie were both missing. I assumed that all three had gone for help. It was possible that one or all of them were returning with fresh oxygen bottles. Dawa and Dorji were still above me. Dawa would not leave the shelf until he was certain that no one was there.

From time to time, I turned my oxygen off and forced myself to breathe without it. I had to conserve every liter of oxygen if I was going to get down. But before long, I had to turn it back on.

Derek spoke finally, enough to tell me he could not move his feet. I told him that he had to stand up, that I would help, and that we had to start moving down, but it was no good. I'm not certain if he even grasped what I said. He was likely too far gone physically at that point.

Shortly after five, Derek's oxygen ran out. I knew I wasn't far behind. Without oxygen, I was as good as dead. It would be dark at six and, if I was still on the shelf, I'd also be dead, as I could not manage the Step alone.

I implored Derek repeatedly, to no avail. At last, accepting that there would be no help, that I had to leave or die, I told him to stand one last time. When he did not, I told him that I had to leave. As I turned to go, perhaps ten minutes from darkness, he placed his hand on my forearm and said, "Don't leave me."

No one wants to die alone, but history is full of men who died needlessly by remaining with the dying. I had to leave. I had to leave or die.

I stayed. I told myself not to, but I stayed.

Until dark.

〜〜〜

The storm did not abate as I sat beside Derek. I'd turned my oxygen up so I'd at least feel better since I knew now that I'd never leave this place. What was the point in conserving it?

But with the greater flow of oxygen, my thinking returned. I could analyze my situation more clearly. If I stayed, I died. If I stayed, Derek died. Derek died if I left. Derek was dying and there was absolutely nothing I could do to save him.

But I couldn't leave him. Not alive. I just couldn't.

In the end, we all do what we must. I was no different. It was dark now and all but a miracle that I was able to find the line at the top of the Step. I hooked myself to it and made my way down in the darkness. Several times the blizzard blew me free of the rock and I found myself spinning. Without my ice ax, it was hard to stop, but each time, I managed to grab at something solid and restore order. Finally, I reached the bottom.

The line was up to the South Summit. I hooked myself to it and walked forward one step at a time. Well above Camp Five, the line went missing again and my oxygen also came to an end. That was the point where I finally gave up and sat down to die. What was one more?

This required no great act of will. Dying on Everest is easy, almost pleasant. It is moving that is hard, living that requires a struggle. Once you resign yourself to no more effort, to accepting the inevitable, you experience a sense of peace. It was over. No more struggling, soon no more cold. I was finished.

The storm picked that moment to ease for the first time since I'd left the summit. The wind diminished noticeably, though it soon resumed its ferocity. But most of all, the snow stopped for several long moments. In the darkness, no longer blind, I saw the lights of Camp Five.

I pushed myself up and began to walk awkwardly down the mountain toward the light, like a drunk leaving a bar. The snow resumed, but I had a fix on the camp now and was oriented by the wind. As long as it didn't change direction, I was going to live.

Calvin was there to greet me. "Where is Derek?" were his first words. Calvin was in trouble, I could see. He was hobbling about, dragging his right leg as if it was a dead weight.

"Dead," was all I managed to say.

"Are you certain?"

"Yes. He's dead."

Calvin took it in as he and a Sherpa moved me to a tent. "Where are Reggie, Dawa, and Dorji?" he asked.

I told him that I didn't know.

"Peer is here with Tsongba." I passed the tent and I saw the Sherpa with his black feet and hand in warm water, tears flowing down his cheeks. "It's a disaster," Calvin said as he pushed me into a sleeping bag and gave me a thermos of hot tea. He drew out a syringe and injected me. "Rest."

Calvin's radio was working and he relayed what I'd reported. Word flashed around the world. Derek Sodoc, the great adventurer, was dead on Everest.

The morning was clear, the storm having blown itself out. The lingering wind was stiff and cold, but nothing to compare with the night before. A Sherpa brought me morning tea, which I took with gratitude. He told me that there were reports of many deaths on Everest. Then I heard shouts of amazement outside. I pulled myself forward and peered out of the tent.

There was Dawa, walking down from the mountain, having survived a night in the blizzard in the Death Zone. A miracle.

NINETEEN

To climb Everest is to dance with death. How many decisions and non-decisions kill someone? The list is endless. It's reckless to go unprepared or in the wrong weather. It's murder to abandon a climber who can still be saved. But on Everest there are rarely witnesses, except for God, and He's not saying.
    —Quentin Stern, www.AbandonedonEverest.com

I could hear Gody and Michael Sodoc talking in hushed voices that night before I fell asleep with my memories and nightmares of the year before. Calvin had given me a pill, which I took along with my antibiotics, and I managed to sleep in the richer air of Base Camp. By morning, I was much improved. I crawled out of the tent in time for breakfast.

Bawu had made his usual fine effort and I actually had an appetite as I sat at the dining table. The two Nepalese pilots from the helicopter were seated at the far end engaged in muted conversation. They were, I noted, army officers—one of relatively high rank—and both were well armed.

Peer had finished breakfast and sat with Gody and Sodoc. Stern was alone off to the side, looking uneasy and a bit forlorn. I assumed that Tarja had already eaten and gone or had had a plate delivered to her tent. Tom was nowhere in sight. They all left me to myself as I drank coffee and tackled a plate piled high with potatoes, eggs, and onions. About halfway through, my hunger vanished, but it was still the most food I'd had in days.

"You seem hearty enough," Sodoc said as I pushed the plate away. He looked enormous, fit, and nasty.

"Better. Last night helped a lot."

He seemed to warm to me as he spoke. "There were those who said you'd never let us recover Derek's body."

"They were wrong, weren't they?"

"You've delivered and I'm prepared to take that as a good sign. My son's body will reach Advanced Base Camp today. There will be a memorial service there before he is brought down. I'll be taking him home for a proper burial."

Peer faced me and said, "Mr. Sodoc's been telling me that he's been in Kathmandu for two weeks, preparing to join us."

"Preparing?" I said.

"Yes," Sodoc said. "I brought a portable parabolic chamber with me. Every day, I spent a few hours in it at simulated altitudes to build my blood count and stamina. The rest of the time I worked out. I'm fit enough to climb this mountain—if that is what I wanted."

"I see."

With breakfast finished, the group scattered about the camp. The sky had a thin veneer of clouds, but in the absence of wind, the day was relatively warm and I lazed outside, grateful to be out of the cold and alive. Stern spent his time blogging in his tent or on his sat phone, arguing with someone. After lunch, I spotted Tom and Tarja talking at length. It looked to me as if she cried before ducking into her tent. Tom joined me.

"She wants me to intercede with Sodoc," he said with a sly smile.

"She thinks you're his man here."

Tom laughed. "She was supposed to be at the memorial service that was to be held here. That's why she didn't go to ABC where the service will actually take place. She's pretty angry about being shut out of the media exposure." I didn't know how to respond to that kind of thinking. "She wants me to fix it with Sodoc."

I shrugged. "So fix it."

He laughed again. "I don't have the kind of influence she thinks I have. Anyway, her problems are more than anyone can set right with him."

"That seems obvious. He didn't approve of the marriage—so what's she expect?"

Tom lowered his voice. "You don't know the half of it. Sodoc told me before I left, but it wasn't something I felt I could talk about. She brought it up just now. She's convinced it's why he's giving her such a bad time."

"I have no idea what you're talking about."

"When Tarja first established herself in Manhattan, she was moving in certain circles."

"Right. She'd paid someone to meet rich men. I think Stern told me that."

"Sodoc was among them."

It was one of those rare moments in life when you suddenly see something from somewhere else, when things that had made little or no sense suddenly took on new meaning. "You're saying ..."

"They had a fling before he married Natasha. It lasted about a week. He told me that he stopped seeing her because she was clearly a gold digger."

I looked toward Tarja's tent in stunned disbelief. "Then she married his son?"

Tom nodded. "Sodoc thinks she went after Derek because she was angry at him for dropping her."

"That's ... that's ..."

"Yes, it struck me the same way."

Derek's frozen body reached ABC late that day. Zhiku and his team had done an extraordinary job managing to get him down so fast. I sat in the media tent at Base Camp with the rest and watched Diana's coverage of the impromptu memorial service. Stern hung over our shoulder, taking notes. Rumor had it that he'd been working for Sodoc—or at least SNS—all along. I didn't believe it. I'd seen the way Sodoc looked at him. But I had to admit that there was something between them, just what I couldn't fathom. Tarja came in, glanced at the screen a moment, muttered something, and stormed out.

Derek's body was draped in the Sodoc Foundation flag, if you can believe that. Harlan read a portion of a generic Christian funeral service, for which Sodoc came to his feet. The rest of us followed, feeling more than a little awkward. On the screen, the recovering team and Calvin stood respectfully about the body as Diana solemnly intoned her coverage. It was ghoulish.

I glanced at Sodoc. His face was stone.

When the service ended, Stern rushed off to blog, while I joined Peer for dinner. Tarja was sitting with Tom, engaged in a fierce conversation that I couldn't hear.

"Why was the service at ABC?" Peer asked. "I thought it was going to be at Base Camp."

I looked about the dining tent. "Nobody's here to speak of. Almost everyone is up the mountain. Maybe that's the reason."

He took a bite of food and asked, "Why's Sodoc even here?"

"To get his son?" I speculated.

"That's what I thought, but he and Gody are having some serious conversations. Something's up, I think. You should be careful."

"Me? Why?"

"I've seen how Sodoc stares at you when your back is turned."

〜〜〜

The next morning over breakfast, I learned that Derek's body was to reach Base Camp that day. It was amazing how fast the Sherpa could descend in the right circumstances—and summit weather had returned.

I could well imagine how grateful they'd be to get down. The divide between Sherpa and Westerners had become even more pronounced the longer we were here. Dawa had told me that one of the Sherpa insisted that he'd seen Laki's ghost and she'd told him that they must turn back or everyone would die. Under the circumstances, it was remarkable that they ascended the mountain at all.

In the valley at Base Camp, the day grew increasingly warm. I drank beer all afternoon, lounging in a comfortable chair with Tom and Peer as the Norwegian discussed mountains he'd climbed. The man's record was impressive.

"What about the army guys?" Tom asked at one point.

"They look tough to me," Peer said.

"What about them?" I said. "They can't be concerned about anything happening here."

"I wouldn't think so," Tom said, "but there's been talk of sabotage and I take it they don't like being cut off this way."

"We're cut off?" I asked.

Tom nodded. "Again. It's all very unusual."

We sat sunning ourselves for a bit. "Why is Harlan doing this?" I asked. "He's moved us up too early, pushing on when circumstances clearly say we should either turn back or wait. I just don't get it."

"I heard it's his wife," Tom said.

"What about her?" Peer asked.

"She's very sick and he needs to be home with her. When Harlan balked at leading this expedition after Sodoc bought it lock, stock, and barrel, his agents offered him a separate and substantial fee to stay on—as well as a bonus if Derek's body was recovered."

"In other words, he's sold his soul," Peer said.

"I wouldn't put it that way," I said. "But it explains a lot."

Stern tried to join us late in the day. He was gaunt and clearly hadn't been sleeping lately.

"How's blogging?" Tom asked.

"Good. You should read the new stuff. Hard-hitting. I've been offered a fee to write a piece for *High Altitude*."

"About what?" Tom said.

"The funeral, of course." His manner brightened and I figured that he wanted something. "Hey, Peer, I'd like an interview for the blog and the piece, okay?"

"I'm busy." Peer leaned back in his chair with a sigh, adjusting his sunglasses.

"I could use some help. Your sponsors are my sponsors. I'd think you'd want to keep the hit count up."

"That's your bag, Stern."

"I think it's going to look a little odd, that's all. I understood you'd be helping me out."

Peer lifted his sunglasses to stare at the man as he answered. "Stern, if you weren't such a disgusting little shit, I might do that. Now move along. You're blocking the sun."

Stern frowned and moved away.

Ten minutes later, we heard sounds coming from the Ice Flow and stood up. The recovery team had emerged, pulling Derek's body along in a sleeping bag. It would still be a frozen block of ice. Zhiku must have realized how that looked because they stopped, lifted the body between them, and carried it the final distance into camp, the Sherpa appearing none too happy about the contact. They'd been a gloomy group for some time and this didn't help. Calvin was bringing up the rear and I was damn happy to see him. I walked out, passing the others.

"I didn't know you were coming down," I said. "Good to see you."

"I was concerned about leaving and have been assured I can go back up in the morning."

"Why? Isn't our job done? I suppose Harlan will move up for his service with Reggie, but that needn't involve you or any of the rest of us."

Calvin gave me an odd look. "You don't know?"

"Don't know what?" I said with a sick feeling in my stomach. I looked toward the Ice Flow. "Where's Diana? And the camera crew?"

"They're going up, Scott. I thought you knew," he said.

"Up? What do you mean 'up'?"

"Diana's going to summit, Scott," Calvin said. "She's planning to make the first live Evening News broadcast from the top of Everest." He paused then added, "Harlan says another storm is moving in. They're pushing to get this done before it hits."

I looked up at the enormous killer mountain with something close to hate. "Haven't they learned anything?"

"That's why I'm returning to ABC as soon as I've finished here," Calvin said. "Then I'll position myself higher up as circumstances suggest."

"Finished? What are you talking about?" I asked.

"The autopsy, Scott. Or as close to one as I can manage in these conditions."

⌐⌐⌐⌐

A new tent had gone up while I'd been lazing in the sun, getting mildly drunk. It was hermetically sealed, a brilliant white with the Red Cross symbol on its roof. Peer explained that it was a state-of-the-art medical facility. Nothing like it had ever been on Everest before.

As I spoke to Calvin, Zhiku and his Sherpa moved Derek's body into the tent. Calvin excused himself and approached Sodoc who was observing with Gody by his side.

This was a development that I'd not anticipated. Deaths on Everest are straightforward. You die of exposure to the high altitude; the symptoms are well known. You fall a long ways or sometimes not so far. You lie down and freeze to death. It was all standard and well documented. What need was there for an examination of the body? And with a frozen body, how much was even possible?

Tom and Peer joined me. Even Tarja came to watch pensively, standing apart, her arms crossed defensively. Stern dutifully snapped pictures, looking very, very intense. I saw him glance down the valley as if staring at something in the distance—or contemplating an escape.

I approached Sodoc. "What's this I hear about Diana broadcasting the news from the summit? There's a front coming in. Do you have any idea how dangerous a stunt this is?"

"That's my business."

"Don't be a fool! Not again. Sending people up in these conditions can be deadly."

His eyes turned dark. "Don't lecture me about the dangers of Everest. You'll recall that I have a very good reason to know them intimately," he said.

"Then call if off before it's too late."

Sodoc pulled himself up indignantly. "Don't be ridiculous. It's already been announced."

"Then unannounce it!" He started to turn from me. I moved to face him. "This is a crazy and very dangerous idea."

He gestured for Gody to stay out of it as he said, "I know my business."

What this man didn't know would fill a library, I thought, but said nothing. Clearly he wasn't going to cancel this photo op. I drew a deep breath and released it slowly before speaking. "Then we need to move the skilled Sherpa climbers, Calvin, and the rest of us up the mountain while you still can. If we aren't needed, then so be it, but when trouble comes, it comes very fast and there will be no time to position help. We already have to be in place. It's the least you can do. We gain nothing by staying here."

Sodoc eyed me steadily. "You seem in a hurry to leave."

I was angry. "Haven't you killed enough people attempting stunts like this one?"

"How dare you—" He stopped as a hand came out of the tent and Gody went up. I moved to Tom before I lost my temper and struck the old man. Gody spoke to Sodoc, then came over to us.

"I want to be clear," Gody said. "Those on the summit who survived the day Derek Sodoc died were you, Peer, and Rusty?"

"There's Tsongba and Dawa, of course. But that's everyone who lived. Why?"

"We'll know in a minute if it's important."

Stern was standing some distance from us as if he didn't want to be included. Gody gave him a look and then ducked back into the tent.

It was longer than a minute. It was another good half an hour before Calvin came out with the oddest expression I've ever seen on anyone's face. He waved for us to gather round and turned to an agitated Stern, who was brandishing a portable recorder, "Turn off that goddamn thing! But you might as well be here so you can learn it directly, as you'll find out anyway."

Calvin looked to Sodoc with enormous sadness and said, "I'm sorry to tell you that Derek was murdered."

TWENTY

For the Sherpa, there is no doubt. The mountain goddess decides who lives and who dies. Like the rest of the alternatives in their short existence, the logic is simple.
—Quentin Stern, www.AbandonedonEverest.com

"No shit!" Stern said. A wide grin of relief spread across his face. "No shit!" he repeated as he nearly jumped in glee.

A warm blush spread across my body. "That can't be," I stammered. "Derek died from high-altitude exposure. He froze to death."

"How do you know?" Sodoc said to Calvin, ignoring me.

"Again, I'm sorry to say it, but murder is always grim. The cause of death, Scott, was not exposure. He was killed when someone planted an ice ax in the middle of his chest. The handle is broken off, but the tip of the ax is quite clear. Once he's thawed a bit, I'll be able to extract it for examination."

There was a pause. Gody snapped, "Who returned without an ice ax?"

No one spoke for a long time. Peer said, "Just a minute. Climbers lose ice axes all the time. It's why we take more than one with us up the mountain."

"Did you lose an ice ax?" Gody asked him.

"No, not on that expedition. But I have in the past."

Again there was silence until I spoke. "I lost my ice ax on summit day." I could feel Sodoc's eyes bore into me. Tarja gasped and seemed to move away from me.

"Tell me about it," Gody said with a measure of malice.

"I lost it on the shelf when I was with Derek. I don't know how or remember when. I just know that when I went to the line to descend in the dark, I reached for it and it was gone."

There was a long moment of silence, then, in a voice I hope never to hear again, Sodoc said, "Tell me you didn't kill my son."

"Just a minute," Calvin said. "I know Scott. He and Derek were friends. Listen to me." He moved directly in front of Sodoc, blocking his view of me. "None of us knows what it was like up there—the hard decisions people had to make."

"I want to hear him say it," Sodoc said in the same voice again.

"Listen to me," Calvin continued. "Let's say someone—all right, Scott here—killed Derek. It was a mercy killing, Mr. Sodoc. Derek was all but frozen in the ice, unable to move. Nothing could be done, nothing!"

"Stand aside, doctor." Sodoc looked at me again. "Tell me."

I couldn't speak at first. I choked back tears. "I didn't kill Derek. I didn't." My words sounded false—even to me.

No one said anything for a very long time. All I could hear was the soft flutter of a tent flapping in the wind.

~ ~ ~

Sodoc and Gody briefly discussed trying to withhold the information, but in the end, Sodoc shook his head in resignation, perhaps understanding for the first time the kind of pain he'd built his fortune inflicting on others. "Word will get out. It always does. If Diana was here, I'd have her break the story."

The men moved away. I'd never seen Stern happier. "What are you so pleased about?" Tom demanded.

Stern appeared as if an enormous weight had been lifted from him. "It's not what you think—though it is a good story. Look, you guys, I know you don't like me. I don't like being here, but I didn't have a choice, you understand?"

"What do you mean?" Tom said.

Stern looked toward Gody and Sodoc and then answered in a whisper. "Gody hunted me down last month. I was scared, okay? Just look at the guy. He wanted to know what I knew and how I knew it. I told him what I'd learned, but that wasn't enough. He just kept boring in on me like he knew I was holding something back. He acted like he knew something. I don't know. But he wasn't taking what I had to say. Finally, I told him what he wanted to hear—that I had sources that said Derek was killed, not just abandoned up there. You have to understand that I thought the guy was going to kill me for writing the book! I was trying to buy time, all right? I gave him what he wanted and it got him to back off. That's all I was after. I've got a little girl to consider! It's not just me. I didn't think it through though. I got a call two days later and was told I was coming along. It's not like I want to be here."

"But you had no source, right? You just made it up," Tom said.

Stern stammered, then finally said, "But I was right, see! I was right!" With that, he skipped off to his tent in a mood approaching ecstasy. I didn't have to imagine the sensational report he'd file or the furor it would create.

No one spoke to me when our little gathering broke up as I went to my tent. I didn't have to wonder what it was like to be considered a murderer.

⌁⌁⌁

I skipped dinner. I didn't want to sit where everyone could look at me, the unspoken questions visible on their faces. I stayed in the tent and considered how this would play out. The more I thought about it, the more certain I was that I'd never leave this mountain alive. Tarja had been right in part, though we weren't all here to be punished. Just one of us. This entire expedition had been meant to catch whoever was responsible for Derek Sodoc's death. Stern had initially planted the seed of doubt in Sodoc's mind that his son had died from neglect and then accused someone of actually murdering him. Knowing the old man, he surely knew that it was speculative, but I could imagine that he'd always intended to hold someone accountable. Maybe I was giving Sodoc too much credit. A paranoid mind might very well have believed his son's death was murder all along. Stern had merely confirmed it.

When it was dark, I dressed quietly, leaving the radio behind. At eight o'clock, I left the tent and, without looking back, set out for the Ice Flow.

I didn't turn my lamp on until I was out of direct sight of Base Camp.

It was insanity, of course. Better to have waited for Gody and his Gurkha knife. Or perhaps he planned to be more subtle—certainly more subtle than he'd been with the Sherpa I now accepted he'd killed. Not that Sodoc would ask for any subtlety up here. But I couldn't go back down the mountain. It was either stay and be killed or move up toward Diana.

I'd been above twice now and both times it had been a frozen, miserable hell. I couldn't imagine her risking her neck for a publicity stunt, but her behavior in Afghanistan came back to me. She'd do it for ratings. She'd done it to get her big break. But it wasn't as if no one had ever broadcast from the summit before. Telephone calls had been made and broadcasts had been recorded. I'd seen live video of Chinese climbers planting the Chinese flag there the May before the Beijing Olympics. Still, a live network television broadcast by the lovely and perky Diana Maurasi would be great drama and make for very high ratings. I wondered what slick suit had dreamed this one up.

The ice canyons were pitch black. It was moonless and only my headlamp marked my passage. I clipped myself to the line, disconnected when reaching the anchor, and re-clipped. All the while, the ice moaned and groaned beneath and about me as the river of ice made its slow way down the mountain. Three times I heard avalanches, though none close to my route.

The most frightening moments were those spent on the aluminum ladder bridges across crevasses. I'd always been roped before and, had I fallen, I knew that I was unlikely to die. Alone, I could not rope myself. The ladders bent beneath my weight, my crampons awkward on the metal, scraping and clattering, the ladder bouncing in response to my weight and effort like a trampoline. But I crossed each of them without incident. It was insanity.

I relived that last afternoon on Everest. I understood it was logical to suspect me, especially since my ice ax was apparently the murder weapon. But from what Gody had said, I wasn't alone. I'd come to know Peer better this year and could not imagine him as a killer. We all have our dark sides though and it was true that he had been involved with Tarja. They were longtime lovers and what did I really know about their relationship?

And Tarja certainly had her reasons. Now I wondered if her attempt to force herself on the summit attempt might not have had another reason than the obvious one I'd assumed at the time. An annulment would have meant not a penny to her, but Derek's tragic death occurring as it did meant a fortune. Had she planned to kill him herself? When she was dropped from the summit attempt, could she have persuaded Peer to do her bidding? You certainly read that scenario often enough—novelists have used it for decades. I just couldn't imagine Peer as a suspect, but I didn't understand how anyone could see me as one—no matter how much incriminating evidence there was.

Then there was Rusty. As I understood it, he and Crystal had been involved in a long affair before she'd succumbed to Derek in New York during the planning meetings. It had been unpleasant and there'd been talk of replacing Rusty with another cameraman, but by the time I met the pair, none of that was apparent. They'd seemed to be good friends and certainly worked as a well-oiled machine.

Still, Crystal had gone running to Derek the moment Tarja took up with Peer. Perhaps Rusty had been thinking that she'd come back to him; maybe he thought that he'd made some progress on the trek to Base Camp, then it had all fallen apart when Derek had been caught.

The reality was that on the shelf, in the blizzard, any of them could have done it, just as much as I could have. Sodoc had been quick to select me as the culprit and I saw a certain logic to it, but I wondered if he'd come to another conclusion once he'd given it some thought.

Benign as the daytime temperatures had been, they plummeted well below zero at night. The snow was firm, the ice rock hard and, away from the ladders, I made steady, if cautious, progress. Except for the luminous patch projected by my lamp, the ice was black as coal. It was like passing slowly through the coldest and darkest cave you can imagine. From time to time, I caught a glimpse of a towering wall leaning over me and wondered if I'd need to wait for Gody. At last, the lights of Camp One came into view. Western climbers typically take half a day to hike from Base Camp to Camp One. It took me until two in the morning and by then I was chilled to my bones and frightened senseless.

They were expecting me.

～～～

I was surprised when Crystal handed me the customary mug of hot tea. "God," she said, "you look like hell."

I took the time to drink and catch my breath before answering. I glanced about. It seemed to me that those in Camp One, all Sherpa, were gawking when they should have been in bed. The only face to which I could put a name was Gametup—after Dawa, perhaps the most skilled climbing Sherpa on the expedition. "What's going on?"

"Harlan called up and said you were coming. I let him know you were arriving when I spotted your light. He sounded strange on the radio. What's going on? And why on earth you are climbing alone and in the dark?"

"Harlan didn't tell you?"

"No. What's happening, Scott?"

"Let's get inside somewhere. I'm freezing." Crystal ordered everyone to turn in and took me to her media tent—she seemed to have one everywhere—and sat me in a camp chair. The wind buckled the nylon every few seconds.

I related to her what had taken place at Base Camp as all the color slowly drained from her face. When I stopped, she placed the fingers of her right hand across her lips and muttered, "My God. Derek was *killed*? How can that be?"

Death and its close proximity is the one great reality on Everest. None of us could escape it. But until these last hours, I'd never given the idea of murder on Everest any thought and neither had Crystal.

For the slightest moment, I wondered who else had been killed up here—deaths we took for accidents.

"It was my ice ax, apparently," I said. "I lost it that final afternoon with Derek. Sodoc is convinced I killed him."

She looked at me in disbelief. "That can't be." I could have kissed her for her unthinking faith in me. "Sodoc can't seriously think you did it, can he?"

"He looked and sounded pretty convincing to me. I decided I was better off moving up the mountain."

She was confused for a moment then said, "But why? What's the point? If you needed to get away, you should be going down, not up."

"The Maoists have us cut off. There's nowhere down the mountain I *can* go. And there's a front coming. Like last year. Sodoc's still insisting that Diana pull off this stunt." I shrugged, making light of my motives. "She may need help."

"Harlan reported that the front is three days or more out."

"You know how quickly things change. And the weather can turn deadly even without the front reaching us."

Crystal became quite solemn. "Who would want to kill Derek?"

I had my list, but only shook my head in bewilderment. She'd have her own names once her thinking cleared.

After a bit, she said, "There's nowhere to go up here, Scott. You know that. Eventually, and that will be soon enough, you'll have to return to Base Camp."

"I'll worry about that when the time comes." Then I laughed, the sound coming out brittle and hollow. "Hell, the way things go up here, it may never be an issue."

Crystal looked at me for a long time, the strain of this last year clearly visible on her face. "Get some sleep if you can," she said finally. "This is going to get very bad for all of us—and you need your rest."

❧❧❧

I was up at dawn with the camp. Over breakfast, I asked Crystal what she was doing here. I'd thought she was set up at ABC to relay the summit broadcast.

"I came down to check supplies. We're having trouble with the mixer and Rusty gave instructions for the duplicate to be brought up. It's here and I'm moving to Camp Two this morning."

"Where's Diana? And who's with her?"

"She spent the night at Camp Four. She's got Rusty, of course, Zhiku, and another Sherpa I don't know."

"When is the summit attempt?"

"They'll spend today at Camp Four. If all goes well, they'll set out for Camp Five tomorrow, then leave at midnight for the summit. You know the drill."

That was cutting it close with the advancing front. "How's she holding up?"

"Good. I won't lie and say she really *wants* to do this. But she's steeled herself for the effort. Rusty and Zhiku will take good care of her. Don't worry."

"I'm going to ABC with you."

She'd already figured that out. "Sure. We're setting out in a bit—so eat up and get ready."

***

Four of us were moving up. The crucial bit of hardware was mounted on Gametup's back since he was the surest of foot. It was one of those clear days on Everest—the kind that lulls you into thinking that everything's going to be okay, that Everest is no different than any other mountain.

About an hour out of camp, we passed three bodies from different decades, based on their clothing. It was always odd how the sight of the dead failed to move you on Everest. See a body anywhere else in the world and you'd have a reaction. Here, they were part of the terrain and we gave them no more thought than the abandoned campsites we occasionally encountered.

At noon, we reached a very hectic Advanced Base Camp. The usual dozen tents were now fifteen and, above the largest, presumably Crystal's, were two sharp antennae. As I understood the process, she'd receive the signal from the summit and forward it on. Ratings would be off the chart and Diana's new career would be well launched.

Crystal consulted with one of the Sherpa and then came to me as I stood sucking air. "Peer is right behind us. He'll be here with a Sherpa in about two hours. He wants to talk to you."

"Okay." I couldn't imagine what he'd want to talk to me about.

"There's more. Tom and Tarja set out late this morning for Camp One along with a Sherpa. They're expected here tomorrow."

"What's going on?"

"I don't know. There aren't any private conversations, so all the information over the radios is very general. Scott, this is it for me. I'm covering the summit climb and broadcast from here. I've got an awful lot to get ready before tomorrow. What are your plans?"

I shrugged. "I'll wait on Peer and see what he wants. But early tomorrow, I'm moving to Camp Four to position myself for the summit attempt. When they start down, I'll move up to Camp Five. Are they still setting out as planned?"

"No changes." She hesitated. "I guess you should know that Sodoc's pretty angry. He's telling everybody up here to stop you."

I smiled. "You mean arrest me?"

She smiled. "Something like that. No one's going to do anything, though. You're safe."

I looked down the mountain. After a moment, I caught sight of Base Camp—a dirty patch against the white snow. "Until Gody catches me."

⌁⌁⌁

After lunch, Peer and Dawa came into view. They were both moving strongly and it was hard to believe that they'd come here directly from Base Camp. At least Peer had the decency to be winded when I handed him the obligatory mug of sweet tea.

"He is all man, Scott," Dawa said with a grin before moving to join the other Sherpa. It was good to see him, good to have at least one friend on the mountain.

"What are you doing here?" I asked.

He smiled. "Staying at Base Camp didn't seem wise."

"What do you mean?"

He leaned on his ice ax. "Sodoc's been using that head of his and came to the conclusion that you, Rusty, and I are all equally guilty. He thinks you killed Derek, but is now open to the possibility that any one of us might have done it. I could see the way he was talking to Gody and decided I was safer up the mountain."

I could only shake my head in disbelief. "Come on. Crissie had the crew save you some lunch."

In the tent, Crystal joined us and Peer related what had happened below. "They realized you'd left about two hours later. Sodoc was furious. He ordered Harlan to send Sherpa after you, but he refused. He told Sodoc to get in his helicopter and get off the mountain, that this was no place for a vendetta. It was pretty ugly."

"Then what?" Crystal asked.

"We all went to bed. By breakfast, Sodoc seemed to have calmed down. Gody had convinced him that there was nowhere for any of us to go, so there was no reason to make a scene. They spoke at some length, joined by the senior officer who flew up with him. I don't think he's a pilot. He kept looking at me and I got the message. I packed up and here I am. Dawa wanted to get away as well. It's pretty unpleasant down there."

"You really think that Sodoc is going to kill you, Scott, and Rusty?" Crystal said.

Peer leaned back in his chair. "I can just say what I saw and that sure is what it looked like to me. The man is a Nazi."

"What are we going to do?" Crystal asked.

"You've got e-mail and a sat phone, don't you?" Peer said.

"Peer, you don't actually *know* anything. None of us does."

"You can alert people. Send for help or something," he said.

She sighed. "First, he is one of the most powerful men on earth. You don't just get on a telephone or send an e-mail accusing him of planning murder. Second, who's going to send anyone up here? There's an insurgency going on, remember? And if they did fly in another helicopter, my guess is that it would be loaded with commandos ready to hunt both of you and Rusty down."

"You're saying that there's nothing you can do?" I asked.

"I can't think of anything, but I'm open to suggestions."

⌇⌇⌇

Afterward, I followed Crystal to her media tent. "Can you access Stern's blog?" I asked.

"Do you really want to read what he says? The man's a cretin."

"He seems to have a free hand down there. There might be something in it that will help."

"I doubt it. And you couldn't trust it if there was. He makes things up." Still, she brought the Web site up on her computer.

Stern's blog was buzzing. From the previous day:

Derek Sodoc murdered!

The news came as a sensation to all at Base Camp. What was to have been his record-setting summit climb last year ended in brutal murder! The great unanswered question is: Who killed Derek Sodoc? And why?

The announcement came just a few moments ago when Dr. Calvin Seavers, expedition physician for this expedition as he was for last year's, informed Michael Sodoc, international philanthropist and entrepreneur, that he'd discovered the tip of an ice ax buried in his son's chest! This word came within one hour of the return of Derek Sodoc's body to Base Camp where, for reasons not explained, an autopsy was performed.

This followed a heroic location and recovery effort of the preceding days. Never before had a body of a fallen climber been brought down from such a high elevation. Even the legendary George Mallory lies above. After a three-day search, Derek's body had been located immediately above the famous Hillary Step, not far from the summit. It was assumed he'd succumbed to the cold and high-altitude sickness. The discovery of an ice ax planted in his chest came as a complete shock to everyone on the expedition.

"I can't imagine anyone would have wanted to kill my husband," Tarja Sodoc said just moments ago. "Everybody loved him."

So she says now, but last year, as described in my best-selling book, Abandoned on Everest, *the international beauty's relationship with her new husband was, shall we say, under great strain.*

Derek had taken up with his producer while a climber was seen darting out of Tarja's tent at odd and suspicious moments. The camp was abuzz with speculation and innuendo.

Last year, it appeared that Derek had been abandoned to his death. This year, we know he was murdered! The abiding question, the one on everyone's lips is: Who killed him? And why?

Was it sexual jealousy brought on by the near constant bed hopping that marked that doomed expedition? Perhaps it was a personal feud brought onto the climb? Or was it, as the Sherpa say, the mountain goddess taking her revenge?

We cannot know, not yet. But the Pandora's box of ancient legend has been opened and trouble now plagues this expedition. How many more lives will Everest claim?

There are no police on Everest, no courts, no prisons. Until today, the great mountain itself has been judge and jury. What can be done here? What should be done? Post your thoughts below.

Meanwhile, a man rich with all the worldly goods and power any single person could ever accumulate walks about in a daze, absorbing the news no parent wants to hear, that his only child was the victim of a brutal murder. No amount of money, no sum of power can take that pain away.

I looked up at Crystal, who'd been reading over my shoulder. "There's more," she said. "Read the next entry."

Murder suspect named!

In a sensational development, just moments ago, Michael Sodoc named decorated war hero and Derek Sodoc pal Scott Devlon as the most likely suspect in the murder of his son last year.

"He was the last to be with him," Mr. Sodoc said. "Until today, I believed he'd left my son to die. In my mind, that was a sort of murder. Today it would seem he actually did the deed himself."

Scott Devlon, a decorated veteran of the Afghanistan campaign and currently a fellow at the Center for Middle Asian Studies in western Massachusetts, joined last year's expedition at Derek's express request. The pair had previously climbed Aconcagua in Argentina, the highest peak in South America, where it was reported that Derek had saved Scott's life.

Suspicion is directed at Scott in part because it is believed that his ice ax served as the murder instrument. It was plunged into the daring adventurer's chest. Then his body was pushed from the shelf above Hillary Step into a bottomless chasm. The only reason the body was discovered was because the line attached to him caught on a rock and prevented its fall into eternity.

Others expressed support for the suspected killer. "I don't believe it," Dr. Calvin Seavers observed. "Those two were close friends. Scott had no reason to kill Derek. Anyway, it was Scott who located his body when all other efforts failed. Is that the action of a killer?"

A good question. But today there will be no answer. Shortly after being branded a murderer, Scott Devlon fled Base Camp and moved in darkness through the treacherous Ice Flow to Camp One. We can only speculate as to his motives, but there are those who believe he is running from his accusers.

Or is he seeking to help the intrepid Diana Maurasi, former anchor of the SNS Evening News, who even now is positioning herself to reach the summit? From there, she will make the world's first regular news broadcast. It is common knowledge here that she and Scott are bed chums. You want to attribute the best motives to the genial Scott, but in these circumstances, it's difficult to know what to believe.

For others here, there is no speculation. They say Scott Devlon killed Derek Sodoc and must pay.

There went my job, I realized. And I certainly wasn't doing Diana any good. There was a final entry from earlier.

Peer Borgen leaves for summit!
World-renowned Alpinist and mountaineer Peer Borgen has left Base Camp in the company of a climbing Sherpa, making his way up the mountain. He told no one his reasons, but given his gallant conduct last year, it is assumed he is moving up to render assistance to Diana Maurasi. A front is closing in and

there is speculation here that we are about to see a repeat of last year's disastrous events. How many more lives will this accursed mountain claim?

In a raging blizzard during last year's tragedy, Peer encountered Tsongba Sherpa, head of the climbing Sherpa above Hillary Step. The Sherpa was in desperate straits and only Peer's prompt action in hoisting him down the Step alone saved the man's life, though tragically Tsongba lost both feet, a hand, and his nose from frostbite. "No other climber in the world could have managed that," a source told me for my best-selling book, Abandoned on Everest, *which gives a complete account of that doomed expedition.*

Given Peer's previous heroism, it can only be assumed that he will rescue someone else before this drama is finished. One cannot but help wonder if it will cost him his life this time.

～～～

Toward dark, Peer summoned me to the edge of camp. The wind was steady now, coming at us from the west. He pointed down the mountain. "Look."

Two figures were making their way slowly toward us. "Who is it? Gody?" I asked.

"No. We'd have heard if he'd set out and they're moving too slowly for it to be Sherpa—even with a heavy load. It must be Tom and Tarja."

"Why are they pushing so hard?" I said.

"We'll ask them when they get here. At the rate they're going, they'll be lucky to make it before sunset."

After our evening meal, we returned to the edge of camp to watch the pair struggle up the mountain. Finally, Tom and Tarja staggered into camp just after dark, exhausted and cold. I thought Tarja would collapse on the spot and Tom looked little better. We helped them to the dining tent to warm up and eat if they could.

"Why are you here?" Crystal asked. "This is absurd."

"That crazy man," Tarja said, still gasping for air. "He was going to kill me. I had no choice. Help me! For God's sake, someone help me!"

"Is that true, Tom?" I asked.

"I don't know, but Michael is acting very oddly. Learning Derek was actually murdered was a shock. He's coming to some very strange conclusions."

"Why turn on Tarja?" Peer asked.

Crystal gave him a look. "Don't be stupid, Peer."

It took a minute before Peer said, "This is preposterous."

Tom said, "I don't think it's that, Peer. Not directly."

"Then what else could it be?"

"Michael's got it in his head that you might have killed Derek because that's what Tarja wanted."

Peer was stunned. "The man must be crazy to think something like that!" He turned to Tarja. "What did you tell him?"

"Nothing, Peer," she said. "He's just nuts. I never said anything to him. Really, Peer. You have to believe me!"

"I don't think it's her, Peer," Tom said. "He's always felt more than a little guilty about neglecting Derek after his first wife's death. Then this happened."

"What's going on with Gody?" I asked.

"He and Michael had an argument with Harlan as we were leaving. As of this morning, Gody, Calvin, Harlan, and a Sherpa were leaving tomorrow for here."

"Why Harlan?" I asked.

"He's trying to rein Gody in, I think. Calvin, of course, is positioning himself to be of assistance."

After a silent moment, Crystal said to Tarja, Peer, and me, "You can't go back down. Any idea about what to do?"

No one had a reply for a long minute. Peer said, "There's an Austrian team on the Tibet side of the mountain. I talked to them two days ago. I know some of the climbers. We can move up to Camp Four. There's a traverse we can follow to meet up with the northern route. Once we join it, we drop down to the Austrians."

I'd scanned every known Everest route and recalled no such traverse. "You say there's a traverse," I said. "How do you know? Has anyone ever used it?"

"I spotted it when I studied the latest photographs of the mountain using three-dimensional image enhancement. It's there."

"I'll take your word for it," I said, "but if no one's ever used it, we can't be certain of the obstacles we might encounter or how far we'd have to climb. The path won't have been cleared or roped. It's going to be very dangerous going. You might make it, but for Tarja and me, it could be too much."

Peer shrugged. "I don't want to try it, don't get me wrong. But I also don't want to face those madmen down below. God alone knows what would happen even if we returned to Base Camp and somehow managed to get back to Kathmandu. This war is the perfect cover for anything Sodoc wants and he controls the media here, obviously." He said the last part looking pointedly at Crystal.

"What about you, Scott?" Tom asked.

"I'm here to help Diana and her team if necessary. I'll decide what to do after that." I said, "Is there any chance I can speak with her, Crystal?"

She shook her head. "She's trying to rest for tomorrow and I couldn't offer you a secure connection."

"Crissie would be fired, Scott," Tom said.

I nodded as I stepped outside. The sky was ebony and the uncommonly bright stars twinkled. A soft, freezing wind blew.

⟿ ⟿ ⟿

At breakfast, Crystal gave us the latest weather report. "Harlan says the front has picked up speed, but isn't expected for another thirty-six hours."

Peer whistled. "That's cutting it close."

"It's New York. They've got a schedule," she said.

I took us all in. We were getting to be a pretty sloppy looking group. Neither of the women wore makeup any longer and both were sunburned. The men all had ragged beards. We all looked exhausted. Every conversation was punctuated with sporadic, violent coughing.

The summit team was leaving for Camp Five and would set out again at midnight. If all went well, Diana would broadcast worldwide sometime between ten o'clock in the morning and one o'clock in the afternoon. That was the slot SNS was planning for. This placed her live broadcast at approximately two o'clock in the morning on the American East Coast, but it would catch the morning broadcasts throughout the United Kingdom and Europe.

The entire affair was absurd. The suits had wanted the broadcast five hours later, but had relented when told that would almost certainly mean Diana's death, as it would put her on the summit at sunset. I'm sure that one of them considered the ratings bump that would mean before realizing that they'd have no star for the new morning program.

Over breakfast, I said, "I'm moving through Camp Three to Camp Four today. I'll wait on word of the summit attempt before deciding what to do. I talked to Dawa and he'll climb with me. Are you still planning the traverse?"

Peer put down his coffee. "I'm moving to Camp Four with you and will think about it. If that's what I decide—and the weather holds—I'll tackle the traverse the next morning. I estimate it will take six hours to reach the north summit route, another six to get to their Advanced Base Camp. Who's joining me?"

Tarja looked up from her plate. "Can we make it?"

Peer shrugged. "I don't see why not. We'll be blazing a new route. At worst, we'll have to turn back." He said the last as if it was a matter of no concern, but in my experience, turning back would likely be as deadly as proceeding.

Tarja shuddered. "I don't …" She stopped, placed a hand to her head, wrapped her arms across her chest, and said nothing.

"What about you?" I asked Tom. "You're Sodoc's friend. You're not running to or away from anything. What are you going to do?"

He glanced at Tarja and said, "I guess I'm going to Camp Four with you all. But I have a very bad feeling about this."

TWENTY-ONE

It was a shock when the new bride, Tarja, set out with her catch to summit Everest. A shock because everyone on the expedition knew what she was up to with her fair-haired stud. When she returned, alone and sullen, the only surprise was that she hadn't died on the mountain. But then they say that only the good die young.
—Quentin Stern, www.AbandonedonEverest.com

The next day was ideal climbing weather; the landscape about us was starkly beautiful and the colors were sharp in the clear air. Ahead was a hard day's climbing, twice as far was Westerners typically attempted. I wasn't looking forward to it.

Gametup, who was staying behind, gave each of us two oxygen bottles, not to use, but to carry to Camp Four. "Need more," he said with that shy Sherpa smile. The amount stockpiled had been earmarked for the search and now for the summit team. We couldn't be certain that there'd be enough in the event of an emergency, with so many climbers at that elevation. Oxygen was the Achilles' heel of every expedition and Harlan had placed a generous supply where we would need it.

Crystal came to bid us farewell and bore news. "Gody will be here this afternoon. Harlan is with him. Calvin's also coming up, but he may have to stop at Camp One for the night. Knowing him, though, he'll press on to here. The good news is that the front's moving as expected, but don't take any chances up there. You all know how quickly things can change. With luck, you won't be needed, and in a couple of days you'll all come back with wide grins. Good luck to you."

I had to admire the way she managed to gloss over the perils. There was only one reason that Gody was climbing to us. There was no getting away from that. And it wasn't just me. Peer and Tarja were equally convinced, enough to consider risking their lives on a dangerous, unproven traverse. As for the weather—counting on good summit weather killed almost everyone who died up there.

Peer set out, leading the way, followed by Tarja, Tom and I, with Dawa bringing up the rear. We moved cautiously up the forty-degree incline of the Lhotse Glacier. Even with our crampons, the ice was slick and uncertain. Still, we made good time, reaching Camp Three before noon. No Westerners were there to greet us—just the flat, expressionless faces of the two Sherpa who manned it. We stopped to collect ourselves, consumed as much of an energy bar as we could force down, had a bit of hot tea, and then set out for Camp Four, perched immediately below the Death Zone.

The second half of the day was longer and more exhausting, especially for Tom and Tarja, who had never acclimatized for the higher elevation. We were climbing without oxygen and even the indomitable Peer, I noticed, was having difficulty. Only Dawa appeared untroubled. We stopped more frequently and, each time, Tom spoke words of encouragement to Tarja, though he looked in no better shape.

I was dehydrated, as we all were, and my head was pounding with the worst headache of my life. Two steps, breathe, two more steps, breathe, and before dark, we finally staggered into Camp Four, our line now well stretched. Dawa lingered back with Tom and Tarja, who arrived a half-hour after Peer and I.

Camp Four is situated on a wind-blasted frozen mesa of the South Col. It has no naturally flat ground, so the few tents were pitched on platforms chopped from the ice. There were no Sherpa to see to our needs, though two were stationed there to maintain the tents and see to emergency needs. Each climber was responsible for boiling his own water, making tea, and preparing a meal if he thought he could manage one. From here up, your body undergoes a slow death. Sleep is all but impossible unless you are on oxygen, and none of us would be.

Only Peer and Tom wore radios. The rest of us had left them behind—and even they'd had them off all day, but now Tom turned his on. Tarja came over to eavesdrop—perhaps to make certain that Tom made no mention of our plans. After a bit, he gave his report. "Gody, Harlan, and Calvin have reached ABC. I'm told to stop everyone. So consider the request made."

"What's the status of the summit team?" I asked.

"They're at Camp Five now. They're setting out at midnight as planned. The front is moving steadily and expected tomorrow night sometime. So we all want to be farther down when it strikes."

As we settled in the tents for the night, I joined Peer who was feeding snow and ice into a metal cup atop a meager flame. "You can't be serious about making this traverse," I said. "There's no established route, no line. It's something for an entire team to undertake—and take a week or more to lay out. If you intend to join the Austrian team on the other side, you should simply summit and then take the route back down. At least that pathway is marked and roped."

He looked up and for once I saw the ever-present certainty absent from his eyes. He grinned. "I will make history."

"More likely, you'll just add to the body count."

It was a wretched night with wind beating at the tent. I kept thinking about Diana above us, knowing she wasn't getting any sleep either. I knew what it was like to lie fully clothed in a sleeping bag, wondering if you could do it, afraid you'd die in the attempt. She was in for a long day. Her publicity stunt would come at the halfway point of her summit effort, with the mostly deadly part to follow. Zhiku and Rusty knew that. I just hoped that she understood that her life was more important than any damn news broadcast.

But I'd seen her in Afghanistan. The broadcast would come first.

⌐⌐⌐

Fate stepped in, as it usually does on Everest. Below us, Harlan refused to continue above ABC, calling Gody a madman. Crystal and Calvin both tried unsuccessfully to convince Gody to turn back. Two hours before dawn, in an apparent attempt to gain ground on us, the former colonel set out for Camp Four, ordering the most experienced climbing Sherpa to go with him, but having no idea who he was. It was Gametup.

As for us, Peer and I rose at dawn. Above, Diana, Rusty, Zhiku, and the Sherpa with them were already at the South Summit, having made excellent time in the dark. From what I've read the world was abuzz with expectation. Tarja and Tom didn't emerge from their tent. Peer and I saw to nature and then hunkered down for a few minutes, taking in the majestic—if desolate—view. Dawa was with the Sherpa, who I understood to be cousins of some kind. They cast looks toward us from time to time and seemed very uneasy over the unfolding events.

Back inside our tent, we munched a chocolate bar as Peer brewed water for tea and our breakfast of climbing porridge laced with a sweet protein. As the meal was nearly ready, Tom poked his head in. "I need you two. I think Tarja's in trouble."

Our Nordic beauty was out of her tent, her climbing suit all askew. She was attempting to walk toward us, but resembled a midnight drunk trying to find a car and could not hold a straight line. She was mumbling to herself. When I reached her, I could make no sense of it. She was breathing fast and shallow and I could detect a slight gurgling in her lungs.

"Her lips are grey. See?" Peer said. "And look at her eyes."

The effect was subtle, but I saw what he meant. Tarja's eyes had a slight bulging look to them. Just then, she coughed spontaneously, bending over at the waist as if she wanted to hack her lungs out. Peer put his arm across her for support. When she finally straightened, Tom pointed and we all saw the pink stain in the snow.

Peer looked to us. "It's HACE," he said, High Altitude Cerebral Edema. "And she has symptoms of HAPE," High Altitude Pulmonary Edema. Both were fatal, in some cases in as little as one or two hours, though occasionally the climber lingered for a full day. But the end was always the same. No matter how experienced or fit a climber, either could attack without warning, typically during sleep. The initial symptoms were usually observed first thing in the morning. There was only one treatment and it had to be implemented immediately.

"We have to get her down," Peer said. "At once, while she's still mobile. Otherwise, we'll have to slide her down the mountain and that will take more manpower than we have. We must get started right away."

"I'll take her," Tom said. "You two need to be up here. Can I get her down with the two Sherpa?"

"I think so," Peer said slowly. "Tarja, you're very sick," he said to her. "You have to go down the mountain. Tom's taking you. Understand?"

She didn't. I was frightened for her. I'd only seen this once before and the stricken Sherpa had died.

"We'll get her ready," Peer said. "Scott, tell the Sherpa to prepare. They have to leave at once."

Five minutes later, Tarja was breathing oxygen—though that alone wasn't enough. Tom and the two Sherpa set out with Tarja short-roped to one of them. She was moving awkwardly, lifting her feet too high as if wading in water, moving oddly side to side, but her feet were under her and she'd improve with every drop in elevation. I told myself that she was young and fit and would be fine. She was in good hands.

It was now just Peer, Dawa and me. In the thin air, even simply standing, we struggled to breathe, coughing intermittently, unwilling to burn bottled oxygen that we might need later. Peer used his radio to alert Crystal as to what was happening and to recommend that she send Sherpa up to meet the descending climbers.

"Look at the sky," Peer said with awe. The sky had turned a burnished azure, an effect I'd never seen on Everest before. After a few minutes, he turned to his radio, listening in above and below.

We hunkered down on the lee side of a tent in what was of the sun to monitor the summit team's status. Every few minutes, I heard an ominous rumble in the distance, though I could see no storm. On Everest, you just never knew. At these altitudes, a storm was as likely to come from below as from above.

Word up the mountain was garbled, but it sounded as if the summit team was making steady progress. By late morning, they'd cleared Hillary Step and there was nothing between them and the summit but the treacherous traverse and the Summit Ridge. If all went well, they'd be on top at noon, their broadcast finished by one o'clock at the latest, and they'd be on their way down.

"I think my traverse to join the Austrians is off," Peer said nonchalantly. "It's just as well. Trailblazers tend to die."

I laughed and clapped him on the back.

As we waited, Dawa was his usual quiet self, but seemed preoccupied. I could certainly understand. This had been a snake-bit expedition with death at every turn. From his viewpoint, the mountain goddess didn't want us here. The proof was all around and strewn down the mountain.

I wasn't one to dispute the Sherpa belief. We were a state-of-the-art expedition with every convenience and advantage modern technology could offer. Of course, that had always been the case for Western climbers. To us, looking back, the efforts of Mallory seemed primitive, climbing as he did in a wool coat and hobnailed boots. But at the time, he'd had the very latest technology possible, including an early oxygen apparatus.

But for all our advantages, we still climbed Everest one step in front of the other. The day would come, I supposed, when some device—a helicopter or rocket or plane of special design—would drop tourists on the summit so they could brag that they'd been there. I didn't doubt for an instant that people would still die.

Peer turned away from his radio. "Bad news, Scott."

"The front?" I'd worried about the weather all morning.

"Maybe. It's picked up speed and is expected in a few hours. But that's not the immediate problem. There's a local pattern we can't see from here, moving up the mountain from the Tibet side. Rusty reports dark thunderclouds and lightning below. He thinks they need to get down fast."

"Where are they?"

"Nearly there. Crystal relayed his recommendation, but Sodoc has ordered them to the top."

The bastard. "Any word on Tarja?"

"Nothing. She hasn't reached Camp Three yet."

"How about our friend Gody?"

"Not a word. Not from him or the Sherpa with him."

I couldn't imagine the Gurkha coming this high. He wasn't a mountaineer and had never scaled such heights before. I figured that he'd wait for me—or us—at Camp Three. I looked up at the sky, now turned a dull slate. "What do you think? Should we move up?"

It was a tough call. As bad as Camp Four was, Camp Five was even worse. We'd be on oxygen there and even colder than we were here. But Camp Five was at least four hours above us, in good conditions. If we waited too long, we'd be no help at all.

Peer spoke into the radio for several minutes, but I couldn't make out what he said. Dawa seemed almost in a trance, mumbling what I took to be prayers. I looked closely at his features and manner. HACE killed as many Sherpa as it did Western climbers, but I saw nothing beyond his state of mind.

Peer leaned toward me. "Harlan says the storm on the north side is moving up fast. The summit team is definitely going to be caught in it, probably in an hour or so. The other front will hit this afternoon. We need to get going."

Two storms merging on the summit was a worst-case scenario. Sodoc was insane to keep Diana and the others up there. I looked at my watch. It was noon. "We're moving up, Dawa. They're going to need help."

He pulled himself back to the present and nodded. "Yes, Scott. I understand." He glanced at the sky. "It is bad above, I think."

Peer broke out the oxygen, since you don't climb above Camp Four without it. Each of us also carried two additional bottles; one we'd plan to use, the other a spare for ourselves or for someone in need. Bottles were stored at Camp Five as well. A few minutes later, we set out, Peer in the lead, me, then Dawa.

Below, Harlan and Crystal were ignoring Sodoc's rant that the broadcast go on as scheduled and ordered the summit team to immediately descend. Peer couldn't make out the response, but the broadcast took place. I saw it later. Diana looked exhausted—despite her best effort to appear perky. The snow had yet to start, but the wind was sharp and she was clearly miserable. She followed the script and did the sign off like the professional she was. It ended with Rusty giving the viewers a sweeping shot of the starkly beautiful world around them. It was heartbreaking to watch in light of what happened.

For us below on oxygen, it was no worse climbing to Camp Five than it had been climbing to Camp Four the day before. Miserable, but not worse. Peer pushed hard since we'd left later than circumstances dictated.

At this elevation, Everest is a barren, God-forsaken place of bare, jagged rock, patches of snow and ice, lethal scree, and exposed narrow ridges. Often the fall to our right was as far as the one to our left and a wrong foot either side could mean death. We were hooked to the line, but when you fell and pulled at it with your full weight, the line didn't always hold. We disconnected and reconnected every fifty to hundred feet—our hands numb and our perception and judgment seriously impaired.

We'd waited too long to move up. Such calls are always difficult. Either the Tibet storm or the front struck us about halfway to Camp Five. First was the battering wind then came the snow, which quickly blinded us. Without the line to follow, we'd have been in very serious trouble.

It was a freezing hell. My lungs burned a cold fire. I slowly lost feeling in my feet, hands, and face—even though we moved steadily. Predictably, Peer lost contact with the summit team. The reach of technology at the top only goes so far.

The weather did not improve and we staggered into Camp Five late that afternoon. I'd hoped to find the summit team there; instead, the four tents were empty. The camp is situated on a windswept saddle and is, I believe, the worst place on earth to layover. We crawled into a slightly larger tent to be less cold and brewed tea while we decided what to do. Peer broke out a small heater and fired it up as Dawa collected snow and ice to melt.

I glanced about and decided that we looked more like survivors than rescuers. Each of us was in bad shape and, to the extent I could think, I wondered how much help we could possibly be to anyone. Still, Peer and Dawa were as good as it got on Everest.

"What do we do now?" I asked. With no communication, anything we did from here on out was either guesswork or a judgment call, depending on your perspective or the outcome.

"Rest a bit," Peer said, "Then move up with spare tanks around. I estimate they left the summit about one. If all had gone well, they should already be here, but in these conditions, things will not go well. Let's hope they're below the Hillary Step at least. I don't want to go above it in this storm and there aren't enough of us to help anyone on the shelf in serious trouble."

That was the cold logic of Everest. If history was any judge—and it usually was at 28,000 feet—rescuers were as likely to die as those in need of rescue. That was our grim reality.

Dawa remained withdrawn. Peer gave me a questioning look at one point, which I shrugged off. In time, the water came to boil and we all drank very sweet tea. Outside, the light grew faint.

"We should move out," Peer said, "before it gets completely dark." He stirred to gather his things and added, "Good luck to us all." Even he was feeling it.

Dawa didn't move, then said, "Scott, Peer, I must speak. It is very bad today. Evil things are taking place and more people will die. It is more than I can bear."

"It's difficult for all of us, my friend," I said. "We must help those above us, if we can. As for Gody, he's below and I'll deal with that when the time comes."

Dawa looked at me with as much pain written across his face as I've ever seen. "You don't understand. I am the cause of this."

"Don't be silly, Dawa," Peer said. "It's the nature of the mountain—of high-altitude climbing. Westerners are foolish enough to come up here and put ourselves and fine men like you in these absurd situations. It's not your fault."

Dawa shook his head. "It is. It is. The mountain goddess, Sagarmatha, my friends, she is taking her justice. I have caused this."

"That's a lot of superstitious nonsense," Peer said. "I don't mean to sound cruel, but that's the truth of it."

"Dawa, you're making no sense," I said.

Dawa said nothing for a long minute, but clearly meant to speak. Finally, "Last year, I felt great shame. The Sherpa goddess Kumari was dishonored. Every Sherpa hung his head. We were mocked by others. My clan, especially my own family, were shamed the most of all. We didn't want to climb with Derek. The priests told us that the mountain would punish us. But we are poor. There was no choice." He looked at me. "You were there. You saw what happened. You know how many died."

"There's nothing to it, Dawa," Peer said. "My people, long ago, had such beliefs. We know better now."

Dawa smiled gently. "You have convinced yourselves of this new way, but the old one was right. Someday you will see."

"It's late, Dawa," I said. "We must leave. This can wait."

He shook his head sadly. "No. That terrible day, I knew it was all true. We had been wrong to come. I was confused. I didn't know what to do. I could see that people were dying, that more would die. It was the worst day of my life." It had been the worst day of my life as well. "I could not find Dorji. I looked and looked, but he was nowhere. I think he walked off the mountain. It was just dark as I gave up and reached the traverse. But the line was gone. I knew Derek had been there, but not what happened after you went to help. My radio didn't work. I wanted to find you so I searched. Instead, I found him against the rock. You were gone by then, Scott. At first I thought Derek was dead. But when I shouted and shook him, he blinked his eyes and I knew he was alive."

"You found Derek after Scott left and he was still alive?" Peer said.

"Yes. I am ashamed I did not speak of this sooner."

"What then?" I asked, though now I knew the rest.

"There was much anger toward Derek. He had defiled the Kumari and shamed every Sherpa. My wives, they could not get baby. The whole village suffered that way. A yak was born blind, a goat with two heads. We all knew the signs. We had to make a sacrifice, but could not agree what offering would be enough? We are just poor people. We didn't know. At Base Camp, we talked of little else. The young men said we would know if we were wrong to climb, to help Derek, because Sagarmatha would punish. I tried to ignore talk, to do my job as you say. But it was no good. Then I found him, the one who defiled our goddess. I believed she had shown me the answer, that she had given me this chance to avenge the great wrong he did us.

I could see what I must do clearly. It was as if she had guided me to that place, at that time."

"What are you saying?" Peer asked.

"There was an ice ax beside him. I'm sorry, Scott, I did not know it was yours. I thought it was Derek's. I prayed and then I killed him with it. He made no sound I could hear. I think he was unconscious. He did not suffer. After that, I pulled him to the edge and pushed him off. I never thought he'd be seen again." Dawa looked up. "Peer, you must remember this. You must tell the others so they will believe and know that Scott did not kill Derek. I did. He was sacrificed for what he did and to save my people."

I put my arm across Dawa's shoulders. "Oh friend, my friend …"

"You killed him?" Peer said. "How could you? It's unthinkable."

"I should never have come back. I should have shaved my head and gone to the temple to live. I caused all of this death, all of this," Dawa said. "I was wrong. It is up to the goddess to take revenge, not an ignorant man like me. I should have left him to her. She was taking him. She would have had him in just a few minutes. Because I killed him, all these others have died. I am very ashamed, Scott. So ashamed." Dawa cried. I'd never seen a Sherpa shed tears before.

Peer met my eyes and shook his head slowly. He was no less stunned than was I. After a few minutes he said, "We must move out, or we'll be too late."

TWENTY-TWO

It snows at Base Camp. Sometimes the wind blows and it snows at the same time. It's not all that different from the Midwest. But above, at the summit, the wind howls and the snow screams across the air. Sometimes, when it's clear at Base Camp, you can see the dark storm above, coiled about the summit like a death mask.
—Quentin Stern, www.AbandonedonEverest.com

It was all but dark by this time. We loaded ourselves with fresh oxygen bottles, abandoning those that we'd used earlier. Then we turned on our headlamps and set out.

To call what we were doing a search is a misnomer. We were connected to the line that stretched from Base Camp to the summit and following it up, as we hoped those descending were also connected to the line and were following it down. Off of that lifeline, I knew from experience how easy it was to pass someone in such conditions without knowing it.

We were two hours to the South Summit. We met no one, not along the route nor at that summit. It had turned dark, however, and any climber even a few feet off the line route would have been a mound in the snow, indistinguishable from one created by nature.

On the razor's edge of a ridge, we climbed from the South Summit to Hillary Step, utterly exposed to the blizzard and violent blasts of wind. Our lights turned the blinding snow into a white glare and most of the time I worked to make out my boots. I moved my ascender along and reconnected to the line by feel, never entirely certain I'd managed it, beyond caring if I hadn't.

Dawa's confession had come as a complete shock. I'd known I hadn't killed Derek, not with my ice ax. I'd always believed, however, that I'd somehow been responsible for his death by abandoning him. Logic said otherwise, but my heart disagreed. Whatever his shortcomings, we'd been friends and friends don't leave each other to their deaths.

Once his body had been recovered and we'd known he was murdered, I'd refused to believe it could have been anyone I knew, certainly not Peer or Rusty. Yet someone *had* killed him, even though he was clearly dying. Someone had found the energy and had the motive to take his life. None of it had made any sense until now. According to Dawa, the murder had been more in the way of a ritual sacrifice. I don't know who I felt sorrier for—Derek or Dawa.

Peer pulled up at the foot of Hillary Step. He gestured for us to gather, moved his oxygen mask aside, and shouted to be heard. "I've seen no one! How about you?"

"Nothing," I shouted.

"No one," Dawa added.

None of us spoke for the longest time. Each of us knew what was coming. The snow struck like sharp pellets and the wind screeched in a way that I've only experienced on Everest.

"We have to climb to the shelf," Peer said at last. "I'll go first."

He fumbled about then attached his ascender and began moving up, with me following. It was difficult climbing and I could tell that Peer was reaching his limit. The Hillary Step is not sheer and, at sea level, its forty feet could easily be climbed without crampons or a line. But here, in the blackest of nights, at nearly 29,000 feet in a gale-force wind and gripped by the blinding fury of the blizzard, it was a daunting task, perhaps impossible even for a man as skilled as Peer. He slipped and stumbled repeatedly. Once I bumped into him as he struggled to get his footing. With a sinking heart, I realized that even if we found someone above here, it would be all but impossible for us to get him or her down.

Peer stopped. He swung back and forth, fumbling with something. I saw his hand gesture down at me, as if he wanted me to come up. I moved closer and realized that two of them were above. We'd found someone from the summit team.

In those conditions, it was impossible to tell who it was, except that the body was small and light, so that eliminated Rusty. Peer rigged a line to whoever it was, tied it to himself, and handed the end down to me. I tied the line to myself and tugged at his leg to let him know I was ready. It took a while with his numbed hands to get out his knife and cut the line that held the body in place. Suddenly it lurched down, the full force striking Peer, who buckled momentarily under the impact. I felt nothing as he took it all himself.

Slowly, awkwardly, I began backing down the Step, as did Dawa. Eventually, we were off the pitch and I helped Peer with whoever it was he'd found.

It was the Sherpa. This was a very bad sign. There was only one reason why a Sherpa would be alone like this. He'd been sent for oxygen bottles and help. That had to be it, as I couldn't imagine a Sherpa abandoning climbers in any circumstances. The Sherpa's presence told me that the summit team was still above us.

He looked dead. His face was encrusted with a mask of ice and snow and I could detect no movement. We sheltered him to the extent that we could with our bodies as Dawa leaned down and called out the man's name repeatedly. "Pemba! Pemba!"

It seemed hopeless. The man was dead. But then I saw his mouth move and his eyelids flicker. Dawa said something to him in Sherpa, then seized him by his clothing and attempted to pull him to his feet. Only those who are ambulatory survive on Everest. If you can't stand upright and walk, you can't be saved. That is the rule. Peer and I reached down, the three of us pulled him to his feet, and we propped him against the rock.

Peer leaned against me, obviously exhausted. "We must take him down!"

"They're on the shelf!" I shouted.

"We don't know that! We have him! In these conditions, with just the three of us, we can't save the others!"

He was right. I knew it. "Ask him about the rest!" I shouted to Dawa as he placed his lips close to Pemba's ear and spoke. After a minute, he looked to me. "He can't talk! I don't think he really understands what I want!"

What else could I do? What choice, really, did I have? "I'm going up!" I shouted.

"You'll die!" Peer said, pulling at my arm to keep me from moving. Dawa straightened. "We must get Pemba down!"

"I'm going to the shelf to search for the others!" I shouted.

I couldn't see his eyes through his goggles, but I heard him say, "I go with you! Peer, take Pemba down. He is stronger than he looks. You can make it!"

This was not a place for an argument. We were all starting to freeze in the cold—even in the short minutes this had taken. Peer was right and we knew it. But he also knew that I wasn't leaving and neither was Dawa.

"You're crazy!" Peer said. "I'll take him! God go with you!"

We short-roped the Sherpa to Peer and hooked him to the line. Dawa shouted into his ear, attempting to make him understand what was happening, set his hands on Peer's shoulders, and they set out down the mountain. I told myself that if anyone could get him to safety it was Peer. But it was insane, one man taking another down from this place in these conditions.

I lifted my watch to my eyes. It was nine o'clock. It would be getting very, very cold soon. I found the line, hooked my ascender, and started up with Dawa following. It was, if anything, even more difficult than earlier. The wind knocked me loose more than once and I found myself spinning freely. Dawa grappled with my legs to get me back against the rock and ice. The footing was unstable and, every foot I moved up, I expected to encounter another body dangling from the line. Instead, I reached the shelf twenty minutes later.

Once on top, I was struck with how much this was like the year before. The conditions were all but identical. I'd never wanted to be here again. Now, in the space of a few short days, I'd been on the shelf twice.

Dawa had been part of the earlier search team for Derek and knew the routine without our speaking. We stretched out our arms and began working our way systematically across the shelf, stumbling more than once. I had no illusions about possible success. Diana, Rusty, or Zhiku could have crumpled to the ice and already be covered in snow—nothing more than one of the lumps we saw everywhere. This assumed that they had even reached the shelf. They could all be dead. There was no way for us to know.

Our visibility was limited to perhaps five feet and even that was uncertain because the snow was so intense and the wind so violent. Still, we made it to the rock face, repositioned ourselves, and moved toward the Step, hoping we'd spot the edge before going over. I knew with absolute certainty that if Diana weren't here, I'd never find her. Going across the traverse toward the summit in these conditions was certain death. I'd managed it once; twice was too much.

I nearly walked over the precipice, spotting it only at the last second, drawing myself up sharply. It had been close. Our second passage away from the Step toward the rock face was as hopeless as the first two. We'd be in the scree soon, where the footing was so unstable that we'd almost certainly be swept away. Then, out of the corner of my eye, I spotted a shape in the snow. It looked like a solitary rock, but I knew that the shelf had no rocks of that height, not standing alone. I turned and moved toward it. As I did, I saw that a light emanated from the top of the rock.

It was a climber, standing alone like a sentinel.

Two feet away, I realized it was Rusty, standing watch as I had, hoping someone would pass by and help him. I threw my arms around him. "Rusty! Rusty! Thank God!"

He was nearly frozen stiff and it took a long moment for him to realize that I was not a phantom. "Scott? Scott, is it really you!" he said in a voice that I could scarcely make out. He gasped for air and coughed violently. He looked spent, all but frozen.

"With Dawa. Where are the rest?" By now Dawa had found me and given Rusty a hug as well.

Rusty drew deep breaths and said, "Pemba went for oxygen and help. Did he send you?"

"No," I shouted. "We found him on the rope going down the Step. He's alive. Peer is taking him down!"

It took a moment for Rusty to understand and then he said, "Over here is better—we can talk." Rusty moved awkwardly away, onto the scree, and we cautiously followed. A few moments later, we were against the rock. He stopped, moved slowly to his left, and halted again at a dark shape huddled against a small ledge only slightly out of the full force of the wind and snow.

I crouched down, touched the hood of the climbing suit, and turned the head. It was Diana. I nearly burst into tears. "I'm here, dear," I said. "I'm here. You're going to be okay. I promise."

She took a long time to register my presence. I saw the slightest trace of a smile as the ice and snow fell away from her face. She struggled to stand and I pulled her up. "Scott," I heard as she came into my arms. "Oh Scott." Then she began coughing.

Rusty and Dawa pressed close so that we could shelter from the storm and hear one another. Over Diana's shoulder, I shouted, "Where's Zhiku?"

"Out there," Rusty said. "We were looking for rescuers. Do you have oxygen? We're both out."

Here we'd made such an effort to find them, to bring them oxygen, and he had to ask for it. Dawa and I removed spare bottles from our backs. He connected his to Rusty, discarding the empty while I attached a spare to Diana, turning the valve to full. I still had one in reserve.

"We have to get down!" I said. "It's going to get very cold. We can't stay here!"

"What about Zhiku?" Diana asked. I could see the life return to her with the flow of oxygen.

"Where is he?" Dawa asked.

"Over there," Rusty said, gesturing vaguely with his arm. "We were trying to cover as much of the shelf as we could. I haven't seen him in over an hour."

"You three go," Dawa said. "I will search for him."

"No, Dawa!" I shouted. "We have to descend. There's no time to search. He should have been where we were before!"

"You go. I will search. He is my uncle." Dawa leaned very close to me. "You understand, Scott? You understand? I stay. I stay."

I understood.

He roped us together, Alpine style. I took the lead, as I was in the best condition; Diana was in the middle, while Rusty brought up the rear. We moved slowly toward the Step. As we reached the line, I looked for Dawa. The last I saw of him he was to my left, disappearing into the blizzard, finally simply winking out like an Everest phantom.

Getting down the Hillary Step was tricky. Both Diana and Rusty had great difficulty with their hands and feet. They moved awkwardly and with incredible slowness. It was going to be a close call, but after a few minutes, I became optimistic that we'd make it.

At the halfway point, Rusty suddenly broke free above me. The line snapped into Diana and she came off the wall of ice and rock. It all happened so fast that I had no time to react. The weight and force of the two tore me away and we all fell crashing down. I struck rock at least twice, perhaps more. I can't say.

I landed partially on top of them both. I felt a dull ache in my right shoulder and a searing pain in my shin where crampons had torn through the jumpsuit. I lay breathless for long minutes, unable to move from the shock, cold, and exhaustion. Finally, I stirred and located Diana nearly beside me.

"Are you all right?" I shouted.

She nodded. "I think so. How's Rusty?"

I got to my feet and pulled her up, positioning her against the wall. I ran my hands over her suit, but everything seemed normal. I leaned down to Rusty who lay unmoving very close. "Rusty! Are you okay?" My light shown onto his ice-encrusted face. His eyes moved, but did not open. "Rusty! Rusty!" I placed my face nearly against his. "Talk to me!"

Slowly, his eyes came open. "Scott," he said softly. "Glad you're here. Find Diana."

"We've got her, Rusty. We fell on the Step. Remember?"

"Fell? No, just the cold. I remember the cold. It hurts."

"Get up! We have to move!"

"Will try. Let me rest first." He spoke so softly that I could scarcely hear him.

"No, Rusty! Stand up! Come on!" I stood, grabbed his arm, and lifted. He shifted his weight as if to help me, but suddenly screamed in pain. I let him go. "What's wrong?"

"My leg. My leg." He gestured toward his left leg.

I reached down and moved my hands along it. The break was major. His leg beneath his knee jutted out at nearly a ninety-degree angle. I sat there numb. Finally, I lifted my head to speak. "It's broken, Rusty. It's broken."

"Hurts like hell."

I straightened up, moved to Diana, and told her. "What can we do?" she asked.

I answered with the last words I wanted to utter. "Nothing. We have to leave him or die with him."

"Oh God," she said. "Oh God, no."

I held her as I struggled with facing the inevitable. There was nothing either of us could do. If by some miracle, Sherpa were at Camp Five, there was a chance that they might find him and get him down. But that was almost the same as no chance at all.

I tried desperately to think of an alternative. Finally, I leaned down so he could hear me. "Rusty! We have to leave. I'll send help!"

I wasn't certain he understood, but in an eerily familiar gesture, he gripped my forearm and, in a choked voice, said, "Don't leave me."

⁓⁓⁓

Diana and I reached Camp Five at two in the morning. There were no Sherpa there.

We crawled into the larger tent. I started a cooker for some warmth and tea and went out to find fresh bottles of oxygen. Back inside, I buttoned us up for the night. I'd had both of our flows to max on the descent and the bottles were all but empty. I set the fresh bottles at a slower pace for rest so they'd last until dawn.

We looked like hell. Inside the less freezing tent, the ice and snow fell away from our faces. We removed our heavy gloves and held our hands close to the scant flame that slowly brought snow and ice to boil. After the tea, I ordered her into a sleeping bag. "And don't forget to put your gloves back on. We'll leave in the morning."

"What about Rusty?" she said.

I shook my head. "Don't think about him. Rest."

She was so spent that, when I checked, she was fast asleep. I recall nodding off a time or two. Mostly I listened to the raging storm and thought about Rusty and Dawa.

TWENTY-THREE

All mountains kill. Everest just happens to be the biggest killer of all.
—Quentin Stern, www.AbandonedonEverest.com

The storm was clearing the next morning, though snow flurries remained. I located the last two fresh bottles. We secured our suits and stomped about in our boots as we made to leave. Neither of us spoke about Rusty or Dawa. The way down was difficult, with banks of knee-high snow from time to time, but the line was in place. We made steady progress, stopping every few minutes to suck air before resuming.

I spotted him at about nine o'clock. He was standing alone, waiting for us, about halfway up from Camp Four. He'd picked his spot well, on a narrow ridge where it was impossible for us to move around.

Diana looked up. "Who is it?"

"Gody."

"What's he doing up here?"

"Stay behind me," I said. I waited for him before realizing that he would not come up to me, so I moved toward him, stopping some twenty feet short.

"The mountain did not kill you after all," he said. "Peer thought you two might be dead."

"You saw him?" He was mummified in a scarlet high-altitude suit, his goggles in place—though he pushed his mask aside to speak as I had.

"Last night. He and the Sherpa stumbled into Camp Four where I was resting with my Sherpa. He told me what happened. I thought I'd wait here in case the mountain didn't do the job."

"What's going on?" Diana shouted. "Let's go! I'm cold."

Gody laughed. "No one is going anywhere, miss. At least, not you two.

"What are you saying?" she demanded.

"I'm saying that the great reporter died on her descent from the biggest story of her life."

Before she could respond I said, "What about Peer?"

With the jumpsuit hood partially covering his face and his dark goggles in place, it was impossible to read his expression. "He and the two Sherpa are dead. It was not difficult."

"I underestimated you," I said.

He smiled broadly. "In every way. I have been climbing these peaks since I was a child. I don't need a filthy Sherpa to drag me to the top and carry me down."

"And Tarja?"

"She's not going anywhere."

"Why?" Diana shouted from behind me. "Why are you doing this?"

"Orders. I have taken my salt and pledged my loyalty. Mr. Sodoc has told me what to do. There is nothing left but to do it."

"Let her go," I said. "I didn't kill Derek—Dawa did—but I can understand why he thinks I have to die. It's crazy, but I understand it. She had nothing to do with it."

He laughed and then coughed. "She is here. It is necessary."

"Was this always the plan?" I asked. "To kill those who climbed with Derek?"

"Oh, yes. Always. When Mr. Sodoc learned one of you actually murdered his son, I thought he'd want you all killed at Base Camp. I told him the mountain would likely see to it and that I would take care of anyone who survived. It's a good place for killing, don't you think? The mountain needs very little help."

From somewhere, Gody pulled his kukri, the same inwardly curved knife with which he'd slaughtered the yak. He slipped his oxygen mask back across his face and assumed the familiar crouch that I thought I'd never see again.

Diana shouted in alarm and backpedaled as best she could in the heavy snow. I pushed my mask in place and hefted my ice ax. He seemed to like that for some reason.

Understand how absurd this was. If either of us misstepped, we'd slip and plunge to oblivion. Both sides were steep and there was little margin for error where we stood. Beneath our feet was thick, untrampled snow, making movement very difficult. Finally, here in the Death Zone, even with oxygen, neither of us was in any condition for a protracted fight. I knew it would end quickly.

I had a slight advantage in that I was a bit uphill from him and I thought the ice ax a superior weapon to his knife. He soon proved me wrong. With blinding speed, he slashed me across my shin, the same one the crampons had sliced the night before, and I stumbled back, nearly falling. Diana screamed.

Had he come in at that moment, I think it would have been over, but he hesitated, fearing my ice ax. I righted myself, ignoring the pain, and moved toward him, swinging the ice ax in a slow, steady motion so he'd not know from what angle my attack would come. When I judged the moment right, I suddenly swung at him, catching him off guard, and felt the tip of the ice ax tear into his jumpsuit. Rather than pull from me, he lunged instinctively with his kukri and I felt the searing pain in my side as the blade sank deeply into my flesh.

I staggered and nearly fell. With what seemed to be lightning speed in these conditions, he slashed again as I pulled away, this time cutting my oxygen hose. I drew a breath of thin air and gasped.

I heard him laugh from behind his mask. He moved back to let the loss of blood and lack of oxygen do his dirty work for him. He pushed his mask aside and said, "My only regret is that in these conditions I cannot enjoy your woman before killing her, as is our custom." He slipped the mask back on and stood waiting.

I placed my left hand to my side where it burned like fire. I drew deep breaths of the meager air and coughed violently. I knew it was over—or would be in the next minute. Delay only worked against me. I slipped the ice ax free from its safety restraint, quickly raised my arm, and, before he could react, threw it at him. It struck his shoulder and glanced off, doing nothing more than distracting him for a vital second. I rushed him like the fullback I'd been in high school, taking him high across the chest before both of us went down.

On the thin ridge, we grappled and wrestled. I was working to hold down his right arm to keep the deadly knife away and he knew it. I was exhausted and felt as if I was suffocating. I managed to knock his mask away. He grunted. We rolled, stopped, rolled back, stopped, then rolled a final time, and kept rolling off the side of the ridge. From somewhere far away, I heard a scream.

We should both have died. That was, I suspect, what I'd had in mind when I'd jumped him. Instead, as we slipped off the ridge and began our death plunge, we struck an outcropping of exposed rock. Gody hit it first and hardest, jolting him severely. I had instinctively clung to his right arm since if he still had his knife that was the side it would come from. The rock held him fast, but I found myself slipping away down the wall of ice and snow.

I could not hold on and we were separated in an instant. I knew I'd lost.

I was sliding feet first, face down, not yet having picked up speed, stabbing at the ice with my crampons. They refused to take, but I had no choice but to keep trying. Then, one stuck and I slowed, the other dug in and I miraculously stopped. I looked up and found I was some thirty feet below Gody.

I saw him ease away from the stone outcropping and move awkwardly on the ice without an ice ax to make the climb possible. He slipped, but caught himself. He looked down toward me and, for a moment, I made out his features clearly. There was no fear, only grim determination. He looked back up, moved a boot, and then abruptly plummeted toward me. I lowered my head in anticipation of the blow, felt something brush as he rushed passed me, and then heard him scream as he fell.

For a very long time, I tried to gather my strength. Diana's voice came from far away. "Are you all right?"

I lifted an arm in signal.

My problem wasn't all that different from the one Gody had faced. Without an ax, I wasn't certain that I could get up this wall of ice and snow. I was considering the problem when Diana shouted again.

"Here!" She held an ice ax up above her head so I could see it. She knelt down and slid it toward me.

It could have caught above me or gone too far left or right of me. I reached for it with my gloved hand, but missed as it struck me full in the face. I managed to ease it under my head and held it in place before slipping the loop around my wrist. A minute later, I started up toward the ridge in traditional style, ice ax into ice, right foot, left foot, ice ax again—all the way up. Once there, Diana helped me to my feet and threw her arms around me. We stood without speaking for a long time as I tried to get my breath, coughing violently every few breaths. I'd never been more spent.

"Let's get moving," she said. "Let's get off this damn mountain."

⚬⚬⚬

We reached Camp Four shortly before noon. It had been tough going. I bled the entire way, the blood filling the inside of my jumpsuit where I felt it slosh, turning quickly to ice wherever it became exposed. When we stopped to rest, Diana had me breathe from her mask to restore my strength before we set out again.

As we entered the camp, there was no sign of Peer or the two Sherpa. Gody must have slipped the bodies off the mountain.

That morning, Calvin and three Sherpa had moved up, unaware of the slaughter that had taken place here the night before. He moved awkwardly in the cold, greeting us with a wide grin. "We thought you were dead! My God, just look at you! Is that blood? Any frostbite? Where are Peer, Rusty, Dawa, and Zhiku? Where are the other Sherpa? God, it's good to see you!"

"We lost Zhiku in the storm," I gasped. "Dawa went after him. Rusty fell coming down the Step and broke his leg. We had to leave him." Diana suddenly burst into tears. "Peer came down with one of the Sherpa."

"We've not seen or heard from Peer since yesterday."

"Gody killed them," Diana said as she regained control of her emotions. "He killed Peer and the Sherpa."

"Gody? My God! Why? You've seen him?"

She told him what had happened as the Sherpa helped Calvin move me into a tent. He ordered them up to find Rusty. I had no expectation of good news, but miracles do occasionally happen on Everest.

Inside the tent, with Diana looking on, Calvin opened my jumpsuit and systematically mopped out the blood without comment. He then went to work on the wound, stitching and bandaging it. "It's unbelievable," he said repeatedly as Diana told the story in greater detail. "You've been lucky," he said to me as he finished, "nothing major was severed, but I don't like the blood loss. Not up here."

Calvin examined us both in detail—expressing surprise at the lack of visible frostbite,—and dressed my leg. He dabbed, cleaned, and muttered, "Shit. That's a knife wound." Then he bandaged it all. When he was finished, he said, "That man nearly did you in. I'm staying here for Rusty and the others, just in case. Do you think you can continue? I'd suggest you stay, but you're much better off below in the richer air—especially you, Scott."

Diana looked at me and said, "We'll manage."

"Calvin," I said a few minutes later as we prepared to set out, "not a word of this to anyone. You understand?"

He nodded lightly. "You two be careful. I have a feeling this isn't over."

⌒⌒⌒

The bandaging held and I did not resume bleeding—though I continued to be in pain. We passed through Camp Three, taking only a mug of tea while standing, afraid that if we sat, we'd never get back up. By late afternoon, we reached Advanced Base Camp, catching Harlan by surprise. He rushed out with a warm, wide grin and shook hands all around. "Capital," he said, "just capital. That blood there. Are you cut?"

"Calvin bandaged it. How's Tarja?" I asked.

"Good. All but recovered. She's at Base Camp."

Crystal rushed out. "Where's Rusty? What happened up there? Why won't Calvin answer the radio?" she asked.

"We had to leave Rusty," Diana said, her voice quivering. She explained the descent, stopping, as I'd cautioned her, before mentioning Gody and anything he'd done.

It was at about this time that the Sherpa found Rusty, dead against the foot of Hillary Step, and eased him away from the route. Their radios were now working and we learned about it almost at once. Harlan ordered them to return to Base Camp.

Crystal went into her tent with Diana. I heard them sobbing for a time, but life goes on—especially at SNS. Diana didn't tell Crystal everything that had taken place, not then at least, because it was business as usual for them. An hour later, Diana emerged from the tent, composed, and freshly scrubbed—even with some makeup applied. With a visibly distraught Crystal operating the camera, she went live, worldwide, seen I'm told in living rooms over breakfast.

"This is Diana Maurasi from near the summit of Everest, where last night my cameraman, Rusty Landon, and I were rescued by legendary mountaineer Peer Borgen and my dear, dear friend, Scott Devlon. Sadly, lost in the summit effort yesterday and during last night's rescue were Zhiku, our expedition's Sherpa leader, and Dawa, one of the most skilled Sherpa guides in the Himalayas. He is believed to have died attempting to rescue Zhiku, who was his uncle." She paused. "Tragically, both Rusty Landon and Peer Borgen perished on the descent in the midst of a blizzard."

There was more, but I wasn't listening. I was so tired that I thought I'd die. I found my tent and crawled in. In the relatively rich air of Camp Two, I fell into a fast sleep.

↤↤↤

I suppose there was radio traffic back and forth. I didn't share in any of it and no one told me what they were talking about—though Diana still said nothing about Gody. For now, it remained our little secret. Sodoc, I heard, radioed up, repeatedly demanding an accounting for Gody's absence.

I ate my first real meal in days and forced myself to drink. My side throbbed, but did not resume bleeding. The fickle mountain had decided to bless us with summit weather. The sky was a glorious blue, free of all clouds, and windless.

Diana checked my bandages just before we set out; Crystal was somber and silent. We reached Camp One at midmorning, paused for tea, and then made our way through the groaning Ice Flow. We emerged at two o'clock that afternoon. Base Camp still looked largely deserted—except for the helicopter squatting beside it.

"I'm glad to see you all," Tom said with a wide grin as he greeted us. "My God," he said when he saw the condition of my suit. "What happened?"

"Who's here?"

"Tarja, of course, Michael, the flight crew, Bawu, and two Sherpa. There's no sign of Gody. I'm really sorry about Dawa and Rusty. Are you certain Peer is gone? The Sherpa didn't report finding his body."

"We're certain. How's Sodoc?" I asked.

"Somber. He's pretty shook up by the disaster and angry about something. It's a bit scary. You'll see. He's leaving in a bit."

Tarja, I noted, was fully recovered as she came over and immediately pressed Crystal for an interview. Both eyes were blue again, but she'd looked better. She was thinner and clearly hadn't been sleeping.

"What happened up there?" Tom asked Diana.

"Sodoc ordered us to the top. Rusty was against it, but you know me." She stopped—perhaps thinking about who would be alive if she'd listened. "The storm hit as we wrapped up the broadcast. It was really bad. When Rusty dumped his camera and equipment, I knew we were in serious trouble. I'm not a climber, not really. I slowed us down terribly. I told the others to go ahead, but Rusty wouldn't. Because of me, we made really slow progress and used up our oxygen."

She stopped to compose herself. "I ... I fell on the traverse." Her voice rose. "If the line hadn't held I'd ... I'd ... Oh God! I can't believe he's dead." She started crying, covering her face with her hands.

"It's okay. It's over now, Diana," I said. "It's over." I placed my arm across her shoulders and she pressed herself against me. I looked at

Tom and said, "After all that, Gody murdered Peer and the two Sherpa. Yesterday, he tried to kill us above Camp Four."

To my surprise, Tom didn't look especially shocked. "What happened?"

"Scott killed him," Diana said more than a trace of pride. It seemed to me that the mountain had actually done the job, but I left it.

"You don't seem surprised," I said to Tom.

He licked his lips. "A few days ago, I would have said this was impossible. Today …" Just then, he spotted Sodoc and moved away toward Tarja. The old man approached aggressively. He glanced at Diana for a moment before turning his attention to me. He looked worn, every bit his age, and more than a bit deranged. "Where's Gody?"

"Dead," I said. "He managed to kill Peer, but came up short with us.

Sodoc looked as if I'd just slapped him. "I don't believe you. He's twice the man you are and skilled at high altitude. That's why I sent him."

"He told us what his orders were," Diana said. "How could you?"

"I don't know what you're talking about." He glared at Diana. "And you'll forget wild talk if you know what's good for you and your career. Now get the hell out of my sight!"

Diana hesitated, looked at me, and walked off. "Killing us all was the plan from the first? That's what Gody told us," I said.

"You murdered my son!"

"The hell I did. You want to know who killed Derek? Is that what this is all about? If that's the case, it's easy enough: go look in the mirror. You killed Derek as surely as if you'd put a gun to his head. In the meanwhile, you can go to hell!"

I turned to walk off, but Sodoc grabbed my shoulder and spun me around to face him. "You think it's this easy, do you?" he whispered in an ominous voice. "You think you get lucky up there and then just walk away? Look over your shoulder and lock the doors. It won't do any good. You're dead. You understand me? You're all dead!"

The senior army officer came up and whispered in Sodoc's ear, looking nervous. Sodoc nodded, rose, and stalked off without a word.

Stern approached and thrust a recorder in my face. "What was it like up there?"

"Screw yourself, Stern," I said.

He grinned. "Can I quote you?"

"Please do."

"I've got another book contract," he said. "It's a hell of a story. I'm wrapping up some interviews here and then I'm off to knock it out." He looked at me through his blue-tinted glasses. "Come on, Scott. You're in the book anyway. You might as well have your say."

"Go to hell, Stern," I said.

Stern laughed. "The old man's taking the body back to bury. I need to get some video. Think about it."

"Guess who gave him the book contract?" Tom said as he joined me with Tarja. "Michael. I suppose he wants to control the story line."

I shook my head in disbelief.

"Not only that, but he's hired the cretin. SNS has decided to move big time onto the Internet and Stern has found a new home with the company."

"Amazing."

"Isn't it, though?"

"What happened?" Tarja demanded. "I've been going crazy down here. He's a madman, Scott. A madman. Have you seen Gody? Is he still looking for us?"

"Gody's dead," I said. "Nothing to worry about."

"What are you talking about?" she said. "Sodoc's alive, isn't he? My God, he's going to kill us. I just know he is. I've got to get out of here!" She wandered away to the edge of the camp and began pacing.

"What's with the army guy?" I asked.

"This is weird. The story is that Gody paid the Maoists to launch their attack. Sodoc didn't want us bothered up here."

"It must be nice to play God." The man actually started an insurgent campaign? It seemed incredible.

Tom shook his head. "Only now it's out of hand."

I told him what Dawa had said that last night.

"Dawa? I can't believe it. I suppose it makes a certain amount of sense though, when you think about it. Why didn't you tell Michael?"

"He wouldn't believe me and, at this point, I'd say it's not even important."

Tom gave me an odd look. "You know, Scott, some people are going to think you did it. There's been plenty of speculation. You need to tell your story."

"In time, Tom. In time. Assuming it even matters."

On the edge of camp, I watched the two pilots checking the aging helicopter before boarding. A minute later, the heavy figure of Sodoc emerged from a tent. I watched as he slowly climbed aboard. I guess Derek's body was already loaded.

You know most of the rest. Diana was covering the liftoff with Crystal on camera. She finished to the whine of the Russian Mi-17 engines as the rotors began to turn. The heavy machine lifted slowly at first, scarcely seeming to rise, then the pilot pointed the craft into the long valley. Crystal was filming as the massive beast moved across the largely abandoned camp, picking up speed as it raced down the valley.

I'd estimate it was about a mile away when it exploded into a ball of bright flame, the sound coming to us a few seconds later, echoing off the flanks of the mountains with a ricocheting boom. Below us, the helicopter crashed onto the rocks and ice, then burned fiercely as a column of black smoke rose into the azure sky.

Crystal caught it perfectly.

Stern was standing beside me, filming as well, and was the first to speak. "Shit, what a story!" Then a moment later: "I wonder if I still have a book deal."

⌁⌁⌁

We were another week at Base Camp. Harlan and three Sherpa took advantage of the weather, climbed to the shelf again, but found neither Zhiku nor Dawa. Harlan held his funeral service for Reggie and, a few days later, we held one for them all at Base Camp. Afterward, Harlan told us that he'd decided to evacuate the Westerners by helicopter.

The government of Nepal created a commission to determine the cause of the explosion that killed Sodoc. It blamed a mechanical malfunction. Having ridden in the thing, it's hard to argue with that, but the finding failed to end speculation. Some are convinced that the Maoists found a way to plant a time bomb on the helicopter. Others say that they shot it down, though I don't believe any of them were that far up and I saw no evidence of a rocket or gunfire.

I personally think it just as likely that the Nepalese government or army planted a delayed bomb in retaliation for Sodoc's dealings with the insurgents. Or perhaps one of his many enemies took the opportunity to get rid of him. There's no way of knowing for certain.

After all, Everest is a good place to kill someone. It's an ideal spot for murder.

But if I was forced to pick a cause, I'd say it was the mountain goddess, Sagarmatha. Dawa would understand—and who's to say he was wrong?

⌐⌐⌐

The legal battle for control of the Sodoc media empire continues, though my money's on the Russian widow and her new son. Tarja was paid off. A story by Stern in the *National Inquisitor* said she got just over $100 million. I believe it. It was peanuts.

Tarja and Tom were an item for a while. I used to catch his self-satisfied smile in any number of magazines and celebrity television shows. He enjoyed his fifteen minutes of fame enormously, he told me on a fishing trip off Baja. Tarja was suitably thankful—until she got the check and vanished without so much as a goodbye. I don't think he minded a bit by then.

A Norwegian team returned to the mountain that fall, but had no luck finding Peer. They held their own memorial service at Base Camp, which was broadcast live over Norwegian and European television.

Crystal left SNS and started her own production team. Her first project is a biography of Tarja, focusing on the last two expeditions. She told me that Tarja's paying well for it.

Gody's murders remain on the mountain. Only Diana and I know of them for a fact. Neither of us has ever spoken publicly about what really happened. Who would believe it? And with Sodoc dead, what would be the point?

The center took me back. In time, I told the story of Derek's death, though not everyone believes it. The Nepalese government condemned me—and the reports that a Sherpa had committed a murder on Everest. When the Western media continued reporting the story, the government canceled all expeditions to Everest for some months. By the following season, economic forces had kicked in and expeditions resumed.

Diana was a sensation for about a week after her return to New York. Then she took a month off and we went to the Bahamas for lazy days in the warm sun and surf and nights of dancing and love. If only life were always like that.

Diana and I talked daily for a while, but she was busy getting her new program ready. It launched last month to good reviews and even better ratings. The last time we spoke, she said she needed to find more time for us.

Tom called last night. He and Calvin are planning to climb Kilimanjaro and wondered if I'd like to come along.

ABOUT THE AUTHORS

Charles G. Irion

Charles G. Irion is an author, adventurer, entrepreneur, and philanthropist. In the 1970s, Irion began his career in commercial real estate development and brokerage. In 1983, he founded U.S. Park Investments, a company that owns and brokers manufactured home and RV communities. In 2007, Irion founded Irion Books and began writing and publishing books. His first book was *Remodeling Hell*—one of four books he authored as part of the Hell Series. This was followed by *Autograph Hell, Car Dealer Hell,* and *Divorce Hell.* Inspired by real-life events, these books are true stories created by actual (hellish) events that infuriated Irion to the point of wanting to expose the demons through his writings. He is donating all of the net proceeds of his Hell Series to victims of fraud.

While writing the Hell Series, Irion began work on the Summit Murder Series. The impetus behind the murder mystery series was his participation in a 1987 expedition to Mount Everest from the China side. Irion couldn't resist creating plot-twisting, adventure-filled stories against the backdrop of the world's deadliest mountains.

Over the past thirty years, Irion has also garnered a large collection of recipes from resident RV campers. More than 350 of these can be found in his book *Roadkill Cooking for Campers: The Best Dang Wild Game Cookbook in the World.*

Irion holds a Masters of Business Administration in International Marketing and Finance from the American Graduate School of International Management and Bachelor of Arts degrees in both Biology and Economics from the University of California, Santa Barbara. As an explorer, Irion has visited more than sixty countries and is an accomplished SCUBA diver. He is also the founder of a children's dictionary charity, a founding member of Phoenix Social Venture Partners, and past president of a local Lions Club. Irion lives in Arizona with his wife, Rose Marie, who he met in Osaka, Japan, at a World Trade Center conference and their beautiful daughter, Chriselle.

To learn more about Charles Irion, please visit: www.CharlesIrion.com

Ronald J. Watkins

Ronald J. Watkins is an American writer of novels and nonfiction. Watkins

has also served as co-author, ghost-writer, collaborator, or editor for more than thirty books. He is the founder and principal writer for Watkins & Associates. In 1993, Watkins published *Birthright*, the saga of the Shoen family, which founded and owned U-Haul International and of the then-unsolved murder of Eva Shoen. When he refused to identify his sources under subpoena, he was twice found in contempt by a federal court, with his position being upheld by the Ninth Circuit on both occasions.

These established case law sustaining the right of authors of non-fiction books to not identify either confidential or non-confidential sources. For Watkins' defense of the First Amendment, he was recognized as a finalist for the PEN/Newman's Own First Amendment Award.

Watkins' first book, *High Crimes and Misdemeanors*, was an account of the impeachment of Arizona governor Evan Mecham. Written just one year after the events, and based on hundreds of interviews with participants, it remains the definitive account of an American impeachment.

He then authored *Evil Intentions*, the story of the brutal murder of Suzanne Rossetti in Phoenix, Arizona. It was followed a few years later by

Against Her Will, the story of the murder of Kelly Tinyes in Valley Stream, Long Island, New York. This was the first murder case in the State of New York solved in large part by DNA testing.

In 2003, John Murray (UK) published Watkins' book, *Unknown Seas: How Vasco da Gama Opened the East*. The following year, Watkins was nominated for the Mountbatten Maritime Prize in the United Kingdom. The book has since been published in Portuguese in Brazil and in Czech in the Czech Republic.

Watkins is co-author with Charles G. Irion on the Summit Murder Series, mystery novels set on the highest mountains in the world. In all, the Series is projected to include eight books. He holds a Bachelor of Arts in History and a Master of Science in Justice Studies. Following university, he worked as a probation officer and presentencing investigator for the Superior Court in Phoenix, Arizona. He is a former chief administrative law judge and was assistant director of the Arizona Department of Insurance where he served as Arizona's chief insurance fraud investigator.

Watkins has been called on by the media and has made a number of television and radio appearances, including Dominick Dunne's Power, Privilege, and Justice; PrimeTime! with Tom Brokaw and Katie Couric; Under Scrutiny with Jane Wallace; Geraldo with Geraldo Rivera, and American Forum national radio program.

To learn more about Ronald J. Watkins, please visit: www.RonaldjWatkins.com

THE SUMMIT MURDER SERIES

Eight plot-twisting mystery novels set against the backdrop of the world's deadliest mountains.

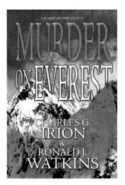

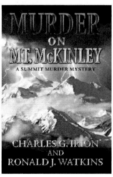
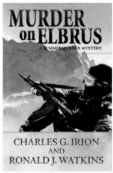

Murder on Everest
Abandoned on Everest, a prequel to Murder on Everest
Murder on Elbrus (Summer 2010)
Murder on Mt. McKinley (Winter 2011)
Murder on Puncak Jaya (Summer 2011)
Murder on Aconcagua (Winter 2012)
Murder on Vinson Massif (Summer 2012)
Murder on Kilimanjaro (Winter 2013)

www.SummitMurders.com
www.AbandonedOnEverest.com
www.IrionBooks.com